Maxwell's Last Will & Testament

By

James Keyse

This book is dedicated to my daughter Loran for giving me the idea without even knowing she had so and to my sister Karen whose words of encouragement got me to the end.

Copyright ©2012

Associate Editor Dr. Karen Keyse Fields

Cover Design and Artwork by Vladimir Milosevic

Prologue

Even as the cadaverous, cancer-ridden shell he clung to expired, Maxwell struggled to extract the last remaining shreds of life left in it. His emaciated body somehow continued to win its battle against the inevitable, defying death in a heroic effort to continue existing for a few precious moments more. That was all he needed. He knew there was no last minute salvation coming, no pardon to be issued seconds before fate cut his thread. He was out of time and for the first time in his life he was powerless to do anything about his situation. Death held the winning hand.

Maxwell was unequipped to deal with his present situation. Oddly, his distress wasn't derived from the fact that he had cancer, or even that he was dying. It was the fact that he had finally encountered something he couldn't buy, cheat, steal, threaten, coerce, or otherwise control. That fact was what had eventually driven him mad. Here, finally, was something more powerful than the almighty Maxwell Bartholomew Alderson, one of the richest and most influential men on the planet. His fragile illusion of control was now completely and utterly shattered. Control, the one thing he believed he held uncontroversial reign over had finally abandoned him like everything else he had ever cared about in his life.

Control was all he had. Maxwell no longer had any other beliefs or emotions that mattered to him. Human emotions such as compassion and guilt were abandoned along with his sanity

2

and morality. In truth, he had left any shred of ethical behavior behind many years before and now he was truly free to act without restraint or conscience.

His inevitable death made no difference to him emotionally other than to free him from any remaining ties to decency that he may have had left. He was free to do whatever he wanted and no one could stop him. You can't put a dead man on trial. That was the liberating truth in his situation, the truth that his demented mind latched onto in the end. Any other emotion was nothing but a pointless indulgence and all that really mattered now was the fact that he was dying and he had unfinished business to which he must attend. That was real. That was immediate. That was tangible. And, that he could still control, if only for a few more moments.

This was what willed his failing heart to continue to beat. He might not be able to cheat Death forever, but even as he slipped inevitably into the abyss, he wasn't completely without power. Yes, the legacy of Maxwell would exist even after he no longer drew breath, at least for a while…

Maxwell snapped back to awareness and pulled himself free of this latest ploy by Death to trick him out of his last moments of life. He struggled against oblivion's relentless call as it attempted to draw him into itself like a siren calling the lonely ship to its demise on the deadly rocks. Even his mind was against him now. "Sleep," it urged soothingly, lulling him into the darkness of eternal rest.

He reflected on his own madness. One can become extremely maniacal when suffering a death that steals away life like a half-clogged sink empties its filthy contents. His sanity was draining out of him like the fetid water, gurgling, belching up its stench, reeking and foul, as it slowly emptied into some unknown pit to rot and fester. Yes, that was how Maxwell was departing this world. That was the state of Maxwell's demented mind as he started down the pipe unwittingly headed for that dark chiasm, his new home for all eternity…

Maxwell resurfaced, gulping for air as he realized he had stopped breathing. Focusing all his attention on the black-suited man in the room with him, he concentrated as the last details of his final transaction where recited. Maxwell knew it was too late to stop it now. He knew they would carry out his wishes now even if he begged them not to. His nod of approval sealed his fate, supplying him with a one way ticket to Hell, condemned to eternal damnation.

It was done.

"*Sharon*…" Maxwell managed weakly.

"As you wish," the short, meticulously groomed man said, turning to leave.

The man turned back toward Maxwell and smiled as he was leaving the room. Maxwell closed his eyes in an attempt to block that vision from his memory. If it persisted, he would spend the last seconds he had left screaming in horror as he faced the truth of what he had just unleashed. That face, devoid of feeling, morally empty, deeply psychopathic, was more than even he could bear. He shouldn't be so reviled by it though, after all, this …man was his creation.

What had he done? He felt as if he was sliding down a greased rope that dangled over a bottomless pit. He could see the end of that slippery lifeline rapidly approaching, writhing snake-like as he fought desperately against the inevitable eternal fall into Hell that would follow when the end passed inexorably from his grasp.

Moments later, a young woman came rushing in. Even through her grief, her beauty was obvious. She quickly made her way to his side, instinctively knowing she was looking at the equivalent of an animated corpse. As she came into view, Maxwell fought past his fading vision to lock her face in his memory in the hope it would later ease the burden on his soul for what he had done, and, more correctly, what he had set in motion.

"Help Sean…" was all he could manage. He had so much left to say but the end was upon him. It began to close in

on him, to drag him into the place the Devil had been gleefully preparing for him. The Devil had been putting Maxwell's accommodations together for a long, long time. Maxwell envisioned the horror that he knew awaited a man like himself. The Devil was a wonderful interior decorator, and Maxwell was sure that he had put some real thought into his new digs.

"Anything you want, Maxwell," Sharon sobbed.

"*Save both...of...you...*

"*Talbert...knows...what...to do,*" he said as he expelled his dying breath.

Those were the last words Maxwell Bartholomew Alderson ever spoke.

Sharon sat there watching Maxwell descend into death through her tears. The life scanner stuttered and skipped. Sharon watched as it missed more beats than it found. Finally, in a chorus of bells and alarms, it finished it's symphony in a flat line and single tone.

Maxwell had departed this world forever.

Maxwell was curiously aware as this new phase of his existence manifested itself. Slipping deeper and deeper into the impending abyss, he thought what was happening odd based on all the stories of people who had supposedly died and returned to life. Instead of watching himself rise above his dying body and ascend into the waiting light, he was watching the world disappear into an ever-diminishing speck of hope above him— once and for all answering the question regarding his final destination.

"This might not be good," he thought as his decent accelerated.

As Maxwell departed this life and went into the next, he watched with interest as the events of that life, the events that had shaped his soul, fast-forwarded past him like a mural being projected onto the wall of a glass elevator as it descended toward some unmentionable final destination. Faster and faster they went by until they were nothing but a blur, a blur that he could see no matter how fast it passed by. It was more than that, though. It was meant to remind him who and what he had chosen to become. A vision that admonished him that he could have been anything he wanted to be but instead, because of the choices he had made with the life he had been granted, a theme emerged.

Regret.

Maxwell was the only passenger on this elevator and discerning its destination was not all that challenging. He would have laughed hysterically at the thought that no one seemed to want to ride down with him but laughter seemed to be forbidden here. How sad that he had died so utterly alone, surrounded by only servants and paid associates and, of course, Sharon. Was Sharon nothing more than a paid servant, too? Was the love that he had seen in her eyes as he died, that he wanted to believe in so badly, real or an illusion? Maxwell was certain that knowledge was restricted where he was headed. It was likely part of the eternal torture planned for his lengthy stay in Hell.

Maxwell despaired for the first and last time. "God, if you are there, make her understand!" Maxwell screamed at Heaven knowing Heaven was no longer listening to him. He had a different master now.

That being said, his personal picture show did attempt to try and flash the occasional good memory on the screen. Ironically, these fleeting and rare memories Maxwell had running through him were so few and far between it had to be another part of the fate he was sure awaited him. His mind envisioned a well filled with the memories of his vile life. In it were a few memories he wanted that never quite got close enough to touch. They would come almost within reach and then plummet back to the bottom before he realized it was happening, sending him into an ever-deepening state of despair.

"This is surely how Hell works," he thought. *"I should warn everyone who has a shortage of good memories!"* he cackled hysterically in his mind.

Sharon did everything she could to block the incredibly potent, visually-damning memory. It had to be her mind playing tricks on her. Still, she couldn't say for sure why his body convulsed, why his face contorted into a grotesque grimace long after she thought he was gone. She couldn't let herself continue to believe he was laughing. That might be more than she could take…

Chapter One

Sean Ryder's day started out pretty much like most of them did nowadays. He woke, seriously hung over and made his way into the tiny kitchen off the side of the main room of the cabin he currently called home. There, he fought his nausea as he made his usual breakfast consisting of coffee, coffee, and more coffee. In the end, he would consider himself lucky to keep even a little of it down, the way he felt right now.

The lake house he currently occupied belonged to his one-time father-in-law Maxwell Alderson. Maxwell never came here anymore so for Sean it was the perfect place to carry out his plans. Maxwell couldn't bear to come here because it reminded him of his daughter, which was exactly why Sean loved it here. This was the one place on earth where he found any solace, and it was the one place that held the few good, albeit, mixed with the very worst memories he had left of his dead wife and the life they once had together.

After he choked down his third cup of coffee he went to shower. He needed to head into town to restock the pantry with his favorite foods, beer and whiskey. Then he would return home and try to catch a few fish to put into his belly to soak up the whisky he would have already started to drink to put his mind back into the oblivion he craved so badly. Yes sir, it was going to be just another day in paradise. Just the way he liked it.

It hadn't always been like this. Once upon a time he was a full fledged member of the rat race just like everyone else. He was once the star executive of Alderson Investments and Maxwell's pride and joy. He was well on his way to one day running the vast empire Maxwell Alderson created at least that was what Maxwell saw in Sean's future, or it had been at one time. Sean remembered that once upon a time he saw that same vision, too. That was until his wife died giving birth to their first child, Maxwell's only hope for a grandchild.

With Angelina's bloody death the tie was broken. At least as far as Sean was concerned it was. He didn't know it yet, but Maxwell had other ideas.

Maxwell was the one person who seemed to actually understand and accept Sean's deep pain and that was why he let him stay here. Sean stayed out here to get his head on straight after the tragic loss of his wife and unborn child and never left. Maxwell's assistant sent him checks on a regular basis to pay the bills and for 'caretaker fees', as she always put it, but Sean knew it for what it was. He never cashed the checks. He didn't need anyone's charity. The remaining hundred thousand or so from his better days tucked away in his bank account should be sufficient for him to finish the task at hand, which was to drink himself to death as quickly as possible.

Maxwell's daughter and Sean's wife, Angelina, was an only child and the source of the bond that had once brought

11

Maxwell and Sean together. Her untimely death was nothing short of tragedy. By sheer coincidence, she left the world in the same manner as her mother, but with one small difference, Angelina didn't leave behind a child to force Sean get over her death the way her mother did for Maxwell. She took the child with her and left Sean to search for a way to accept what had happened and to find some sort of salvation on his own. It was something he desperately needed and was never going to find on the road he was going down now. He had totally missed the boat and so far, he was failing miserably.

What he had been able to accomplish was several near death experiences, just not close enough to choke on his own vomit. No, he was working on it but so far death eluded him. Too many outside influences in his little endeavor kept him from getting there.

After he finished the last cup of coffee, Sean headed up the narrow path towards the garage off the main house. His head was still pounding with a vengeance and he chewed several baby aspirin as he walked towards the garage on unsteady legs. He liked them because he could chew them until the pain left him. He had no delusions about feeling better later on today though. The headaches were not going to leave. He knew the only thing that was going to help was more of the same. He also knew more of the same was killing him very slowly. But that was the plan, after all, wasn't it?

He walked by the hulking lake house, clean, well preserved. He never went into the main house. It remained dark, silent, and empty. Angelina loved it here more than any other place on earth. They spent every spare moment they could steal from their busy lives here when they could have stayed in any of the plush estates throughout the world Maxwell owned. They even came here to have the baby. Perhaps if they would have stayed in New York to have the baby as Sean so painfully knew they should have, the birth of the child would have not ended in both their deaths.

Sean now had to live with the knowledge that Angelina's death was entirely his fault. True or not, that didn't change how he felt. He let her talk him into having the baby here even though he never felt right about it. If only he would have been more of a man and stood up to her just once. He should have forced her to have the baby in a hospital instead of here, with nothing but a midwife, who just stood there and watched her die as everything went wrong. If only he had done the right thing, she would still be here, and so would the baby.

Sean could not bring himself to go into that house. It just sat there like a white mausoleum. All of the furniture covered to protect it from the dust, the home sealed and silent. The only residents in that house were the spirits of his dead wife and their unborn child beckoning for him to join them. He intended to oblige them, soon. He would get back to work on that task later today.

The garage held three of Sean's favorite possessions, even though technically, they weren't his. The first was a baby blue 66 Ford Mustang convertible. The second, an original AC Cobra 427, red, of course, with bold white stripes down the hood. A car with very few siblings left alive. The third and most prized was a blue Harley Davidson Electra-Glide, a copy of a bike from an old movie Maxwell loved. It was the latter of the three Sean loved the most as well. The feeling he got riding that massive, powerful beast of a bike was the closest he came to happy these days.

He opened the garage door and fired Big Blue, as he called it up. The rumble of the engine immediately woke his senses and sent a rush up and down his spine to match the heartbeat in his temples. Unfortunately today that rush ended up shaking his throbbing skull and almost making him wince with the pain but he was not getting off, he might ride to Lake Michigan if he had to in order to clear his head. All so he could start all over.

Regardless of his motive or feelings, he put it in gear and let it roar out of the garage and down the long drive leading out onto the road towards town. To the innocent bystander you would have thought he had the look of an intensely happy man, gritting his teeth against the sheer power and majesty of the ride.

The reality was he was in serious pain and was fighting to keep consciousness.

Maybe he would stop at the Valley Tavern to catch up on things before he came back to get on with the days task of searching for solace and oblivion. It had been quite a while since he spoke with another human being and sometimes he did miss it. There were times he still thought about trying to rejoin the human race even if they grew more and more infrequent as he sunk into the self administered death sentence he was carrying out.

The lake house property lay about twenty-five miles south of Munising, Michigan, along the border of the Hiawatha National Forest. It was not what you would call an estate per say. It was not ostentatious, opulent, or well-manicured, with servants running here and there. It had a more sublime charm to it, especially to Sean. It sat on a rather large expanse of land and there was no one was around for miles providing the beloved isolation Sean craved.

The house was simple and was not a place you would associate with a billionaire. Compared with Maxwell's other properties it was downright provincial but it was heaven to Sean. No other dwellings existed for miles. It was just Sean, the birds, the animals, and the fish, lots and lots of fish, all waiting for him to pull them from the lake as he sipped his whiskey.

The calming waters of the lake as they slapped the shore and the whisper of wind through the ancient trees accented by the occasional chirps and caws of the birds brought Sean the peace and tranquility he needed to forget what lie in his past. If you drank enough in that calm setting to stop thinking, eventually, peace would come, even to a killer like Sean. Either that or you passed out. Both served the same purpose and Sean didn't really care which came first as long as his brain shut down for another day, another day closer to death.

He began to feel better as he made his way along the empty road. Closer to town, he passed Hanley Field where a corporate jet once waited to ferry him back and forth on the various missions Maxwell sent him on to further expand his empire of "restructured" businesses, or as some preferred to call them, stolen businesses. A jet sat there now as he rode past, waiting for its precious corporate cargo or some other high end master to tell it to take to the skies.

All of that 'stolen' talk was merely caused by ignorance, a big misunderstanding of course. They were simply opportunities others would not, or could not see or realize themselves just sitting there waiting for Maxwell to unleash their hidden worth, or as he called it, "failures in need of new management".

Maxwell built his empire out of the small fortune his father left him. A hard earned bounty gleaned from the hills in the Northwest Territories back during the gold rush days. Alderson Investments was now one of the largest capitol investment firms in the world. Hundreds of businesses owed their new lease on life to Alderson Investments, whether they wanted to admit it or not. Yes, Maxwell served a purpose in this life. He saved what was worth saving and tore apart the dead soldiers, and those who killed them in the first place in order to build new additions to his vast empire. The people he ran off had a different picture of Maxwell, that's for sure! Maxwell didn't care. He simply did what came natural.

Maxwell's father was an inspiration to Maxwell and the reason he saw the world as he did. He has been one of the smarter ones back during the gold rush. Rather than search for the gold himself, he made his fortune selling the perspective miners the equipment they needed to play in the dirt, searching for what few would ever find in any meaningful abundance. They did find enough to pay for more supplies and that was all that mattered to Maxwell's father. A lot of gold went through his hands but not one nugget did he dig or pan for himself. He simply converted them into goods. It was a wonderful symbiotic relationship in Maxwell's mind and a wonderful lesson as well. There are, after all, many forms of hard work and not all of them involve digging and other forms of arduous labor. Some of them even dig away at your soul rather than the ground. But the result is the same, everyone ends up dead but some end up rich before they die.

Alderson Investments was a life Sean married into. In the process he became the son Maxwell never had, but so desperately wanted. Sean was never truly comfortable with the type of business dealings Maxwell lusted after, though. Working in a company that specialized in takeovers and acquisitions took a certain kind of personality. It was one you were born with or one you decided you could stomach. You could not be merciful to the ones that got themselves into the position where they needed a capitalist investment firm to come in and take over. These latter day managers and CEO's were the problem, not the solution. You were the solution, and the game was to rebuild or demolish. The only decision was which one was the more profitable avenue. Either one was going to shake up the lives of those involved to the core. Inevitably it could be an utter blood bath at times. "It isn't called investment capital for nothing. Always remember we are not in the charity business and we must protect our own interests first so we can continue to assist the ignorant. We will provide charity to the poor workers they failed to take care of, but the hell with the assholes that ran something worth having into the ground. They deserve nothing, not even our pity," Maxwell was very fond of saying this. When you worked for Maxwell you had to be willing to be ruthless if necessary. It was for the good of the many, after all.

Maxwell understood well the principle of sacrificing the few, for the good of the many. Besides, the ones he put on the chopping block were the same ones that put the companies he bought out in trouble in the first place, weren't they? Why did they deserve his, or anyone's mercy? How many lives had they destroyed running the companies they lost into the ground? No, mercy was definitely not on the 'to do' list in this game, and although Sean was not the naturally ruthless type, it wasn't odd that it never became easy for him. He had to work at it and work at it he did.

When Angelina died, his name was being whispered in all the appropriate places. He was the next candidate for any and every race out there. Hell, he was expected to be seen on every 'Man of the year' list in existence! When that list came out if he was on it he intended to cry. He wouldn't cry for joy, he would cry because the world idolized a man who learned how to rip the lives of the weak apart!

Sean studied law at Harvard and this is where he and Angelina met. He was a 'scholarship case' as they were sometimes called so it didn't ring of charity. What it really meant was he was not part of the ruling class that was so deeply embedded in that world.

When they met he took a liking to Maxwell immediately. Maxwell didn't know Sean had already cracked the secret code of Angelina's pants so, of course, he didn't know he was just trying to impress him. Sean was hoping the man would be his father in law one day.

The unintended affect was that it didn't hurt that Maxwell was a rather famous alumni and he, Sean Rider, Scholarship case, poor as dirt and he was dating the iconic Maxwell Alderson's only daughter. Life at Harvard seemed to improve from then on.

That was never why Sean dated Angelina. He truly loved her. Long before he knew who she was, he loved her. It was just a side benefit that opened doors in a closed world for an outsider like Sean and he had no choice but to jump in all the way.

He didn't work for Maxwell until several years later. Not even after he graduated did he go straight to work for him. It was his desire to make his own way, no push-ups for him. The last time he worked for another client was when he came up against Maxell himself.

He first tried his hand at 'real' law. He majored in corporate law but stuck to the lighter side of it taking his first job with an insurance company as a lackey lawyer working petty cases against people who just wanted their lives returned to them by the ones who took them. Sean's job was to see to it that their needs being met never came to pass. It left such a bad taste in his mouth it was easy for Maxwell to persuade him to come to work for him. That and the day Maxwell pulled him aside and told him if he ever wanted to marry his daughter he had no choice. It was not a threat, it was a promise.

Sean showed up at the office bright and early after an all expense paid trip to the Bahamas with Angelina. They stayed there two weeks in Maxwell's private suite. Sean took advantage of the moment and made Angelina his wife. A small ceremony, Maxwell was not invited. Sean wondered how close he came to death pulling that last act of defiance off. Luckily Angelina would not let her father break her husband's legs or worse, disappear like some of her fathers enemies had throughout the years. That little fact and the fact that Sean knew that deep down, Maxwell actually seemed to like him kept him alive, at least for now.

Still, Sean knew a different Maxwell than most. He got to see the man's behavior around his beloved daughter, Angelina, and Sharon, the daughter of one of his servants who had grown up with Angelina. Sharon was like the sister Angelina never had and they were treated in this manner by all of Maxwell's servants. They were close, closer than many a sister who share actual blood.

Sean grew to love Maxwell because he could see past the hard exterior formed when Maxwell's own wife died giving birth to Angelina. Maxwell spoke of it only once. Sean sat in total disbelief as Maxwell sobbed after finishing the story. He didn't think that depth of emotion Maxwell was displaying was possible for a man like him, but it was.

The truth was that Maxwell was a loving, doting father and had been a devoted happy husband once, too. Sean realized that life had soured or changed for Maxwell without the guidance of Martha, a supposed charitable and unselfishly kind woman who was no longer around to exhibit her calming effect on Maxwell. Had she lived, he may have become a different man than he was today but she was gone, and along with her, any semblance of mercy or charity Maxwell had for the doomed souls he would spend his lifetime toiling against.

Yes, Sean was one of the few who had seen that side of Maxwell and the charitable part of Sean knew he had to forgive Maxwell. Unfortunately, all of that was before the tragedy of losing Angelina. All of that was before Sean deprived Maxwell of the last thing on earth he loved, driving out what was left of Maxwell's soul. That was ultimately why Sean left him. He could no longer face Maxwell, let alone keep working with him.

After that, Maxwell had become driven. Sean knew when Angelina died he would never go back. He knew he had been assigned a locker in hell but still, he refused to assist Maxwell in seeing how many lives he could ruin. Maxwell locked himself away after that. Only Sharon got close to him after that.

One thing never changed though. Sean respected Maxwell's keen sense of purpose, despite how ruthless he was in his business dealings. Where others simply saw a tyrant and a hermit who reveled in the pain of others, Sean saw a shrewd, if not visionary man. Bad tempered? Always! But that didn't change the fact he was a genius when it came to business.

Sean knew him for what he was, not the man others saw. He was a lonely man who frankly knew what it took to take a run down business and make it thrive, throwing out the trash when needed along the way, and selling it when it was viable so he could move on to his next conquest. Like it or not, Maxwell actually took a vast number of failed enterprises and turned them around. In all honesty, this was why people really hated him. He was better than them!

Sean hadn't quite fully developed the love of the kill that was necessary to take control the way Maxwell had but under Maxwell's wing, he was on his way to becoming just like him. The feeling of power one gets wading through the bodies... Feeding on the carnage and coming out victorious can be a bit addictive. As he looked back, in a lot of ways, he was becoming just like Maxwell. He could see the changes now that he was out. He could see what had been taking place to him. He had begun to harden and worse had become capable of great cruelty, all in the name of success. He was becoming many things, and some of them he didn't very much like. He now saw he had begun to adhere to, and to accept, Maxwell's famous philosophy... "Kill the ones that need to be killed. It strengthens the herd and lets

23

lions like us eat too. That's why the weak and the slow exist, to feed the strong.

"Don't just be faster than the slowest antelope, if you are then you are still just an antelope. You are no better than feed for the lion, dinner, satisfied with the herd mentality and secure in the belief that there is strength in numbers and you are not the slowest one there so not on the menu tonight!

"Instead be the fastest lion and don't worry about needing anyone else. Feed yourself. The world is filled with antelope. Eat and live to hunt another day!"

Sean had a much less adversarial personality then Maxwell back then. His cynicism had to be cultivated and nurtured or he would be of no use to Maxwell down the road! The other necessary ingredient was that Sean needed to feel as if it was all his desire. Yes, how to turn a soul? Do it under cover of darkness.

It was too late now, everyone had their view. Nice guy or not, the fact he believed he was one didn't save him from being looked at as a monster in the business world, let alone within the company. Just working for Maxwell automatically qualified one for a certain label and to be his heir apparent?

Sean carried that label along with two others these days. The first one was that he was the man that killed Angelina. It wasn't important that he gave this label to himself and no one else felt that way, not even Maxwell. Sean did, and that was all that mattered. It was now the label he would carry to his death.

As for the other label, Maxwell's relatives simply called him 'That freeloading murderer sucking off of Maxwell's teat.' A rather long title, true, and one Sean couldn't care less about. To the relatives of Maxwell Bartholomew Alderson though, it was a seriously important fact, a fact that they were keenly aware of.

It was all just another great reason to knock a few back and obliviate the memories. Besides, when it came to Maxwell's relatives, they all hated Maxwell and he hated them so it was a wash. They wanted his money and used him every chance they got and they provided him with a free-flowing wellspring for his hatred. It was a win/win all the way. Maxwell hated everyone and everyone hated him.

Maxwell's hatred of his relatives was a passionate. They were always looking for a handout, showing up uninvited at any one of his various estates. It was common for them to stay for months and even years at a time. Most of them never worked a day in their lives once they figured out how to freeload, or more appropriately, steal from Maxwell. They were simply waiting for the old tightwad to croak so they could divide up his estate and split all his wealth, and most importantly, liquidate his company.

The lake house was, of course, first on their list of assets needing to be liquefied along with its current resident who needed to be kicked out and sent packing with nothing but the clothes on his back, well, maybe not even the clothes on his back.

Because of his desire to be as far from any of his wonderful relatives as possible, Maxwell no longer went to any of his estates. Maxwell now spent all of his time the one place they were never welcome. He made it abundantly clear that this was the case. These days he rarely stepped foot off of the 'Me Lady'. The yacht, if you could call it that, was the one safe place left in his life and he took her all over the world. She and her crew were the only company he needed, having given up on Sean over a year ago.

Sean drug himself up out of the morass of memories as he pulled into the parking lot of the Valley Tavern. He shut the massive bike down after one last twist of the throttle which produced a deep throated, satisfying roar. He sat there a moment hoping the aspirin would soon begin to do their job, yet certain only one thing would take the pain away.

Katy would be working, as usual, and she would try and get him to eat something, as usual. He would quietly decline, as usual, and she would break down and hand him a beer before he could ask for a shot, as usual, and they would keep this little dance up for an hour or so, as usual, at which point Sean would then disappear for a few more weeks, as usual, and Katy would wonder if he was still alive, as usual.

After their initial ritual dance, what happened next would depend on her mood though. The as usual was not always as usual! Sometimes she got mad at him and sometimes she just complied. He tolerated her constant barrage of motherly love and sometimes even complied with her extra demands for one reason. She had been Angelina's best friend and she could not bear to watch what Sean was doing to himself without trying to stop it and he could never hurt her, not really.

It was always the same though. It would start out as small talk and turn into a well-intentioned lecture and then she would cry. That was when he would give in most of the time. She had a way of getting him to do what she wanted.

The one thing that Sean hated about her meddling was the fact that she kept making attempts to play matchmaker and find him someone to help him forget Angelina. Of course, it never worked. He never forgot her. He tried a few times and actually came close to a relationship with one of her many 'friends' she would introduce him to.

One of them was a sweet woman his age that was actually very appealing. She was also not what you would call shy. She seemed more than willing to reacquaint him with the pleasures of the flesh. Hell, he saw her from time to time and it was obvious it was a standing offer. Who was he to turn down a little extracurricular activity? After all, it didn't keep him from his primary goal of self-destruction, instead it added to his self-loathing and usually fueled a really deep depression in which he could double his effort!

Even now though, Sean just could not bring himself to love anyone. He couldn't care less about women, love, or relationships anymore and finally both he and Katy gave up, Katy much more reluctantly than Sean.

Sean was a lost case and so far no one had been able to change that. Katy still tried on occasion, but she wasn't stupid. She could see she was wasting her time, even though that knowledge hurt her deeply. She knew only Sean could fix Sean. And he didn't seem to want fixing.

Sean snapped awake. He realized he had been standing there stroking the seat on the bike and felt a little embarrassed hoping no one had witnessed his mental lapse. Even though he was trying to kill himself with alcohol he didn't want anyone to know it. He didn't want to be the guy sitting in the gutter no longer able to buy booze. He wanted to be the guy who was dead and buried because he finally got to a point he consumed enough to kill himself. You know, choke on his own vomit or something like that.

Embarrassed, he quickly made his way to the door and into the familiar main room of the Valley Tavern taking his usual place at the bar. Katy met him with a menu and a set of silverware, as usual. He smiled and shook his head in resignation reaching for the menu and pretending he was going to order something.

"I'll start with a shot of your best house bourbon," he said, staring her down with all of the defiance his pounding head could manage. He knew it was going to be a waste of time by the scowl that made its way across her care-worn, yet still pretty face. She had always been a beautiful woman.

"Milk," she threw back more defiantly than he could ever be.

"Beer!" he countered, really getting the game rolling.

Katy was older than Sean but still quite attractive. She was slim and statuesque and possessed a wonderfully bubbly personality, most of the time. She was patient and with everyone and loved to talk. The only one Sean ever saw her get mad at was Sean, well, there was the occasional brawl or too. You didn't mess around in her place though. You were respectful or you were not allowed in, period, and of course there was always Ben and his famous bat.

"You'll get one after you eat, Sean, maybe and that is a really big maybe. You look like shit!" she shot back, daring him to argue with her.

"Alright, give me a burger and fries, and a beer. Bring the beer now and I promise I'll actually eat the burger and fries," he offered in truce, making one last attempt to challenge her obvious authority over this situation.

"I'm going to hold you to it, mister. Don't mess with me or I'll stop giving a damn and I mean it this time!" she growled, unconvincingly.

She opened the cooler below the bar and took out a bottle of beer and set it in front of him without removing the cap. He laughed and took the beer. He opened it and threw the cap in the ash tray on the bar. Katy just shook her head and disappeared into the kitchen.

Sean loved this place and so had Angelina. They shared many good times here and ate many good meals. Katy and her husband, Ben, owned the place. She tended the bar and played hostess and Ben ran the kitchen just like Ben's father and mother before them. Ben was an excellent cook. The fare was simple and delicious and the place was usually packed once the residents knocked off from their jobs and crowded in for grub, gossip, and a few well deserved rounds of cheer.

As he sipped the cold and refreshing beer he looked around the place. It hadn't changed a bit in all the years he'd been coming in here. It was an old stone and Tudor building, a little on the rustic side and age worn, which just added to its charm. It was not the best lit place but that too was part of the charm. One of the few adornments on the wall was a large deer head Ben bagged many years ago. It hung accusingly over the fireplace looking down on a few old, well-worn chairs that sat waiting for someone to plop down in them for a bit of conversation and lie swapping.

The walls were covered with a dark, rich wood paneling above the stone with a ledge and several dozen bar stools running the entire way around the main room and in the adjacent rooms as well. The wood plank floors were well-oiled and carefully maintained. The bar matched the paneling on the walls as did four booths buy the front door and the various tables and chairs scattered in a seemingly haphazard manner around the room. The room had a warm, dusky glow provided by the only real update Ben did to the place, which was to put in some recessed lighting to add a back glow to the few ancient chandeliers hanging from the off white, smoke stained ceiling.

Katy and Ben lived above the place in the second floor rooms which were simple but comfortable. The building had been in Ben's family for three generations and his father was the one who decided to convert the first floor to a pub and grub. Ben was a natural at running the place as was Katy. They loved this life and this place and wouldn't trade it for the world.

On the main floor, off to the side was a game room. It held a few tables and bar stools, a pool table, two dart boards, and a shuffle board Ben's father bought years ago, a favorite of the older customers that frequented the place. The venerable games all sat idle for now waiting patiently until later in the day when they would be visited by the local men and women as they drank and talked about work, the men puffing on the cigars taken from the well-stocked humidor Ben kept just as his father had. It was one of the town's oldest establishments and Ben and Katy took great pride in that.

One day their son would take it over just as they had from Ben's father who now spent his days stealing beers when Katy wasn't looking, which, of course, she always was. She pretended to scold him and threatened to kick him and his cronies out. They, of course, just laughed and went on with their fish stories. Nothing he tried got past her but she knew her role in this little game. She was supposed to be shocked and annoyed and chase the old fart but it was all for show. Ben senior lost his wife a few years back and Katy would never do anything to hurt the old man. She loved him as much as she did her own husband and son and besides, he was actually good for business! He and his buddies played many games of shuffleboard and he always had a crowd when he began to deal out his lies. He was the best liar in town when it came to the size of his fish and the heroic battles he fought to land them. All the time they all bought food and drink, all except Ben senior that is.

Usually if Ben senior wasn't here sneaking beers, lying, or playing shuffleboard with his buddies he was down at the lake with Sean catching his next big lie. He was probably the only other person Sean saw on a regular basis and they were the only real friends Sean had left. When you were trying to kill yourself friends just got in the way so the fewer the better.

Several minutes passed as Sean sat reflecting before Katy re-emerged from the kitchen with a steaming platter of fresh cut fries and a burger so large it was in danger of falling over and would have to be smashed to fit in his mouth. Sean's stomach growled as she came over to him and he realized he was indeed starving and admittedly needed the nourishment. She set the platter down in front of him and he greedily began shoving the hot fries in his mouth without a word or a glance up. Katy smiled and walked down the bar to the register where she grabbed a pile of mail and a bottle of ketchup.

"I almost forgot. I picked up your mail today. I was going to bring it out to you later today or have dad bring it. I was trying to get up the courage to get out there and check and see if you were still breathing," she snorted sarcastically, making her way back towards him.

"Thanks Katy. How is the old fart? I haven't seen him in a few weeks," he managed between mouthfuls.

"He's been laid up ill with a cold but is sick of being cooped up. I was figuring I could get him to come out with me to check on you. Hasn't stopped him from coming down and stealing a beer though. He's getting older, you know. It takes him a long time to recover these days," she replied in a more conversational tone.

He hadn't realized how hungry he was until she brought the food out. The juicy hamburger dripped as he savored the delicious blend of juicy meat, melted cheese and catsup mingled with mayo, pickle and a juicy slice of tomato. Rivulet of the savory mixture coursed down his chin as he stuffed the mouthwatering feast into his mouth.

After several large bites he stopped to wipe his chin and turned his attention to the stack of mail she set down next to the plate. He never read any of it but he always took it with him to throw away just to keep from having to listen to Katy accuse him of wasting her time. There was a large manila envelope from Talbert, Gibbins and Talbert, the law firm that represented Alderson Investments and also tended to Maxwell's personal affairs. Sean just stared at it. That envelope for sure would never be opened. It would make a nice starter for the fire tonight though.

"By the way, what did the suits want?" Katy asked, pulling him out of his silence, busy at her business of cleaning and polishing the handsome, use-worn bar.

"What suits are those?" Sean asked, not grasping the question.

"The big city suit types that were in here earlier looking for you. They didn't come out to the house?" She stopped rubbing the bar and looked over at him, raising her left eyebrow quizzically.

"Not that I know of, no. I haven't seen anyone for weeks," he shrugged, taking another bite of the burger while it was still hot and juicy. He even forgot about the beer sitting there waiting on him, giving the plate of food his full attention.

"Well they asked for you by name and I told them where they could find you. That was about two hours ago. They said it was urgent they find you," she said, returning her attention to what she was doing.

"Well if it was urgent for them then I am glad they missed me."

"Sean, you can't hide forever," Katy scolded, growing slightly agitated.

Sean had other ideas. He could and would hide forever and hopefully forever wasn't that far off. "We'll see about that!" he said, under his breath. Sean shrugged and worked on the burger and fries avoiding both her sweltering gaze and the growing list motherly responses he knew she was formulating just in case he had the nerve to continue to banter with her.

He would need to find a way to avoid them. It was most likely another one of Maxwell's attempts to lure him back. Going back was never going to happen no matter what the Old Fart did. Sean was through with him and more importantly, through with that life. He wasn't proud of his current existence, in fact, he was downright ashamed of it and worse yet, he knew what his deceased wife would say to him if she were here. But that didn't change the fact that he couldn't face Maxwell or the rest of them any more. He lost his nerve and he was ashamed of himself.

When he finished eating he sat back and reached for the beer. "Thanks Katy, that was really good."

Katy was out on the floor serving a young couple that had just come in and she looked over and smiled at him warmly. Sean hoped all the comments he knew were building up in her had been washed away with the gesture of submission he just tossed her. He could tell she was quite pleased with herself for getting him to eat. She couldn't stand the way he was trying to kill himself and she constantly berated him for the injustice he was doing to Angelina's memory. Thank goodness the two customers came in. That was the only thing saving him from a good ass chewing. He was sure of it. That and the peace gesture he had just made.

He sat quietly sipping his beer and just enjoying the nearness of people without feeling any need, or being forced, to interact with them in any way when the two men came into the tavern. Although the second one that come through the door blocked enough sunlight to make Sean think the earth was in the middle of an eclipse, he could make out the suits and knew his planned escape had been abruptly cancelled. It was obvious they were the ones Katy was talking about. He had no intention of speaking with them and reached into his pocket for his wallet so he could pay Katy and sneak out the side door and hop on Big Blue before they realized he was the one they were looking for. Katy spoiled his retreat by pointing her finger at him though and Sean swore under his breath. The two men looked down the bar at him and headed briskly in his direction.

"Mr. Ryder. We work for Maxwell Alderson. We are here to see you on his behalf," the short, round one of the two told him.

"I don't have any dealings with Maxwell or Alderson Investments these days, gentlemen. Now if you will excuse me," he responded dismissively, trying to push past them.

"I see you have received your plane tickets and room reservations, Mr. Ryder. Since you should have had those days ago and already been in New York, we were sent to find out why you had not come as directed," the shorter man said to him in his best business tone.

Sean knew the formal tone well and knew the little errand boy was going to have his say and deliver his message whether Sean liked it or not. He didn't seem the type to take no for an answer and he had a rather large assistant to make sure he was listened to. He was vaguely familiar too. Sean was certain he had seen the man before and not in a good way. At least he remembered thinking it would not very pleasant for whomever Maxwell had him going to visit. He remembered the aloof, distant air and the harsh almost gleeful twinkle that come into the man's eyes when Maxwell was whispering in his ear. Sean found himself unable to hold back the little shiver, just like the last time.

"As long as we are already here, we can provide you with transportation when you are ready," the man's associate chimed in. He was much larger but had the same look, and that look said Sean had better not refuse. He would be getting into their car. The only question was if he wanted to get into the car under his own power.

Except for the obvious size differences, they both looked like near identical clones in their priceless black suits. It didn't take long for Sean to recognize them despite his long absence from the firm. Well, not these two specifically, the small one, yes, but not his over-developed partner. Yes, maybe the short one, but the general type was unmistakable. He was sure he semi-recognized the shorter of the two men. He was sure he had seen this man before, with Maxwell.

Maxwell had a well hidden cadre of these goons. He never let anyone talk to them so Sean had no idea who they were or what, specifically, Maxwell employed them for. He did have his suspicions. Based on several events throughout Sean's employment he may not have known their specific purpose, but he had some rather distasteful ideas.

It seemed they did certain 'things' for Maxwell from time to time. They all dressed, walked, talked, and Sean was sure killed in the same way and you would never see them coming or going. They were ghosts. Sean knew the type well. He also knew he would not shake them unless he at least let them say what they were here for.

"I am not going anywhere unless you are here to kick me off of the lake property. Deliver your message and leave me alone. Like I said, I am not beholden to Maxwell anymore," Sean said defiantly, feeling a little on edge at the tension he was creating and having a pretty good idea where it could get him.

"It is obvious you have not heard of Maxwell's demise, Sir. If you had I am certain your behavior would be much less confrontational and not nearly as rude. So, in order to get us back on the right track, let me be the first to offer you my condolences," the shorter one said, trying to defuse the situation but still making sure Sean knew who was in charge right now. There is nothing quite like a subtle hint at where things might be heading to calm most men down.

The big one apparently was not allowed to open his mouth very often. He was definitely not allowed to speak without permission and then only on certain subjects. His conversational skills were likely more along subject lines like, "Which leg would you like broken first?" Or, "Do you not have a preference? I could do them both together to save time if that works for you. Just let me know, meat sack!"

It was not a true test of the imagination to come to that conclusion concerning Mr. Big. He likely possessed talents reserved for the truly uncooperative. Sean saw several moods cross the man's face and was sure one was delight. That was probably the end of a thought involving something to do with Sean that Sean did not want any details of, let alone any first hand knowledge. These were not lawyers or businessmen in the normal sense. These were what were commonly referred to as errand boys or more appropriately in their case, fixers. They would do whatever you wanted, to whomever you wanted, in any manner you wanted it done for a price, maybe for free if it was going to be really fun. They also didn't take no for an answer, and, they never failed at their task. It was time to back off or suffer the consequences.

Sean looked at the two men for a minute. Even though the bar was dark, they both were still wearing their sunglasses. This and the dark suits they were wearing and meticulous grooming both exhibited was totally overshadowed by the otherwise unremarkable nature they displayed, but Sean wasn't fooled. These two were Maxwell's private thugs.

Neither of them had a clue what a smile was. Well maybe they did, but you wouldn't want be around to see it if they did. That smile would most likely be one of the last things you ever saw. You were better off keeping them wearing the blank expression they were wearing now, if you knew what was good for you. Sean had a pretty good idea how they thought and how they worked and he also knew it would not be wise to rile them up.

They were just another reason he never wanted to go back. The fact that Maxwell had assets like these at his disposal was one of the reasons Sean walked away. Maxwell always kept a few "special" assistants around. They belonged to some firm or more likely some secret fraternity Maxwell dealt with. No one knew for sure where they came from. It was Maxwell's little secret. How and why Maxwell knew them, or even why had them around was not something Sean was never privy to.

If and when they were used was strictly between Maxwell and them. No one else was ever involved in any of the details or had any clue what he used them for. Sean just knew that if they were seen around, whatever roadblock to whatever project they were currently working on simply seemed to suddenly disappear and everything fell into place. It was as if their mere presence smoothed negotiations over no matter how reluctant the target was. You wouldn't see or hear from them again until some other resistance needed special consideration and then wham bam, thank you ma'am, there they were, Maxwell whispering sweet nothings in their ears.

Katy closed some of the distance between her and Sean and was listening intently. Sean got a little nervous. Katy was not the type to sit there and allow one of her customers to be mistreated in her establishment, especially one like Sean, whom she considered almost like family. Sean decided to finish this little exchange quickly.

"OK. So where are we going?"

"We have a private jet waiting at the airport and we are under strict instructions to escort you to New York where the reading of Maxwell Alderson's will is scheduled for tomorrow. I am certain, now that you are aware of the circumstances of this visit you are most anxious to comply with."

Sean shivered as he saw the man glance in Katy's direction. He let his gaze linger there just long enough to make Sean nervous before returning it squarely on Sean, making firm eye contact to drive home the potential outcome of a wrong answer. A funny tick came to the corner of the man's mouth as he must have contemplated how she might die. Oh, he was fast and he was shrewd and he didn't miss the fact that she was hovering over them and getting a little worked up. He knew they cared for each other and that put Katy in danger. They were experts in the mechanics of leverage, PhD, all the way.

"What's going on Sean? You need me to call the sheriff?" Katy asked, as she worked her way over to the phone.

"No Katy. It's all right. I guess I'll be making a trip to New York. It seems Maxwell died."

"Do you require anything from home or can we just proceed from here? We are under orders to provide you with anything you might need and we are running out of time," the little mouthpiece said trying to sound magnanimous. What he was really saying was, "get in the car, before I break more than your legs."

"Is there a bar on the plane?" Sean asked.

"Of course there is, Sir. It's fully stocked for your comfort and convenience. As I said, we are here to see to your complete comfort during this time of mourning," Little Big Man informed him, the sarcasm barely contained in his high, almost feminine voice.

"Katy, I'll get back in a few days. Can you and Ben watch the place for me and take Big Blue home?"

"Of course, Sean, but are you sure you'll be OK? These two well-manicured thugs don't seem to have very good manners to me," she barked, eyeing the two defiantly.

"Ah, they're completely harmless. They're just here on orders doing their job like good little errand boys. Isn't that right, boys?"

Sean enjoyed the look that crossed Big Little Man's face. H was trying to rile them just a little to redirect their attention away from Katy. She didn't understand what she was dealing with and he didn't want them returning to educate her.

"That is correct, Mr. Ryder. We are just doing our job. Now then, if you are ready, we have a car outside."

Little Big Man gestured towards the door as Big Little Man uncrossed his rather large arms letting the super sized fists at their ends slowly drop to his sides. Sean knew a physical threat, or promise, when he saw one. He knew what would bring a smile to that face right about now. A little blood dripping from Sean's smart mouth would do the trick. Maybe add a large bruise that would follow the lump on his skull after that appeared after he was unceremoniously tossed in the back seat, well maybe the trunk. That would make him just as happy as can be. A few broken ribs and he'd be howling and slapping his knee for sure.

Quietly, without glancing back, Sean headed for the door. He wanted them out of this neck of the woods as soon as possible. Katy was a strong woman and Ben was a big brute of a man but they didn't understand what these boys did for a living and if they even so much as thought a lesson in manners was due, Sean would be finding another tavern to visit and be short a few friends.

As he crawled into the back of the black sedan, he couldn't help but wonder why such a fuss over his appearance at the reading of Maxwell's will. What had the old man done to interfere with his mission of self destruction now? Knowing Maxwell, he had done plenty and Sean was helpless for the time being.

Chapter Two

Sean woke around noon having nearly forgotten where he was. His head pounded with the after effects of the night before. The plane ride had been one long sampling of the bar followed by the further sampling of the equally well-stocked bar in the suite he had been dumped in at the Waldorf Astoria. That of course was before, or maybe after, he couldn't remember exactly, but he knew that somewhere in there a trip down to the hotel bar had taken place, where he was sure he made an ass out of himself. To think he accomplished all that in one night and still found the time to wake up this morning! Paradise was a wonderful place!

There was a small table near the window which held an assortment of pastries and a pot of coffee which he staggered over too, filling one of the dainty cups in hopes the black liquid could quell the pulsing in his head. He didn't bother to wonder why it was there or who had brought it in. He just took what was given gratefully. He sat down in one of the chairs and cradled his head in his hands in an attempt to squeeze the pain from it as he fought back the bile churning ever more fiercely in his stomach, threatening to rise up in an uncontrollable bout of nauseous rebellion. Yes sir, just another day in paradise, he thought.

After the plane ride and the trip from the airport which he barely recalled, Little Big Man and Big Little Man

45

unceremoniously dropped him in the suite to further drown in the self-pity he cloaked his dying heart in on a daily basis. They avoided every question and attempt at conversation he tried but at least, thankfully, they had refrained from beating the crap out of him as he was well aware they would thoroughly enjoy doing. It would have made a nice fringe benefit to the unsavory task of delivering him here. He was sure of that much. Especially, after he made it a point to get them good and pissed at him in hopes they would forget about Munising and Katy all together. All he needed was for them to be passing through and decide to stay for a day or two to educate Katy. But he knew he probably didn't have to worry. These guys most likely had more than enough business to keep their blood lust sated and he didn't think returning to Munising would be professionally correct from their point of view and they were always professional, that much was obvious. They would do whatever it took to remove a roadblock but to bring attention to their little guild when otherwise avoidable would most likely be frowned upon. Still, one should not take chances with the likes of them.

He picked up the cup of coffee and the carafe that contained the remaining black magic and stumbled into the bathroom where he unceremoniously emptied the contents of his stomach for several minutes until the waves of nausea and dizziness left him. The shower was a large marbled walk in room with several shower heads that he turned on to let the water warm as he stripped off his clothes, shoes included, that he had failed to remove the night before when he passed out. He vaguely remembered being on the couch in the sitting room and wondered how he got into bed and why he was still dressed if he had been helped into the sack. There were no bruises so it must have been someone other than his two escorts.

He spent a good fifteen minutes standing in the warm streams of water which thankfully washed the stench of sweat and alcohol from his body. As he began to feel a little better he constantly lowered the water temperature hoping the cold would chase away the funk of his pounding brain and wake him enough to get to the bar to start another round of "Drink till you pass out," his favorite daytime game show here in paradise.

Finally, semi-refreshed, he turned the water off and grabbed one of the large soft towels hanging from the golden hooks next to the shower door and dried himself off. There was a soft, comfortable robe waiting there which he ignored. He headed to the sink where he found a tooth brush and slew of other toiletries waiting which he gratefully put to use, fighting to keep his hands from shaking lest he lose a little skin. He was used to this daily battle though. Just one of the perks of living in paradise! Yes sir! Here in paradise, shaving could be especially interesting, even entertaining, on days like this! He opened the door leading back into the bedroom and strode into it naked except the towel draped around his neck.

He was considering going out into the main room to see what was left to sample on the bar in hopes he could steady his nerves and sooth his aching head when he glanced over at the table where he found the coffee earlier. Sitting there looking at his naked body was a woman dressed in a charcoal grey suit, her legs crossed at the ankles and tucked gingerly under her chair, and her hands laid in her lap. She was regarding him with barely concealed interest, or, was it amusement he sensed, disgust maybe? It was hard to tell what that look meant. Figuring out which was made even more difficult by the fact that he could barely focus his eyes.

She was an extraordinarily attractive woman, an exotic beauty of Asian and Caucasian decent. Her long black hair was pulled back into a pony tail except for a few locks that escaped to frame her delicate face and the large eyes which regarded him with open distaste over a pair of stylish glasses sitting low on her nose. She looked like the classical librarian as she watched him over her spectacles, barely controlling the amusement she was getting out of the situation, openly taking in his nakedness. Yet, he could also see obvious signs of disgust curling up the edges of her tightly pursed lips as if to fight back the urge to vomit. He felt immediate shame.

"Good morning, Mr. Ryder. I trust you slept well, although I would describe it more like a coma than actual, restful, sleep. I took the liberty last night of having a tailor measure you after you passed out. He was a really sweet and

48

gentle man and seemed to enjoy it quite a bit. He spent a lot of time on the pants for some reason. He was very worried about something to do with needing to determine the proper tuck or something, that's when I had to step out for a time.

"Oh well. Anyway, you will find fresh clothes in the closet over there. Shall I send your other clothes out for cleaning or should I just have them burned before the vermin in them get a chance to infest the entire city?" she said curling her nose up in a gesture of open disgust and still managing to look down it at him, all at the same time.

Sean suddenly felt like a little boy standing in front of the principle. On one hand, he was very attracted to the woman. On the other hand, she made him feel like a bad little boy that needed to be paddled, the prospect of which, he would not be totally against, if delivered by her. Yes, this woman could get a young man to do pretty much anything she wanted, he thought, amused by his own confused emotions.

"By all means, Sharon, have my real clothes sent out for cleaning. I'll need something to wear when I get paroled," he countered, not bothering to cover his exposed body in an attempt to shock her. It wasn't having the desired affect.

Sharon just shook her head and turned her attention back to the laptop sitting on the table.

"Let me know when you are coherent enough for me to fill you in on the details, Sean," she said as she typed.

Sean made his way to the closet and found several suits hanging there along with shoes, undergarments, and all of the trimmings and trappings of the life he left behind. He sighed as he pulled on the boxers and pulled one of the dark grey suits off the hook and took it back out into the bedroom. The color of the suit, like Sharon's own, was a uniform he no longer wanted to wear. Leave it to her to be the one he would have to deal with. This was going to be a long day and he was tempted to just walk out into the main room and get two or three of the tiny little bottles and down them so he could start the shutting out process before this went any further.

"So Maxwell is gone," he said, unable to hide the hint of genuine regret in his voice.

"He died quietly. He'd been fighting cancer for a while but he wouldn't accept any more treatment. I was with him, he asked for you, Sean. You broke what was left of his heart," she said looking up at him accusingly, the loss welling up in her golden, almond shaped eyes.

"I know. I turned out to be such a disappointment."

"You made your bed. You could have come back any time you wanted. He kept hoping you would snap out of it, but you just gave up."

"I killed his daughter. I wasn't about to come back!" Sean growled. Sharon's voice had a sharp hint of anger in it that made him wince but his response answered it tone for tone.

It was more than she could hide even though she wished with all her might she could. She hated Sean right now. She really, really, hated him. It would be so much easier if that was the only emotion she had towards him but unfortunately, it wasn't.

"He asked me for one last favor, or, assigned me one last task I should say. Look at it however you want. He made me promise I would see to it that you were here for the reading of his will. I hope the escorts weren't too hard on you," she sneered, a hint of pleasure seeping out at the thought of his possible rough handling by the two thugs.

"OK. I'm here. You're free to go," he threw at her, gesturing towards the door.

"It's not that easy. I am to be your personal assistant until this is all settled. Like it or not I am going to see to it that this is done. I have been very well compensated and as you know I am persistent, if nothing else. I will earn the money paid me."

"I remember that much about you and a whole lot more," Sean said, a rueful smile coming to his face.

"What happened to you Sean? I used to have so much respect for you. Hell, you mentored me! You just gave up. How do you think that would make Angelina feel?"

"Keep her out of this!" he snapped, turning and heading back into the bathroom.

"Just stay away from the bar, Sean. I mean it! I took everything from the room and if you so much as look at alcohol for the next six hours I'll make your life a living hell. You know I can. You're in no shape to fight me, Sean Ryder!"

Sharon was on her feet with her arms rigid at her sides, her tiny fists clenched. She let out a small scream and stomped her foot in frustration at her situation then stormed from the room slamming the door hard. A few seconds later she opened the door and came back in to retrieve her trusty laptop followed by an equally splendid exit and a second satisfying slam of the innocent door.

Sean listened to her swear under her breath and winced with each stomp and slam but didn't dare leave the bathroom. Some things never changed. One thing for sure, you made that little lady mad at your own peril! Sean smiled remembering several occasions when he had been witness to similar displays of aggression. Sharon had more facets than the Hope Diamond and every one of them simply added to her charm.

Sean stood there staring at his reflection. The memories were flooding back and he wanted to drown them out of his mind but he knew she meant what she said. He half expected a guard at his door, one of her trusty assistants. Sharon had been Maxwell's personal assistant and a very close associate of Sean's for many years and she was not one to be taken lightly. Once upon a time the two of them made up a pretty formidable team.

Sean knew she would gladly have the boys return and restrain him if that was what it took. He let out a sigh and finished dressing. He might as well be in prison, so much for another day in paradise. All he had to look forward to now was a long day nursing a pounding head.

When he finally got up the courage and emerged from the bedroom, he found Sharon sitting on the couch. She paid him no attention, her laptop open as usual as she tended to the affairs of her dead boss or some other matter of trumped up importance.

Sharon was a small woman, but not as small as many women of Asian descent thanks to her American father. Her father must have been quite tall and had passed that attribute along. Mother Nature could be very proud of this work of art. She was a well crafted and flawlessly executed mixture of traits. Her form and face defined perfection. Her body was well proportioned, nothing too large or too small and she was taut from years of meticulous care and exercise. Her face sat atop a long, slender neck which gave way to full lips beneath high cheekbones, all of which culminated at the eyes which could pass for golden jewels. Sean had to admit she was still one of the most beautiful women he had ever seen.

She completely ignored him as he entered the room, her small hands with their fastidiously manicured, long pale nails clicked away at her keyboard. She was totally focused on whatever it was she was doing. Her keen sense of purpose was a

53

trait that had served her well in her years with Maxwell. Sean quietly made his way over to the sitting area and took a chair off to her left, his eyes automatically straying to the now empty glass shelves that the night before held a mountain of tiny bottles of the elixir of life he craved. Sharon reached over and tossed a bottle of chewable baby aspirin at him and began to speak never looking up. Her tone was both businesslike and filled with regret all at once.

"The reading of the will is going to start at six tonight. Maxwell didn't bother sharing the details with me so don't bother asking. In the end, he was bitter and withdrawn and the details of his will were kept completely secret. He wasn't himself at the end, Sean. Something was driving and consuming him and he wouldn't let me in on any of it. He even sent me away for a while. He was a tired man, filled with hate and disappointment and a lot of that disappointment was aimed at you. You were supposed to be there to take his place," she finished, glancing up to see what affect her words were having on him.

"I admit I have made some mistakes in my life and maybe I have sort of lost my way. I could never return though. I couldn't face him. I killed his daughter! As a matter of fact, I am still not sure why I'm even sitting here! I don't have to take this shit from you, from him, or from anyone else for that matter. I will say it again. I don't want this, any of it!" Sean shouted suddenly growing intensely and almost uncontrollably angry at his situation, but feeling more like a peevish, spoiled child than anything else after his little tirade.

"You could have come back. I would have helped you, Sean. I would have been there for you. You know I always cared about you and when Angelina passed I tried to be there for you. All you did was spit on her memory you self loathing piece of shit! You didn't kill her and you know it. SO GROW UP! Maxwell never blamed you, either. He loved you Sean! I wanted to…," she stopped and shook her head. "Oh never mind," she finished, tears glistening in her eyes as she stood, preparing to flee from the room.

She stopped only for a second at the door. Without turning she addressed him one last time in a voice so cold it made him shiver. "You just stay sober for a few hours and we can get this over with. Then, you can drink yourself to death for all I care and good riddance when you're gone!" Sharon was openly crying now as she again, ran from the room slamming the door in her most formidable display of frustration and hatred yet. She slammed it so hard he was surprised she didn't break it. She always did have a bit of a hot button, he recalled. That's why she always got what she wanted in the end. No man, or woman for that matter, could withstand her for long.

Sean sat there trying to absorb what she said and feeling every bit the heel. Why did he come back? This was going to be harder than he thought now that Sharon was in the picture. He felt the noose around his neck pull just a little tighter. He could never hurt Sharon. He cared for her a great deal. He had tried so hard to forget that, and now here he was, stuck with her.

"Oh thanks a heap Maxwell, you old son of a bitch this is just what I need!" he thought to himself. *"Leave it to you to find a way to take a few more jabs at my soul even from your damn grave!"*

Sean grabbed the bottle of aspirin she had thrown at him and chewed several with no water, his mind reeling and throbbing. Eventually, he fell asleep. He was overwhelmed with the emotions that sped through his fogged brain unchecked, like wildfire. What he didn't know was Maxwell had indeed known how difficult this would be for Sean. In fact, he was counting on it.

Chapter Three

Several hours later Sean was awakened by the door
opening. A waiter dressed in heavily starched, perfectly white
attire was pushing a cart into the room. He left it there by the
table and silently walked out of the room not even stopping to be
tipped. Sean rubbed his eyes and got to his feet, making his way
to the table, the smells issuing from the covered dishes making
his mouth water.

As he lifted the lid from the large plate in the center he
had to smile. It was obvious who did the ordering for him.
Sharon had the memory of an elephant and provided him with
one of his favorite meals. There was a thick slab of prime rib
smothered in au jus accompanied by garlic mashed potatoes and
a wonderful medley of steamed broccoli, cauliflower, carrots and
pearl onions in a buttery sauce. Warm bread, the steam rolling
from it, was waiting in a basket wrapped in a dark red cloth with
a pitcher of iced tea to wash it all down. Another smaller dish of
freshly made strawberry shortcake waited topped with a wisp of
whipped cream. No salad was included with the meal, Sharon
knowing it would most likely go to waste. Sharon would know
Sean was not fond of rabbit food. Even the vegetables on the
plate, with the exception of the potatoes, carrots and maybe
onions were a stretch for Sean. He and Sharon had shared many a

meal together as they worked the long, arduous hours while in Maxwell's employ.

He greedily dug in cutting into the perfectly done meat making his way greedily through the meal. As he savored the last of the shortcake and strawberries Sharon came into the room. She seemed a little apprehensive and withdrawn. Sean knew he needed to apologize to her and sometime tonight that might happen, depending on how the evening progressed. Not now, maybe not at all. He was still steaming mad at being thrust into this predicament and part of it seemed to be her fault.

"Well at least your appetite is still intact," she said approvingly, noting the empty plates in front of him.

"It was delicious, and, thank you," he responded genuinely. Like it or not he couldn't help but apologize to her in some small way and if that was simply by being kind, then so be it. They knew each other too well and for too long to do anything less and the reality was she was probably as unhappy about this situation as he was. Oh well, he was just not a vindictive person.

"It's time," she said gesturing to the door.

He followed her out and they got into the elevator. They rode down to the second floor in silence. Sean could not bring himself to look at her as he struggled with the regret and embarrassment from his earlier behavior. He could feel her looking at him though, and he knew the look she would be wearing, pity. For a split second he began to get angry again. He didn't want her pity and he didn't want anything Maxwell had to offer him either. It took all of his will not to start screaming and clawing at the wells like a madman, unable to escape his situation.

They entered one of the many conference rooms. This one had a long central table and off to the side were two smaller tables, one of which had several small packages on it and next to it another with glasses and various beverages on it, none of them alcoholic Sean noted ruefully. The room wasn't empty. Sitting at the long table were several people Sean recognized but had no desire to ever see again. This was going to be another red letter day in the life of Sean Ryder. Oh, could it get any worse? If Maxwell is involved, the answer is a definite... YES!

Martin Alderson and his wife Jessica looked up, Martin shot him a look that would have frozen the devil's heart. Martin was Maxwell's brother's only son and one of the many relatives Maxwell had tried to avoid his entire life. Maxwell never hid his feelings and when it came to Martin, the feeling was one of pure loathing.

Jessica was an enigma to Sean on some ways. He recalled hearing many nasty stories and once upon a time she even tried to seduce him. Sean almost laughed at the thought. Angelina was pregnant at the time if he recalled it right. That is really all one needs to know about her.

Next to Jessica sat Melissa Alderson, their daughter. She was notoriously known throughout the world, an artist at freeloading and jet setting on Maxwell's dime. Her entire life was one big mooch fest, just like mommy and daddies. None of them had the faintest idea what the word work meant. Melissa was very familiar with the words addict and prostitute though, and it looked like that was still true. Once beautiful she was now little more than a shell filled to the brim with chemicals. Sean wondered how anyone would want to be with her.

Across from them sat Brett Madison and on a special bench brought in for her, his grotesquely obese wife, Beatrice. Beatrice was Maxwell's sister's offspring and although she was not creative enough to steal from Maxwell herself, her husband was. She didn't delude herself and they all knew why Brett stayed. It was the potential of getting his hands on Maxwell's money. That's what he married, not her.

Of all the relatives, Maxwell reviled the two of them the most, if the degree of revulsion he felt for any of them varied. The sight of Beatrice almost culminated in Sean losing the meal he had just devoured. He sympathized with Maxwell on that account but knew that Martin was by far the vilest of them all.

There were two others in the room which Sean hadn't seen in a long time but recognized without any trouble whatsoever. They had to be the long lost children of Brett and Beatrice. He only met them a few times and it was years before but he had listened to endless ravings from Maxwell about how they had literally taken over his estate in Monaco. Maxwell loved that place and their presence had forced him to avoid it or suffer their unwanted company. Why Maxwell never kicked them out was beyond Sean. Why did Maxwell put up with any of them if he really didn't want them there? Sean never understood that.

The resemblance of the two twins to their parents and to each other was unmistakable. Identical or not, one was his father's son, the plain and vacant expression on his face was probably the most memorable trait he had, and the only thing not like his father. He was built like his father, an athlete's body really, if he would have taken care of himself. Unlike his father, it seemed he sort of missed out in the brains department.

The other was a massively obese young man just like his mother. Unlike his mother though, he was an openly cruel man and where his mother was weak, he was cold, especially when it came to using his less fortunate brother to do his dirty work.

It was odd to see the twins together. They were a set of identical twins that could not be more different if you tried. Dress them up and put them on stage, mean and fat and dumb and skinny, a tried and true formula for laughs.

Sean looked at the six of them and they stared at him. Sean fought the urge to laugh hysterically as he wondered if they all rode the elevator down together or if the attendant made them split up so as not to overload the car.

Sean took one of the seats as far from them all as possible and focused his attention on the water glass in front of him. Sharon sat down next to him.

"Well look at what the cat drug in. If I didn't know better I'd say we were in the presence of the fallen heir to the throne. But we all know what you really are, eh Sean?" Brett spat, glaring at him, the pure hatred unmistakable in his tone.

"What are you doing here?" Martin hissed at him to keep the attack alive. "You're not family. You have no business here. Go back and get your things. You're going to be evicted here shortly anyway. I won't even piss on that lake house after I light it on fire. Before I light it maybe I will. I'll clear it of the horrors that it holds once and for all."

Sharon instinctively reached out and laid a calming hand on Sean's as she saw him tense.

"Easy Sean," she whispered. "Let it pass."

"Oh, I just couldn't pass up the opportunity to be in the presence of all of Maxwell's loved ones one more time. I was sure it would warm my heart, being here in your presence to bask in the deep, abiding love you all had for him. I'm sure your not here because of his money! After all, you all showed so much feeling for him and cared so deeply for the late, great, Maxwell Alderson," Sean tossed back at them, laced in an extra-thick coating of sarcasm.

Jessica let out an unladylike snort and turned her nose up at him. Martin started to formulate a response. Brett was getting up to take it to the next level when the door at the head of the table opened.

"He is here at the behest of Maxwell, as are you," a portly gentleman explained as he entered the room, making his way to the head of the table. "Please try and be civil, or you will be asked to leave. I don't think any of you want that, am I right?"

They all settled down.

"Let's get started, shall we?" the tweed jacketed gentleman said, as he positioned himself at the head of the table.

Sean again fought back hysterical laughter looking at the suited lawyer whose apparel was straight out of the 1940's. Sean met him before, a bigwig at Talbert, Gibbins and Talbert. In fact Talbert himself, if memory served, and these days it didn't always serve. Talbert always made Sean think of something out of an old Alfred Hitchcock movie.

"As you are all aware Maxwell Alderson has passed. I have been given very specific instructions on how these proceedings are to be carried out. Each of you has been specifically chosen by Maxwell to attend these proceedings and I must inform you that if you fail to remain until I dismiss you, you will be heretofore and forevermore excluded from his will."

There was a long pause as Talbert stopped and looked at them. He was trying very hard to be enigmatic, but was failing badly in his acting. Sean only saw a pompous idiot. He obviously needed to go watch some more old movies and practice in front of the mirror.

"Do you all understand that?" Talbert said, in his best big boy voice.

Everyone looked around the room a little confused by the strange beginning and nodded.

"In a few moments, I will play a video made by Maxwell. The video represents his last wishes and has been certified as legal and binding by no less than three persons, of which, I am one," he crowed, as if that little piece of intelligence sealed the deal.

Sean remembered he was always a little full of himself. This was actually sort of amusing. He decided he could sit here and watch the show. He hadn't had this much fun in quite some time.

He was definitely one of the founders. Talbert, yes that was his name for sure and he was not just one of the bigwigs, he was the original Talbert for sure. Maxwell owned this man lock, stock, and barrel. He began back up after a nice pause intended to allow them to bask in his glorious presence.

"The last will and testament of Maxwell Alderson is completely legitimate, and iron clad I might add," he finished, reaching for a remote, and gesturing for the lights to be dimmed. One of the several suited attendants reached over and hit the light switch.

"May I remind you that failure to remain for the entire presentation will result in your being declared ineligible and will result in you forfeiting any inheritance you may have otherwise

64

received. These are the conditions I was sworn to carry out," he said again, using his 'don't question me, peasant, I am your liege' voice.

After another sufficient pause to let everything he had conveyed and his power over the situation thoroughly sink in, he turned towards the screen and hit the 'play' button before anyone had the opportunity to protest, or question his authority over the proceedings. He was quite in his element.

The screen flared to life and Sean found himself looking at a ghost from another life. Maxwell sat in a chair in the state room of the Me Lady. For a second he didn't speak, he sat there with a wide grin on his face, a lot like Talbert, Sean thought, almost laughing out loud. He hunched down in his seat and tried to cover his amusement with an unconvincing cough. He glanced over and saw Sharon staring at him disapprovingly. She made him feel like he had just been caught with a straw and a spit-wad ready to it shoot at Talbert.

Well. It would appear I will finally get the last word with all of you. Let me start by apologizing for the intrigue and mystery. I wanted to make sure that you all got the opportunity, no, the pleasure, of hearing my last words.

I trust you are all enjoying your stay at my favorite haunt, if I may use the word, in New York. My staff has been instructed to see to your every need during your short stay and in the days to come as the provisions of my last will and testament are carried out. I also trust I have not put you out too badly by forcing you to come here against your will. I know you are all very disturbed at the news of my passing and I truly regret having dragged you away from the comfort you are all so accustomed to, at my expense, of course.

As most of you know, or suspect, my holdings are worth somewhere in the range of eighteen billion dollars. Before I provide each of you with your inheritance, I wish to spend a little time recapping our long and glorious lives together starting with my beloved nephew, Martin. Let me assure you all, the order in which I address you does not have anything to do with your standing. In my memories and in my will, you are all equals! In no way does the order reflect your eventual receipt of my properties, should there be anything in it for you, that is.

Martin, I have chosen you to start with, and for good reason. Let me begin by saying you are one of, no, you are the most foul and disgusting man I have ever had to look at. You make me sick and your lazy cheating wife is hardly any better. I know how sick you really are. I trust that thing you call a daughter is still alive. I would have thought by now she would be dead of AIDS or hepatitis or some other disease equally as unpleasant. Well, maybe she just overdosed. I guess she is at least smart enough to buy and use clean needles as she fills her whorish body with the drugs she gets from stealing and selling

off my possessions. Ah well, enough of the reminiscing. I hope
you enjoy what I have to give to you.

     No offense Melissa, I am sure you could not help it. After
all, look at what you had for role models? Your father is a
gutless wimp, a foul little man with a diseased mind. Your
mother is the last whore of Babylon. Who can blame you for
following in their footsteps? I am sure Jessica was a good
mother, when she wasn't busy spreading her legs for every man
she encountered. And I'm sure your father spent many hours
coaching and mentoring you in the facts of life. I even have some
pictures of you and your father's encounters along with many
others for each of you.

     As an added bonus here is a little extra gift from me to
the three of you for your viewing pleasure. Martin, Jessica,
Melissa, Thomas will now hand you all envelopes filled with
photos of your various past and many indiscretions. I trust you
will enjoy them as I know how close a family you are. You
deserve each other and I wish you all the very best in life.
Thomas? If you would please give them the envelopes I provided
you?"

     Talbert got to his feet, his face devoid of all emotion as
he delivered the promised envelopes from the pile of papers in
front of him.

"This is outrageous!" Martin yelled. "I don't have to sit here and take this. Come Jessica, Melissa, we are leaving. Send us whatever he left us. I am not going to sit here and take this outrageous defamation of our characters!"

"Must I remind you that if you leave you forfeit your inheritance? As distasteful as this is I am bound to uphold his wishes," Thomas said quickly.

Martin promptly sat back down and shut his mouth. He could take anything the old fart threw at him as long as it was paid for in cash in the end.

There was about ten seconds of pause as Maxwell sat there staring at the camera, a big smile on his face as he must have been visualizing the effect his words would be having on them.

"Ah, Jessica, I am truly sorry for divulging your many indiscretions. I am guessing Martin knows about them anyway. In fact, I know he put you up to many of them. You have just allowed yourself to become an amoral, sex starved, slave. His slave, to be exact! I don't dislike you. But I do wonder what kind of a reaction Martin will have when I disclose how you tried to seduce even me! Oh, and even Sean when his wife, my own daughter, was carrying his child!

Sean looked over at Sharon who sat there with a look of utter incredulity on her face. Sean simply put his brows up, pursed his lips in a gesture of utter distaste and nodded imperceptibly to which Sharon let out a tiny shiver.

"Ah, too bad you could not get right to the source of the thing you crave most, my money! I know what you really crave. You crave your freedom and soul back and you think this money can help. Stick around. You'll get your chance at both. Freedom you have now because Martin no longer has anything to offer you. As for your soul, I can't help you there. That is up to you.

Don't fret, my dear, the package I gave you could put him away for a very long time. If you decide you can no longer bear the endless torture and abuse, you could be free in an instant. If not, rest assured anything Martin receives you will share in equally. I just gave you power over him. Use it if there is one shred of decency left in you. Do it for her. You know what I am talking about.

Maybe some of the smarter people in the room are realizing I am handing out power. Technically, none of you need each other anymore, as you will soon be rewarded with your own inheritance. You can be free of him now Jessica and you too Melissa, and if you find the strength to redeem yourself you will receive your true inheritance unlike the rest of the pigs in the room with you, a few exceptions to that rule, mind you.

I realize that as of now, most of you don't understand. Trust me, soon, you will. In the end you will all get exactly what you deserve, even if it is not what you expected. For you, Jessica my dear, I pray there may still be hope. Melissa, you too but for you it will be a much more difficult set of choices.

Sean, I imagine you are just about fed up and I do apologize for you having to sit through this but it cannot be helped. You are not a blood relative but I want you to know that I still think of you as a son and I do not pity you, by the way, I never did, and, I never blamed you for what happened. I am still hoping you will come to your senses. In fact, I am counting on it.

I have forced Sharon, whom I must now apologize to most deeply of all, to remain with you until this business is over. Don't be angry with her. This was all my doing. I know you won't hurt her, so yes, I used her. When this is over, she will receive a bonus of two hundred and fifty million dollars. Nothing can change that. If you do not comply and you force her from you before you are given permission to do so, you will again be hurting someone who loves you and whom I know you love too. Stop making the same mistakes over and over, my boy. For now, sit back and enjoy the show. You and Sharon are not in it.

Sean truly hated him for the first time in his life. How dare he do this to him! He had indeed been on the verge of getting up, his hands clenching the arms of the chair. He had no intention of staying here. Now, if he left he would be hurting Sharon. Oh, he hated Maxwell in that moment all right, but he wouldn't do any harm to Sharon. Sean realized how pleased

Maxwell would be to know that again, as usual, in the end the old bastard won.

Well, at least it seemed he would not be the brunt of the cruel joke Maxwell was playing out so he might as well enjoy the show as Maxwell suggested. So far it had been a little entertaining he had to admit, besides, what choice did he have?

Sean wondered at the fact that Maxwell had obviously thought this through very carefully right down to how long and when they would each react to his well-rehearsed shots. But we were talking about Maxwell after all. Of course it had to be planned down to the second. Maxwell would accept no less than perfect.

The pause again ended and Maxwell picked back up where he had left off. The difference was there was no look of happiness or triumph on his face, only regret and pain showed there. Apparently, he did still have something of a heart left and found this a little distasteful himself.

"I do deeply apologize, Sean, but as I said, you are just going to have to sit there. I knew how to keep you in your chair and I know you did. You and Sharon are the only two people there who still have souls, even though you misplaced yours. That, my boy, is a problem I will remedy for you. Sit back and relax for now and maybe in the end you will again find true happiness like the happiness you once had with my Angelina.

You were good to her, Sean. Fate got in the way and you simply were not equipped to deal with it.

Incredibly, Sean watched as Maxwell wiped his eyes. Sean had no idea what to think at this point but he knew one thing. This was ugly business Maxwell was dealing with but he had to see how it ended. He had seen Maxwell make a few people cry in his day but to see him cry was something he knew was a very rare sight.

"Now, let me turn my attentions to my darling cousin, Melissa. No, I did not forget you. I hope you are finding everything to your tastes. I hear the drugs in New York are among the finest in the world if you know where to look, and I am sure you do.

As a bonus gift I have paid the Betty Ford Clinic enough money in the form of a very hefty grant to allow you to spend the remainder of your life there if that is what you choose to do. If not, I am sure they will use it to help someone who wants to be saved. As I said, what chance did you ever have? I recommend you check yourself in before it is too late. Please?

Brett. How are you, dear fellow? I hope you are doing well. I am sure you are. After all you have been stealing from me for years. Did you think I was stupid? The one thing that truly breaks my heart when I think of you is the fact that it is ultimately my fault that my dear sister's daughter is so large and

*disgusting. I wish I had put you in your place long ago before
you had a chance to destroy her.*

*If I thought I could keep from getting sick I would try and
imagine what it would be like to actually have sex with your wife
but you don't do that do you? No, you just feed her and control
her and make her feel like she is less than human. That is usually
when you go and screw the secretary that I pay for by default
with the money you stole from me. That is a nice car dealership
by the way. How is that business going? I spoke to friend of mine
and the wind is going to soon shift direction for you, my friend.
Don't hold it against me, but it is time the IRS took a look at your
operation. Might need to close the doors for say, oh, forever.
Don't play with the big boys if you don't know the game. I think
we can both agree I am a true expert. Good luck.*

*Beatrice. What can I say? Sorry you had to find out your
hubby was cheating on you with that little red headed gold
digger down at the dealership. But I guess you knew that
already. You are not stupid, you are just weak. You too have a
permanent invitation to the clinic. They can help you. It's not too
late. Kick that ass to the curb where he belongs and free
yourself.*

*I am offering you a chance to prove you are not a
disgrace to my sister's memory. Think about it. Find the inner
strength you have buried in that heap of flesh you carry. Well, I
am sure you won't listen to reason so chow down and rock on*

you disgusting pig of a woman! Oh, enjoy the photos. Thomas has a package for you too.

Last but definitely not least, by any stretch of the imagination, definitely not the least in my list of favorites is the two twin turds! Hey boys, how you been? When I said you were the twin turds I didn't mean it, honest! All you two are guilty of is being greedy and having stupid parents. The stupid parents I forgive you for the greed, I do not. Daddy taught you well, one is a master thief and the other is a fat master thief. See you soon, boys.

Ah, I kill myself! Well, I would if I was still alive anyway, but I digress.

Ah, the hell with picking on the two of you, it wouldn't do any good anyway. You have spent the last decade or so stealing and whoring, just like your dad. What makes me think anything I said to you would matter?

Let's get down to business, shall we?

Thomas will soon be handing each of you a small box and issuing some instructions. In the box you will find a key. I bet you all wonder what the key will open! To find that out, you will need to search your hearts and minds and figure out what the most precious thing in my life was. One thing remained that meant more to me than anything else on the face of the earth. If you can figure out what it was you can figure out how to find my true will and the keys to the kingdom. Only there will you find the true inheritance I am leaving but I warn you, if you are wrong you may find more or less, in some cases, than you bargained for. This is all you get to help you.

Melissa, I will plead with you one more time. I truly blame your father and your mother because of her weakness to stand up to the monster she calls a husband for your problems. I want to see you get help. Do as I said. If you do that and remain sober for one year allowing yourself to be tested for drug use and getting psychiatric help for the entire year to rid your mind of the poison your parents planted in it I have set aside fifty million dollars for you. If not, it goes to any charity Thomas chooses. It is your life. Choose wisely.

Jessica. I know I said some cruel things, true, but cruel. But I feel the same thing in your case. Brett and his clan of thieves can rot in Hell but I know one other thing Martin was responsible for. I know you spent a large portion of your life as his punching bag and I know he has convinced you that you are nothing and keeps you scared into submission, forcing you to be a party to his sick perversions. I wish I had the courage in life to do what I am doing now, I am sorry, I was too weak.

Beatrice. One time deal, you take it or you leave it. Go to the clinic and lose half your weight. Just half, and get the same help I want to see Melissa get and you get the same thing I offered her. I loved my sister and you have to help yourself or it is all over for you.

So there it is in a nutshell. Now I am pretty much done. Talbert will take over now. Ladies, take what is offered, don't play the game. Decide tonight or the choices are gone. The hell with any standing promises. You don't deserve that much.

You are all such a disappointment to me. Get free of each other and look for a new beginning. All of you better do as I say. Sean, I mean you too. Break the cycle. Money, this money solves nothing and gives nothing if you don't change who you are right now, before it is too late.

I, Maxwell Bartholomew Alderson, being of sound mind and body do hereby bequeath whatever your key unlocks to each of you, and you alone. So it is written, so shall it be done.

I always loved a good scavenger hunt. You are the scavengers. Happy hunting!

The video abruptly ended filling the room with a silence so complete it was palpable. Thomas, true to Maxwell's wishes got up and went over to the table where the small packages waited. He set one box in front of each of them then delivered the promised envelope to Beatrice.

When he was done handing everything out he made his way, in as stately a fashion as one could manage under the circumstances, back to the head of the table where he stood and looked at them all. Sean recognized the signs that this was a disgusting task, even for him. How much did Maxwell pay him to do this little piece of dirty work?

"The keys are identical and will all open the same lock or locks as the case may be. I cannot help you in any way. Maxwell never divulged what the keys were for to me or anyone on my staff. He simply told us to deliver them, along with the message."

"This is outrageous," Martin fumed, getting rapidly to his feet and pounding his fists on the table. "It is obvious he was out of his mind when he did this. I am going to get my lawyer."

"Let me assure you it will do no good. At the time of this taping, he had insisted on a full mental evaluation and the results prove his sanity and are being held as a matter of record in our vault. He also took the time and effort to have this video and the remaining instructions reviewed by several judges and other experts and they all agreed that it is perfectly legal," Thomas said, sitting back down in his chair.

"Each of you will be given the use of a private jet and each of you has been assigned a personal assistant of Maxwell's choosing to help you in any way you require. You can use and search any of his estates and travel anywhere in the world you require, until the provisions of the will have been fulfilled. Afterwards only those properties or monies which become legally yours are you allowed to control or remain on. You will all be removed from any other holdings that do not belong to you by whatever means is necessary. I warn you, the assistants are also to see to it that you do not attempt to steal from his estates. They will remain with you until this business is over. Maxwell was very specific about this. When the provisions are fulfilled, the losers are all out on their ears, as he put it."

He raised his hand and gestured to the various people that had up till now stood silently at the back of the room. All of them closely resembled the ones Sean had been brought here by. Six black suited, nearly identical twins.

Sharon reached over and put her hand on top of Sean's. He was still reeling from the disgusting diatribe he had just witnessed but was awfully glad he did not have one of Maxwell's thugs for an assistant. He knew how Maxwell felt about these other fools but he had no idea Maxwell would end his life on such a cruel and vindictive note. Sean was ashamed of him at that moment and wanted nothing to do with this.

Thomas got up and went to leave the room having completed the utterly disgusting task he had been so handsomely paid to perform.

"I will be keeping tabs on all of you via your assistants and I will make sure you are all kept up to date on any developments in the search that I am aware of if you desire the information. Now, you are dismissed," he decreed, leaving them staring at his back as he strolled out of the room.

Sean looked around the room. Jessica was staring blankly at the photos in front of her and Martin was following suit. Beatrice was openly weeping, as usual. Brett was reading an obviously well timed email informing him his dealership had been revoked and was being reported to the authorities for suspicion of tax evasion. Melissa was rifling through her purse which was filled with a myriad of bottles. She was having trouble finding just the right pill for the occasion. The twin turds just sat there staring greedily at their respective keys.

Sean struggled to keep from breaking into wild laughter. He knew what had just taken place was one of the meanest tricks Maxwell could have ever played on them and he in some deep down place felt sorry for them. The problem was, not one thing Maxwell said was a lie. He simply put it out there for everyone to see. Hell, Jessica had tried to seduce him once and he had driven Melissa to the hospital after one rather nasty party she had thrown at Maxwell's Florida estate. To tell the truth, he didn't feel sorry for any of them.

He didn't wait to see what would happen next. He got up and made for the door.

"Where do you think you're going, Sean?" Martin hurled at his back.

Sean stopped but didn't turn when he answered, "I'm going home."

As he left the room he could hear Martin yelling after him.

"It won't be your home for long, Mr. Perfect! Not if I have anything to say about it. I'll see you in a while, that's the first place I'm looking!" Martin yelled as Sean made his way as quickly as possible from the room in an effort to escape what he was sure would follow.

Damn it! He hadn't considered that. Oh, thanks a heap Max, old buddy, he thought as he made his way down the stairs headed for the bar, Sharon at his back trying to keep up with him.

"Sean, wait! I didn't know. I swear to you. I had no idea."

Sean stopped and spun around.

"That, them, I did not miss. That is what I never wanted to be a part of, ever again. That is why I never came back. My god, he was sicker than ever!" Sean spat at her vehemently. "How on earth did you stay with him?"

"Sean, I'm sorry," she said to him again weakly, "I know he put you through a lot just now." Sharon's demeanor suddenly shifted, startling Sean, "He put me though it too! So don't be all high and mighty with me, Sean Ryder! At least I was still living, even if my boss had become a madman!" she threw at him, balling her fists and crossing her arms.

Sean knew what that meant and backed down quickly. He turned and started back down the hall towards his original destination leaving Sharon dangerously, and unchecked, at his back. Maybe not the brightest thing he had ever done, but he wasn't going to get in another fight with her.

"Where are you going?" she demanded of him, "don't do this to me, Sean, please."

"I'm not going to do anything just now. I'm going to the bar, to think. Coming?" he said over his shoulder trying to defuse the situation and calm her back down. He again turned and headed in the direction of the bar.

Sharon stood there a moment, a deep purple flush coming over her face before she was able to regain her usually indomitable self restraint. Sean was always the one person that could set her off, and she hated it. It was like he knew exactly what to say to boil her blood. Not this time, she decided.

"Yes, I think I am. Make mine a double, please," she said.

He stopped and turned to her. Smiling in a disarming way, he put his hand on the small of her back and nodded his head in the direction of the bar.

"Well, come on, then. I need to sort this out. I can't go home right now. He made sure to screw that up for me just by being nice to me and making them all think I had some advantage. They are all scurrying to Michigan right now to find the hidden treasure they all believe he would want me to find first."

Sharon laughed, "I hadn't thought of that."

"How do you feel about the ocean?" he asked her casually, "I suddenly have a craving to see the sea."

Sharon liked seeing a bit of the old Sean shine through.

"Well, that depends on what you have in mind, Mr. Ryder. I guess I am at your disposal. Shall we?"

Sharon casually hooked her arm in his and together they made their way down the hall to the bar where piano music was softly spilling out of the open door inviting them in with its soothing, mellow tones. She was not about to let him sit there and get sloppy drunk if that was what he had in mind. She would let him have a few drinks. Hell, she wanted one too! But at the same time it was time he rejoined the human race.

She walked quietly next to him and began making some plans of her own.

Chapter Four

The Me Lady was a beautiful yacht if you could call her that, a cruise ship would be more appropriate. She was not the largest boat floating off the shores of Cannes, France but she had all the trimmings. At over two hundred and seventy feet bow to stern she was listed in the Who's Who of boats.

She had a beautifully sculpted, navy blue hull which blended perfectly with the turquoise water accenting the blinding white decks above with their generous expanses of glass. Equipped with two jet skis, a launch that was over thirty feet long, a helipad, and a cruising range of thousands of miles she was fully self-sufficient and could cover vast distances without returning to port or refueling.

She had a full-time staff consisting of a captain, a world class chef, and numerous deck hands, waiters, maids, and engineering staff. In the end of his life, this was home to Maxwell. He ran his extensive empire right here from this ship. Sharon, his personal assistant, spent nearly as much time here as he did when she was not off on one of his errands or overseeing one of his business deals.

Sean had no idea how many state rooms and cabins she had total or how big the crew was but he had met the Captain on many occasions back when he was still working for Maxwell. He was an older man and had been the captain since the day the hull was laid. Many of the crew had been with him as long as he had been there and for most of them, the boat was what they called home. Maxwell did not like change or surprises so he liked that arrangement very much. The crew was loyal and discrete, just the way Maxwell expected them to be.

Sharon took the liberty of phoning ahead to make the arrangements for them to be picked up at the airport where they had just landed. Sean was spitting mad with her at this point and was planning an escape the second they opened the jets door. He was in bad shape now and suffering from the effects of alcohol withdrawal. Sharon gave instructions that all alcohol be removed from the jet and he suspected she had done the same on Me Lady too. Well, he was willing to bet they had plenty in town and right now he badly needed a drink.

Unbeknownst to him, she had his passport and any other papers he might need with her and so far she'd been leading him around by his nose. He felt bad every time he snapped at her and he backed down just as quickly but she had the uncanny ability to rekindle his bad mood in a matter of seconds. All it took was that familiar wave her delicate hand in dismissal, not even bothering to get upset, she was in total control and he didn't like it very much. So far he succeeded in calling her pretty much every bad name he could think of, some of them bad enough to make him blush himself. She seemed determined to sober him up and was mercilessly controlling him and his actions to that end, and it was taking its toll.

"Well, assistant, what would you have me do now?" he asked in mock submission.

"Get off the jet, get into the car and get on the boat. Go onto Me Lady and let's finish getting that poison out of your body so you can think clearly," she instructed, not even bothering to look at him.

"Sounds fine for you, but I have other...," he started.

"And don't even think about going into town or trying to leave the boat once we get there. I will have you watched, and unless you're ready for a mile swim, which from the look of you I would say is not possible right now, you're stuck, end of subject," she said, again not even looking at him. He could see the stress well up in her, but tough shit! He needed a drink! He was going to try and escape.

Sean looked out the window of the jet and there was a black limo and wouldn't you know it, the two drivers were Little Big Man and Big Little Man he noted amused. Sean knew his trip into town was cancelled. Damn that woman!

"Some assistant you are. I thought you were supposed to provide me with anything I needed," he said peevishly, feeling like a little boy who had just been grounded.

"I am!" Sharon shot back smiling. It was the first time she looked at him and she seemed quite pleased with his obvious pain.

85

"I hate you right now you know that? You are the devil. A very beautiful devil, but the devil just the same," he sighed, surrendering.

"Sean! Was that a compliment? I knew there was still a gentleman hiding in there somewhere. Progress, however slight, is still progress," she said surprised, softening just a little, for the first time in two days.

"Don't get used to it. I still want to throttle you right now," he growled sullenly.

Sean departed the plane and headed straight for the terminal at a brisk walk before anyone could react. He had to at least test what would happen if he didn't head for the car. He barely finished the first step in the wrong direction before Big Little Man uncrossed his rather large arms and began to intercept him. Sean adjusted course and with a large smile on his face, he climbed into the back seat with Sharon.

They cleared customs in a matter of seconds, the official actually coming out to the car to do it. He smiled at Sharon as if they were old friends and stamped both of their passports waving them on. They rode silently towards the shore and the waiting launch to take them out to Me Lady.

Maxwell hadn't always kept her here, he actually moved around a lot, the boat acting as his own floating citadel and mobile office. Sean visited him here many times in the long forgotten past but he rarely spent any time here always choosing to stay in town. He loved boats but he disliked the idea he was stuck here so preferred the freedom of his own rooms.

Sean was a little surly and a little bored and he couldn't pass up the opportunity to play with the two errand boys just a little.

"So what are your names, if you don't mind my asking? I am tired of calling you my two tormentors or Big Little Man and Little Big Man. I have a few others I was working on but they aren't ready for prime time yet," he asked conversationally.

"It is not necessary for you know our names, Mr. Ryder," Little Big Man said in his flat tone while looking straight ahead, "but if you must have a name to call us by, you can call me Mr. Smith and my associate, Mr. Brown." With the last, he turned and smiled at Sean in a way that let Sean know he would be better off not asking any more questions along those lines.

Sharon reached over and poked him in the side. She furled her brows and shook her head at him. Sean decided not to play that game anymore. He liked the shoes he had on. Concrete shoes were not good to wear around the water and it was a very small leap of logic to assume Mr. Smith and Mr. Brown were both well versed in the theory and application of cement shoes.

Sean almost lost it. All he could do at that point was envision the two men sitting in a classroom, their notebooks opened and pencils freshly sharpened. At the front of the room stood an equally well attired thug pointing to the inscription on the blackboard that read, 'Anti-flotation Clothing 101'.

As the car approached the dock, Sean looked out over the crystal clear water. He'd forgotten how truly majestic the Me Lady was. The last of the sun was hitting her and she sparkled like a mammoth jewel floating in the distance.

The car came to a stop and they got out and headed for the launch. Sean was tempted to run again and steal the car when they all got out but unfortunately, Sharon dismissed the two men and his only form of escape sped off. Sean stood watching as it disappeared into the distance leaving him stranded with his lovely tormentor.

They boarded the launch appropriately named Me Lil Lady. It would be misleading to call it a dinghy or even a launch. It served the purpose of both though, but was actually more of a sport-fisher or cruiser and when Me Lady was underway it sat in a niche at the stern of the ship blending into the hull below the helipad. A dinghy yes, but for all intents and proposes it was a very versatile craft. The main cabin could easily hold twelve or more comfortably and it had a full kitchen, bar, and two small state rooms in case you wanted to take it out for a day or twelve. The color scheme matched Me Lady's perfectly and it was fully equipped as a sport fisher which did actually hold a certain charm for Sean. He did love to fish.

Sean was standing on the back deck watching the effervescence bubble out from beneath the stern as the boat made its way to the Me Lady when Sharon walked out onto the stern deck. Sharon watched curiously as Sean stared at the crisp, clear, water seemingly mystified. What she didn't know, was that he was actually contemplating jumping and swimming back to shore.

"Sean. I am sorry I am being so difficult. I made a promise and I intend to keep it. Then you can do whatever you want. I won't stop you and I won't try and help you if that is what you choose," Sharon whispered sadly, ready to cry. The sight of Maxwell begging her to try and save him brutally pushing its way to the front of her thoughts.

"It's OK Sharon. Maxwell was no fool. He knew there was only one person I might listen to, and that is who he sent."

"Sean... I... What I said about Angelina, back in New York. I really do apologize for that. I was just so angry with you."

Sean turned and looked at her. He walked over and took both of her hands in his.

"Sharon. It's OK. I know I have been acting like a fool. You can't fathom the way it affected me, no one can," Sean blinked his eyes to stop them from tearing. "Right now, I still want to kill you, though. You have no idea how bad I want a drink. I can't stop shaking and…," he said apologetically, looking at his hands.

He was ashamed of himself now that his mind was clearing somewhat. This didn't happen if you just stayed drunk. You could make it go away. You could overcome the guilt and embarrassment with a few more drinks. He was not sure he could he could do this. It hurt too much.

"It will pass," she said lifting her face up to his.

In an act of pure, motherly love, she kissed him gently on the cheek. She then reached up and put the back of her hand gingerly on his forehead and then turned and headed back into the cabin. Sean looked after her a little surprised at the sudden, but brief, show of kindness.

Sean reached up and touched his cheek where she had kissed him. The sensation still lingered there and was not unpleasant. Sean sighed and turned back to watch the water light up as the boat cut through its calm surface.

They reached the ship and pulled alongside. As they made their way up the gangplank, Captain Scott Spencer waited on the deck to greet them when they came on board. He immediately grabbed Sharon up and gave her a big bear hug and kiss, laughing and smiling.

"Oh, Cherry Blossom, I missed you. Where have you been?" he asked her. "It wasn't the same not having you around here."

"Maxwell had some post mortem business he wanted me to attend to," she said hugging him back and planting a kiss of her own on his tan, ruddy cheek.

"Yes, he was very fond of you. At least you were here in the end. I know that meant the world to him," he said, patting her lightly on the back to comfort her.

"I hope so," was all she could say, lowering her gaze to the deck to hide the tears.

"Mr. Ryder! My, it has been a long time! You don't look at all the way Sharon described you. I was expecting a half dead man," he barked, taking his hand and vigorously shaking it.

"Oh?" he asked, looking at Sharon sideways, "I can just imagine."

"Your state room is ready, Sharon, and it is just the way you left it, as always. You will be staying in Maxwell's old rooms, Mr. Ryder," he informed them.

"I am not sure I am comfortable with that arrangement, captain, and call me Sean, please."

"Maxwell insisted and made me promise if you were to visit after he passed that I would put you in there. It was one of his last wishes. Please, you must. It's back to the way it was before he got sick, the way you would remember it," he said, half insisting, half begging.

Sean was not in any mood to argue. He didn't get any sleep on the plane and he was tired enough to sleep anywhere. He wanted sleep so badly. He would take any relief he could get as his body revolted from the forced sobriety he had to endure under Sharon's iron fist. He could also use some reprieve from this tyrannical devil in a woman's body.

"OK. I am about ready for bed now. Can I get some food brought in? I'll take it in the room."

The captain held up his hand as if to stop him and shook his head.

"That won't do at all on your first night back, sir. The chef has been working very hard to prepare a wonderful meal for you and Miss Hu. Please, it would not do to disappoint him. Afterwards, the doctor will see you and then you can sleep for two days, if you like. Please. It means a lot to the crew.

"You were always very nice to us all, and we did missed having you pop in and divert Maxwell's attention from us for a few days with your antics," he smiled, "besides, the fishing here is really good," he whispered conspiratorially under his breath, raising his hand to hide his mouth from Sharon's sight.

"Fine, but I don't need a doctor," he said smiling, just a little.

"That's my doing, Sean. I am worried about you and he will give you something to help you through this," Sharon said.

Sean knew he wasn't going to get anywhere so he just let out a sigh and gestured for them to lead the way.

Sean thoroughly enjoyed the meal and had unceremoniously gotten up to go to bed when the chef appeared out of the kitchen followed by his assistant chef and the crepe table.

"I pray you have enjoyed the meal! It has been quite some time since I have had guests to cook for. These vermin do not appreciate my artful cooking!" he sniffed, gesturing in a manner that implicated the entire crew.

"It is by far the best food I've had in a long, long time," Sean replied honestly.

"I am so glad! Now one last course and I will feel that I have fulfilled my duty!" he stated, reaching for a bottle of Dom and four fluted glasses from the cart.

"I gave strict orders there was to be no alcohol on board!" Sharon shrieked, leaping from her chair.

"Calm down, Miss Hu. It is only champagne. It is all safely locked up, and only I have the key. I need some things for cooking and it is not civilized to serve a crepe without champagne. You would not deny me this necessary ingredient would you?" he demanded, getting agitated with her obvious lack of knowledge on proper serving and etiquette.

"Yes, I would," Sharon shot back, staring him down.

"I assure you no one is going to die from one small glass of champagne or a single bottle of beer for that matter, and besides, I refuse to make a crepe without having it to enhance the flavor!"

"Well, I suppose it's OK this time!" Sharon said resignedly. Knowing she was overreacting slightly, she opted for a dignified retreat. She dropped her guard, just a little, and sat back down.

The chef filled four glasses as he barked out orders to his assistant who began to make the crepes. He handed them each a glass and sat down himself. "Good, now let us have a toast to Miss Hu and Mr. Ryder!" he said, raising his glass for a toast.

They all raised their glasses in acknowledgement of the toast then they all took small sips of the delicious nectar, except Sean, who suddenly stopped. He was suddenly holding the glass out in front of him, gripping it hard in his shaking hand, glaring at it as if it were a viper trying to strike. He looked at the crisp cold liquid for just a moment and then, fighting with every ounce of restraint he had in him, he set the glass down in shame. He knew if it touched his lips he would not be able to stop himself, and the shame and self loathing that made him feel was turning his face a mottled shade of bruised cherries.

"I'll just have a tiny sip, in a minute with my crepe, to enhance the flavor, as you said," he apologized, ashamed.

Searching for his dignity, he set the glass down. He looked sheepishly at Sharon who was doing a very good job hiding her satisfaction and admiration at his sudden courage. That somehow made it better, but, on the other hand, it made it worse, too. It made him angry or shamed him. He couldn't tell which one for sure. He could barely stand the fact that she was there seeing that for some reason. She was the last person on earth he wanted to see him at a weak moment right now.

He wasn't sure why he did it. Maybe it was because he was starting to feel a little differently about his life and his self-destructive behavior since his wife's death. He still hated his life, but maybe he really was doing Angelina's memory an injustice. He looked again at Sharon and saw the tear coursing down her cheek before she could wipe it away. That was all he could take.

"I hope I am not offending anyone but I am just not in the mood," he said getting rapidly to his feet. He fled their company and made his way to Maxwell's state room before any of them could protest. He had to get away before he said, or did, anything else embarrassing. He was not enjoying having to reexamine his behavior over the last year or so. It hurt.

When he opened the door to the state room, an older, well-dressed, gentleman was sitting in one of the plush chairs near the entry to the cabin. Sean had always loved this room, he had to admit. The man was seated in the state rooms sitting area. There was a large coffee table inlaid with mother of pearl residing in the center of the area surrounded by four pure white chairs in a semi-circle on three sides. The chairs faced a large fish tank on the wall. The tank was loaded with exotic creatures which Maxwell had always insisted on caring for himself.

The room was devoid of carpet or rugs. Instead, there was a spiral pattern of lightly colored marble tiles of pinks and whites that started in the middle of the room and spread out in an ever enlarging circle. The colors were all of light and effervescence, hues one would associate with the inside of a shell and they set the tone for the rest of the room.

The state room was actually one of only two spaces on the top level, the wheelhouse being one deck down. Maxwell's state room overlooked the bow where a beautiful pool and small garden awaited. There was a massive bed centered on the rear wall which, like the other walls, was of the purest white. Various pieces of lightly colored furniture and artwork were scattered tastefully throughout the expansive space to create a peaceful spacious ambiance intended to make one feel as if they were living beneath the waves in a giant shell. What he always loved about the room most was not so much the décor, although it was very beautifully done. What he loved was the view. The room looked out over the front of the boat with nothing but glass on three sides surrounding you with the unobstructed beauty of the ocean everywhere you looked. All these features served the purpose for which they were intended which was to make one feel as if they were living in a shell, peacefully looking out over the ocean.

At the rear were the only other doors. They were a set of matching, massive, white doors on either side of the bed. One lead to the equally opulent bathroom and the other to a mahogany meeting room Maxwell used as his board room.

A door off to the side of the board room led to one of the most beautiful studies Sean had ever had the pleasure of working in. It contained all mahogany wood furniture to match the board room including a truly massive desk. There was shelve upon shelve of books accompanied by a number of oddities which Maxwell had collected in his long, fruitful life.

If he remembered right, the door to the rear of the board room led to Sharon's similarly appointed state room and private study. Maxwell insisted on having her near and unfortunately for Sharon, he also had a direct intercom to her rooms. She would be required to answer day or night in order to act on the many ideas that popped into his head. Sean could imagine Maxwell leaping out of bed and hitting the intercom button calling to his faithful assistant so he would not lose the ideas he was constantly coming up with.

He pulled himself back from his reverie and turned to the man sitting in the main chamber. "I don't need a doctor," he said dismissively.

"Of course you don't," the man answered, getting up, "so this should be a very short and sweet encounter. But I am going to accomplish what I have been paid to do. Mr. Ryder, I presume?" he said walking over and pointing towards the bed.

"Why yes, indeed, Dr. Livingston!" Sean said, mocking the man.

The doctor, ignoring Sean's wit, stood there holding his bag in his hand. He made his way over to him, opening the top.

"How cliché," Sean thought, it really was a little black bag.

Dr. Livingston pulled out a stethoscope and set the bag down on the edge of the bed. "Strip to your briefs, sit on the bed, and let's have a look, shall we?"

Tired and wanting nothing but sleep, Sean reluctantly complied. He had already made a big enough ass of himself at dinner, so why fight? Better to get it over with so he could just plunge into a deep sleep. He wasn't stupid. If the doctor didn't report back to Sharon he was done, Sean was in for a real rough time.

The examination lasted about fifteen minutes. The doctor looked him over and poked and prodded Sean asking if this or that hurt. In the end the good doctor took out a syringe and a small bottle of something Sean could not quite make out the label on.

"It's just a special vitamin supplement and a mild sedative to help you sleep. I give it to a lot of patients in your condition. You're fine, but the lack of certain vitamins that were lacking in your obvious diet of pure alcohol must be dealt with. You have a full blown case of Delirium Tremors right now which is only going to get worse for a few days. I am sure it hurts, I am sure you are about to crawl out of your skin, and you are nearly depleted."

"Thank you for putting it so delicately, doc," Sean snorted.

"A few more months of that and I think your liver would have begun to shut down. I think you will be fine though, as long as you don't relapse," he said as he filled the rather disturbing syringe. "By the way, you really should consider thanking whoever pulled you out of the gutter. They probably saved your life," he informed Sean.

"Liver failure was actually the general goal," Sean informed him. He was more than a little ashamed as he said it.

"Well, I promise when you wake, you will feel like a new man. I can't stop you from killing yourself, if that is what you choose. I can arrest, and even partially erase, the damage you have done so far and give you another chance. I suggest you wise up take it," the doctor said in a perfectly professional tone stabbing him mercilessly and rapidly injecting the concoction into his behind.

"Ah!" Sean cried out, "easy there, Dr. Livingston!" he begged in helpless protest.

Sean was rubbing his butt-cheek trying to stop the growing sting there when Sharon strode into the room from the back door, "how is he?" she asked the good doctor.

"He is weak, depleted, but nothing time, rest, and a little infusion of the right vitamins and a mild sedative won't cure. I was just in the process of administering them, one down, one to go," he said, speaking as if Sean was not sitting there on the edge of the bed in front of them, rubbing his violated nether parts.

Annoyed that he was being treated like a child again, Sean began to stand, "and I was just about to say no! Not if it hurts as bad as the first one did!" he blurted defiantly before he had a chance to think it through.

"Oh my god!" he thought to himself. Had he really sunk this low? Was he really going to act like such a child? He wasn't sure if he should be ashamed, or just tell them all to go to hell and leave him to his death. He was a grown man, after all.

Sean started laughing hysterically as the two stood there and looked at him in complete dismay. He had no idea why he was laughing. He wanted to get up and run. He wanted to escape but he also knew that he was being completely irrational. He could not believe what he had become. Again, the shame washed over him and then he began to cry.

Sharon just looked at him. She felt pity but knew that showing it was the last thing Sean needed just then. Something told her she had to go the other way, she didn't know why, but she let her anger come out instead.

She slowly crossed her arms in front of her, tapped her delicate foot, and bore into him with her eyes. It was a look that let Sean know he was getting the second shot. If she had to call in the entire crew to restrain him he was going to get the shot. Her tan, almond shaped face with its matching almond shaped eyes seemed to float slightly back and forth hovering over her folded arms. She looked like a cat ready to pounce.

"Sean, that is about enough. Do I have to restrain you?" she asked, "or should I just slap you across the face and bring you back that way?"

Sean looked at her and he was suddenly aware again of how beautiful she was. Her anger was not completely expected. At that point in time he had been looking for a little sympathy, he got zero. This puzzled him. He did the only thing he could in the situation. He tried to laugh it off.

"Well it might help. Please, be gentle," he said lying back on the bed.

She just stood there looking at him. She was not amused. He knew that look! He could not explain it, but it was 'The Look'! He'd seen that look before when they argued about how to proceed on the details of a job they worked on together. He knew right away she was the Rock of Gibraltar and didn't find him the least bit funny and had no intention whatsoever of putting up with his shit any longer. In that moment he knew she was immovable, impenetrable, and primed to get her way.

"Do it already and let me get some sleep, please," he said in resignation. He rolled onto his side and exposing the yet unmolested butt cheek for the needle soon to come.

The doctor rubbed his target with alcohol and plunged the second needle abruptly into his cheek. Sean swore it was bigger than the last one. The doctor was pinching and pulling the skin around it in an unsuccessful attempt to ease the pain somewhat, but a cold sensation, followed by a searing burning sensation spread out from the spot anyway. Sean mashed his teeth hard, unwilling to show the slightest sign of pain to Sharon, who was watching with a smug, satisfied look on her face. Finally, the needle was withdrawn and the doctor packed up his little black bag and strode out as Sean's head began to swim in earnest.

"Happy?" Sean asked.

"No, not yet I'm not," Sharon said as she helped him up to the pillows and covered his legs and torso with the blanket.

"There, are you happy now?" Sean asked her again, trying to redeem himself somewhat.

"I'm getting there," she said putting the back of her hand lightly on his forehead as she had done earlier, looking for fever, like a mother checking her young. She let her hand sit there a moment and then moved it down towards his cheek. Suddenly she smacked him lightly on the cheek where her hand had so recently been gently touching him, "go to sleep now."

As the sedative took hold, Sean started to feel as if he was a head floating along on the sea. He followed Sharon's blurring shape as she walked around the room closing the blinds. His sight got more and more blurred, he began to think she was an angel, trails of color were following her and he wondered at her beauty as he slipped into a deep sleep.

For a long time, Sean slept, just as Sharon planned it.

Chapter Five

Maxwell Alderson saw the end coming. He learned he had cancer just before his daughter died but he told no one. Sean disappeared after the death of his daughter and it became apparent he would never return. That was over a year ago, closer to two.

That was when Maxwell decided it was time to hang it up, or, possibly he took matters into his own hands. It all depends on your outlook. Maxwell would have gladly handed Sean the reins of the company but Sean was not willing to take them. Sharon could do it but that is not what Maxwell wanted, no, that was not at all what he wanted. The board would take her apart little by little and he had to protect her at all costs, even after he was gone.

When he made up his mind to sell out his share of the company he didn't make any big announcements about his plans. In fact, he swore them all to secrecy as part of the deal, making sure they would make no announcements until he was dead. They even had to lie to all of the employees and make them believe Maxwell was still in charge.

The only ones he would have felt the need to tell about the cancer were Sharon, and maybe Sean, but Sean was lost in his misery and it would have been pointless and Sharon didn't need the burden then. He lured Sharon away from the company to continue to be his private assistant and see to his affairs until after he died, including the ones she knew nothing about at the time that she was now forced to carry out pretty much against her will. He swore her to secrecy about selling the company and up until now she hadn't told a soul.

He quietly turned the company over to the board of directors who gladly bought him out, anything to get rid of the old tyrant. Sharon had been with him for several years now and when he left she was perfectly willing to go with him, especially for what he was paying her. She loved her work, she loved working period. Besides, it wasn't as if the board of directors would allow her to keep running the business the way she was doing for Maxwell when his health really started to fail him. They saw her as one of Maxwell's pets and would not tolerate her being in charge. He paid her very substantial amounts of money to see to his business with the big bonus at the end of all of this mess, once she carried out the last assignment. She would be able to do anything she wanted including start her own company if that was what she decided to do. She was young and full of ideas and Maxwell had seen to it she would be taken care of for the rest of her life.

Maxwell, and by extension Sharon, were lying to all of the potential inheritors. None of them, Sean included, knew he had long before quit running the company, let alone even owning it anymore. He forced Sharon to keep it secret and to keep up the appearance until he died. Not one of them suspected and in some ways it shamed Sharon deeply that she had to lie to them all, especially Sean. What really bothered her was she had no idea why Maxwell insisted it be this way. Most likely pride, but possibly to hide the fact his assets were now very much liquid and no longer tied up in the company he had built from practically nothing. She tended to believe this was the reason.. His greedy relatives would find some way to wrest his fortune from him if they knew it was all liquid assets.

One of the worst aspects of this entire ordeal was Mr. Smith and Mr. Brown and the other thugs Maxwell was using to carry out all of this nonsense. He didn't allow Sharon to have any knowledge of their part in this and he assigned her to be Sean's personal assistant upon his death until all of the provisions of the will were carried out. They were to steer clear of her and Sean. That much she knew. This whole thing was tied to the bonus she would receive, a last minute "Got Cha!" thrown in there by Maxwell but a rather heafty one she was willing to work for, at least for the time being. So far, nothing seemed out of the ordinary apart from the surrealistic treasure hunt Maxwell had them all participating in.

The others all had someone that worked for Mr. Smith assigned to them. Sharon shivered any time she was around them. There was something very sinister about them, even though they came across as the nicest, most professional group of men and women you would ever want to meet. But Sharon knew better. She knew more than Maxwell thought she did.

What Sharon didn't know was the details to Maxwell's little treasure hunt or even that this is where it was all headed, at least not until the other night at the reading of the will. She only knew what Maxwell had instructed her to do via Mr. Talbert. It was her job to see to it that Sean was cleaned up and helped in any way she could help him, and for this she would become filthy rich and none of them could protest because it was paid to her for services rendered and completely above board and legal. The money sat in escrow now waiting for her to finish with this nasty business.

Sharon imagined Maxwell sitting in whatever space was provided for people like him in Hell laughing at them all. She was sure he'd be pleased with himself. Yes, Maxwell was a real son of a bitch. Sharon knew he was getting exactly what he wanted and it made her furious. He would surely be laughing right now as his twisted plans unfolded. What exactly did he have in mind, she wondered? Would it ruin everything for Maxwell if she walked away from the money and told Talbert to go fuck himself, and use Maxwell's rotten prick to do it!

Sharon had known Maxwell her entire life. Her mother was Angelina's nanny from the moment she was born. She had been there when Martha, Angelina's mother died and had seen to it that Angelina was taken care of while Maxwell grieved for his dead wife.

After Sharon was born, both she and Angelina had been raised as sisters. Sharon had even been the maid of honor at Angelina's wedding to Sean. She was on her way to be with her for the birth of their child when Angelina died. The news devastated her and the demise of Sean that followed was more than she could bear. She loved them both very much.

Sharon's mother never would talk about her father and she never saw him or met him. It seems it was a source of disgrace for her mother. An oriental woman with an illegitimate child was not tolerated very well, especially when the child was of mixed blood. But, thanks to Maxwell, no one he could control ever looked at Sharon as the illegitimate child of a house servant. She was always treated like a member of the family by Maxwell and because of that, anyone that Maxwell did business was expected to do the same. Maxwell was very fond of Sharon and her mother and grateful for the fact that they treated Angelina like their own flesh and blood. In return for Maxwell's kindness, Sharon's mother loved Angelina and treated her as if she were her own daughter.

Maxwell loved Sharon so much people found it strange and as a result, there were many rumors. He paid her way through college, private schools, a bill any billionaire could cover and he gave her everything a child could have wanted or needed. Back in those days, after the death of Angelina's real mother, Maxwell lived at the estate outside Hong Kong as much as possible and spent as much time there as he could so he could be with Angelina and by extension, Sharon. It was as if no other place mattered to him and he found happiness there with his strange little family of necessity. When Sharon finished with school he offered her a job as his personal assistant and protégé and she worked for him from then on.

She had enough money to never work another day in her life but she was a workaholic. She loved what she did, and in the end, Maxwell gave her free reign over the company, much to the chagrin of most of the board members. Most of them despised her because of it and treated her with disdain when Maxwell was not around to cover her anymore. They began to exercise their own ideals and Sharon began to struggle to keep control. Maxwell ended it all pretty much right there. It was then Maxwell knew he wasn't that powerful anymore and he could no longer protect Sharon from the word he created and now had no choice but to relinquish control of. It was not a good day for Maxwell or his sanity.

Maxwell couldn't have cared less what the others thought. He had complete power over the company and kept the board in place only as a symbol, more or less. He made them all very rich so they put up with whatever he said. This was not a public company. There was no voting Maxwell out. If he wanted Sharon or even Sean for that matter to run things, they were powerless to stop him. But that is not to say they couldn't make them miserable. Maxwell knew Sean could have controlled them, but Sharon was not just a shrewd businesswoman, she was a delicate flower and Maxwell did not want to see that flower crushed and discarded. He knew it would find its own path, not the one he went down, but a better one.

Law, it was law he feared and the experts that twisted it. You did what Maxwell said or you found yourself looking for work elsewhere. They had no real power that didn't come from him. But they did have power and they would never stop until Sharon, and possibly even Sean were completely and utterly destroyed.

Sharon ruled the company for him after Sean disappeared and carried out his wishes and plans. She had complete control most of the time but always saw to it any ideas Maxwell had or any wishes he had were carried out. Even when he was dying, his mind was ten steps ahead of everyone else's and Sharon was his staff and shield.

Her mother had been just as beautiful as she was and her father must have been a handsome man, too. Most of her features tended towards her mother and were very oriental but she did get some complimentary traits from her American father. She had no way of knowing anything other than he was American. That was all her mother would tell her and now she was gone too and Sharon would never know who he was. She died five years earlier, never divulging who her father was.

Sharon was taller than most Chinese women but that didn't mean her body was disproportionate. She had a full and flawless figure that she took great care in maintaining and she carried herself with undeniable grace. Her skin was a luminous brown and her oval face rode like a perfect beacon above her perfect body. Her large almond shaped eyes were almost gold in color and almost difficult to look at for too long. They were framed by her lustrous black hair. Her gaze could burn a hole right through your heart, and she knew it.

She was not a vain woman but her beauty, it seemed, was intoxicating. Men had trouble concentrating in her presence and in business she learned to shamelessly use that to her advantage whenever the need presented itself. Maxwell taught her to use all of her gifts, all of the time. "Never show mercy!" he would tell her, over and over.

Vanity or not, she reveled in her ability to completely unhinge a man, taking pleasure in seeing their bodies shake uncontrollably when she purposely got too close to work her magic on them. Maxwell was no fool. He used her to break down some of his toughest opponents. She didn't mind, although she always felt a little dirty afterwards, like she was nothing more than a tool for him to use.

Feeling dirty on occasion was one of the many side effects of working for Maxwell. She had to admit though, that she loved seeing what her mere presence could do to a man. It was in many ways, entirely flattering, immoral, maybe, but none-the-less, flattering. She couldn't help it if god graced her with beauty, and brains.

So it was she found herself drugging Sean so he would sleep for several days while she ordered the Me Lady out to sea to make the journey to America. This would give her enough time to convince Sean he needed to play Maxwell's little game. Right now all Sean still wanted was to crawl back in his hole, or the nearest bottle, and continue his slow attempt at suicide. He was making progress, but, Sharon knew the slightest slip and he would slide right back into the life she was trying to save him from. He still wanted that self-destructive life he chose to live. The one that would provide the death he had chosen to seek.

As he lay there sleeping she looked at him. He was the only thing Angelina ever had that she was jealous of. She would have never done anything to hurt Angelina but she had always been irresistibly attracted to Sean and she knew he was attracted to her, too. There wasn't a man alive she had met that did not find her attractive and Sean was no exception. After all, she was an extremely beautiful woman and she was not afraid to show it. But Sean's deep love for Angelina kept him from acting on that attraction, even though Sharon sometimes fantasized about it and was certain he would have welcomed it.

Sean was totally devoted to his beautiful wife and for Sharon it was the same. She would never hurt the closest thing she had to family, no matter how she felt about Sean. That was not her style. Even the long hours they spent together could never make either of them go down that road. It was just a fact they dealt with as they worked together. It was strictly platonic and above board, always. Just two people who respected the others good looks, is all. It is just a fact of human nature to see the beauty in one another she told herself over and over. No harm in fantasizing. No promise was ever broken to her dear sister. But Angelina was gone and Sean was here and his need was blatantly obvious. Could he?

Over the years they became Maxwell's star team, his only confidants. That is, until Angelina's death. When Angelina died, Sharon considered going to Sean and telling him how she felt, but Sean was a changed man. He was a broken shell of the man he had been and for Sharon, the attraction disappeared as she watched him sink into depression and despair. Sean couldn't get past the memory of his dead wife and the ludicrous belief he was somehow to blame for it, and now, Sharon felt only pity for him. At least she tried to convince herself that was true. She knew somewhere deep down both of them still harbored feelings for each other, even if they would always remain platonic in nature.

Seeing him lying there was bringing many of those feelings back, and remaining detached was turning out to be more difficult than she expected. Damn it! She did feel for him still to this day. Damn you Maxwell! She couldn't help but wonder what he had been thinking when he set her up like this!

Sharon had rarely been intimate with any man. Yes, there were occasional flings here and there but for the most part she was pure business and could not be tied down like that. Why now was she finding herself lying at arm's length, facing this fool, stroking his cheek? Why were there tears in her eyes, and why did she have the overwhelming desire to undress and pull his head to her breast and cradle him in her arms as he slept?

As the events of the last several days caught up with her she fell asleep there in his bed. Overwhelmed with exhaustion, she drifted off into a deep and peaceful sleep, her hand lying against his chest, feeling it rise and fall, as he slept in the drug induced coma she had ordered for him.

Her last thought was a good one and made her smile. When Sean finally did wake he would find himself far out to sea with no escape. He might be angry at first but as soon as she explained to him her reasoning she was sure he would agree with her short-term plans. She was just hoping he would give her the chance to explain it all to him and accept that she really was trying to help him.

Chapter Six

Melissa sat in a drug-induced haze of shame and anger, lost in her own thoughts as the others raged and argued around her. How could the old fart be so cruel! He had ripped her heart out, even if it was all true. That didn't change the fact that he had revealed her deepest darkest secrets, her child abuse at the hands of her father.

After a while Brett, Beatrice, and their two grotesque children they had produced all stomped out of the room. She wondered at the fact that Beatrice seemed to be ignoring the news that her husband was cheating on her with his secretary. Oh well, she must be that pitiful, and needful, she thought.

Her mother and father were still in the room squabbling with each other. Did either one even give a damn about her? She was the one who had been abused all of her life. If Maxwell wanted to know why she stole from him, it was to get away from these two, especially him. She was deathly afraid of her father. He was mad.

Everything Maxwell said was true. She knew she was a slut and a drug addict and she also had to face the fact that she had allowed her father to sleep with her many times. It started when she was around thirteen and became a normal part of her life. He would sneak into her room and make her do terrible things. Eventually, she grew to like or at least accept it and that set the stage for her life. The first man she charged for sex was a fifteen year old boy under the bridge behind the school. She knew so many wonderful ways to pleasure a man, thanks to good ole Martin that she became a local legend.

By the time she was eighteen she had a nice little bank account and a nice little drug problem. She also had the label of the biggest whore in school, which was a matter of pride in some ways. She was good looking and men willingly did what she wanted. She made it a point to try and have sex with every kid in high school, especially the ones that already had girlfriends. She relished in their pain as she let slip the sexual encounters to this girl or that, knowing full well what the outcome would be. Strangely, even after the boys knew that she would tell, they still came around, so much for young love. Young sex, that's what they wanted, not some altruistic girlfriend to hold hands with and swap spit with before they got on their perspective busses for the ride home.

It was her plan that when she reached the age of eighteen she would use that money to get the hell out of dodge. Mommy and Daddy taught her well. All you had to do was drop in at one of Maxwell's estates and you were treated like royalty, no questions asked. With digs like those it was easy to move from estate to estate taking things and selling them for drug money or providing her special brand of company to the many jet setters she ran with for the gifts they provided her. She did whatever she had to do to stay away from that monster and her mother.

One time she had been given a fifty thousand dollar necklace for a mere nights worth of pleasure. She sold it and snorted it all in a matter of two weeks. It ended in a forced rehab, after her first overdose. She knew then that she had a death wish. That someplace deep ion her she didn't want to live. She also knew she was too big a coward to take her life. This weakness, this constant struggle with her inner demons set the real tone of her sub-human existence.

She also knew she wasn't Martin's real daughter and she supposed that made it all OK in his eyes. It wasn't really like he was having sex with his own daughter. Her mother had to know about it but, of course, they would have never admitted to it at the risk of Maxwell cutting them off. So they all played the game. Well, the game just changed. She began to realize how right Maxwell was about one thing. She didn't need them, never had.

If she could somehow be the one to find the secret of the key she could rid herself of these monsters she called her family once and for all. She would get started right away, well, tomorrow, that is. Tonight she was going to get as stoned as she could and party till dawn at one of the many haunts she knew about here in New York. The Big Apple was full of men who would gladly provide her with what she wanted in return for what she provided. It was the only tool she had, and she knew how to use it, even if it was getting a bit worn.

She wasn't an unattractive woman. She'd been considered quite stunning as a young woman and at the age of twenty five, she was not so far gone yet to have lost her looks from the abuse she continually inflicted on herself. As for Maxwell's suggestion that she check herself into the Betty Ford Clinic at his expense, well, that was not even a consideration at this point. She could clean herself up if necessary long enough to become filthy rich then maybe she would see about trying to change her ways. Right after she destroyed her mother and father, that is. She was now on a mission. She had a purpose. Something she hadn't had for a long time. She would see them dead and buried before this was all over if she had her way.

Martin and Jessica were still at it. Whispering now, their faces close together thinking they were not being overheard, they argued about how to best deal with this new development. True to form, they would just ignore the truth about all of the affairs and other little indiscretions and work together to get their hands on Maxwell's fortune. Would they even offer to include her? She doubted it very much. They had never been good parents anyway, they were just the people that raised her and then proceeded to torture her until she was the thing she was today.

Melissa got up to leave the room.

"Where do you think your going?" Jessica asked her.

"As far away from the two of you as I can get, mother dear," she said, walking out of the room, leaving them to their own misery. She had enough of her own and didn't need whatever it was they had to offer her. Hadn't they done enough for her already? She almost laughed at that.

As she walked down the hall towards the elevator she finally realized she was being followed by her supposed personal assistant. She stopped and stood there for a minute. She took a step and then stopped, playing with him. She spun around, nearly losing her balance.

"What do you think you're doing?" she asked him as he stood there, an emotionless look on his face.

"I am assigned to work with you miss. If you do not require my services right now I can wait wherever you want me too," he responded in a cold indifferent tone.

"So you will do whatever I tell you to do?" she asked as they boarded the elevator.

"I will make any arrangements you require. Travel, meals, whatever you need. My job is to make sure your needs are met to allow you to concentrate on your task," he said in the same dead tone.

"What if I tell you I have no intention of participating in this madness?" she asked, becoming more and more amused by the prospect of having a personal servant.

"I am required to remain at your disposal until the provisions of the will have been met. Even if you did not want to use me, I have to remain available to you."

"I bet that just pisses you off," Melissa said laughing. "Imagine someone being stuck with me. Pretty funny, if you ask me."

"I don't see any humor in it at all. I am being paid for this service, so it makes no difference to me one way or the other what you do with that time, miss," he said to her in a tone that chilled her to the bone.

"Fine, have it your way. What's your name?" Melissa asked as the doors opened to her floor. She was going to get herself presentable and hopefully find a good party.

"You may call me Mr. Smith." he said.

Melissa looked at him and began laughing so hard she almost cried.

"Oh, I bet," she said. "OK. Mr. Smith. I need some money. Are you supposed to take care of that need too?" Melissa asked once she got hold of herself. She knew many Mr. Smiths, why should he be any different.

"I can get you anything you need but I am not authorized to provide you with cash beyond certain levels deemed necessary to conduct your search, miss," he replied, still playing the role of stoic ass.

"Well then, get me an ounce of cocaine!" she ordered, testing the limits of what this pretty boy in the black suit would do. If she saw him on the street she would think he was one of the infamous Men in Black.

"That would not be legal miss, I'm sorry. I will not interfere in your personal business but I will not participate in any illegal activity. I am not here to judge or interfere, but I will not do anything considered a violation of current laws. I hope you understand."

"So I guess an orgasm is out of the question," she said sarcastically.

"Yes, miss. You will need to take care of that yourself as well," he said with a little bit of disgust leaking out in his normally flat response. That in some way angered her.

"Just have a car waiting out front in one hour then, Mr. Smith," she spat, turning to go to her rooms.

He turned and walked back down the hall towards the elevator. Melissa watched him go and wanted to just throw something at the back of that perfectly groomed head. Well, she would see just exactly what he was good for later. He apparently wouldn't give her money but she was willing to bet he would buy her all the drinks she could handle. Call it a liquid dinner paid for by Maxwell's personal assistant. She knew places she could tack many thing onto her bill here in the Big Apple and beyond. At least she could count on a party for a while out of Maxwell.

Melissa did her best for the next several days to drink all of the alcohol in New York. She found several men willing to supply her with some multi-colored party favors, a dominate color of white to balance it all out. She in turn faked a number of orgasms that of course, they paid for dearly, and in the end provided her some additional spending money for her efforts. She could still turn their heads and make them pay. It was her only talent.

Melissa was a tall, statuesque woman with long, honey blond hair. She was neither skinny nor voluptuous but rather a woman whose proportions fit her height and gave her just the right natural wiggle when she walked to turn the heads of most men. She had blue eyes when they were not too bloodshot to tell the color and she almost always wore her skirts just above the knee with loose open collared shirts sans bra to accent her walk coming and going. She called it the good girl being bad look. As long as she didn't let herself get too emaciated, a nagging side effect from the cocaine and methamphetamines she so dearly loved, she had a well-rounded set of breasts that continued to defy gravity. Recently she noticed diet alone was no longer capable of controlling the sag of her once supple breasts. Ah, just one of the many perks to growing old.

Had she lived a cleaner life she would be rich right now, but most of the money she got in her hand went to new clothes to keep them attracted, or, to lining the inside of her nose with whatever she could get her hands on. She wasn't picky when it came to drugs. She liked them all, as long as they made her forget who she was for a while, that is.

True to his word, Mr. Smith took her wherever she wanted to go. He paid for everything, even when she bought drinks for the entire bar for the night he picked up the tab without blinking. She was eating in the finest restaurants and partying with the jet setters just like she'd always done. But even she knew it had to end sometime and the longer she kept this up the better the odds became that someone else would figure it all out and beat her to the big prize. Knowing Maxwell, no one would figure it out overnight but the longer she kept this up the more the odds turned against her.

She hadn't seen nor heard from anyone else since the night of the reading and didn't care to. All of her questions to Mr. Smith on the subject told her no one had been successful yet. Well, she was smarter than all of them put together, and now she was going to beat the old bastard one last time. When she did find it her next action was going to be to hire Mr. Smith to kill her parents. She was pretty sure he would do it for the right sum of money.

The night she decided to take her break from destroying herself she was with a gentleman who decided she wasn't worth the five hundred bucks he had been forced to give her as a gift for her company and he started to smack her around as a little bonus. Melissa was amazed when Mr. Smith showed up in the room asking if she was OK. The gentleman went for him and Mr. Smith casually pulled a gun out of his jacket and proceeded to use it to beat the man to a bloody pulp after which, he escorted her back to her bedroom, put her in bed and called a private doctor up there to tend to her.

That was when she decided it was time to take a break from her normal routine. She didn't have any illusions that Mr. Smith gave a damn one way or the other what happened to her, but at least she was sure he would keep her out of trouble until this was over. He could be a very nice friend to have around in her profession, she thought. She had always shied away from having a 'driver'. It was simple greed really. She didn't want to share.

Melissa was lying on the couch in the main room of her suite holding the key up and letting the light from the window hit it and reflect into her eyes. It was a small silver key with no markings on it whatsoever. The mechanism it would fit was ultra-simplistic. The lock would be a child's toy or something, she surmised.

She had already tried the safe deposit box in the hotel and every other possible place she could think of including lockers in train stations, subways, anywhere she could think of. She kept thinking that it was right here in New York because of what Maxwell said in his video, "His Favorite Haunt."

The others were all heading to various properties Maxwell owned following their own hunches, all except Sean and Joel, that is. Mr. Smith reported Sean had gone to Cannes and taken the Me Lady out to sea and Melissa smiled as she tried to picture the faces of the others and how furious they would be at this little turn of events. As long as he stayed far enough from shore they couldn't touch him that would drive them all completely bats. Way to go, Sean!

After the reading of the will they all ran up to Michigan expecting to find something there because of Maxwell's obvious love of Sean, but so far they found nothing. The only one still there was one of the twins and Melissa could just imagine him stumbling around and tearing things up trying to find some hidden treasure. The vision made her laugh. He was definitely not the sharpest knife in the drawer. She pictured him just digging and digging until he got all the way to China and never once thinking he might need to look somewhere else or even start a new hole. Him, she was not worried about. His brother on the other hand, she did worry about. They might be identical twins but that didn't mean they were equally intelligent, or unintelligent, as the case may be.

William got the brains his brother didn't have and he was a devious scam artist. He kept up the façade that he looked after his mentally inept brother, if you wanted to call it that. Joel wasn't handicapped in any way, he was just naive. But even still, she knew how it really was between them. William teased, taunted and pried his brother. His methods were utterly cruel and his brother always fell for it and out of love went along with whatever plan he got sucked into. This had gone on for years and even to the tune of going to jail for his cruel brother. Afterwards Joel would forgive his brother just as quickly, William promising never to do it again while he planned his next coup. William took full advantage of Joel's love, and Joel was not smart enough to accept the simple fact that his brother used him. Melissa felt sorry for him but at the same time loathed him. They were dirty. Not in the figurative sense either. They were both pigs and usually smelled like they hadn't showered in weeks. William was grossly obese, and they were both greedy, and disgusting. One was just more so than the other.

Melissa snapped out of her revelry and dropped the key on the coffee table next to the couch. She looked over at Mr. Smith. He was capable of just sitting there and not doing a thing as usual intrigued her. How he could just sit and maintain the role he was playing, never once breaking character was a wonder to her. He wouldn't tell her a thing about himself. He was a complete enigma. She had once seen the palm of his hands and was not shocked to see the tips of his fingers and the soles of his hands were devoid of traceable markings as if they had been burned by acid or sanded smooth like a woman would do to the bottoms of her feet. Maybe it was like a nightly thing he did. She fixed her hair, he fixed his fingerprints.

She knew exactly what he was and it chilled her to the bone. He was a ghost and didn't really exist. If something happened while he was around people would say they saw this guy in a black suit with black hair and sunglasses and a vacant, expressionless look on his ageless face and that would be the extent of the description they could give. No trace of him would be found and the "Agency" he worked for would be just as impossible to find. He would have, for all practical purposes, disappeared into thin air. But he did come in handy. If she won this thing she might just hire him if he could be bought. She wasn't sure he could, though. She figured he already was. The only question was who truly owned him. For now, it appeared to be Maxwell.

"Well then, my good man, what am I missing?" she asked, not expecting an answer.

"I cannot say miss. You never told me what you were thinking," he responded as he sat there staring at her.

"If I did would it make a difference? You aren't allowed to help me," she said.

"That is true, but asking me if your logic makes sense is not the same thing as my helping you. No rule there."

"Why didn't you tell me that before? Never mind. I didn't ask, right?" she deduced, answering her own question.

"That is correct, miss. All you have asked me to do so far is pay the bar tabs you have been running up. You never asked me for anything other than what I could physically provide you with," he told her, never once breaking character. He was as cool and calm as ever, this one, a real cold fish. It made Melissa's skin crawl.

"OK, so here goes," Melissa said. Her brow furrowing as she tried to think through the drugged fog she was always in.

"I am listening."

"I am here because I think it is here. My reasoning is based off of what he said about this hotel being his favorite haunt. He went to a lot of trouble to bring us all here. He could have just as easily sent us all a representative and done it that way. I realize he wanted to embarrass us all, but at the same time, he wanted us all specifically in this hotel, so why?"

"Your logic is sound, but not thorough," Mr. Smith replied.

"Oh? Prey, tell? Why not," Melissa replied in a voice drenched with cynicism.

"You misquoted him, that's why, he said, 'his favorite haunt in New York'. That's not the same as the thing he most loves, which is what you are supposed to be looking for," he informed her, making more sense than she cared to admit.

"You may be right. So what did he love the most?" she asked herself out load.

"That, I am afraid I cannot help you with, Miss Alderson. I never met him and that would be interfering, if I knew and told you," he said. The old Mr. Smith resurfacing after he finished

127

speaking he most words he had spoken since he started following her around.

"Gee thanks," she said shaking her head.

"You're welcome," he said back in that utterly emotionless tone of his.

"If I was a nicer person and cleaned up would you consider me attractive?" she asked to see if she could throw him off his guard.

"That question I consider personal miss, and as I have said before, I am not required to provide you with any personal information. My personal life and my feelings about any of this, one way or another are completely irrelevant to my performance as it pertains to this assignment," he said, so bluntly she wanted to throw something at him. But she was sure he was poised and waiting for that very thing to happen.

"Well you can at least answer this question. Do you have a personal life or does your 'Agency' or whoever you work for dictate that, too?"

Mr. Smith indeed had a personal life, but for him his work and his personal life were one in the same. He chose to not even respond to that question because what he would have told her is how much he would personally enjoy stripping the flesh from her abhorrent bones and feeding it to his pet fish, after sterilizing and detoxifying it first, of course. Right now his personal life consisted of sitting here with this whore and contemplating the many ways he could kill her for his own enjoyment while he slowly drove her mad with his best super, secret, agent routine, one of his personal favorite personas.

He was hoping the ordeal would end soon though. She seemed close to throwing herself out the window. If he was lucky he would be down below so he could watch the body as it hit the pavement. That was his idea of a good time!

Melissa waited for a response, but knew it wouldn't come. This man was as cold as they came. She sat for several minutes thinking about what he said. He had a good point and she needed to rethink her logic.

"So the thing he loved the most, money, his dead wife or his equally dead daughter?" she didn't realize she had spoken aloud.

"Those do have more potential than New York, miss," Mr. Smith said startling her.

"Yes, but the wife and daughter are dead and I don't think it was money he loved, just the amassing of it through his business deals," she mussed.

"Well if I may say so. You have at your disposal a jet and any other form of transportation you require, I can arrange for you. If you can think of a place where one of those loves could be manifested I would suggest you go there and investigate it," he offered, not even blinking.

"Sounds like you're helping me, Mr. Smith," she said jokingly.

"Not at all miss. I was simply responding and trying to remind you that you have at your fingertips all of the resources you could ever want to assist you. I never said where you should go or which resources you should use, or how," he said.

"So I need to take it one step at a time. Well, maybe not. They are both, no, all three, buried in Oregon where Maxwell was born and no one has apparently thought of that. I think a visit to their graves is in order."

"Shall I get your plane ready, miss?" Mr. Smith almost sounded excited.

"Yes. When can we leave?" she asked him.

"In about two hours we can be in the air. I will have the car ready for you within the hour. The trip should take about six hours. It is Gold Beach you want to go to, correct miss?" he asked her, and yes, there was a hint of excitement in his voice.

"Yes, that's the place. How did you know?" she asked him suspiciously.

"I was thoroughly briefed on these matters," he shrugged dismissively.

"I see," Melissa said. She wondered just exactly what he knew that he was not sharing.

One thing that would make the trip worth while at least, was the opportunity to spit on Maxwell's grave while she was there, as a thank you, of course. Even if she was wrong it was at least a start and the fringe benefits would be worth the time and trouble. She owed Maxwell at least that much.

Chapter Seven

Eventually, Sean started coming around. He felt groggy but refreshed. It seemed especially difficult to wake though. It was as if he was climbing out of a deep, dark hole that fought to suck him back down into its depths. He felt as if someone, or something, had hold of his legs and was trying to pull him back down and see to it he never woke. He almost forgot for a moment where he was but the gentle rocking and ocean sounds refreshed his memory and he reached over and hit the button that raised the blinds exposing a spectacularly blue sky. The view almost blinded him but his eyes soon adjusted to it and he climbed out of bed feeling better than he could remember.

He made his way over to the windows and noticed the expected scenery was no longer there. The view was one of open water and this brought his confusion back. Why had they left port? He went into the bathroom and showered, shaved, and brushed his teeth, noticing his hands were no longer shaking. He had to admit, even if he didn't want to, that he felt pretty good.

Not surprisingly, when he came out he found a tray of food and a pot of coffee waiting on him over by the fish tank. There was no privacy here! He didn't care just then, though. He could never remember being this hungry. He greedily worked his way through several of the home made pastries while he filled his plate with eggs and sausages and poured himself a steaming cup of coffee to wash it all down with.

He half expected Sharon to come into the room and when she didn't he was a little surprised and possibly, a bit disappointed. He convinced himself it was for the best. She would have just gloated over the fact of how much better he looked and make sure he knew he had her to thank for it. That would have most likely begun the next round of cat and mouse between them.

After he ate and drank his fill, he made his way to the wheelhouse to find out where they were and where they were headed. He was a bit put out by this new turn of events. His plan was to act indignant and finally put the woman in her place once and for all. She was his assistant now, not the other way around. That was about to change because he was in charge now. That damn woman was going to get a piece of his mind!

"Ah! Good morning Mr. Ryder," the captain greeted him. "You are looking quite fit today, I must say."

"Good morning," Sean replied, making his way over to stand next to the captain, "I feel pretty good I must admit, and thanks!"

He looked out the wheelhouse for any sign of land and then finally turned to the captain. "I was just curious. Where are we and where are we headed?" he asked casually, trying not to show his anger.

"We are about four hundred miles off the coast of Portugal headed west to Virginia. It should take us about a week or so to get there, if I push her. I am not pushing her right now though, and I am avoiding the shipping lanes," the captain replied.

"Why are we headed there?" Sean asked him.

"Sharon's orders, Sir," he said, "If you want any more information you'll need to ask her, because she didn't tell me anything else."

"Where is she? Do you know?"

"She was sunning herself up on the private deck a little earlier. I would guess she is still there," he said turning back to his charts, effectively ending the conversation.

Sean could not help but feel that he was still being manipulated by them all. He was glad the captain was not looking at him as he began to turn red in the face. They both knew that Sean knew the truth. He was as much a party to Sharon's manipulating plans as she was.

Sean walked out of the room highly annoyed. Sharon was supposed to do what he asked her to do, not the other way around. He took the ladder up, and sure enough, there she was sunning herself without a care in the world. Her trusty laptop sat idle on a small table next to her. She was not working but was instead just lying there absorbing the sun. Sean could not help but admire her. He had always found her beautiful. It was just never a subject that was considered acceptable. But just then, there was no denying she was strikingly beautiful, and her suit, or lach thereof, did little to hide the fact.

She wore a blindingly white hat which was tied with a bow under her chin. The large, wide brim flapped in the wind. Dark shades reflected the sun as she lay there with her face turned up towards the sky. Her mouth had an easy smile on it as she consumed the heat of the mid-morning sun. Her enjoyment was obvious as she reveled in the rays of the unobstructed sun.

She was wearing a tiny white bikini that left little to the imagination and her body glistened in the sun, heavy with oil from head to toe. Sean could not help but get aroused when he saw her, but he reminded himself that he was angry with her. His resolve slowly dwindling, as he admired her flawless body lying there, drenched in the warmth of the sun. Sharon looked up grabbing the rim of her hat so it would not blow away, lifting the glasses, she squinted at him.

"Well, it's alive!" she said sarcastically. That was all it took to remind Sean he was mad as hell.

"Yes, it is. It would like to know what the hell is going on here?" he said tensely.

"Don't get all excited, Sean. I did it to protect you. You were in no shape to think for yourself."

"Protect me from what? So far, the only thing I've needed protection from is you, and those thugs that work for you," he said, the anger building in him over the last few days' events.

"They don't work for me. They work for Maxwell. I was saving you from an unwanted visit from one or all of Maxwell's family members. You guessed right. You never told anyone where we were headed, and neither did I. Not even Thomas. Would you like to guess where they all headed as soon as they left New York?"

"Let me see… Michigan," he guessed, seceding to her logic.

"Ding, Ding, Ding! Give the man a prize. I took the Me Lady out to sea so none of them could come here, because as soon as they figured out where you were, I figured at least one would be coming to tail you. As you said before, they all have this belief that Maxwell rigged it so you would find whatever the key opens first. We are too far out for a helicopter to make the trip and I told the captain to take it slow and easy so we have about two weeks of peace while you figure out what your next move should be," she said smiling innocently up at him.

"You could have told me, Sharon. I'm not stupid, you know," he said plopping down in a seat next to her.

He looked over at her as she lay there. Her barely covered body made his clear head pulse with desire. He hadn't felt like this in a long time and it wasn't as unwelcome as he expected it might be.

"You still needed some time, and we didn't have any. I see you're not shaking any more. Congratulations, you're clean and sober!" she said sarcastically, looking him directly in the eyes.

Sean had noticed it before when he was shaving and again he had to admit he actually felt pretty good.

"How long was I asleep?" he finally asked.

"Four days. I had the doctor give you a sedative along with the vitamin concoction to make you sleep, and to help you through the hard part of drying out. I dosed you myself several times."

"That would explain the bruises on my ass."

"You were shaking and sweating. It was terrible to watch, but thankfully, it passed yesterday," She said shyly. "I was very worried about you, and I stayed with you the entire time."

She was looking over at him demurely. Sean could see that watching him 'dry out' had not been very pleasant for her and it helped him to forgiver her. She really was trying to help him, he admitted reluctantly to himself.

"Please don't be mad at me, Sean. I really was doing it for you. I was afraid what might happen if any of them got around you and messed you up again," she said almost pleadingly. She hid her face as the tears began to trickle down her cheeks in an unwelcome and barely controlled flood.

He was still a little angry about being shanghaied. She could be so devious, but he just couldn't stay mad at her, and, in fact, he was beginning to realize he probably should thank her. He did feel pretty good and he was starting to like the feeling. It was a hell of a lot better than waking up puking and hitting the bottle first thing in the morning.

"I forgive you, and, I guess I ought to thank you, too," he grudgingly admitted. "You are still the devil, but at least you're on my side in this. That makes me feel better," he said softly. "I need a friend, and I can't think of a better person to have around to help me."

Sharon smiled and sat up. She folded up her laptop and put on her sunglasses again.

"You are very welcome, boss. It's almost lunchtime. Care to join me?" she asked him happily.

"Well, I just had something but what the hell. I still feel like I could eat a horse. I haven't eaten in four days after all!" he said getting up.

"Well just because your sober doesn't mean I'm going to let you get all fat. I'll have some sandwiches brought to the study. We can have a working lunch," Sharon said, all business.

Sean followed her down towards Maxwell's study, work being the farthest thing from his mind as he nearly stumbled, unable to take his eyes off of her. She had a way of walking that drew and held your eyes whether you liked it or not. There was a terrible conflict raging in him over his sudden depth of feeling for her and his feelings for Angelina. All he knew for sure was he wasn't sure how he should feel about anything anymore.

As they sat eating a light lunch of sandwiches and iced tea to wash it down, Sharon filled him in with what she did know, and what she surmised. He listened in amazement over the families antics she revealed from the scant details she had. As he sat there listening, he took out his key and played with it. He stared at it and tried to figure out what it might do, his curiosity growing at the prospect of the challenge. That much about him hadn't changed. He loved a good challenge and he thrived on winning, even under the mysterious circumstances he found himself trapped in. In some ways, it was like a surreal nightmare, monsters and all, but that wasn't enough to scare him off.

"Sean, I have to admit, and you need to understand, that I have no idea what this is about. Maxwell had your buddy, Mr. Smith, making these arrangements, and he refused to speak to me about it. I am going to let you in on a little secret. Maxwell hasn't been with the company for about a year now. He let them buy him out not long after you left and he resigned himself to the fact you wouldn't come back," she was fiddling around with her computer again as she spoke to him.

"Why would he want to do that?" Sean asked, still distracted by the key.

"I haven't the faintest idea, but I think it was to keep the family from knowing he had those kinds of liquid assets. Along with the nine estates and Me Lady he had somewhere in the vicinity of eighteen billion dollars in various banks and other monetary instruments. He had around twenty billion, but spent a lot of it on this little game. As his assistant, the only thing I was involved in when it came to all of this, was paying Mr. Smith and all of the lawyers, and let me tell you, they were paid a lot."

Sean was still staring at the key and only half listening to her. It was a small silver key with absolutely no markings on it. It was not a door key that was for sure. A safe deposit box, maybe, or a train station locker, possibly. He put nothing past Maxwell at this point. It was a small key and would most likely fit some type of box or other container. Being completely devoid of markings, it would be impossible to trace it to its maker. Whatever it was, it was made for a very specific purpose. Maybe he could torture Mr. Smith into telling him. As much as the idea amused him, he doubted that very much.

"Sean! You're not listening to me!" Sharon accused, annoyed.

"I'm sorry. What were you saying?" he said, snapping out of his obvious daydream. He had been in the process of sticking a hot poker into Mr. Smith's side yelling at him, in some foreign language, to tell him what he wanted to know.

"Thomas sort of let on that the keys all worked in one or several locations, right? He also said that the true prize was related to what Maxwell loved best. I wonder what he meant by that."

"It's hard for me to tell. I haven't been around him for a few years but I know what he used to love. The real riddle is

139

what did he love the most and was it a thing, a person, a place. Who can tell?"

"The other question is, 'when,' was he talking about? I got the impression he was referring to the now, otherwise, I would have said it was his wife, or maybe Angelina, that he loved the most. But he loved this boat, too, and several of his estates," Sharon said, obviously thinking aloud.

"I think that goes too far back or is too broad. I doubt it's a place. It could be that it's in one of those places for a very specific reason, but it's not a place in, and of itself. It makes more sense to relate it to a reason rather than a place. That is a guess, but it seems right. If you ask me what he loved the most was being Maxwell Alderson. He loved screwing with peoples heads most of all!" Sean said laughing.

"Well, we have to start someplace so I have put this spreadsheet together so we can start cataloging information and pieces to the puzzle. Come have a look," Sharon directed, beckoning him over to the side of the table where she sat.

Sean got up and stood behind her and off to one side, so he could look at the screen. His face was uncomfortably close to hers and she was still in what little there was of her bathing suit and smelled like coconuts from the oil she rubbed on her smooth skin to protect it earlier. He wasn't having a lot of success concentrating on the computer screen with her sitting between him and it like that. His eyes kept wandering over her luscious frame and he knew he was staring but he just couldn't stop.

"I set it up to let us break it down into various categories, we can then… Sean, stop staring at me," she said, looking up at his face, annoyed, but also highly amused.

"Oh. Uh, I'm sorry. I didn't. Sorry."

Sharon stood up and faced him. She was still in her bathing suit and Sean was fighting with his eyes to keep them from looking where they really wanted to be looking. Sharon locked his gaze with those golden eyes of hers and gave him that look he dreaded. Her gaze bore straight into his muddled brain, and he was powerless. She had complete control over him and he knew it. He was locked in her gaze, firmly fixed, escape was impossible.

"Well, if you're ever going to be able to work with me you need to get a handle on your hormones. You used to be able to do it. Although, I know you always struggled," she teased, a mischievous little smile forming on her lips.

Sean closed his eyes and shook his head vigorously trying to block the vision of her and break her hold on him, unsuccessfully. She was staring at him openly, her brow furled in thought and she was biting her lower lip and that always drove him nuts. It wasn't bad enough he had to deal with all of this other crap, now he had to deal with her, and he was completely unprepared for it.

"Sean. I think it's time you evaluate your situation, and your life, and face up to something I know is painful. I loved

Angelina, you know that. She was the only sister I ever had, and I loved her as much as you did, but, she is gone, nothing can change that. You can't blame yourself for the rest of your life, for something that was never your fault in the first place. Damn it! You need to get on with your life!"

Sharon turned away from him and paced back and forth with her tiny fists clenched at her sides. She was on the brink of exploding again. How long could this go on? She was visualizing the satisfaction beating his chest with her fists would give her right now.

Sharon stopped inches from him, fists at her sides, eyes ablaze.

"We can both still love her memory and keep her in our hearts, but guess what! I have always loved you, too. Not so much in a sexual way, but there is that, too,' she said offhandedly. "Most of all, I don't think Angie would approve at all of how you chose to grieve her loss. I think you need to accept the fact that we, you and I, are all each other really has right now, and I don't want to lose you again. I like to think Angelina would approve, and she most certainly deserves better than you have given her so far! I know she would want us both to be happy. She would not approve of the way you have behaved. You know that's true. Search your heart, Sean."

Sean stared at her in awe. He wasn't even really listening to her any more although he knew somehow what she was saying. All he could do just then was stand there, looking at her.

142

She had her eyes locked to his and it seemed to him she was just moving her lips and he was deaf. Part of him listened and knew she was completely right. The other part simply was thinking she was just too beautiful and he should let her know he agreed with her analogy. But there was another part. There was the part that still lived in deep despair and wasn't able to climb out of that dark place he had existed in for so long now. He simply wasn't ready yet.

Sharon moved a little closer to him and took his hand and brought it to her cheek brushing her lips gently across the palm of his hand. Her nearly naked body and that small, soft touch set Sean on fire. It shot from his hand moving with lightening speed up his arm and then it radiated out of every nerve in his body like fireworks engulfing his entire being. He wanted to take her in his arms and kiss her greedily, letting their bodies melt together, but he just couldn't do it!

"I can't," he cried out, breaking the spell. He was shaking with desire as he pulled his hand away from her and quickly left the room before his resolve weakened, and he gave into her, gave into himself.

Sharon plopped down in the chair and cradled her head in her hands. She fought the urge to weep, eventually losing the battle. How was she going to ever bring him back to the living? He had to see she loved him. He had to see Angelina's death was not his fault! What she feared, more than anything, was that she might have to watch as he went back down the rabbit hole again. She wouldn't allow that. He needed time and he needed her to be patient, too. He needed her to guide him back to the land of the living.

Sharon hated Maxwell at that moment for placing her in this situation. It was as if he knew how she felt and knew this would be the hardest thing she ever did. Why on earth couldn't he have just died and left her alone! She gathered up her things and ran into her private quarters so have a good, long cry.

Chapter Eight

Sharon knew Sean needed some space and time to think. She went out of her way to avoid him for the rest of the day and she put on the most conservative clothes she could find. They had a lot of work to do and sooner or later they were going to need to get down to business.

That evening, when she went to the dining room for dinner she got a little worried when he didn't show up. Earlier she made sure to tell the captain to have someone keep an eye on him and to make sure he came to eat with the rest of them. All day she went to the captain for progress reports. So far he reported nothing that alarmed her.

Sean had been in his state room for a few hours sleeping again. He had gone to the gym, which was encouraging, she thought. He sat for a long time on the front deck by the pool and then went back to his state room around five, hopefully to dress for dinner, but, so far he was a no show.

She was tempted to go get him and force him to come to dinner but she was afraid he would get angry. She knew she could no longer force him into anything. She was powerless and hated the feeling. It was up to him now. She kidded herself that it didn't matter, but she knew she was lying to herself. Why had she let her feelings out? It was very unprofessional of her.

The captain watched her and waited. He was getting on her nerves as he sat there and sheepishly avoided looking at her, fiddling with his water glass to pass the time and keep his hands busy. He was not about to speak until she did so they sat there for about ten minutes playing this little game. Finally, Sharon decided it was time to get the meal started.

"Well, I guess it's just us," she said.

"It sort of looks that way," Captain Spencer said noncommittally.

Sharon raised her hand and gestured for the waiter to begin with the first course. He quietly moved in and provided them with a salad, offering fresh grated cheese and pepper to each. Afterwards, he retreated back into the corner and waited.

Sharon wanted to scream! The Captain kept sneaking glances at her trying not to get caught. He was just trying to figure out how to proceed, she knew, but she would prefer he just be himself. She tried to break the silence.

"So where exactly are we?" she asked, reaching for her fork to get them both started.

"I am only doing six knots so we will make about, let me see, I'd say, three hundred fifty miles or so today with the tail wind we have. We will need several weeks at this speed, if that suits you. I can kick it up if you like but we burn fuel faster that way," he informed her, digging into the salad, still averting his eyes.

Just then Sean strode in as if there was nothing amiss. He made his way to the remaining place setting and sat down ignoring the eyes on him. He was dressed in a pair of shorts and a shirt he must have dug out of one of the state rooms.

"Sorry I'm late I was combing the place for something to wear. You sort of missed that need, Sharon, I can't parade around in my birthday suit, you know," he said smiling.

"We will remedy that when we get the chance," she replied casually, trying to act just a tiny bit indignant to hide the flood of relief she felt when he walked in.

After that conversation slowly returned to normal and the tension dropped. Both Sean and Sharon were smart enough not to let what had happened earlier show. 'Drop it and move on.' Sharon heard Maxwell saying in her head as he had done so many times in life when things were not going the way he intended and a course adjustment was in order.

After the meal the chef appeared, as usual. He had in tow a bottle of Dom, as usual, and Sharon winced but kept her mouth shut, not as usual!

"Was everything to your liking?" he asked, as he deftly worked the cork free.

"Everything was wonderful, as usual, sir," Sean replied.

Sean wasn't stupid. He knew Sharon was watching to see what he would do. He had already made up his mind what he was going to do but she didn't' need to know that. Not just yet anyway. He was enjoying watching her squirm and he knew she wanted to say something. It was burning on her lips and he almost lost it and laughed at the inner turmoil she was unable to completely hide. He was allowed to have a little fun, after all.

The Chef made his way around the table filling the as of yet unused wine glasses starting with Sharon. He then moved around to the Captain working his way around to the empty seat he would take when he finished his task. As he moved over to fill Sean's glass Sean stopped him by putting his hand over his glass and waving him on. The chef passed him by and Sean was sure he heard Sharon finally breathe. He was extremely pleased with himself. It served her right for torturing him.

They all sat there in silence for a while. It felt lighter in the room. Sharon was smiling and the Captain was telling dirty jokes just to see if he could shock her, which, of course, she wasn't but pretended to be just for him. The chef would shake his head and let out little ticking sounds each time he spilled his punch line.

Afterwards Sean got up and thanked them all.

"Sharon, we have a few more hours we can get some work done if you are up to it," he said casually.

"You're the boss!" she said getting up and following him out the door.

They headed up towards their staterooms in silence. Sharon walked behind Sean. She was feeling somehow, she had been the brunt of some joke, or game he was playing. It would be just like him! To sit there and make her wonder where he was and what he was up to and that thing with the wine glass! He must be really proud of himself right now, she thought, anger welling up in her just a little.

He didn't say a word until they reached the study. The whole time Sharon was working herself up into a fury with him. Finally, they entered the study and Sharon just couldn't hold back any longer.

"Well?" she said to his back. Her arms automatically crossing themselves below her breasts as a frown took over her normally sweet little face.

"Well what?" Sean responded, trying to pretend he didn't know what was going on.

"Sean!"

"Look. I heard everything you said and I spent the day thinking. I also spent some time searching the yacht for clues to pass the time," he started.

"I was worried about you and you were playing games with my feelings, Sean!" she accused, trying not to let the strength of her anger overwhelm her. Most of all, she was trying really hard not to cry.

"No, I wasn't. I wanted to see what you were going to do, just as much as you wanted to see what I was going to do. Tit for tat, Sharon, and don't deny it," he said calling her bluff. "As for being late to supper, I am sorry. I was digging around in here and lost track of time," he said semi-enjoying her overreaction.

"Well, don't do that again. I was so afraid you would slip back into your depression," she said succumbing to the tears as the stress gushed out of her. Damn it, she hated these feelings. Damn you, Maxwell.

"I'm really sorry, Sharon," he replied softly. "I didn't mean to hurt you. I just needed time to think."

"So what are you thinking?" she asked, wiping her eyes on the backs of her hands, trying to regain her dignity.

"I am thinking you are probably right, as usual," he informed her, leaning up against the long table.

"Of course I am," she said, taking advantage of, and grateful for the offered opportunity to regain her composure.

"Let's keep this on a strictly business level. OK? I am just not prepared for anything more than that right now. I may never be," he said quietly.

"OK," she said moving closer to him, "I just want you to be the old Sean I used to love to work with. We had a lot of good times, didn't we?" she asked, still sounding vulnerable.

"Yes we did. We kicked a lot of ass in those days, if I remember correctly. So why not do it with this too?" he said relaxing a little, now that the tension had passed.

Sharon just nodded and went over and hugged him. He felt that jolt of electricity course through him again and gingerly, he put his arms around her and hugged her back. He was still fighting his own demons, this wasn't helping him any.

"This is not very professional, you know," he chided to cover his feelings.

"Sorry," she apologized, moving away, head down.

"It's late, and I am still feeling like a bag of crap. I think I am going to bed now. Good night." Sean said making his way to the door to his stateroom.

"OK, but tomorrow we need to get a plan together. I will see if there is any new news. I'm not really tired yet," Sharon said, returning to her usual self.

Sean left the room without glancing back. Sharon was a mess but she didn't want him to know that. She had to get her composure back. All of this had taken a tremendous toll on her. She never expected this and she hated Maxwell for doing this to her. She would have been much better off if she had never seen Sean again.

Sean was right. Keep it professional and get her bonus. That was the key. Then she could do anything she wanted and get far away from them all, from Maxwell, too. Tomorrow she would fix it once and for all. Now she just wanted to sleep. She had lied. She was really dead tired.

As Sharon slept she dreamt of Maxwell. He was sitting in a big easy chair in his own private theater in Hell eating popcorn and watching the festivities as the intricate plot he had set up before he died unraveled on the big screen, in high definition, of course. Satan was patting him on the back in a congratulatory way.

Sharon looked at the screen and saw herself running back and forth, this way and that, like one of the Keystone Cops. Sean was standing there watching her, his head going side to side as if he was watching a tennis match. Maxwell just laughed and laughed.

Then the scene changed and Angelina was standing there crying. She held her arms out as if she was pleading for something but Sharon was not able to hear what she was asking her to do. All of a sudden the entire family was there, Sean, Angelina, Martha, and even her mother was there along with all of the others. They all stood there slapping their knees as if they were watching the funniest thing they had ever seen.

It took a moment for her to see what was so funny but when she looked behind her she saw an old time puppet stage with Maxwell at the top. Sharon realized she was what they were all laughing at. She knew why she had been running back and forth and this way and that. She was on strings and Maxwell was pulling them, trying to make her dance but all she did was flop around as she fought to break free with Maxwell repeating over and over, "You can't get free from me. I own you." He laughed and jerked and laughed some more until she thought she was going to go crazy. His laughter was finally drowned out by someone's screams, hers, and she jerked awake renewing her vow to keep it professional. She wasn't sure she could take much more of this.

Chapter Nine

Joel was glad to be rid of all of them, especially his fat, lazy brother. They all took their jets and flew directly to Michigan after the reading of Maxwell's so called will, all expecting to find the treasure where Sean was staying. None of them trusted Maxwell and fully expected he had rigged the game in Sean's favor after the little display of affection and kindness he showed him while ripping the rest of them to shreds with his little display of childish hate. He should have just given them all some of his fortune and they would have left him alone. What a greedy man Sean was! One thing they all agreed on. He would never get a penny, if they could help it. Joel just sometimes forgot why he was supposed to hate Sean so much. He'd never done anything, mean to him, in fact, he was kind of nice. But everyone hated him so there must be a good reason.

The main house was now in a total shambles. All of them, even Joel took great pleasure in ripping through every inch of it. Too bad they ended up not finding anything. Not even a plug nickel! Every piece of the long covered and unused furniture had been exposed, searched, and some of it even torn apart. No room was left untouched. The attic floor was covered with boxes and papers and old books thrown everywhere and the other rooms were pretty much the same.

Some bitch named Katy finally showed up with her rather large husband in tow, not to mention the local Sheriff and they put a stop to it. She was livid when she saw what they had done to the place. She even pulled an old sword off the wall from over the mantle of the fireplace and chased them all around with it. Apparently she was supposed to watch the place. After that, Joel decided he would stay at a hotel and just come out during the day to continue his personal search.

The others gave up way to easily. They all left after the run in with Katy. Not him, no, he was certain it had to be here. Nothing else made any sense, and when he found it he would finally be able to show them all he was no dummy. He could read Maxwell like a book. That old fart intended for that loser, Sean to get all his money. It was so obvious it was a joke. All Joel had to do was find it before that fool came back here to be victorious.

He found the keys to the two cars and the bike in the garage and pocketed them before anyone else saw them. They were his little secret! Yes indeedy, Joel had a secret of his own! The others looked for the keys and finally gave up. He wanted to tell them, just so he could prove he was superior to them, but he stopped himself and kept them hidden until they left.

He was now riding back and forth in style. He was the proud owner of a cherry red 427 Cobra! For now, he was, anyway. Boy, it was a sweet ride. That's for sure.

Katy disapproved of his use of the car but he pointed out to her that she really didn't have any say in the matter. He was allowed to use anything, go anywhere, and do whatever he wanted. Maxwell said so. Those were the rules. He heard them plain and simple, and no country bumpkin was going to get in his way. No brother either, for that matter. He had an idea!

He had been alone now for a day with the exception of his nasty assistant. He was a cruel looking man in a black suit who always wore sunglasses. Joel didn't really care for his type of help. He seemed to grimace any time he even spoke to him and their relationship had become one of Joel giving, and Mr. Brown taking orders, if that was even his name. Joel doubted it was. After all, he wasn't as stupid as they all thought he was.

Joel was staying in the local Holiday Inn. Not what he was accustomed to, but adequate for his needs. What he was accustomed to was the palatial estate in Monaco that he and his asshole brother took over long ago to spite Maxwell. He knew Maxwell liked that place and he knew that it drove him mad that they were always there. To be honest, he was surprised they hadn't been forced to leave. Maxwell avoided the place like the plague after they showed up, and as a result, they used it for their home base, raping, plundering, and pillaging the local village. All that and more could be yours! All that, all on Maxwell's tab. Joel thought, smiling. He was a heck of a lot smarter than they all realized. That was his little secret.

It's pretty easy to steal from a place like that, and pretty hard to prove. No one even seemed to care anyway. If they took something, it was magically replaced with something new and equally valuable for them to take later on, and that is how their lives pretty much went, his and his brother's. Steal, sell, gamble, and buy women. That was life in Maxwell's wonderful world of the disgustingly rich and colossally stupid.

The real irony was they all thought he was the stupid one, well not Joel Madison. He played his role well and his brother took all the heat. Now who's the dummy! Maxwell had no clue how much they took. He was the stupid one, not Joel.

Joel spent a lot of time, too much really, dreaming about what he would do when he got all of Maxwell's money. First, there was what to do about his lying, cheating father. Maybe death was too good for him. Maybe he should have thought twice before he did to Joel's mother what he had done. Not that Joel could totally blame his father, Betty, his secretary was pretty hot. Joel would have 50 secretaries hotter than her when he was super rich though. His father would look at him different then.

His mother, of course, he would take care of. His father on the other hand had to go. Oh yes, he had to go straight to hell. That's where he had to go. It was going to happen you know. Joel would make sure of it.

Joel had all sorts of tortures planned for his dear old dad. The man hated him with a passion anyway, and he knew it. He saw him and his brother as huge, fat, failures. Maybe they were failures, but his brother was the fat one, not Joel! He didn't let himself get fat like his stupid brother.

Well, Maxwell got the last laugh on his dad already, by taking his business away. Joel had to admit that was some really sweet icing on the cake, there! Even if he got some small compensation for it, he was essentially broke now, just like the rest of them. But, he could still think of several other indignities he could lay on the stupid jackass. There could never be enough salt poured in that bastard's wounds. Yes. His dear old dad was in for a rude awakening at the hands of his new master, and son, Joel the magnificent!

His brother was another matter altogether. Joel wouldn't rest until his asshole of a brother was completely destroyed. Nothing as simple as a little salt would do for him. All the years of playing his fool and taking all of the crap he dished out were at an end. When he found the answer to Maxwell's puzzle, his brother would find himself the man without a home, a hopeless loser, totally dependent on the generosity of his brother and of course, master, Joel the benevolent.

But no, not really, Joel had no intention of sharing with him even though they had made a secret pact to share. Joel knew his brother was lying to him, just like he knew his brother knew he was lying, too. Or his brother lied and he knew his brother lied or he lied to his brother or… enough! He shook his head in confusion.

"Well, I will be the one, not him. That's all that I got to say!" he said aloud to himself.

The promise was the kind of game they played all the time. William thinking he was so smart and Joel letting him think so. It would be like a dream come true for Joel, when he finally got the upper hand.

"End of the line, Willie, my boy! Bow to your superiors!" Joel told himself aloud again, lost in his warped day dreams.

First things first, he was hungry and there wasn't much to eat out there, so he needed to go into town and get something before he went out there. Seemed Sean was not much of an eater. He was most definitely a drinker. He was pretty far gone from what Joel saw in New York. He was not a concern, really. Apparently, he wasn't even trying to find it. He just slipped out of sight.

Joel had taken to getting his meals at the Village Tavern, partly because the food was good, and partly because Katy, the owner hated him. He wouldn't be surprised if she was spitting in his food. He hopped into the 427 knowing how much it bothered Katy he was driving it, and headed over for some brunch.

He parked the car near the front door and revved it several times just to further annoy her then he shut it down and went into the tavern. He took a booth near the door, also knowing his stench would hit any other customers that came in, even further annoying her. He hadn't bathed for several days now. He was usually too busy and too tired after a full day to worry about the little things like that. Actually, he almost never bathed, if you wanted to know the truth. He so badly wanted her to tell him to leave. It would be all the satisfaction he needed to make him happy, at least for a little while. But, for some reason she was still putting up with him.

Katy stared at him as he slipped into the booth, pushing the table back and centering himself on the bench. She made her way over with a grimace on her face.

"I think it is time I exercise my right to refuse you service," she said staring at him in defiance.

"Oh, why is that?" he asked innocently.

"Because, the other customers are complaining and you are damaging my property, not to mention, ruining my business. The smell of you is permanently embedded into the furniture and I am running out of money trying to disinfect everything you touch, so it is a pure business decision. You understand," she said in the most sarcastic tone he had ever heard. Man, she was good at being mean.

"Fine, I'll just hop back in my car and go down the road. Your food sucks anyway," he said vehemently.

"Your car, what's that supposed to mean? You shouldn't even touch that thing. It was Maxwell's most beloved possession. Sean's too!" she said angrily. "All you are doing is ruining it."

Joel didn't respond. He just sat there for a moment. Of course! Why hadn't he figured it out sooner! The cars and the bike! He knew Maxwell loved them. He remembered being a small child back when Maxwell actually enjoyed having him visit and taking him for rides in this very car. Always telling him what a wonderful machine it was, and how much he loved it. All the money and possessions he had were nothing compared to that car, he once said to Joel. He was addicted to the sheer power of thing.

"Well, if you insist, I'll leave," he said trying to hide his excitement.

He got up and left, forgetting all about his hunger and headed back down towards the lake house with Mr. Brown in tow in his black sedan. He was going to go over every inch of this car and the others if necessary. This had to be it!

When he arrived back at the lake house, he made his way into the garage and shut the door behind him to keep Mr. Brown out. He was not going to have him watching and learning what he did. For all Joel knew and suspected, there was a stash of gold or Platinum or other equally valuable commodity hidden somewhere in the cars or the garage and Mr. Brown might rob him if he found it. There wasn't anyone around to stop him and that thought scared Joel just a little. It hadn't occurred to him that a check was probably more like what he should be looking for.

Joel's mind began to wander again. Maybe it was a certificate saying, 'Congratulations Joel! I knew you could do it. Here is your 18 billion dollars! Thank you for playing Maxwell's game of Joel wins!'

Mr. Brown sat in his car and watched as Joel made his way into the garage and quietly drove off with an uncharacteristic smile on his normally expressionless face. Thank god the smelly idiot hadn't wanted him to chauffer him around. He gagged every time he got downwind of him.

He headed back towards town and he made his way into the Village Tavern for a little lunch leaving his charge alone for the first time in days. He was sick of rubbing menthol in his nose to cover the smell of this grotesque human.

Joel stood staring at the car after he made sure he was alone. He saw Mr. Brown leave and was glad for it. The man gave him chills. With him gone, Joel could load up his gold and drive away. How much gold was 18 billion dollars anyway, he wondered? Would it fit in the trunk or would he find a treasure map maybe! That would be pretty cool! Joel's mind drifted into a fantasy which had him dressed like a pirate digging on a golden beach.

"Snap out of it, Joel! You have to find the damn map first, you know!" he said aloud

Ah, but it would be so much like the games he and his brother played to steal. They had to catch you and they had it down. One made a big stink usually his big, fat brother and Joel lifted a few treasures from the palace to sell to the local hock shop.

"Focus, Joel!"

162

He first looked in the glove box, nothing there. He then opened the trunk, still no magic box or stack of glistening ingots with his name on it. He knew Maxwell was not that stupid. No, he would hide it very well. It would be some secret compartment he would have to find. If he had to, he would dismantle this piece of crap to find it. It had to be here!

Joel opened the hood of the car. The glistening, perfectly maintained motor filled the space below the hood and Joel dug around looking for some sort of place to stick his key. He had to be right! There was nothing there, but he wasn't ready to give up just yet.

Next he went over the Mustang. He went through the same routine with it, checking under the hood, in the trunk and all of the other common spaces. His observation of the bike was equally fruitless. He was just about to give up when an idea struck him. If it was all of them then it might just be here in the garage someplace. There was an attic and a lot of drawers and lockers filled with tools. Many were strewn around the floor because the others had at least gone through those but one more look couldn't hurt.

Joel dug through the drawers and the cabinets and was still coming up empty handed. He was getting seriously annoyed, now. Damn him! It had to be here.

He was sweating profusely from the exertion and his stomach was sending spasms of hunger to his brain. This could at least wait until after lunch. He wasn't in that big a hurry to get what he had coming to him and he had forgotten to eat after Katy kicked him out.

He made his way to the small lake cottage that Sean had obviously been living in. Smiling at the destruction he and the others had caused the place. Sean would be a little upset when he saw this, he thought, happily. He, Joel Madison, personally ripped through his clothes leaving nothing but a pile of rags for him to find. Served him right, teacher's pet, and all!

The pantry was barely stocked. There was a garbage pail full of whiskey bottles but not much food. He found some soup and crackers and figured that would have to suffice. As he sat there sucking down his soup, which he didn't even bother to warm, he put together his next move. It had to be a hidden panel or fake wall. Where would you put that in a car? He began to tick through the possibilities.

"Trunk?" he said out loud to himself. He would tear the carpet out of it next, same with the floorboards. 'Junk in the trunk, you skunk!"

Joel spit a mouthful of soup out all over the table as he laughed hysterically at his own incredible wit. The soup made him laugh even harder.

"Doors!" it could be in the doors. There was a lot of space there! Drug dealers hid stuff there. He saw it in a movie!

"Good plan, my main man! Is your name Stan? Have I got me a fan?" he howled flinging a spoonful of soup at the wall.

"Seats, now that's a good one, Joel my boy!" he quipped as he shoveled more of the soup and cracker mush he was swilling down into his mouth.

"Back seat, front seat, Jeez oh Pete, sit in your seat!" he said pouring some soup on the floor in tribute to his unrivaled humor.

"Wheel wells! That's the ticket!" he said as he finished the last of the bowl of slop. Maxwell would hide it in the wheel wells or somewhere like that before he would hurt his precious little car. He had to be right. He and only he knew what Maxwell would do. He wouldn't damage his precious little hot rod.

"I got you right where I want you. Joel, master of ceremonies, will now simultaneously dance and pee on Maxwell's grave with his eighteen billion dollar weenie, wearing nothing but his alligator tap shoes."

He threw the bowl towards the sink intentionally missing and laughed as it broke against the backsplash throwing shards of ceramic all over the countertop and headed back out to claim his well-deserved prize.

First things first, he tried to lift the carpet and see if there was something under it. It had to be the Cobra. That was the one Maxwell really loved. Nothing so far was working, time to move onto the wheel wells.

As he began to feel around the wheel wells of the Cobra his heart was pounding like a jack hammer. He was completely convinced if his superior mental prowess. He had the old fuck face now! After he found it, he was going to take a sledge hammer to this pile of shit just to spite the old man and prove his superiority over them all once and for all. Who cares if there were almost none of them left in the world? This one was on its last life!

It never occurred to him he would be destroying his own property.

He carefully felt all along the inside of both of the front wheel wells and so far found nothing. Not to worry though. He was right! It was just a matter of time now. One of the rear wheel wells was just as unproductive as the two front wheel wells. One more on this heap of shit then he would check the Mustang.

He pushed the gas can out of his way that Mr. Brown had left sitting there. That idiot! He told him to fill the tank from the supply that was kept there and the idiot just left the can out almost all the way full too. He kicked it out of the way and it fell over spilling gas on the floor. The smell was very strong, but Joel wasn't stopping now. No, he was going to get his prize.

He began to daydream again. Maybe he would burn the place down instead of using the sledge hammer. Hell, the gas was already there and he could burn it if he wanted to, after it was his, you know. No law against it. He didn't want this place! Plus it would be less exertion and a hell of a lot more fun to watch he thought, as he smiled at the vision he created in his fetid mind.

"Back to work, you smelly jerk!" he told himself.

He was feeling around and at the front of the wheel well there it was! A small bump that certainly felt like it didn't belong there! Oh man! Was that a keyhole he felt? It most certainly felt like it. There was a small little panel in there. There was a slot just the right length to be a keyhole and it definitely did not belong there. He couldn't see it but he could sure feel it. Well, it might have remained hidden for most, but not super Joel!

"I got you now you pile of rotting flesh!" He yelled as he got off his knees. He danced around for a minute even doing a little jig in the gas before kicking the can a second time into the cupboard sending gas splashing everywhere.

"I wonder what will happen when I open it! I bet a secret panel lifts and reveals the gold, all stashed in the wheel wells. They will all pop and I will be rolling in the dough! More Dough for Joe, don't cha know!" he howled as he danced around.

Joel dug into his pocket to retrieve his key. Shaking with excitement, he got back down on his knees and felt around for the spot again. If only he had a mirror to see with. He lay down on his back to see if he could get a better look. It was a tight fit but there it was! He could just make it out, a small, round silver button with a key slit in it.

His hand shaking almost too violently to hold the key, Joel reached up and pushed the key into the hole. At first, the lock seemed to be rusted or something because the key was difficult to get in. By god! It was going in!

"Fuck you all! I win!" he yelled as he pushed the key home in the lock.

Picric acid has some very unique qualities. It was discovered in the 1800's and soon became the explosive of choice. It has one major drawback though. It is extremely volatile, especially when it is allowed to dry out. It's relatively safe, if kept in glass, or plastic, and usually it's kept in water to make sure it doesn't become unstable.

It was widely used until the discovery of TNT and generally fell out of use except for things like blasting caps and fireworks. It is still widely used in the manufacture of fireworks. When ignited, it produces a satisfying hissing noise when it is burned in the air. Always a crowd pleaser!

As the blast engulfed his hand, one of the last things Joel heard was a whistling noise followed by his own screams. Just the right amount of friction is all it took to ignite a glass tube of Picric acid crystals running along the gas tank's fill spout and down to the tank. The small explosion was enough to split the seams and ignite the tank. The ensuing conflagration from the full tank of gas and the now flaming floor where the gas was spilled earlier engulfed Joel Madison in an intense blaze.

One would never think it was true, but the human body is also relatively flammable, once the fats begin to dissolve and burn and Joel Madison was burning quite well. He never even got a chance to try and put himself out.

Mr. Brown sat in the Village Tavern, a paper in front of his face as he enjoyed the delicious burger and fries he was eating. He lost his appetite having to be around Joel but today was proving to be a very special day and suddenly, he was very hungry. The idiot had finally made the right choice. He was sure of it, and the credit all went to the semi-attractive woman running this fine establishment.

At least, he hoped he made the right choice. If he got back and the idiot was still looking, he would need to start dropping hints. He was a patient man. It went with the job. But this was one he was willing to kibitz on just a little, even if it was against the rules. He couldn't take much more of this guy.

The phone rang and the woman, Katy, picked it up and Mr. Brown peeked over the paper, reveling in the look of surprise that made its way across her face. She was taking off her apron with one hand, holding the phone with the other. She hung up and yelled at the back room and the cook, her husband, came running out with a ball bat. Obviously, he was used to breaking up an occasional fight in here among the locals. She whispered something in his ear and ran out of the tavern.

Mr. Smith waited as the man ran back into the kitchen, most likely to shut down the fryers and grill. Calmly, he stood and stuffed the last few fries in his mouth and reached into his pocket pulling out a ten. He stuffed it under the plate where they would find it later. He wasn't the type to not pay his bills. You never, ever, ever, drew attention to yourself.

He got into his waiting sedan and started down the road. He could drive close enough to possibly get a good look at the fireworks show which hopefully, he hadn't missed. If he timed it all right, it should happen any second now and he wasn't the type to time things wrong. He wouldn't stop, of course. They had seen the last of him around here. All of the hotel arrangements were made under the name Alderson and he left behind no trace of himself. The route he was going to take would get him east to Sault Ste. Marie, across the Canadian border, after a nice leisurely drive in this beautiful country. From there, he would get on a plane and make his way back.

As he passed within a few miles of the lake house, he saw several flares go up, one was even a whistler and although it was daytime, the show was still a good one. When they investigated, all they would find was a destroyed car with a destroyed gas tank and a ruined gas can nearby and a pile of whatever was left of Mr. Joel Madison which, he figured, wouldn't be much. Nothing strange would be found, it was just one of those tragic accidents that happens from time to time. The lock was actually just a formed piece of glass tubing covered with a light piece of plastic filled with the highly unstable Picric acid so common in fireworks. The glass tube would have totally disintegrated. Any forensics would simply find the combustion by-products of the fireworks that had, by some coincidence, been stored in the nearby closet which ignited right on cue, shortly after Joel Madison began cooking in earnest.

Yes, it had been some show, and Mr. Brown was finally free to move on to his next assignment. Hopefully, it had nothing more to do with this bunch of idiots. He did love killing, it was almost as much fun as torture, but he preferred a more apt opponent, and something just a little more personal and up close. At least he won the pool. The others better pay up. He finished his assignment first, and he didn't even have to cheat.

Chapter Ten

Sharon found Sean in Maxwell's study pouring through his desk. Thankfully, he hadn't heard her scream the night before. She was trying hard to forget the dream and she certainly didn't want to try and figure out its meaning. She was totally prepared to handle things a little differently today. That was her plan, and under no circumstances was she going to deviate from it. Sean made it pretty clear where his head was last night. Maybe that would change later, but for now, she was just happy he was acting like his old self.

She was wearing a plush pink robe that was loosely tied at the waste and although she didn't intend it she looked absolutely delicious in it, her fine dark hair spilling down around her glowing face as she combed it out. She hadn't thought about how her appearance would affect Sean. She was just trying to get herself together for the new day.

Sean was wearing a pair of swim trunks he found that seemed to be his size. He was still in fair shape. Just because he was busy trying to drink himself to death, didn't mean he hadn't been active. He killed many an hour doing yard work and chopping down trees to make fire wood and pass the long lonely hours. He loved chopping wood, lots and lots of wood for the cold nights during the winters in Michigan and if not for the lack of proper nutrition, he would be in top shape instead of having the obvious look of malnutrition he was still sporting. A few more weeks and he would be his old self again, he thought. Oddly enough, he suddenly wanted to be his old self.

Sharon sat on the edge of the vast desk and watched him. A satisfied look on her face brought on by his noticeable progress and renewed drive. It was obvious she had just showered, her long black hair falling wet and free she smelled faintly of cherry blossoms, her signature scent. It came from a special hair shampoo she used. Nothing else ever touched her hair! It was the source of her nickname with the Captain.

"What are you looking for?" she asked him.

"I have no clue!" he said laughing and sitting back shaking his head.

He got up and to her shock and amazement, hugged her. "Thank you, Sharon," he said sincerely, kissing her cheek softly.

She liked the way it felt. Not a good start to being a total professional, she chided herself. She got the sudden urge to bolt from the room and put a habit on.

"Thank me for what?" she said confused, pulling the robe tightly around her in a self conscience gesture.

"Thank you for not losing faith in me, and for saving my life. I was lost for a long time. I owe you a lot," he said softly smiling at her.

"Oh, it was my pleasure, Sean," she said, wagging her hand at him in dismissal.

"Yea, but I think you actually enjoyed making me suffer. That, I won't forgive you for," he countered.

"I am not the one needing forgiving here, Sean. Besides, that is what assistants are for! You know, we can just forget all this nonsense. I am not exactly poor and with us back on the same team we could start our own business. There is no way we would not be successful. Maxwell taught us both well. If you want to, that is," Sharon offered, dipping her head in a gesture of total vulnerability.

"Oh, that is a sweet offer, but what fun would that be? Besides, you don't owe me anything. That's your money. I would much rather have my own. That old fart is not going to get the best of me. I loved him, but he is not going to have the last laugh. How does eighteen billion dollars sound to you instead? That ought to get us off to a roaring start!" he smiled at her and sat back, putting his hands behind his head in a show of total confidence.

"It sounds like a challenge, and I never back away from a challenge!" she said with a sly smile on her face.

Sharon was totally little taken aback with the sudden mood change. My goodness! Sharon thought. He must have come to some sort of reconciliation last night while she was screaming from her nightmares. Somehow, it didn't seem fair to her. He was obviously having the time of his life and she was again feeling off guard. "By the way, thank you as well," she said quietly.

"What do you need to thank me for?" he asked.

"For showing me the old Sean was still in there and I wasn't wasting my time. I was about ready to give up on you yesterday," she said quietly.

He reached out and touched her cheek softly, kindly. "Don't give up on me just yet. I have a lot to deal with, Maxwell not withstanding. Let's concentrate on one thing at a time for now. We have a lot of work to do."

"Sounds like a plan I can live with!" Sharon said happily.

"I want to view that video again," Sean said absently. He was speaking more to himself, than to her.

"I was thinking the same thing. I just happen to have a copy of it on my laptop, thought it might come in handy at some point," she told him getting up and heading towards her study next door where she had left it earlier, "let me get dressed and I'll be back with it in a few minutes."

"Don't get dressed on my account!" Sean teased throwing her even further off guard.

"I'll be back in a few minutes, too. I need to talk to the captain," he said to her as she was walking out of the study.

"What do you need to talk to him about?" Sharon asked doing a 180 spin, the tension showing in her stance.

"That is none of your business! I am allowed to have a few secrets too, you know," he informed her mysteriously.

"Just don't do anything stupid, Sean, or you will be right back in hot water with me again. You know ...," she started to lay into him but he just smiled and closed the door on her. Damn him! Now what?

Sean found Sharon in the study pouring over the video and taking notes on her laptop. It was a little unnerving to see Maxwell's face on the big screen in the study.

"Leave it for now. It can wait," he said to her.

"Hmm?" she responded, barely hearing him.

"Come on. Me Lil Lady is in the water. I want to catch some fresh fish for dinner," he said trying to pull her out of the chair, reaching to drop the screen down to break her trance.

"Sounds like fun," she said absently, still staring at the computer.

"Earth to Sharon, come in Sharon," he said waving his hand in front of her face.

"Oh. Sorry. I was just looking at the video," she said finally snapping awake. "Now what were you saying?"

"Fish… I said we are going fishing," he said laughing.

"Why on earth are we doing that? We have too much work to do. You said it yourself!"

"All work and no play, makes for a dull day!" he said, still laughing. "Indulge me. Do I need to remind you that you are supposed to do anything I tell you to do?" he said in a mock stern tone.

"I thought that is what I have been doing. Just look at yourself. You look ten times better," she countered. "But if you insist I'll humor you a little just this once. Just remember who is really in charge here, Mr. Ryder!"

"I feel a hell of a lot better too, so let's have a little fun," he responded.

After changing, they made their way to the catwalk and down onto Me Lil Lady where the first mate, a thin man named Jack waited to pilot for them. Several of the crew had already gotten out the rarely used equipment and rigged up the fighting chair.

"Good spot for Mahi-mahi," Jack said as they came onboard.

"Then Mahi-mahi for dinner it is!" Sean said smiling at the prospect of the fight to come.

They went to the stern and Sean showed Sharon how to get all the lines out in the water as the first mate took them out away from the Ship to open waters. It was a beautiful day. Large, puffy clouds rolling along in an azure blue sky above the crystal clear water as far as the eye could see. They headed west out ahead of the Me Lady which was getting back underway to follow them as they progressed.

Sharon looked a little apprehensive. She was out of her element here and she knew it. Sean enjoyed seeing her off guard. He was also enjoying the way she looked. Wearing a florescent orange bikini with a white sarong wrapped around her slim waste. She was as always, very beautiful and completely alive.

Sean, knowing that Sharon had never fished a day in her life wanted her to experience how fun it was. He hoped she liked it as much as he did. So when the first one got on the hook he held onto it, letting it run perhaps a little farther than he should have, while the crew set her up in the chair. Her face was filled with a mixture of fear and exhilaration and Sean loved watching her toil with her emotions. When she was set, he handed her the pole right as the fish jerked the line and she let out a squeal of excitement, her eyes as big twin moons, radiating a brilliant, golden glow, as if they had their own inner source of energy.

"Now hang on and just keep pulling the tip up until it is at the top then take up the line real fast by dipping your pole and reeling it in as fast as you can. If he goes airborne, get the tip up fast then take up the slack. If he runs let him go then take advantage of when he is tired. Whatever you do, don't let go!" he yelled in her ear over the roar of the engines. The exuberant look on her face told him she loved it. It wasn't hard to see she was having the time of her life.

Sure enough, it was a beautiful Mahi-mahi. It went airborne several times, Sharon screaming with delight each time it took flight. It took her about 30 minutes to reel it in, about five foot long tip to tail, not a huge one, but enough for a first timer. Sean just sat back and watched the entire time as the look on Sharon's face changed from fear and excitement to pure adrenaline laced fierceness as she battled the powerful fish. She was definitely in her element and he could tell she was enjoying herself even though the fight had drained her to the point of temporary exhaustion.

"Again!" she said laughing.

"Not bad for a first timer. I think she likes it," Sean said patting her heartily on the back. "Now it's my turn!"

It didn't take long to hook another and Sean took the chair. As he battled the fish, a slightly larger one than Sharon's, she stood there clapping and jumping as the fish tried to get free.

"Go Sean!" she yelled with delight as he worked the fish.

Caught up in the moment Sharon came up behind him and put her arms around his neck and hugged him from behind. He could feel her breasts against the back of his head and the sensation drove him mad. The mixture of that sensation, his desire, the battling fish, and the memories all came crashing in on him and for a few seconds he lost his concentration, almost losing the fish. He realized he was losing his willpower and a strange sense of desire he had forgotten was welling up in him, in more ways than one.

As Sean battled the fish, Sharon jumped around the deck like a little girl and kept telling him to hurry up so she could have another turn. Sean just laughed and in a split second the massive fish jumped and in a colossal effort, snapped the line. The pole and Sean reeled backwards and Sharon howled in laughter.

"Now you're going to tell me about the one that got away! Mine was bigger!" she said teasing him.

"No way, that one was at least fifty pounds heavier. I don't think you could have taken him either. Besides the line is old and it must have been rotted." He said sullenly.

"Excuses, excuses, just like a man!" she chided. "Poor Sean bested by a first timer," she teased as she came over and put her arms around him while he was still strapped in and kissed his cheek.

"My turn again!" she said trying to pull him out of the chair.

"At least unhook me first. Now aren't you glad we took a little time for some fun?" he said enjoying the moment immensely.

They caught three all told getting hits one right after the other and then they turned it over to the crew wanting to give them all a chance too. On Sean's orders, no one was to come home without catching a fish even though they only kept the first one to cook. It was more than enough for the entire crew to have some.

As the crew fished and yelled enjoying the break from their usual tasks, Sean and Sharon made their way to the main cabin to relax for a while and just kick back. Everything was perfect and Sean was happy Sharon had found it so enjoyable. He wanted to share something he loved with her and this was just the thing.

"Sean. I don't ever remember being this happy and I mean that with all my heart. But I have to admit I am at a loss for how to proceed. I can't figure you out and I don't understand what I am supposed to do. It is driving me nuts," she said losing the battle with the tear in her eye.

She was not used to the amount of emotion she was dealing with since this all started. It was a bit like a roller coaster ride right now. She was giddy with happiness, gorged with adrenaline, and yet still filled with a sense of foreboding. She feared what getting involved with him and his dark emotions could do to her. It could be a train wreck for her personally. Hell, she didn't even know if he wanted that still. It was a real mess. That much was for sure.

"Good. Then my sneaking was all well worth it. As for being off balance, try wearing my shoes," he said smiling at her.

"Thanks for doing this, Sean. I think we both needed it," she said.

Sharon had been getting them a couple of sodas and now came over and set them down on the table and sat down next to Sean. Sean immediately felt the heat from her adrenaline-laced body. A scant few feet separated them, and that was not enough to allow the heat to dissipate. He looked at her and saw the flush in her cheeks and realized she was extremely aroused. It was almost more than he could bear and he felt the same thing happening to him. Oh, if only. He knew what he wanted but the demons were still sticking their pitchforks in his heart and he didn't want to regret doing something he was not prepared deal with.

"Sharon, I got to go shower. I feel really dirty and smelly," he stammered, trying to avoid her gaze. If he looked into her eyes he would be lost.

"Please do! You smell like fish guts," she said moving just a little closer and poking him in the side a couple of times making him grab her hand to stop her.

"You're not exactly fresh as a daisy," he countered keeping hold of her hand. He made the mistake of looking at her face and wham! Those eyes drew him right in. My goodness, she was beautiful. No doubt about that and right now he could feel the heat of her body intensify as she leaned ever closer. That was about all he could take.

Neither one said a word. They just sat there, eyes locked and like two magnets, their faces drew closer and closer until finally, their lips met. It was soft and light and Sean lingered there for a moment, wanting to take her in his arms and run away all at once.

She put her hand on the back of his neck and let her head fall back parting her lips as they kissed. They drew apart and Sean involuntarily looked down at her body, her breath coming in a slow, deep, rhythmic dance, making her breasts rise and fall enticingly.

She would let him take her if he wanted, he knew. That little fact was excruciatingly apparent unless he was misreading her. He didn't think he was misreading her at all, though. The heat coming from her was absolutely intense and he was losing control.

Sharon didn't know what to do. She was extremely aroused and she wanted Sean to make love to her more than ever. So much for keeping it platonic, she thought! This was not what was supposed to be happening today. He threw her off balance again with this little fishing expedition. She had no idea it would affect her this way and part of her was angry with him for it, but most of her was on fire with desire.

She knew she needed to get up and run into one of the state rooms and take the coldest shower she could stand, but her heart and body were betraying her mind. She reached up and put her hand on his neck turning slightly towards him. She wanted him to make love to her, fishy smell and all.

Sean reached down and cupped her hand pulling it towards his mouth he kissed the back of it softly and held it to his cheek. They both shivered at the same time and Sean knew he had to break this up now, or live with the consequences later. His only real reason for stopping was the fear he would resent it later, or be noticed by the crew, and that was not what he wanted. He got up quickly and left the room before she could say anything.

Sean made his way up to the bridge and told Jack to return to the Me Lady.

As they went back on board the Me Lady, Sean turned to Sharon when they got to the top of the gangplank.

"Dress nice for dinner tonight Sharon," Sean said turning and leaving her in the lurch.

Sharon was about to explode at him, for what reason she could not fathom. Maybe it was that he had left her sitting there ready to give herself to him, or maybe it was because he had made her want him when she had just finished convincing herself she should not! Whatever the reason, she was feeling a bit put off just now and wasn't sure she should comply with his request. She needed to get a little control back. She was already feeling every bit the puppet from her nightmare last night.

It was nearly dark when Sean was ready to head up for dinner. Sharon went into her rooms when they returned and had not made a peep for hours. He was pacing back and forth trying to figure out what he should do when he decided to use Maxwell's intercom.

"Sharon, if you are ready, I would like to escort you to dinner, if that is alright with you," he said feeling a little like he was picking up his prom date.

"A Lady needs time to get ready. I'll meet you and the captain when I am good and ready," she said abruptly in the speaker putting an end to the conversation.

Sean smiled. He could tell by her voice she was trying to exercise a little control over the situation. She was obviously off balance, and although he felt a little sorry for her, he was enjoying it, maybe, just a hair too much. He didn't want her to know how she was affecting him either. He still felt a little guilty but the more time he spent with her the more he realized just how right she was about the whole situation. Just don't let her know that. She would never let him forget it!

When she told him she needed a little time to get ready he didn't know it would be close to an hour! He had been dressed for two hours, wearing one of the suits Sharon had made for him back in New York he headed up to sit with the captain, thinking she would be right behind him. By the time she made her appearance, he was pacing back and forth until finally, when she must have decided they waited long enough, she graced them with her presence.

Sean just stood there next to the captain gawking at her, the captain who was equally enthralled by her beauty stood there smiling. She had her hair up and off her long thin neck and the pale, pink colored dress complemented her golden complexion beautifully. She had on a dainty tiara. It sat glistening in the dark folds of her hair matched by a necklace that drew the eyes unwillingly to her long, sensual throat. As she walked towards them the dress moved enticingly around her like a gossamer veil. Sean was at a total loss for words and she just smiled at the unspoken complements every eye on the boat gave her.

The captain came to his senses first and held out his hand to her.

"May I have the honor of seating you, my dear?" he said mustering every bit of gentleman he had in him.

"You may, kind Sir. It is good to know that the world is not without chivalry," she responded in an equally formal tone holding out her hand to him and looking sideways at Sean at the same time to see what kind of reaction she would get. He didn't move or blink.

The captain pulled out her chair and helped to seat her while Sean still just stood there gawking at her.

"Sean. Put your tongue back in your empty head and sit down, please. Where are your manners?" she said teasing him.

185

She was thoroughly enjoying the affect she was having on him. Served him right! He had it coming after what he did to her earlier.

He laughed and sat down, one of the crew assisting him with his chair.

"You look absolutely radiant, Sharon," he finally mustered.

"Thank you, Sean. You look quite handsome yourself."

"Shall we start with a toast?" The captain asked, looking to Sharon for approval.

"Yes, we shall," she said. A glass of champagne seemed in order.

The waiter came around and filled each of their glasses and withdrew again. Sean didn't cover his this time and Sharon made no notice or sign she disapproved. He would only have one or two glasses but he didn't want to spoil the mood.

The captain lifted his glass in salute. "Well then. I would like to propose a toast to my little Cherry Blossom. Thank you, for making these many years on this barge bearable. You were the bright spot in Maxwell's life, and as he confided in me many times, the most precious thing in his life."

"Thank you, captain," Sharon said tapping her glass gently against his. Sean had forgotten to answer the toast. He was sitting there staring at the captain.

"Sean! You're doing it again. Where is your head tonight?" she chided.

Sean broke his stare and tapped both of their glasses. "Yes, to Sharon," he said still lost in thought. Something important had just taken place and his mind raced to figure out what it was.

Sharon stared at Sean wondering what was going through his head. She didn't think it had anything to do with the champagne. One glass wasn't going to send him back into his self-inflicted hell now. He seemed to be well over that. She now understood it wasn't addiction he had suffered from but instead, a form of depression and a feeble attempt to commit suicide. He had his mind back and that depression seemed to be gone. That wasn't the issue here. It was something totally different. He looked like his mind was going a mile a minute. That was a look she had seen before when he had a breakthrough or a really important idea came to him.

"What it is Sean? You look like you just saw a ghost!" she said, slightly concerned.

"Oh, it's nothing really. I'll tell you later. Just was thinking is all," he said noncommittally. "Let's eat!"

The meal was exceptional and of course the best part was the fresh Mahi-mahi steaks, perfectly seared and drenched in a savory butter sauce. Finally, the waiter brought out a sumptuous Crème Brule for dessert and the head chef made his entry triumphantly.

"I hope you enjoyed the meal!" he said as if he really cared what they thought.

"Wonderful. Please sit and join us for a toast to your brilliance topped only of course my expert fishing skills. If we waited for Sean to catch dinner we would have all gone hungry!" Sharon said sarcastically.

They all laughed as he took a seat at the end of the long table and motioned to the waiter to come fill his glass. They all raised their glasses nodding in his direction in a silent toast.

"Now if you will excuse us I need to get some work done today. I can't spend all day just giving fishing lessons, you know. If you're up to it, that is, Sharon," Sean said smiling at Sharon.

"Why don't you take this with you?" Captain Spencer said holding out the bottle of champagne. He had a knowing look on his face. What he didn't know was Sean really did want to discuss something with her. He was sure he had made a breakthrough.

"That won't be necessary, Captain. You two enjoy it or give it to the crew," Sean said dismissively.

"Come on Sharon. Let's go to Maxwell's study," Sean said offering her his hand.

Sharon took the offered hand and got up following him out.

"Sharon, I've got something I want to bounce off of you," Sean said walking out the door at a rapid pace.

"Sean, slow down!" Sharon said trying to keep up.

They went into the state room and Sean quickly closed the door behind them barely able to contain his excitement.

"Here, just sit over here with me," Sean gestured to the sitting area by the fish tank.

He had taken up Maxwell's task and was caring for them himself now. He knew why Maxwell loved the fish and he had to admit it was fun to watch them. Sharon sat down rather heavily. She looked a little exhausted now after the long day.

"I'm not sure I can take much more," she said as she sat down.

"Oh, this may or may not upset you. I guess it depends on how you look at it. I'm sure of one thing though. I am sure it's very important," he said taking the chair next to her and turning so he could grasp her hand. He was pleased when she didn't pull away from him. Good. This might upset her a little.

"Well, what is it already? I can't stand much more suspense. You already have me completely off my guard and I am not sure I like the feeling, Sean!" she said as her emotions began to well up again.

"Listen, I think I know what Maxwell was referring to, you know, what he loved most in the end. I think I know what that thing he loved the most was, but more importantly, I think I know why. God, I can't believe I never figured it out before!" he said. "I can't be sure yet, but it makes reasonable sense if you think it through."

189

Sharon looked at him, her curiosity peaking as she perked up a little at the news. "What?" she asked.

"It was you, Sharon! You were the thing he loved most, in the end," Sean said in an excited voice, sounding a little like a child on his birthday that just got exactly what he wanted.

"Me? What are you talking about?" she asked surprised and confused, immediately dismissing the idea. "That's silly!"

"It was what the Captain said when he toasted you that got me to thinking. I don't think you were really listening. Probably too engrossed with my good looks. You could barely keep your eyes off me, you know," he said trying to lighten the mood a little.

"I didn't see you exactly minding the way I looked either, Sean," she shot back in a sassy, dignified tone, pulling her hand away she turned her little nose up at him and unconsciously began adjusting her dress with nervous hands.

"He said, and I quote, as he confided in me many times you were the most precious thing in his life."

"Oh, that doesn't mean anything. Besides, what do I have to do with a silly key?" she asked disappointed, expecting something a little more tangible for evidence.

"I don't know that yet, but you didn't ask the most important question of all. Why is it you?"

"OK, Mr. Know It All. Why is it me?" she asked mocking him a little.

"Because, you are the daughter of the late, great, Maxwell Alderson," he said simply sitting back in the chair and again, putting his hands behind his head in that gesture of total confidence.

Sharon sat there staring at him in disbelief. It was totally outrageous and inconceivable but he completely believed what he was telling her. That was more than apparent in his mannerisms. She had just assumed Maxwell was always nice to her because her mother took care of Angelina and she had no father to speak of. Was it possible?

"Then why didn't he tell me after my mother died? If it was some pact they had, why didn't he tell me then, or at least before he died? Why didn't he just will everything to me? It's not possible, Sean," she said shaking her head, looking down as her mind raced to get where his was.

"Oh, I believe he never told you when he was alive because he liked things just the way they were. He had one of the best personal assistants and partners a man could ever want and got to keep his daughter close in the bargain. Pretty convenient wouldn't you say? Any number of things could have happened that could backfire on Maxwell if others knew about it, or if you knew about it. You might have left his side, not being comfortable as his assistant, or working for him in the company. He didn't want to lose his hold on you. I can't say as I blame him for that. You are awfully nice to have around. I can sympathize with him there," Sean said innocently.

Sean continued to talk while Sharon tried to absorb it all.

"He definitely didn't want you to take over the company. That much is pretty obvious. I guess he was afraid it might turn you into him eventually and he couldn't bear the thought of that. It could have been because he knew the board would eat you alive, not to mention his loving family, if he was not there to prevent it. After you roll it all up into a nice little package, I think he just wanted things his way, as usual, and this is his way of telling you in the end. I think this is all for your benefit, and maybe it's me supposed to help you and not the other way around. Think about it this way. The only two people on the face of the earth that could figure that out or would even have a clue about you were the two of us."

Sharon was on her feet now pacing as Sean filled her with his hypothesis. He was an extremely intelligent man and it was beginning to make some sense in a sick sort of way. When it came to Maxwell sometimes being able to think in sick ways was the only way to understand his mind.

"It's all hypothetical of course, but still, if you are right, what does the key have to do with me and why didn't he just will me everything? I accept the theory that it could be me, but that I might be his daughter? How did you arrive at that conclusion? That is just absurd! Are you feeling ok? You got a lot of sun today," she said teasing, playfully reaching up to check for a fever. She had to admit though, the idea intrigued her.

"I'm serious!" Sean said. "To the first part of the question, I don't know, but I think we can narrow the search down immensely if we use that logic. The answer is either here, on this boat or, more likely, in Hong Kong. The place he deeply associated with you and of course, your mother! For the second part of the question, I just think he didn't want to let them all drag you through the mud. You know how his relatives are, and the board? They would have been all over you, and there would be a big court battle and the whole nine yards. Instead, he decided to use me, and let me take the heat. He threw us together as if he knew what would happen between us, and as for why? It just feels right. Look at how he treated you all your life. He never did those things for any of the other children of his employees, and he could have done it for them all."

"You said threw us together knowing what would happen between us. Is there something happening between us, Sean? I could have sworn you spurned me earlier today. In fact, that is about all you've done," Sharon said, turning her face down to hide her pain.

In that moment he knew he could love her. He also knew he could not keep pulling away from her every time they got close. He wanted to be close to her and she obviously wanted that, too. He didn't want to dredge through his memories of

Angelina any longer and he was now able to see that was exactly what he was doing. Katy tried to find him a new companion on more than one occasion and he was always pleasant but there was no spark. There was never anything that could break the spell, until now. Angelina and Sharon both deserved better and he had mourned her long enough. It was time to live again.

"Why do I get the feeling that he is leading us both exactly where he wants us to go and he knew exactly what we would do?" Sharon asked, a little anger seeping into her voice as she clenched her tiny fists.

"Because he was, and he did," Sean said a rueful smile on his lips. "Jesus, the man is dead, and he's still running everyone's lives. But you know what the worst part of the whole thing is?"

"What's that?" Sharon asked him.

"I wish he were here so I could thank him from the bottom of my heart for sending you to rescue me," he reached out to her and pulled her to him, gently, he kissed her soft, sweet lips.

Sharon melted into him, her soft, sumptuous body pressing against him as she kissed him back, her lips parting, hungry. Sean's head spun as he let her press hard against him, desire overwhelming him. They stayed that way for a long time. Both of them giving and taking with a deep need to be loved, caressing, gently touching each other.

"Stay with me, Sharon. I don't want to be alone tonight," Sean said vulnerably. "We don't have to make love. I can wait and maybe we should, but stay here with me. I need you."

"Shut up Sean. You'll ruin it. Give me a few minutes. I am not going to ruin one of my favorite dresses. Besides, we should do this right, if we are going to do it," she said primly. She turned and headed for the door leading to her own chambers. "Brush your teeth. You taste all fishy and take off that suit and hang it up before you ruin it," she said over her shoulder as she went through the door.

Sean did as he was told. His head was spinning, and his body on fire. He knew he had lost the battle between need and restraint but what amazed him most was he was glad. He was falling in love with Sharon. He hoped Angelina would not be upset and again, he tried to fight back the feelings he had lived with for so long. This was going to take time but he wanted Sharon, he didn't know what he would do without her. Everything was different now.

He knew it was stupid, but he still saw Angelina lying there dying in a pool of blood in his nightmares, and right now he wished he could block that vision out forever. It was not the memory he should carry. He should carry the one of her sitting on the back of a horse, smiling over at him. The sun was behind her that day and Sean recalled thinking he was seeing an angel. That was the one he was going to keep in his heart. Not the other.

He sat there waiting and silently he forced himself to see Angelina young, happy, and full of life. That was what he wanted to remember from here on out. For some reason, he was no longer afraid that the nightmares would happen tonight. Please god, no more nightmares. Silently, he prayed for peace for both himself and Angelina.

As he sorted through his feelings, a tiny knock came to the door. Slowly, Sharon opened it and peeked in. He could sense her vulnerability. It was as palpable as his own was. She was just as lost and maybe, they really did need each other. Sean knew he needed her. Of that he had no doubts. Still, he never considered how alone she must be feeling until just now. He should have considered that a long time ago. His capacity for selfishness disgusted him.

Sharon had on a robe, but Sean could see a long lacey black negligee underneath it. She tip toed into the room in her bare feet and stood just inside, not knowing exactly what to do. For a few seconds they just looked at each other, not speaking.

Sean was sitting on the edge of the bed in a pair of long pajama bottoms. His arousal was so thorough he was afraid to stand up. He tried hard to hide the fact without much success. He held out his arms to Sharon, beckoning her to him, and she came over dropping the robe to reveal the long transparent gown she wore and the wonderland beneath it. Her breasts strained against the delicate cloth, begging to be free, begging to be caressed. She stopped and stood in front of him. Sean's eyes roamed up and down her perfect frame taking in her beauty. He wanted to reach out and tear the flimsy cloth from her shaking body but he fought the urge with all his willpower. He wanted this to be perfect.

After what seemed an eternity to Sean, Sharon reached down with one hand and pushed him back on the bed, coming down on top of him. Her body covered him as she slid her leg between his, lightly touching his burning loins. Her hair, free now, fell down and tickled his face and neck sending shivers down his spine as she hovered just over him looking into his eyes, smiling.

She put her head down and greedily took his mouth to hers. Her hand roamed over his chest raking the light hairs there then moving on, she reached down and caressed his stomach. Slowly, her hand made its way down his body all the while she held his mouth to hers, her breasts barely touching his chest sending shock waves through his body. Sean pulled her closer and they opened their mouths to each other even further, the hunger deepening with each beat of their hearts and each soft flick of their tongues as they explored each other with complete abandon.

Sean was lost then, and knew he was far beyond the point of no return. He could no longer ignore how he felt. Sharon was willingly giving herself to him and he was willingly taking what she offered. He was still fighting off a flood of emotions. One of which was a nagging guilt he knew was irrational but he couldn't help it. It wasn't guilt over Angelina or a sense he was cheating. It was guilt that he was taking Sharon this way and he was afraid they would not feel the same about each other tomorrow. He knew it was silly and was determined to ignore it. As he struggled to be completely there with Sharon, she sensed his turmoil and pulled away from him. Gently, she disengaged herself and stood again, looking down at him as he lay there breathing heavily.

"Sean, you don't have to do this, but I really wish you would. Oh, how I wish you would," she said, a liquid glaze forming in her eyes, the tears threatening to break free and course down her soft cheeks.

"It's been a long time since I let myself love anything, let alone anyone, but right now I don't think I have ever wanted anything more than I want to make love you. I couldn't stop if I wanted to," he said, sitting up and taking her chin in his hand drawing her face to his as he kissed her softly.

Sharon pulled away from him and ran her hands down her sides grabbing the diaphanous gown that tried unsuccessfully to cover her trembling, yet willing, body. Lifting the gown slowly, irresistibly, up her luscious frame she revealed herself to him inch by excruciating inch, until she pulled it over her head, baring herself completely. She smiled as he sat there seemingly unable to move, mouth agape, eyes roaming over her hungrily. The look of utter admiration in his eyes said all she needed to hear.

Sean sat mystified as she removed her gown and sighed softly, completely taken by her beauty. After what seemed like an eternity, he pulled himself out of the dream and stood. He picked her up in his arms. She let him hold her, giving herself completely to his desire. He held her there for a moment, her face buried in his neck and then he laid her gently on the bed. He stood there for just a moment looking down at her flushed, burning body. Again, he wondered at her passion, he would have sworn he could feel the heat radiate from her as she became more and more aroused. Her insatiable fire called out to him as he greedily took in her splendor.

Lust for her overwhelmed him as he crawled onto the bed and leaned down to take her breasts into his hungry mouth. His hands and lips tried to touch every inch of her soft body. He wanted to know every inch of her perfect frame and store it forever in his mind.

Sharon laid there and let him explore her body. The sensations he was giving her heightened her arousal and she pulled his head into her flesh as he relished in the sheer taste of her arousal. He took what she offered and let out a tiny sigh of appreciation, driving her further into a state of total sexual awakening.

Working his way softly back up, he lightly brushed his lips on her shoulders moving towards her neck and face and eventually he let her searching mouth find his. They came together as she strained up towards him, engulfing him in the exquisite tangle of her arms and legs. She pulled him into herself and he let her have anything she wanted.

Sharon's desire was now completely out of control, she pulled at his pajamas and once free, he melted into her flesh, throbbing from head to toe as she wrapped herself around him like a velvet vise. Her hands wildly gripped his brown, curly hair as she arched up writhing in pure lust, her legs straining to encircle him. Thrusting her hips up into him, she opened herself to him, all the while, her mouth pulling at his hungrily as they both tried desperately to breathe each other in.

His heart would never forget that time and place, the point where the melding of their souls happened. He was forever trapped there as she gripped him and begged him to take her. He no longer had any will to resist and together their passion filled the room like a cloud of steam, their bodies burning from within. All he wanted was to remain there like that forever, but she would have none of it. She continued to drive into him, begging him to succumb to her need.

Slowly, he gave himself completely to her as she pleaded and whimpered her need. Little by little he let himself go deeper and deeper into her waiting flesh, fighting the urge to plunge into her while his entire being quivered from the sensations emanating from the sweltering oven between her legs. Locked in that fiery chasm between her open thighs, he struggled to control the waves of passion that coursed through him unfettered.

Sean labored to retain his sanity as she clung desperately to him, trying to pull him deeper into her steaming depths. His mind and body careened wildly on the fringe of their mutual pleasure. Barely able to control himself, he battled with all of his will to remain there eternally. He clung to her desperately to prolong the inevitable in a vain attempt to control her as she quivered violently below him, completely lost now in her own need. Holding back as long as possible, their passion relentlessly growing more desperate by the second, Sharon unabashedly spurned him on, moving beneath him, waves of unbridled desire emanating from her flesh. Suddenly, with a need that was almost savage, she pulled him deep within herself. He let out a cry of pure pleasure as their bodies melted to become one, Sharon softly moaning rapturously in his ear as she clutched at him trying to absorb him into herself.

Her breathing grew more desperate as they moved together and all at once, moaning in carnal delight, she succumbed in one phenomenal release of pure erotic elation. As her pleasure grew more intense, she cried out to him, as her raked body bucked and quivered. Sharon was completely lost in her desire and need and no longer controlled her own body.

For a small eternity Sean fought as her enraptured body writhed violently in waves of exquisite release. It was more than he could take. Sean could hold back no longer. Eyes glazing over he buried his face in her neck to stifle his own whimpers of ecstasy as she forced her will upon him. In a pure flash of volcanic eruption he exploded into her. They gripped each other tightly sharing in the impassioned moment of mutual release, one wave after another crashing through their entwined souls, until they were both spent.

Neither of them could remember a release so powerful or so profound. It was more than either of them was prepared for. Neither moved for several minutes as they tried to come to grips with the powerful flood of emotions attached to that simple act of love they had just shared.

For a long time, they lay there, still intimately entwined. Sean remained in her and she lay there cooing as she twirled his curls in her fingers, her arms wrapped around his head, her lips searching for his. Sean's face was buried in her neck. He could feel her pulse throb as he relished the feel of her long, silky hair falling wildly around his face. Sean couldn't help himself. He began to cry.

Sean struggled to regain control, his spent body shaking in ecstasy, unable to move. Sharon began to weep with him and they lay there holding each other, completely drained and completely satiated. Sean knew he would never forget this memory, nor would Sharon. Despite the long held feelings he had been harboring all these years, he had fallen completely into her trap and he knew he never wanted to be free.

Sean realized it was time to be happy again. He loved this woman with all his soul and he desperately needed her to love him too. He needed her. They lay there together for a long time, caressing, talking, crying, and making love. That was fine, but what Sean really remembered was how she held him. How she gave herself to him and loved him, no questions asked. He knew he finally had a new home and part of him thanked Maxwell for somehow knowing how badly he needed Sharon.

Later, as they basked in the afterglow of their lovemaking and the unequivocal, emotional connection they now had to each other, Sean finally did find his freedom. Sharon was right. He could honor Angelina's memory and again, find happiness. He wanted nothing more than to spend the rest of his life with this wonderful woman. He could let the ghosts of his past find peace and rest now.

Sharon finally gave in to her need to sleep and Sean lay there on his back with her curled up under his arm all moist and warm, her leg and arm thrown possessively over him. Her warm soft body pressed against his side, her face buried in his flesh, her soft breath tickling his skin. As she drifted off to sleep, Sean realized he was too energized to sleep. After all, he'd been asleep for three days. Slowly, reluctantly, he slipped out of her grasp and went for a shower.

After he showered, he made his way back to find Sharon still fast asleep. As the lovemaking took its toll on him he realized he really was tired, carefully, he slipped back into bed and worked his way back into her warm grasp. Sharon woke just enough to pull him to her again, pulling him possessively to herself, she folded herself into his arms and wrapped her legs around him and fell back into deep sleep. Sean was at peace and Sharon's unconscious response made him feel as if she were trying to protect him. She lay there dreaming and cooing softly, snuggling. An indescribable state of contentment fell over Sean and he fell deeply asleep.

Sean woke to find Sharon sitting at the coffee table devouring a full breakfast of eggs, bacon, toast, fruit, coffee and orange juice. There was a rather large spread sitting there waiting for him as well. He walked on unsteady legs towards the sitting area, the seas rough from a passing storm that both of them had slept right through.

"Good morning sleepy head," Sharon said between mouthfuls.

"Good morning my little dove. Did you know you coo when your content?" he said teasing her.

"Do I?" she said wonderingly. "I was really tired. I was having nightmares the night before," she said suppressing a little shiver. "I slept better than I think I ever have last night though. So I guess, thank you for providing me with such a wonderful, restful, night, my love."

"I'm glad you slept better last night. I know I slept like a rock, although, it was not the best kind of sleep," he said pretending to be sad.

"What's wrong?" Sharon asked concerned.

"I dreamt I was drained of half my life force by a beautiful succubus and now she has me completely in her power," Sean said waiting for her reaction.

"Well I must not have gotten enough of it because I am still hungry for more this morning!" Sharon shot back at him laughing playfully.

"Well let me recharge my batteries and we can see about fixing that," Sean said laughing.

"You started it with that damn fishing trip and then you just left me hanging. I was pretty mad at you, but worse, I don't think I have ever been that aroused. It was probably better we didn't make love then. I think I might have killed you in the process. But I am still a little mad at you for leaving me sitting there wanting to tear your clothes off. That wasn't very nice, Sean," Sharon said trying to sound indignant with a slice of aggravation on the side.

"I didn't want the crew to catch us," Sean said. "Besides I was a little confused."

"Well too bad about the crew. They know we spent the night together. You should have seen the look on Rita's face when she brought in breakfast. By the way, I have two questions for you. One, are you still confused? And two, are your hormones under control now so we can get some actual work done?" she said with a sly smile.

"Well yes. I am still confused, but I will get past it, in time. Two, do you have any more of that vitamin supplement? I am feeling just a little weak. I will need all of my strength to complete my hormone therapy."

Sharon laughed at that and got up and kissed him. She sat in his lap and held him close.

"At least let me eat first. You already got yours!" Sean said as he pretended to get ready to take a bite out of her neck, making her giggle.

Sharon sprung to her feet running out of the room towards the bathroom. Sean set into the food like a starved madman. It was delicious. When he was almost finished Sharon came back in, fully dressed, and looking like she was ready for a board meeting.

"Well, now it's my turn to make some plans. I want to visit Hong Kong," Sharon said.

"I was thinking the same thing," Sean said smiling and nodding his head. "We are good together."

"Yes, we always were. I missed working with you. Anyway, it should take us several weeks at least to get there, considering we need to make a complete course change, probably get fuel, secretly, of course and…"

"Slow down there!" Let's just tell the captain where, and how fast, and secretly, and let him worry about it," Sean said laughing. "That is what he does for a living, you know."

"I suppose that will do. In the meantime we make sure no one finds out where we are going, like you said. They will just have to wait it out. I have a wonderful idea. Bad news! I think the satellite communications just went out. Darn! I won't be able to report any messages now."

"Sharon, I just said that." Sean said teasing.

"I know. I am just thinking out loud, Mr. Ryder. It's my job, remember?"

"Devious behavior, I like it. Well then, down to business. How do we prove me right or wrong?"

"The more I think about it the more right it feels. I hadn't thought about it in a long time but I remember being a child in that house and I remember sometimes running into Maxwell and my mother and they would quickly move away from each other. I even think I remember seeing them kissing, and more than once. I was just too little to put two and two together at the time, and eventually, those memories slipped away." She said reminiscing.

Sharon began to recount her early years and her memories slowly flowed out or her. Sean listened intently as she shared what she remembered. All of it could be very important.

"I saw the two of them holding hands too, and when I think on it, I remember them always having a certain look when they were around each other. The same look I will have when I see you now." She said with a whimsical look on her face.

"Focus dear. Keep thinking, Sharon. You might remember something important." Sean said.

"If they were together they were always careful, and you know something? Think about Angelina's age and mine. They were at it before Martha died, Sean! If any of the other servants knew, they never spoke of it. I never put two and two together but it is very possible that they were secretly lovers all those years. I think I really could be Maxwell's illegitimate daughter! How strange would that be?" Sharon said in amazement.

"Well, I don't care who your father is," Sean said.

"I have just one more question," Sharon said.

"OK, but this is your last one," Sean said shaking his finger at her.

"Sean. This happened kind of fast. It's not too fast, is it?"

She looked like a little girl to him now, afraid of the possible answer. Sean took her in his arms and held her. He stroked her hair and then he took her chin and forced her to look in his eyes. He wanted to make sure there was no mistake in how he felt and he was sure his eyes would tell the story more effectively than he could ever do with words.

"Sharon. I am going to need some time. I completely lost control last night. I barely held back after fishing. You were so aroused. I could feel the heat coming off of you and it about drove me mad. I had to get out of there," he said shaking his head and smiling. "I have never seen a woman that aroused before and it sort of scared me. I was scared of my feelings. I'm not now, though. I know exactly how I feel. I am deeply in love with you."

"I hoped you would say that but in all fairness I was full of adrenaline. What did you expect?" Sharon said indignant at how easily he read her.

"I still do have nightmares over her death, and that is the really hard part. You can't know how horrible it was. I don't want you to," he was nearly ready to cry but he went on. "I watched helplessly as the life drained from her, while she struggled to give birth to my child," Sean said, eventually losing control, he wept.

The pain came in overwhelming waves but also leaving in waves just as powerful. His soul finally worked to cleanse itself, letting him get on with his life. Sean waited for control to come back but he didn't rush it. The release seemed right and seemed to help. He was safe now. Safe with someone that loved him and cared. It was a slow and painful process, but it was finally happening.

Sharon waited patiently for him to work through his grief, she wanted to hold him and just letting him mourn but she held back. She wondered at the depth of his pain and realized it had been pent up in him all this time. He had never released his grief until now and it had simply been festering away like bad blood inside him. She knew he needed this and she wanted it to run its entire course. Eventually he calmed himself and aside from a few hitching breaths, he became still.

"You can't imagine how guilty I felt. It was my fault she was pregnant to begin with, and if I would have insisted she stay in New York, she might be alive today. It is a huge burden to carry. It nearly killed me," he said quietly hiding his face.

Sharon went to him and sat in his lap pulling him to her breast, cradling his head in her arms, she stroked and shushed him. He broke down and buried his face between her breasts and cried again. His body wracked with tears, he let go of everything he had held inside himself all this time. He never cried when she died. He never mourned her. He just tried to kill himself. He let go of it all now, here, safe with Sharon.

Rocking him gently, Sharon spoke to him in a soft, motherly tone. He was still crying and she wanted him to get it all out. She had never seen another human being in so much pain and her heart was filled with love for him.

"You can't blame yourself for that. I very much remember how she was. I grew up with her, remember? If she wanted to have an old fashioned birth, she was going to have it. As for getting her pregnant she told me she was going to have ten babies, so you can stop feeling guilty about that. She wanted lots of children. Plus, I spoke with the doctor. There was no indication of trouble and she was as healthy as an Ox. It was just one of those freak things that happen and no one can explain it. More importantly, no one ever blamed you for it," she said trying to make him understand. "Even Maxwell knew that it wasn't your fault. He just didn't know how to get through to you. He suffered too, Sean."

Sean was still sobbing, his body hitching and he was angry with himself for being so weak but he took Sharon and the comfort she offered and let go until it was out of his system. He fought to regain control after a while, but laying there, letting Sharon hold him and letting his feelings gush out without fear actually made him feel a little better, no, a lot better. He held her as tight as he could.

"I know you're right. I guess I always knew that, but I just sort of gave up. I really did want to die," Sean said as he fought to regain control, his body shaking as he tried to speak.

"Put it behind you now. It really just shows how much you cared. Now, I need you. Angelina needs to be allowed to rest in peace and not because of last night, or whatever happens between us from here on out. She's at peace because you are finally letting her have peace, and because you are finally finding it for yourself. That would have made her happy. I know how she thought," Sharon continued to hold him to her. Gently, she kissed his cheek and her own tears began to run down his face to mingle with his own.

"I am falling in love with you, Sharon," Sean said looking into her eyes. "It scares me."

"Don't worry. It's a safe thing to do. I already loved you," Sharon said smiling down at him. "Now, let me go bark a few orders at the captain and then let's see what we should do today."

Nodding, Sean smiled and wiped himself clean. He would never forget this moment. He knew they loved each other and he knew instinctively they would be together forever.

Sean had an uncontrollable urge to work out, so he went first to the gym. Afterwards, he went and cleaned himself up. Today he was going to go exploring the ship. There might be something here, but, knowing Maxwell, that was too easy and out of character, it seemed. Maxwell would have expected everyone to catch his little ploy that set Sean up as his number one pick. He would have expected them to rush off to wherever Sean went and to the lake house. But, he could not have foreseen the little trick of going out to sea to lose them that Sharon devised. He would have counted on the two of them putting it together before anyone else could and heading to Hong Kong. A place none of them, including Maxwell, ever went to anymore. None of the relatives, besides Sharon, would recall the memories that place would hold for Maxwell, let alone his secret love and the unknown love child that none of them even guessed at. If

Sean was right, that is. They may go there because Angelina grew up there but they would likely look in the wrong places.

When he came out of the shower, Sharon was not in the state room so he went into the study to have yet another look at that damn tape. There had to be a clue there, or somewhere in the study. He figured that was his best chance on the boat of finding anything.

When he got to the study he found Sharon there, hunched down over her laptop, her granny glasses on. She looked beautiful to him, even dressed like that. He noticed she was frowning and reading something.

"What you got?" he asked.

"Sean, you need to see this," was all she said, obviously concerned.

Chapter Eleven

Sean worked with Sharon for many years. He knew the look on her face was one you took serious. He went over to where she sat and put his hands on her shoulders. He leaned and kissed her gently on the side of her head as he read over her shoulder. On the screen was an internet news article.

"Billionaire's House in remote Hiawatha National Forest incinerated:

On May 21st, 2011, a major fire was reported to the Munising, Michigan Fire Department on the property of the recently deceased multi-billionaire Maxwell Alderson. By the time the fire department arrived, the blaze was completely out of control and efforts to put it out were unsuccessful.

Both the main house and garage, where the blaze is believed to have begun, were completely destroyed in the conflagration. The extent of the damage was made that much more spectacular by the presence of fireworks that had apparently been stored in the garage. The combination resulted in a display of destruction that could be seen for miles. The blaze has been ruled accidental and is believed to have been started as one of the several vehicles in the garage was being serviced.

The fire took the life a man believed to be Joel Madison, a distant relative of Maxwell Alderson. Joel Madison, Son of Brett and Beatrice Madison, was completely consumed in the blaze. A conclusive identification is waiting on dental records due to the extreme condition of the body.

The possible identification was made by a woman claiming to be a close friend of the family who was watching the property while the caretaker, Sean Ryder, was away to attend the reading of Maxwell Alderson's will, according to the source.

The source of the identification, also reported there had been several of Maxwell Alderson's relatives staying at the home recently and that they had been responsible for major vandalism on the property. According to the source, she was forced to remove them from the property in order to put a stop to the vandalism, but that Joel Madison, the deceased, had remained in town at one of the local hotels.

Evidence of the mistreatment of the property was apparent in the only building left standing, a tiny lake cabin, which was heavily vandalized corroborating the claims that mistreatment of the property was taking place. The source also reported another man had been staying with Mr. Madison, but he has, so far, been unable to be located for questioning and was apparently not present when the accident took place as the source, a local restaurant owner, reported he had been at her establishment when the report came that the property was ablaze. He is not under suspicion and no warrant has been issued.

Billionaire Maxwell Alderson was a successful capitol investor who died of cancer recently. His fortune was believed to be in the vicinity of twenty billion dollars. The mistreatment of his property by his relatives has yet to be explained."

Sean stared at the report incredulously. He had to read it twice to accept what it said.

"Damn them. They destroyed the place. Thanks a lot, Max!" he said angrily.

"I'm so sorry, Sean," Sharon said not knowing what else to do. She knew how much that place meant to Sean.

"Well I won't be going back there ever again," he said sadly.

Sean walked over and sat at the desk slumping down in the chair in resignation. He didn't say anything for several minutes and Sharon just let him sit there and sort through his thoughts. Both of them knew something wasn't quite right. They sat in silence trying to figure out what it was but it was just out of reach of either of their minds.

Sean was distraught. His mental state so vulnerable he couldn't help himself. He began to let the guilt seep back in. Was this his fault? Was this punishment?

"Are you OK?" Sharon asked him in a tiny voice trying to break the silence and bring him out of his depression.

"I was just thinking. Something in that sounded a little off. It's bad enough they destroyed the place but to burn it down?" he said the anger beginning to well up in him at the picture of them defiling that house where he had so many memories. "No. I am not OK."

"Well at least the cabin was spared. I remember my visits there when Angelina was still alive. I used to love that place, it was so peaceful. Those fireworks could have caught that on fire, too," Sharon said reminiscing.

They were both searching desperately for something good to say about it all.

"That's what is so strange. That's what I can't figure out. Where did the fireworks come from? Where did his 'Personal Assistant' get off to?"

Sean remembered Mr. Smith and Mr. Brown and a shiver went down his spine. Thank the good lord in heaven he had Sharon and not one of those nasty characters following him around. No, he was not going to let himself slip into depression again. He was going to fight, damn it.

"He went back to wherever he came from I would guess. He had no reason to be there anymore," she said shrugging her shoulders.

"Sharon. I knew every inch of that place. There weren't any fireworks in that garage," he said turning his gaze up to her.

"Your not suggesting that it wasn't an accident, are you?" Sharon asked looking at him. "That's ridiculous. You probably just never noticed them before."

"I suppose you're right. It just seems odd to me, that's all," he said getting up. "Join me for a swim?" he said holding his hand out to her. "I need to think and clear my head. This hurts. I admit it."

"I know it does, Sean. It was a special place for you, for me, too. Don't let them take that away from you. Not now."

"I won't. But if I find out there was some type of dirty dealings here, I can't promise I won't do something I may need legal representation for later on."

"Don't worry my love. I have a legal degree and a lot of high powered friends." Sharon said going to him and putting her arms around his neck."

Sean looked at the truth in her gaze, and smiled. He put his forehead to hers, and they stood that way until Sean finally initiated a kiss. They held each other for several minutes.

"Pool, now," Sean said.

"Yes Sir!" Sharon said. "Whatever you command, master."

After a swim, they spent the next several days exploring every inch of the Me Lady just to pass the time and take their minds off of all of this. Sharon knew Maxwell better than anyone and they methodically searched the ship to make sure it wasn't holding any secrets they could use in their search for the mysterious lock they were supposed to find. More and more, they became convinced they were heading in the right direction by going to Hong Kong.

Maxwell loved this boat. You could say the same about the estate in Hong Kong. He spent many long years of bliss there and for Sharon it was the only true home she had ever really known. It all made a lot of sense and the more they analyzed what facts they did have, the more they were convinced Hong Kong was the right destination. In reality, it had nothing to do with the estate, Sean and Sharon both knew that. It was as Sean said. It was really a question of whom, not where.

Sharon's rooms there would still be intact, just the way she left them the last time she was there. Her rooms there were off limits to visitors and always held in reserve for her. It had been a while, but they would never do anything to them without her permission. Angelina's had been locked up and closed for years. As for her mother's rooms, they were now for use by the new housemother.

Sharon kept very close track from then on what the others were doing. Martin and Jessica were currently in Monaco. She was amazed that they were still able to remain together. William was in Fort Lauderdale for some unknown reason. She wasn't surprised to learn that neither him, nor Joel's parents, had gone back to claim the remains. It spoke volumes about their true character.

Brett had taken off for Devonshire, England and Beatrice, of course, followed him a day later. Brett no longer caring what she did, but, she seemed to be determined to follow him around. She always was weak.

Sharon imagined how annoyed Brett would be at this point. Saddled with this ball and chain and out of a job all at once, it had to be a little bit uncomfortable for him. She wasn't the vindictive type, neither was Sean, but, they weren't immune to the comic aspect of it all.

Melissa seemed to be getting nowhere fast. She spent several days in New York before heading to Las Angeles. Why there, was beyond both of them.

As the Me Lady made her way relentlessly towards Hong Kong, the time they spent together was one big blur. They made love often and poured over anything they could find that might help. Sean was becoming more the man Sharon used to know every day, and, she had no doubts he loved her deeply. He was focused and exuberant when they worked and infinitely gentle when they didn't, well, except when she requested he not be so gentle. He was starting to look to tomorrow, and the little game Maxwell had set up was becoming less important to him as the days passed, although he was determined to solve the mystery. Now, it was more a matter of principle than the money.

They were already making plans for their future. If they were successful they were going to keep only three things of

Maxwell's, the, lake house, rebuilt of course, the Me Lady, and the estate in Hong Kong.

Sharon mentioned marriage and children only one time and Sean grimaced and told her he couldn't bear the thought of her dying like Angelina had. Sharon knew it was going to take time, but she wanted to give him children, badly, and wasn't the type to take no for an answer. He was just going to have to trust her and get used to the idea. It could wait, but not forever.

They were now steaming at full speed for Hong Kong but their destination was still a secret. There was little news coming in from the law firm and in the last three days, no one had moved. It was still amazing how callous they all were in the case of Joel. Greed was an ugly bedfellow. Sean was actually a little upset that they were not able to go and fix the problem. Someone should have cared, anyone, even him. Sharon was proud of him for his compassion towards someone she knew he loathed.

Both Sean and Sharon were convinced at this point that the answer was not on the Me Lady. They had gone over it with a fine toothed comb and it seemed out of character for Maxwell to make it that easy with all of them knowing he spent the last years of his life here. He was way too complicated for that. So they decided to just enjoy themselves for the remaining ten days it would take to get to Hong Kong. They did feel a little bad having told the captain to push the Me Lady to get there. He frowned but complied.

Time was something they could not afford to waste now. Sooner or later, the others would make their way there. What they were counting on was being right. The others would look in the wrong places, not even taking Sharon into account. That was all they really had going for them at this point.

Sharon wanted to fish again. Sean laughed at her new found love for sport fishing and teased her, pointing out it was just an aphrodisiac for her. He wouldn't let them take the time to drop Me Lil Lady into the water for it though. Sharon protested his unwillingness to give in to her and her desires but he found other equally interesting ways to sate her desires. He was completely taken with her, and spent a lot of his time thinking of new ways to make her smile.

As several days past, all of the reports they were getting still had the others pretty much in the same places. In a hilarious turn of events, William was arrested in Fort Lauderdale. Apparently, he had decided the continued trashing of Maxwell's estates was not only fun, but allowed. It seemed the head of the staff there felt otherwise, though.

They weren't surprised. Now that Maxwell was dead, the staff really didn't see the reason to put up with his crap anymore. He and his brother had terrorized them for many years when not harassing the staff in Monaco and now William apparently returned and was ripping through the place like a madman. The police were called and he was unceremoniously thrown in jail.

According to Thomas, they were trying to arrange for his freedom which was proving somewhat complicated. It seemed the police there were familiar with him from previous dealings and were in no hurry to release him, damages paid for, or not. Thomas included a warning for them to refrain from any activity of this nature, stating that after this event, no further intervention on their behalf would be forthcoming, legalese for cut the crap or deal with the consequences yourself.

The only real news was that Melissa had left Los Angeles. Whatever she was up to there obviously hadn't produced any results. She was headed to Oregon, according to the reports. Sean gave her credit for that move, so did Sharon. It had occurred to them to look there where Maxwell, his parents, Martha, and Angelina were all entombed but they set it aside as plan "B".

On the fifteenth day since they left port, they again woke to find more disturbing news.

Chapter Twelve

Melissa finally woke when the plane touched down at the Gold Beach Municipal Airport in Oregon just as the sun was beginning to make its decent. Not the smoothest of landings, thanks to a strong cross-wind, it had been sufficient to raise her from the coma she was in for the entire trip from Los Angeles. Her stomach jumped up into her throat and she shakily rose to her feet and made her way into the bathroom of the plane to expel the bile in her stomach, followed by a generous powdering of her nose from her special compact.

After they left New York, she decided a quick stop in LA was in order. Her funds limited, and her need for medication outweighing her desire to find Maxwell's will, she needed to get a refill before continuing on. LA was another wonderful place to find the things that made her existence bearable.

She wasn't planning on staying as long as she had, but she ran into one of her occasional companions. He had been more than willing to see to her needs in exchange for her "services". She was well stocked now, with enough medicine to last her through the dismal trip ahead of her.

She was very proud of herself. None of the others had even considered this location, or come to the realization of what she was sure was the answer. It wouldn't be long now, she would be kicking the rest of them off of her various properties, sending them all off to figure out their own miserable lives, while she lived out her days in the lap of luxury.

Her life would be far from miserable. She was going to kick Sean off of her yacht and throw the biggest party the world had ever seen on it, as she made her way around the Caribbean Islands. Right after she put the hit out on her loving father and mother, that is.

Mr. Smith seemed to be agitated with her and she was enjoying making him suffer. When she announced their little detour he had shown possibly the first sign of emotion she remembered seeing. Oh, she was taking full advantage of his situation!

When she got off of the plane he was standing next to a black Lincoln, his apparent car of choice, waiting for her. She did a lot of things in the back seat of his cars, trying to see if she could get him to react in some way other than fight back the desire to strangle her. She had sex several times glancing up to see if he was watching, and had even done some things to herself just to see what he would do. Some emotion, any emotion, she could get out of him made her feel superior to the aloof attitude he sported like a suit of armor to guard him from her outrageous behavior. It pissed her off though that she never even got him to blink. He never even seemed to look. All work and no play. That was Mr. Smith's way!

The only time she'd seen any emotion was last night when she was so high she was afraid she might have to ask him to take her to the hospital. Something told her he wouldn't do it. He would simply wait until she was good and dead and explain it away by telling them that she frequently passed out in the back seat, and he would be absolutely right. That look, that emotion, she saw in his eyes told her everything she needed to know about the mysterious Mr. Smith. She decided she needed to be a little more careful around him. She wasn't quite ready to fall off a cliff just yet.

As soon as they were in the car she told him to go directly to the memorial. She had no intention of staying in this hellhole any longer than was necessary. The way she figured it, she would be in and out in a matter of hours and on her way back to New York to start giving a few orders of her own.

Maxwell had purchased the land where the house he grew up in was and turned it into his own private cemetery. His mother, father, wife, and child all resided there. The place was located about one hour east of Gold Beach the way the crow flies, but took longer through the sparse and twisting roads. Why on earth anyone would want to be buried here was beyond Melissa, she didn't even want to be here. She did have to admit it was typical of Maxwell. He was mean as hell, but he was also a sentimental fool. That is why they got away with so much under his nose all these years.

As the car rolled through the hills Melissa decided she needed to refresh her nose and wake her senses with a bit of magic powder. She took out her "compact" and began preparing several thick lines of something even she couldn't know for sure what it was, and proceeded to snort away. As the rush hit her, she sat back smiling and considered if she should try and shock Mr. Smith one more time before they parted ways.

She had long ago changed her mind about hiring him to do her dirty work. She wanted someone that at least had the common decency to be human while killing her family for her, not some schmuck that would revel in the task getting much more pleasure out of it than she would. That would ruin it for her! Instead of doing what she was considering, she sat back and watched the lush greenery roll past and daydreamed about her billions.

The gravesite was built on a hill. It had a small parking lot and a well manicured pathway leading up to the lonesome crypts, here, in the middle of nowhere. The pathway was lined by a beautiful wrought iron fence. The majestic trees made a soft sound that was almost pleasant to her ears. Mr. Smith hadn't come up with her. She figured he would consider that helping so she just walked away not even bothering to try. She would be rid of him soon enough.

Maxwell built this place a long time ago and moved his parents here after their deaths. Maxwell's father was every bit as strange as Maxwell and had bought this land and built a home here after he made his fortune with dreams of turning it into an orchard. He didn't live long enough to do much more than build the house, and after he died his wife moved into town and sold the land. Maxwell bought it back at twice the price to turn it into a monument for his parents when he made his money. After his wife died, he built the rest of it including the future resting place for himself. A place for his daughter was added after she died. Sean was too distraught to figure out what to do with her remains so Maxwell stepped in and took care of it himself.

Melissa stopped and lit a cigarette. The walk up the hill was making her head pound furiously. There was no place to sit so she leaned up against the iron fence for a little break digging in her purse for a few aspirin, which, she promptly put in her mouth and chewed without water. The bitter taste was one she was infinitely familiar with.

Finishing the cigarette, she threw it carelessly to the path and moved on up the hill towards the cemetery. A Large monolith was centered at the rear of the yard surrounded on each side by three large crypts and one even larger walk in crypt in the center that had its own gate surrounding it.

"That one has to be Maxwell's," she said out loud to herself looking at the main crypt.

The light would be totally gone soon and she had no desire to return tomorrow, and no desire to stay here in the dark either, so she picked up the pace and made her way to the left most crypt.

"Penelope Alderson" She read on the crypt, "Loving wife and mother."

"How sweet, Maxi. I bet it took you all day to come up with that one!" she said sarcastically.

The next one had the name of Maxwell's father on it, Harvey Alderson and an equally plain inscription. The trees were bringing a pre-dusk darkness to the place even sooner than she expected it on this hill. She was running out of time. She made her way past the center one to the two larger crypts on the right side of Maxwell's and began to look more closely at them.

The farthest one from the middle was Angelina's. She thoroughly went over it looking for any sign of a hidden door or recess but the solid stone faces held nothing she could find. She had no idea what to even look for really, she simply hoped she would know it when she saw it.

The same proved to be true of his wife's and a quick check of his mother and father's resulted in no great revelation either. Swearing, she sat down against Harvey Alderson's crypt where she was shielded from the wind and took out her handy nose compact and helped herself to a few more doses to help her think.

"Fuck you, Maxwell," she said as she stared at the monstrosity that he built for himself. She had actually considered that once or twice in her lifetime but apparently, her mother had beaten her to the punch line there. She laughed hysterically at her own wit.

"Maxwell, you self righteous pig, where is it?" she said, still looking at the main crypt.

Maxwell's was different than the others. It had a gate around it and was actually more than just a crypt. This was a marble monstrosity with a massive metal door covered with ornate designs and his name carved deeply over the door.

"No way!" she said her eyes widening. "Were you that full of yourself?"

She got up and put away her case and went around through the gate to the front door. There was a lock on it but it didn't look like her key would fit it. She tried the door knob and it turned with only a little protest. Pushing on the door it slowly and noisily opened onto the dark interior of Maxwell's personal mausoleum. The door was fighting back very hard so she only pushed it far enough to allow her access into the tomb. This did little to let light into the dark interior.

In the dim, almost non-existent light, she could see a sarcophagus in the center and two alabaster white benches on the sides with candelabras on either side of the benches. She was about to run and get Mr. Smith so he could go in and light them when she remembered, through the fog of her abused brain, the lighter she had in her purse. Addicts always carry a lighter. She carefully made her way to one of them and lit it. After several minutes she got them all lit and she looked around the room.

"I got to give you credit Max. This is quite a place you've got here," she said again laughing but more to control her anxiety and fear than out of respect for her sense of humor.

She started to examine the crypt in the center and found nothing unusual there. She decided, if she had to, she would push the damn lid off before she left. On the back wall was a massive relief of what had to be Maxwell's own version of himself carved into the wall, and she went to it and began to study it. She was sure it would hold some clue for her. It had to be here!

The relief had Maxwell standing on top of a mountain that she could only guess was supposed to be Olympus. The elementals all crushed beneath his feet, he had his arms held out from his sides. In one hand, was a scale, it was as if he was some just and powerful god of righteousness, which humored her to no end. In the other hand, he held an old fashioned briefcase. Beams of light shot from a halo around his head to finish off the vision of Maxwell as none other than, the mighty Zeus! The detail was very meticulous. As she scanned over it she noticed the briefcase and its little locking strap, and low and behold, was that what she thought it was? Was that a tiny, barely noticeable keyhole on the clasp?

"I win you old bastard!" she said, in a derisive tone, the sneer on her face one of true hatred and triumph all at once.

She was shaking as she pulled her key out. Barely able to contain her joy, she fought to keep her hand steady as she worked to insert her key into the hole on the briefcase. Finally, she got it lined up and with one push it went smoothly into the lock.

"Here's to you Maxwell," she said as it bottomed out in the lock.

If only the wind didn't' make so damn much noise as it whistled through the dense conifer trees. If only she could see straight and her mind wasn't so muddled up by all of the drugs and alcohol. If, if, if, there are always so many ifs. If she had taken a little time to observe before acting, she might have heard the scratching and other small noises coming from behind the wall. If she was a little more cautious, she might have had a chance to avoid what happened next.

As the key bottomed out in the lock and tripped the latch. The satchel was forced open and flipped up because of the weight of the rattlesnakes in the compartment behind it and a cleverly rigged counterweight. She automatically pulled her hand back and stepped back, but there were several dozen snakes pouring out around her feet, and they were not happy they had been disturbed. As they hit the floor, many of them struck at the first thing they saw which happened to be Melissa's bare legs. Jumping and hopping and screaming wildly seemed to only infuriate them more, and the biting continued even as she fell to the floor, rolling and lashing out as best she could. She was bitten, according to the coroner, over fifty times.

The last thing she saw before she was bitten in the eye by one of the unhappy residents was the satchel swinging back into place shutting again as the last of its hidden residents fell to the floor and promptly struck at her arm. Her key still in the slot seemed to be glowing and calling to her. How odd, she thought. The last thing she heard was the upset rattles of the snakes lulling her into a deep sleep as the considerable pain finally started to subside.

The last thing she thought was something she had read about their fangs. They were like hypodermic needles. That was it. They could penetrate a balloon and not pop it, they were so sharp. She thought about the tracks between her toes and other common places to hide such nasty little things. She thought about how many needles she had willingly stuck into her own flesh over the years as she died. If she could have, she would have laughed at the irony of that, but movement was no longer possible.

Mr. Smith heard the screams and for the first time in many days was truly happy. The only bad part was that he didn't get to see what happened, or see her die before him. Too bad she hadn't jumped back in New York. But he knew what his associate had rigged and he shivered at the thought of what she must have just gone through. He admitted reluctantly to himself he hated snakes.

Casually, he pulled his cell phone out and made a call. It took only five minutes for the car to arrive. They were waiting just up the road for the call. While he waited, he made a second call to an anonymous number with an operator on the other end.

"Seven is available," he said and then hung up.

Two men got out of a black Lincoln exactly like the one they left the airport in and went around and opened the trunk. A small case was taken out and one of the men opened it and took out a pair of gloves. They were strange looking gloves made of some latex material and if one looked closely enough they would see the odd imprints of Melissa's hands on them. He went into the car Melissa and her assistant had come in and fiddled with the steering wheel, radio and numerous other knobs and controls. If you saw this you would think he had lost his mind and was playing car like a little boy, not old enough to drive would do as he pretended to be dad on his way to work. At least he wasn't making car noises while he played in order to add an additional semblance of realism. He opened the glove box and handled the rental agreement that was there and then got out. The other man opened a plastic bag and sprinkled out the hairs and flakes of skin that were in it. They also belonged to Melissa. Gathering these things is very easy to accomplish when someone is comatose. The prints were perfect and the hairs were an added nice touch. Just for kicks Mr. Smith sprinkled a little white powder that was from Melissa's compact he obtained earlier as she lay passed out on the plane. They all stood around for a minute more as Mr. Smith closed the trunk and wiped it off.

"Should we go and check?" one of the newcomers asked.

"Be my guest. I wouldn't go near that place for a week. You like snakes, you go right on ahead. I hate them with a passion," Mr. Smith said shivering.

"If I didn't know better I'd say you were afraid," the other laughed.

"I call it being smart, not afraid. Besides, Peter built the mechanism and you know Peter. It worked just fine. If someone pulls the key out and tried to reinsert it nothing is going to happen and you would have to knock the wall down to know the compartment was there, and no one is going do that. I checked out the old caretaker and he is half blind and usually tanked up when he comes up here. He will just think it was vandals sticking it in or that he missed it all these years and it is nothing more than a nice touch to the artwork. There is no indication of a hidden compartment now. I couldn't even find a seam when I was here before. She is dead or will be in a minute or two. Besides, you know better than to go back and risk leaving something contrary to what we want the scene to look like. Are you slipping and going senile on me, or do you want to see her laying there?" Mr. Smith reached into his pocket and took out the keys. "You drive. Get us someplace I can shower. I have been stuck with that piece of shit for longer than I want to remember, and I can't remember ever feeling this dirty."

The three men got into the other car and drove off.

It wasn't until the following week she was found. The caretaker had just been there earlier on the day she came and only came up once a week to tend the place. He always came, even when he was sick, he came, or he got his son to come for him. He received a nice check in the mail once a month for the service as he always had and it was a sizable amount. He wasn't going to risk losing that.

As he came around the final bend he noticed a black car in the parking lot. His first thought was kids up here again but the car was a black Lincoln, so he wondered if it might be a rich relative or something. No kids around here had access to a car like that. But the local kids came up here to party all the time, and even though they never did any real damage, he hated cleaning up after them.

He pulled his worn out pick-up, with its small trailer carrying his mower and other lawn tools into the parking lot and finished off the last of the flask he had in his pocket. It was a bit chilly this morning, rain most likely, he thought. Hopefully he would catch them and he could make them clean up their own mess and give them a good scare to boot! He also usually made them leave their beer or whatever else they had when he kicked them out. An added bonus for him!

When he got up to the plot he didn't see anyone but he noticed right away the door on the mausoleum was ajar. Damn kids! It was one thing to come up here, another altogether to go in there. They were going to get a real talking too, that's for sure!

He caught them up here a few times having sex. It was hilarious to watch them scramble for their clothes and he usually got a nice eyeful in the process. He quietly moved closer to the mausoleum and was just about to peek in and see if he could catch them at it when he heard a sound he had heard one other time in his life. It wasn't a sound you forgot, even if it wasn't that common in these parts. Rattlers! Sounded like more than one, too.

He ran back down to his truck and took out the high intensity flashlight he kept there and a rake with a nice long handle on it and ran back up the hill, stopping once, to catch his breath.

"Is there anybody in there?" he called. Damn, if they were bitten, it was going to be a mess.

There was no answer so he held the rake out in front of him and began to force the door all the way open with it. It protested loudly but was moving. He was half tempted to run back and get some help, but if there was someone in there, and they were bitten, he would need to help them right away. This is, of course, if they were still alive.

What light there was shown into the room and even with his flashlight, he couldn't see any snakes near the front, so he cautiously moved a little closer. It smelled of urine and feces, and god knows what else. Rotted flesh! The putrid odor hit his senses hard and made him nearly puke right there. He knew that smell as well as he knew the sound. It was death and it would be dancing the jig, maggots making the skin crawl, nasty juices running out of it. All depended on how long since they died. Yep, he knew what he was going to find, several tours in Nam taught him that smell. He had smelled it over and over again. His light hit the woman's body lying behind the crypt. Oh she was dead, all right. No doubt about it, she had to be. Her body was sprawled out and bloated. She was staring with one gruesome eye while the other dripped its matter down her pallid, swollen cheek. A rather large rattler was curled up between her spread legs just daring him to go in. He didn't take him up on it.

He ran back to his truck and picked up his cell phone calling 911 hoping he could get reception this far out. He never tried before, and they were pretty far from civilization here. No such luck. He got into his truck and made his way back to town and straight to the Sheriff's office.

Later that day after the dozen snakes were cleared out, they hauled out the body. She must have walked in unknowingly on the nest. It was a little strange to see so many snakes here. Usually, they were more in the mountains, than this close to the coast, but some kids must have left the door ajar and they used the mausoleum to get out of the weather, odd though, to see so many.

He got a good look at the body when they brought it out. It was covered from head to toe in bites. She died a fast and painful death. No one could survive that many bites for long. What was most disturbing to him was the one eye. It had been punctured and the juices had oozed out and down her face but you could still see the deflated shape of it. He almost went into hysterics when he saw it. Like a balloon, but no longer filled with air. The other eye was still intact, still open, its glazed hazy stare still holding a look of surprise in it.

He followed the Sherriff into the mausoleum to see if anything was missing or damaged after being assured five or six times the snakes had all been cleared out. Everything seemed as it should, nothing was broken or out of place. He would have to replace the candles again, though and he would need to scrub the damn place to get rid of the stains and that awful stench! Damn kids, always lighting them when they came in to party.

No one even noticed the key stuck in the wall. He would find it months later, after he got up the courage to go back in. He stuck it in several times and nothing happened. Kids must have put it there, he thought, and threw it away. He considered it might be part of the relief carved on the wall but he would have noticed it before. Oh well, no biggie, and no harm done.

The incident was in the paper the next day and it turns out she was some relative of the Alderson's had come to pay her respects. Terrible way to go, he thought. He was a lot more careful from then on when he went up to do his job. He carried a small pistol with bird shot in it with him, and good thing too, he found three more of the damn things. He took them out with the little pistol filled with its scatter shot, and buried them where they lie. He would just keep killing them, until whatever nest they had was emptied out but always, now, he wore some thick tall boots when he was up there. The check was still too good to pass up.

Chapter Thirteen

After reading about Melissa's death, Sean wanted nothing further to do with this business. Sure, it was listed as an unfortunate event, an accidental death, but the circumstances were just too coincidental for his tastes. No mention of her supposed assistant was anywhere to be found, just like before, and when Sean researched the snakes on line, it seemed that although feasible, it would be rare in that area to see so many. Unless, of course, one was unfortunate enough to stumble into a nest as was suggested by the police. It wasn't, after all, unheard of.

Sharon was just as convinced as Sean was that something was wrong though about the whole thing. For a few days she became withdrawn and distant and Sean was afraid she was having second thoughts about the two of them. Sean had to admit, he had become a little introverted too, though, after this last bit of news.

Neither one spoke to the other about their thoughts for some time, but both were thinking the same thing. Maxwell was toying with them all, and worse, he was toying with their lives, and it was straining their relationship. The longer this went on, the worst it could get. Both of them knew they had to face it head on, but neither one knew where to start.

After a few days of this, Sharon went looking for Sean. She wasn't going to let this go on, and she figured it was up to her to get them back on the same track again. Sean was in the gym working out. He was pushing himself at a fever pitch, sweating profusely.

"Sean. Stop for a minute, please," she said, walking over to him. She had half expected him to start drinking again, but he hadn't, so far.

Sean ignored her for a minute and finished his reps. He was breathing hard and had to sit there for a minute before he could talk.

"Sharon, what the hell is going on?" he said, looking at her as his breath returned. "The second we get to Hong Kong, I want us to get far away from anything Maxwell touched. Fuck the money, and fuck him."

"I couldn't agree with you more," she said. "There is one slight problem."

"Oh?" he said half expecting her to tell him that she wanted to get away from him, too.

"Well. I have been thinking," she said. He mistook her pause, and her facial expression for bad news.

"Sharon, please don't say it. I don't know what's going on, but I don't want you to leave me," he said choking on the words.

"Don't be silly," she said dismissively. "Did you think?" the look on his face melted her heart. He thought she wanted to get away from him too, she realized. Oh, men were so obtuse! She almost laughed realizing she had been thinking the same thing. That he might want to get away from her. Ok, she was being a little obtuse too, she reluctantly admitted to herself.

"Sean, you're stuck with me. What were you thinking?" she said. "I'd hug you but you're all sweaty and nasty so you will just have to wait till later, when you're cleaned up. Now, you listen to me. Do you remember what you said to me the morning after we, well, you know? You told me you were falling in love with me and I said what? I said it was a perfectly safe thing to do. So stop being an idiot. It is not becoming. I love you."

Sean let his guard down, and sighed. For a minute he was two years old, and totally vulnerable. If he lost her, he didn't know what he would do. He couldn't help it, he jumped up and took her in his arms and held her there as close as he could. Finally she pushed him away.

"Now you got me all sweaty. I don't mind, but I prefer we get sweaty in a more mutually pleasurable way. Now settle down and listen, please?" she said all business again. He nodded afraid that if he spoke he would cry.

"I know you are thinking the same thing I am. Maxwell orchestrated this whole thing, and has his little army of assassins working to carry it all out. You noticed they never seem to be around after something bad happens. They just disappear into thin air."

"Oh, you bet I noticed," he said. "I remember Mr. Smith, and his goon assistant, Mr. Brown. I knew what they were when I met them. I never met those two personally, but met plenty of their associates sneaking in and out of Maxwell's company doing his little errands. I knew what was going on, and it gave me chills. Maxwell had a personal army of thugs."

"So ask yourself. Where is your Mr. Smith, or Mr. Brown?" She asked him. Her brow raised above her almond eyes inquisitively.

"Well, they were in Monaco," he said trying to puzzle it out.

"Yes, and we are here. I just needed them to arrange some transportation. They are not assigned to you. I was assigned as your assistant, not one of those goons, and I can't wait to see if they even show up to meet us when we pull in. You know, I bet they know where we are, and where we are going. I'd bet my life on it. But, if they are not there, then I don't think we have anything to worry about."

"That doesn't mean we're not in danger," he said, shaking his head. He was through with this. He could get a job anywhere he wanted, and so could she. They didn't need this mess.

"So, you think you are wrong about me then? Or, you think Maxwell would kill his own daughter?" she said shivering.

"No, but Mr. Smith would," he said disgusted. "Probably like it too. Remember, he may have been loyal to Maxwell but Maxwell is no longer here."

"I asked the Captain who has been on board since Maxwell died and he said no one. Not one soul has stepped foot on this boat since the day he died, unless they snuck on board."

"Well, you wouldn't expect them to come in through the front door, would you?" Sean said sarcastically.

"No, I think we are safe here," Sharon said to him.

"OK, but what about when we get off the ship?"

"We will just need to be careful. If, no when, we find something we can deal with it then. My guess is that using the keys had something to do with it, booby traps or something. So, we just don't use it until we can make sure it is safe. How could Maxwell be so cruel?"

"Should we warn the others?" Sean asked.

"Would they listen? Or, more likely, would they think you were pulling a fast one?" Sharon asked back. "Maybe we're reading more into this than we should. I find it hard to believe Maxwell was that sick in the end," Sharon said wishing she could believe herself.

"You forget how much he hated most of them," Sean reminded her.

"Go get cleaned up Sean. We can talk about it later," Sharon said to him, giving him a little peck on the cheek.

"I need my back scrubbed. Can you send my assistant in to help me shower please?" Sean said mischievously.

"You have a one track mind," she said smiling at him. "But I find I have no choice but to comply with your request! But only because you got me all stinky, too."

They were still about six days from port. Sharon sent a long message to Thomas. His response was exactly what she and Sean both expected. The deaths had been thoroughly investigated, by local authorities, and no evidence of foul play was suspected.

Both tragedies seemed to be completely legitimate accidents, although he could not explain why the assistants assigned seemed to be gone when it happened, both times. Maxwell made the arrangements with a firm he did not even know the name of. Either that or they worked directly for Maxwell. He didn't know which was true. It didn't concern his part in this. If they were no longer required to be present, he could not see why they would have stuck around. In both cases, they were not present anyway, which, is more than enough to vindicate them. As he said numerous times, he was not privy to those arrangements, so didn't know what their instructions were. His job was to see the proper heir was rewarded and the rules were followed, only. Besides, Melissa had taken her own car. He wasn't even sure her assistant had been in town. From all the receipts Thomas had been dealing with from Melissa's assistant, she seemed to simply be having one big party. For all he knew, she sent him for drugs, or whatever, while she looked.

In the end Sharon and Sean decided to drop it but to keep their guard up from here on out. It seemed somehow too convenient that her assistant had witnesses and such a great alibi. When they got to Hong Kong, they would stay in a hotel which Sharon would arrange for in the moment. They could use taxis to get around, if they were that paranoid about the whole thing. When they investigated the property, they would do it together, and watch each other's backs. If Mr. Smith, or Mr. Brown, or anyone looking like them showed up, they would get away as fast as possible.

They were determined to find the truth, and Sharon still had many sources and contacts in Hong Kong that would do whatever she asked them to do, for a fee, of course. She wanted to find her birth records and anything else she could get her hands on. But anything she did from here on out she would do herself and on the down low. Thomas was not going to know what they were up to. She knew of no requirement to report her every move to him, or to anyone else, for that matter. She had sent him a message but had in no way given away their position or their intentions. There was no way that the message could be traced wither. It came via satellite.

She and Sean would be the only ones who knew their movements. Sharon had an especially appropriate friend she was going to contact. He worked for her many times in the past "researching" her foes for the ammunition she needed to make them more pliable during negotiations. He would be the first person they contacted when they got into port. If they were being watched or followed, he would know. He was the best. He was in the same business as Maxwell's associates, and very well acquainted with unsavory types and tasks and best of all, he worked on a cash only basis!

She wanted to call him, but Sean wouldn't let her. He didn't trust any form of communication they had right now and almost regretted sending the query to Thomas. If Maxwell's "friends" knew they were suspicious, who knows what they might do. No. They needed complete anonymity from here on out, everything they did would be through Sharon's friend, Mr. Kim, for the time being. Sharon was even going to pay him out of her bank account, not through Thomas.

One thing was certain. Sean planted the seed Sharon might learn who her father was, after all these years, and now she was as entangled as him. Money, or no money, she needed to find out if he was right. The answer had to be right there, in Hong Kong. Of that, they were both sure, now.

Chapter Fourteen

Brett was nearly out of patience with Beatrice. She was like an incurable disease! No matter how mean he was, no matter what he said or did to her, she stuck to him like glue. Well, he really had no one to blame for it but the man in the mirror. He made sure, long ago, she was completely dependant on him. It was his way of making sure he would get his hands on some of Maxwell's money someday, without having to steal it from the old tightwad any more.

The fact that she was so obese was his doing, too. Feed her and keep her locked up in the house, fully dependant on him, for company, and of course... her favorite vice, food! She had gotten so fat it was difficult for her to get out, so he made sure she was kept in bonbons all the time. As long he kept her locked up like he did, she would not argue with him on what they did with any money they eventually got from Maxwell. Leave her and he would be out in the cold. That was no longer true, but for now, it seemed he couldn't get rid of her. Besides, keeping up at least some slight appearance he cared was still in his best interests.

His sons on the other hand were of no use to him whatsoever. They were quite the disappointment to him. He wrote them off long ago, and Joel's death was of no concern to him, and certainly didn't warrant his changing his plans. He didn't even feel any remorse, which was driving Beatrice even deeper into the depression he made sure was a daily part of her life. William could rot, too. Both of them took after their mother as far as their weakness was concerned, and William was nearly as grotesque as her, maybe more so because he was a nasty, unclean man too, as was his brother.

Beatrice begged him to go back with her, and honor their son, but he vehemently refused her request. He promised her they would fix it when this was over, and promised her he would stay with her which, of course, was a complete lie, on both counts. He had no use for her now, but he couldn't shake her. Not yet, anyway. He just kept up the façade in case by some off chance she was to find the money before him. That would be bad. He would then have to bleed her, kill her, or steal her blind. Possibly it would be a combination of the three, with the killing taking place as soon as possible, before she could dump him, or make arrangements for William to get it first. He tried to get her to go back and let him keep looking for both of them, just to get rid of her, but it didn't work. She was like glue.

'*Well, glue can be removed,*' he thought.

The estate in Devonshire was a very old monstrosity of a manor home once owned by some Duke or something, it didn't matter to him. What mattered to him were the photos he found in Michigan showing Martha here, lots and lots of photos. Martha in the garden, Martha in the home, Martha on a horse, dressed for a fox hunt, Martha very, very happy. Guess who else was in many of those pictures smiling like there wasn't a care in the world?

Before Martha died, she loved living here. They moved to Hong Kong only because Maxwell was in the middle of some major business there, and had to remain there almost all of the time. He bought the place there, and turned it into a palace for her to make her happy, but she always missed England. She was born there, and loved it there.

As far as Brett knew, Maxwell rarely, if ever, came here after she died. But what stuck in Brett's mind was Martha. Maxwell doted on her, even after she died giving birth to Angelina, in Hong Kong. She had to be the thing he was referring to and where better to search than her true home, the place she loved most. Hong Kong was a possibility, but this was where her spirit lived and Maxwell knew that very well.

He had some other ideas but for now he needed to exhaust this one fully. Going to Michigan had been a huge mistake. It was way to obvious a place, if you knew how the old fart thought, and he could have put the time to better use. He could have had at least a day of peace, too, if he told Beatrice he was headed there. She would have run after him, and he would have been far away.

Beatrice spent most of her time crying over her son, and avoiding facing her problems with food, as always. She knew

Brett was a cruel man. She knew all about his little secretary, too. Brett spent more time at his precious dealership than with her. But she knew why that was, too. He hated her, and she knew it. Her world was not one where she deluded herself that she was any great prize. On the contrary, she was ashamed of what she had become over the years. Always a little on the plump side, she buried her head in the sand long ago, just glad she had a man, and this is where it got her.

Brett had never been faithful to her, and she knew it. He only married her in the first place because of her name, and the potential wealth he would someday get access to by being her husband. If she didn't find it first, Brett would send her packing, of that, she was sure. Maxwell had ruined her already less than perfect life. She couldn't bear the thought of being alone, money or no money. Even having him dependant on her was better than that. Maybe she could change things, too. She could be hopeful that she would have control, if she controlled the purse strings. It was all she had to cling to.

The manor had a beautifully equipped media room, as the servants called it, where she was spending a very large portion of her time. The chairs were wide and comfortable and had trays on the side to hold the goodies she constantly called for. The servants came when she called and looked at her with open disgust, she could see it, as she ordered everything from ice cream to baked chicken, with all of the fixings.

Right now, she was working on an entire casserole dish of bread pudding. She had to admit, the English had some pretty tasty dishes. Thanks to the modern invention of satellite TV she could even sit here and watch all of her favorite shows. Today's topic was "Am I the father of my step mother's child?" and the DNA results would soon be revealed. She anticipated at least one more juicy twist in this plot. Right now, two men were trying to kill each other while the security guys held them just far enough apart to control them, but not far enough apart to prevent them from still hitting each other once or twice. They let them connect, but not seriously. It has too still look like they were trying to prevent it. It all lent itself to a good day's ratings, here on Trailer Trash TV.

Brett hadn't even come by to check on her, but she had her own personal assistant to keep tabs on him. The man was no better than any other man. Even his cool, professional attitude could not completely hide his absolute disgust when he was around her. But Beatrice didn't care. As long as he had to do whatever she wanted he could hate her all he wanted. Why should he be any different?

As soon as she got here, she had her assistant arrange for her to get Martha's old quarters. Ha! That one she got over on her smug husband. He didn't think about it until two days later, and by then, she had secretly gone over the entire room. He thought she was just sitting here eating her way through all the food in England, but she was no fool. She might be sitting here now, but it was a place she could think. While Brett chased the young maids and haphazardly searched the house and grounds she took a much more reserved, and much less exhaustive, approach.

As the host of the daytime trash TV show she was watching finally revealed the result of the DNA tests, which, of course, sent the audience into a frenzy of boos and cat calls at the fact that he and his own step mother had borne a child, Beatrice came up with her next move. She reached over and picked up the bell she confiscated to summon her assistant and rang it. In a minute, he came slowly into the room and stood waiting for the next order of food he was sure was coming to refill the pig's endless trough.

"Please summon the Head of household for me," she said trying to sound regal.

"Yes Ma'am," he responded almost surprised. She knew what he was thinking. She always knew what they all thought about her.

Beatrice was actually afraid of him. It wasn't the way he looked at her. It was the cold calculated way he treated her, well, it was the way he looked at her, too. She could imagine him strangling her in her sleep, just to get away from her. She saw the same look many times in her loving husband, and she knew what he was thinking.

While she waited, she flipped through the channels. It was difficult to find some of her favorite TV shows. They were all over the place. Ah. Here was her favorite judge, telling it like it is. Chewing out some poor loser who was dumb enough to put himself in the position where he could be bantered and made fun of, for the viewing pleasure of people like Beatrice whose entire existence was enriched through seeing more pitiful people than themselves.

Finally, the Head Mistress came in. Beatrice knew the look on her face, too. Before she came up she spent several minutes telling the rest of the staff of her misfortune at having to be in the same room as this vile woman and if she could figure out how to do it, she would give her the boot, but good!

"Yes mum," she said coldly.

"Tell me everything you remember about Martha Alderson, please," Beatrice asked her in an unusually stern tone.

"Well. Let me see. She was a very kind woman and always treated the staff here like family," she said pointedly.

"What were her favorite things to do?" Beatrice asked.

"She loved horses and of course, her gardens. She spent many long hours there tending her roses, and other treasures. She was an avid wine collector. The cellars are full of many fine wines she personally selected, to this day, some of them very rare indeed. Oh. She also enjoyed playing bridge. She played bridge every Saturday as I recall," the woman said reminiscing of the

woman she so dearly missed. She wouldn't have tolerated this…
thing here, or her letch of a husband, either. She would have sent
them packing on the first train out of town, and that was
something the banker could put in his vault, for sure.

"Is that all you remember?" Beatrice asked her.

"She was a very thin woman, mum. She kept herself in
good condition. Appearances were important to her," she said the
last with a very noticeable emphasis.

"That will be all. Thank you," Beatrice said, anger
threatening to well up in her until she would cry. How dare she
speak to her like that! Who does she think she is anyway? If she
found the will, or whatever it was she was looking for, and
gained control of this place, that woman would find herself out
on her ear so fast her smug head would turn right off her
shoulders. After she and the assistant left the room together, no
doubt to laugh at the way the mistress had treated her, Beatrice
reached down and grabbed the box of chocolates she had hidden
under the pudding dish she had just finished, and began to
console herself, one piece at a time.

As she unconsciously watched her court show, the judge
reprimanded another unfortunate loser, while Beatrice ran the
information through her mind. Where to begin? She mentioned
the horses, and there was a stable. That could wait until
tomorrow. It was a very long walk to the stables. Gardens
seemed like a very good possibility, and a good place to hide

something. But it was a large garden, and that would have to wait, too. It would be dark soon, anyway.

Bridge made no sense to her, so for now, it had to be the wine cellars she would investigate next. They were close enough to be easy to do today and like a garden, it was full of places to hide something. As soon as she finished this box of chocolates, she would head down there. Most of the staff would go home soon. They didn't stay all night, except the night maid who hid from her anyway. She dozed off with a chocolate still in her mouth.

Brett was going purely on the photos he found in Michigan. He already covered the entire garden and he already worked his way through the barn. There was a greenhouse filled with roses and his search there had proven to be fruitless, too. The entire house yielded nothing, and he was down to the attic and the cellars, which were on his to do list. His disgusting wife beat him to Martha's bedroom so that was pretty much a wash, too. Tomorrow, he would move on to Hong Kong. He would send Beatrice to Fort Lauderdale by telling her he was headed there. That would buy him a few days peace.

Right now it was time to spy on Beatrice, he decided. God forbid she beat him to the punch. He would be stuck with her forever then. Well, forever was far too long to even think about. He would be stuck with her until he could figure out how to get rid of her was a much better way to look at it. He heard a lot of people like her choked on their food. Oh, yes. Being that obese carried terrible health risks. It might be something as simple as a chicken bone lodged in her throat. Yes, the possibilities, and risks were endless for someone like her.

When he quietly peeked in on her he found her right where he expected, asleep with food smeared on her lips, a box of chocolates still in her grip. My god, the woman was really out of control. He thought he might just say the hell with her and this place now while he had the chance and look elsewhere. He would at least have a day or two of peace before she found out where he was. He was finishing tonight and taking off first thing in the morning.

Sean was still out on the Me Lady and that just royally chapped his ass! The second he pulled in someplace Brett was planning on descending on him like a vulture on a rotting carcass. Who did he think he was, anyway? He basically stole the Me Lady so no one else could look there. He had to hand it to him, though. It was a pretty slick move, when they all threatened to swoop down on the Michigan property. What a hovel, that place was. It deserved its fate, just as Joel deserved his.

Beatrice was awakened by the door to the media room closing. It must have been Brett because it was 6PM and the staff would be gone by now. She waited just a moment and tinkled her little bell. No one came. Damn that supposed assistant. He disappeared a lot. She was going to complain to him next time she saw him. If she could get up the courage to do it, that is.

She quietly got up and made her way slowly down the main stairs towards the kitchen. Earlier she saw the door leading down to the cellars when she was poking around in there for something to eat. It looked old and dark but there were lights. She knew where a flashlight was too, and decided lights or not, she would grab that just in case. What she was looking for was liable to be difficult to see with good light, let alone the semi-dark of the cellar she was expecting to encounter.

There was a noise in the upper floor of the house and she stopped to listen. It sounded like a door creaking. Good. Brett was poking around up stairs or maybe in the attic, so she was free to explore and not be caught.

She made her way into the kitchen and opened the drawer by the cellar door where she saw the flashlight earlier and switched it on. Carefully, she opened the door so it wouldn't make any noise. The cellar was pitch-black and she searched for the light switch. She knew there were lights but she couldn't find the switch. Finally, the beam from her flashlight illuminated a switch at the bottom of the stairs. Why on earth it was there, she didn't know. She stepped as gingerly as her tremendous girth would allow onto the first step which gave out a small creaking protest at the weight, but held. Slowly, she went down with the flashlight aimed at the switch, each step making the staircase cry out in protest at the burden she put on it. At the bottom, she reached over and hit the switch and a series of bare bulbs came to life supplying a weak, but sufficient glow in the cellar.

She stood there a moment looking around. There were all sorts of baskets and barrels stacked around, some so covered in cobwebs you could just imagine how long they must have been sitting there. But there was no sign of wine racks, or anything like the head mistress described. At least, not what she envisioned she would find. She saw several doors off of the room she was in and tried each of them only to find more piles of useless, ancient junk. Hopefully, she wasn't going to end up looking through them. She did not like spiders at all and apparently, the spiders liked it here quite a bit.

After trying every door and not finding the wine cellar, Beatrice was beginning to think there must be another cellar somewhere. In a house this big and this old, you never knew, and it was obvious these rooms she found were not the entire extent of the underground chambers that could be present under this house. She turned to leave and saw one last door she hadn't noticed recessed in an arched cavity next to the stairs. That had to be it.

She made her way to the door and saw a light switch there. She opened the door and flipped the switch and a room of racks and bottles stood before her. There were no windows, but in here, there were more lights and she didn't need the flashlight. He heart was pounding in her chest as she made her way through aisle after aisle of wine racks, many full, some with only a few bottles on them. One thing for sure was no one came in here very often. The bottles were covered with dust and it looked as if nothing had been touched for years. The only exception was the floor. At least they kept that clean!

She knew absolutely nothing about wine, but could imagine this room alone was worth a fortune. Some of the bottles had thick layers of dust on them, and the labels were almost unreadable. Some, it was obvious, were newer and for general use, but even these were now covered in a light coating of fine dust. She imagined the hostess being able to ask for just about anything, and it would be in here.

Several areas in the place were dark and she had to turn the flashlight back on. At the end of one of the rows was an ornate wooden cabinet, and oh my, it had a small keyhole! This could be it! So far, it was the only thing even she'd seen even remotely having potential, and it was in a place that made a lot of sense. Maybe it had been placed there on purpose. She reached her shaking hands into the pocket of her dress, a billowy massive piece of cloth with pockets on it to retrieve her key.

She wore these dresses all the time. What were they called? She believed the common term was Mumu or something like that? It was about all she could find that fit her. Brett called them tents to hurt her feelings, she recalled, letting it distract her for a moment. She stood there trying to find the key in all of the empty wrappers and other things she had hidden in the pockets, remnants of her emergency stash.

Slowly she was making her way down the row when she heard something behind her. She let out a little yelp and turned and aimed the flashlight back. Brett was standing at the end of the row looking at her.

"What are you doing down here?" he asked, the anger in his voice barely controlled. "I just saw you asleep in the media room, not fifteen minutes ago."

"You woke me up, and I had an idea," she said glancing back over her shoulder, then realizing she didn't want him to know she may have found something. She tried to lie to him. "There is nothing down here, though," she said trying to sound disappointed.

"You're lying," he said automatically. "After all of the times I have caught you hiding food, you don't think I can tell when you're lying?" he said sneering at her.

Brett started down the row and Beatrice turned her entire girth to block his path.

"I found the case. I'm going to open it, and if there is something in there, it's mine," she said defiantly. "I know what will happen if you find the money. You are not going to get rid of me that easily!" she shrieked, holding the fear back as well as she could.

"Beatrice. Don't be silly. Come on, we will do it together, and share everything, just like I said," he said trying to sooth her.

He was usually able to calm her, but this time she was shaking her head at him and the anger was welling up in him. He should just kill her now, he thought visualizing a heavy rack of wine falling and trapping her beneath it.

"No, this time you will leave me. I know that. I'm not as dumb as you think I am," she said, starting to cry.

God! He hated that! She was so supremely pitiful he could just puke right here, right now. He steeled himself.

"Beatrice. I fucking said... I would not leave you. If we find the money, we will share it, and you can have an entire staff of waiters at your beck and call," he said moving towards her.

Beatrice was backing up towards the end of the row which of course, was a dead end. There was nothing there but racks of wine and the wooden cabinet.

"I said move, you fat bitch!" Brett said clenching his fists.

Beatrice was openly crying now. She was always afraid and right now she was very afraid of what he might do.

"You promise we will share?" she said shyly, the moisture pouring from her eyes and nose, she wiped at it with her arm making Brett grimace in disgust.

"Yes. I promise, now move aside and let me in there," he said trying to sound reassuring.

She turned her body sideways giving him just enough room to pass her and he walked towards the cabinet.

"There is no guarantee this is it anyway," he said.

Beatrice was not going to be left behind. She was right at his back. If he found anything at all, she was going to see exactly what it was.

Many older homes at one time were built over top of wells. It was an old practice from medieval days which ensured an internal water supply and later, was done to have water available in the home, especially the older homes of the well to do. It was as close as you could get to running water, back then. A pump in the kitchen eliminated the need to go outside to retrieve water. Larger homes like this one may have had several wells in them, feeding bathrooms and other areas of the home. The wealthier the home, the more wells and water services they put into them. Most of it now no longer even used, replaced with modern water service.

With the advent of running water and electricity many were covered, but not all were filled in. That was a hell of a lot of dirt to carry into the house to fill it so a framework and a cover were used to do the same task. The fellow who covered this one used a wooden frame to hold the stone and mortar he covered it over with. The household staff didn't even know it was there. It would take a trained eye to find it. You would need to know what you were looking for, and need to be actively looking for it. The stones blended in but the round outline remained, if one was looking for it.

One aspect of geology is the study of erosion. Some older versions of mortar had a large amount of lime in them so the mortar and the limestone blocks used were very susceptible to erosion. The water in this area was very acidic and very easily ate the wood and mortar, especially when it had a little help or was accelerated by some means.

There was the outside chance that the floor might have possibly held Brett alone, if he was careful, but the two of them together was far beyond what it could support. The weight of the racks on the sides of the covered well added even more load and the recently relocated cabinet was heavy with bottles of wine. It might have held, but with Beatrice's added weight, there was zero chance it would be able to support the load.

Neither one of them got to see what was in the cabinet. All they would have found was a few bottles of wine and the key wouldn't have opened it anyway. It wasn't even locked and they would most assuredly be just a little put out to find the contents consisted of just a few bottles of a not even expensive wine. No matter. Actually though, they did get a chance to see, but it wasn't what either one of them were thinking about at the time.

As the floor gave way Beatrice instinctively reached for Brett, Brett instinctively reached for the wooden cabinet and the three of them were closely followed by the bottles of wine disturbed from their long sleep on the tumbling racks surrounding the crumbling floor of the ancient well. In a tremendous clang and clatter of breaking glass accentuated by screams followed by the distant splash of the entire conglomeration of flesh, stone, glass, and some rather expensive wine they hit the bottom of the well together.

Beatrice hit her head as she fell backwards on the edge of the now exposed pit and was immediately unconscious. The screaming was Brett as he flailed his arms and fell in a shower of bottles and glass, Beatrice's massive bulk underneath him still clinging to him. She made a wonderful raft and at first she softened the landing for Brett, as a result, he might have survived, thanks to her. That is, if it wasn't for the cabinet coming down on him pushing them both beneath the surface of the water and trapping them there as more bottles fell and broke against the walls and cabinet.

Beatrice finally got what she wanted, to be with her husband, and Brett, well, he got the last thing on earth he wanted, to be close to her. To make it worse, as he tried to get free, he instinctively rolled over and found himself on top of her as if he were having sex with her. He died flailing in all of her voluminous flesh. Suffocated in the bosom of the woman he hated.

The two assistants, number 5 and number 6, or Mr. Smith and Mr. Brown, if you prefer, made sure they were seen leaving the estate with the other servants. They made sure they were seen in town and in the rooms they had rented for just such an occasion. A little birdie they knew told them of the tragic deaths of their charges and removed the other "potential" hazards from the estate as they stayed in the hotel for several days until finally, one of the staff found the tragic site and called the police down to the estate to investigate and retrieve the bodies.

The town was abuzz with the story, and the two assistants just sat quietly in the corner, unnoticed and unrecognized, and listened as they talked. The police, upon pulling out the bodies and seeing the massive weight of Beatrice knew exactly what had happened. They were both snooping around where they had no business being in the first place, according to the hired help, and had unfortunately, discovered the old well. Well, the bright side was that none of the local staff had fallen in. From what they all said, it was no great loss and good riddance.

Mr. Jones, and Mr. Young, or Mr. Smith and Mr. Brown, if you preferred, checked out the next morning leaving a rather nice tip for the maid and were never seen there again. As for the little birdie, Mr. Doe, he flew away the night of the tragedy.

Life at the estate returned to normal rather quickly. The place was cleaned and scrubbed to rid it of the smell of that woman, and the town quickly moved on to the next topic they found to gossip about over their nightly pints at the hotel pub. The staff got a lot of free pints for sharing their stories about the two, until the regular crowd got tired of hearing it. It was still a small but appreciated consolation prize for having had to put up with them.

Chapter Fifteen

Sean was feeling better than he had in years. His body was responding well to the good food, hard exercise, and good love he was receiving. He had gotten into a daily routine of waking up and making love to Sharon and then working out for an hour or so and then digging into things trying to find some kind of answer to the puzzle.

Sharon of course was becoming even more obsessive with the research than he was and he found himself constantly dragging her away from her laptop and the study forcing her to have some fun. There was no question they were happy together and Sharon kept throwing little hints about her honor and biological clocks. Sean was still most likely never going to be able to fully embrace the idea of her getting with child. Marriage, no problem, but her persistence had at least gotten a "we will worry about that when this is all over" out of him which she knew was going to have to suffice.

When the news about Brett and Beatrice came in they had little doubt they were right. Now there was no question Maxwell was playing a very nasty game. Sean and Sharon felt trapped in a surreal world in which they were being led by Maxwell the puppeteer. Sean used those exact words and Sharon shivered as she remembered and shared her dream with him. The fact he would say that very thing sent chills through them both as Sharon told Sean about her dream.

Thomas sent a note on the subject pointing out how the floor had given out under Beatrice's weight when they stumbled onto an old covered well. Again, it was just another unfortunate accident and all in a days work. Yes sir, nothing wrong here! Just a lot of dead folks that all happened to be searching for the same thing. They were just a bunch of expendable puppets being manipulated by Maxwell, the master puppeteer, in the final act of "Maxwell's Last Act", sure to be a massive Broadway hit.

Neither Sharon nor Sean bought it anymore and they were sure none of the others did either. It wasn't like they were the only ones who ever went into the wine cellar. It was all too coincidental and too convenient that Maxwell's beloved relatives were all of a sudden so accident prone. Thomas could play the blind man all he wanted or more likely, as he was paid to do but it didn't fool either one of them. After all, he was being paid a hell of a lot to play his part. Sharon knew what he was being paid, she wrote the check.

They were now genuinely afraid for their lives and had finally decided to confide in Captain Spencer. They were feeling isolated and the world was closing in around them. A friend or two was something they both needed right now and they knew they could trust him.

At first the man was incredulous. He looked at them both like they must have placed their minds in a lock box for safe keeping but as Sharon pulled up all of her notes and showed him the video Maxwell made he began to get a little afraid himself. What if the Me Lady was in danger? He cared about the ship more than he did his own life. Hell, he helped design it, it was his whole life!

Both Sean and Sharon made a pact with him. Keep the mouths shut and the eyes open. Keep the Me Lady safe. Keep the crew alive but don't breathe a single word to any of them. One of them could be a spy. People get bought all the time and they knew they had to keep this quite and just keep alert for anything out of the ordinary.

They promised the captain that if there was any way to do it, one or both of them would be the new owners and he would never have to worry about a thing. As far as they were concerned, it was his home and he could stay there for the rest of his life. All they knew was they had to have some allies.

They were now four days out of Hong Kong and the captain was dreading the day they would pull in. He wasn't stupid. Now that he knew some of what was going on, he knew the others, the ones still alive anyway, would be descending on them the minute they could, and he wasn't about to roll out the red carpet. He would make their stay here miserable and get them gone as soon as possible.

So far they successfully hid their destination and the timing of their return to port so there would be at least a day or two before anyone found out where they were. Not a single communication to the outside world left the ship since the query to Thomas and that was heavily regretted just then. Until they hit coastal waters there was no requirement to report their intentions or location to any authority and even if there was, the worst that would happen is a rebuke from the maritime authorities.

Sharon was still itching to get in touch with Mr. Kim but Sean refused to let her. As soon as they docked they would get in a taxi and head to a large, busy hotel and from there they would get in touch with him. It was time they had their own Mr. Smith working on their behalf. They considered staying on the ship but decided the constant barrage and spying they knew was coming would be too much to bear. Although the number of potential visitors was shrinking rapidly!

Bringing the captain in was something they thought through long and hard. He had to know what to watch out for. If Mr. Smith or his crew of thugs came around he had to know he was in danger and so was the crew, even though it appeared no collateral damage happened in these little "accidents". In the end, they all decided the crew would be taken off of the ship, if, or when, the inevitable happened. The captain had access to repair and replenishment funds and seemed to think the ship was in bad need of a little refurbishment, hell, it might need fumigating too! This would give him a good reason to get everyone off and put a security team on to watch the ship and control the comings and goings of anyone other than Sean, Sharon, or his own staff.

Besides, the crew deserved some long overdue R&R in Hong Kong.

In the end they decided rather than fumigate the ship to go ahead and get it put in some kind of quarantine. If it was under quarantine and off limits only those cleared could come and go! Sharon was almost certain that if she called Mr. Kim he would be able to get it held in quarantine for at least a short amount of time. He had connections all over Hong Kong. Sharon was willing to bet that included Customs.

There was nothing to do now but wait.

Chapter Sixteen

As soon as he was released from the county lock-up, William high tailed it out of the states and headed straight for Monaco. He had a lot of time to think on the subject while in jail and had several ideas. Pity about his mother and father, he thought. The good news there was he wouldn't need to even consider sharing with them or his half witted brother now, for that matter. They were out of the race, so to speak.

Before William and his poor deceased brother had basically taken over the Monaco estate it was one of Maxwell's favorite places. He lived there after Angelina was grown and kept the Me Lady anchored there almost all of the time. Maxwell didn't like to fly and used the Me Lady extensively. Maxwell stayed in Monaco even after he and his brother took it over. That had to mean something in this crazy little game, he was sure of it. It might have been on the Me Lady but he was in Monaco a hell of a lot of the time, too.

The Me Lady is where he would go if his current hunch was wrong. As soon as that sneaky ass Sean pulled it into port, he would get on the ship. Sean was a smart one. That much credit he had to give him even if he couldn't stand the smug bastard. What Sean didn't know was he was smarter!

William was going to go there right off the bat, but by now Sean had almost certainly picked it over from stem to stern. The good news was that apparently he hadn't found anything, so far. The only things found were untimely deaths, and this was beginning to bother William just a bit. At least as much as he was certain the others had noticed.

So what was the pattern? What was the secret that Maxwell was dangling in front of them all? It would appear to be related to Sean but so far, it appeared that path wasn't bearing any more fruit than any other path. No one was dying around him. That much was true. Was that the point? He needed to think so. To begin again he went where he was comfortable, Monaco.

His mother and father, HA! It was easy to see what happened and quite believable, actually. She was so large she fell through the rickety old floor and took her loving husband with her. But Billy wasn't buying it. The game was for real and he was afraid.

The snake bite was really the one that scared him. It was very hard to swallow. It was true many people unwittingly stumbled into snake dens from time to time, and a crypt was a perfect place for that. They loved places like that, dark and quiet. A place a snake would find quite cozy. But still it didn't sit quite right. Not when one considers the number of bites. One or two of the nasty little creatures he could buy, but not ten or twenty. Although the bitch was most assuredly stoned out of her gourd at the time as usual, and very easily could have walked in on them before she realized what was going on.

His brother's death was easily understandable. The guy was a true moron. William had put up with him forever. So, if he tried real hard he could believe it was an accident. William tore that garage apart and he remembered the fire works, he considered lighting a few off until that bitch Katy chased him off with a sword. His dunce of a brother refused to follow him even though he promised to share with him. Oh well, Joel was stupid but he was not blind. He knew William didn't care a lick about him. He couldn't blame him for wanting to beat him to the prize, even though he would have found a way to take it from him anyway. If he did keep his halfwit brother around for his own personal amusement, he would have lived his life at William's mercy anyway. Maybe it was better he was dead, at least for him, anyway. Now William would need to do his own dirty work.

Summing up his theories in jail, William surmised two things. Maxwell loved himself or Maxwell loved his dead wife or daughter. The question was which one? The places to look were not that hard to figure out if you reasoned out the places that Maxwell would most closely associate with happiness and the two women he loved, or, of course, himself.

Martha spent a lot of time before her death in Devonshire. He knew that but she lived in Monaco just as long, maybe longer, than in Devonshire. Devonshire held more meaning for her than for Maxwell, he surmised. Besides, apparently, his mother and father didn't find anything in Devonshire other than their tickets to hell to be reunited with the bastard. Going near that place would be his last resort. No need to go to places already scrubbed for him unless he ran out of ideas and he never ran out of ideas, no sir, he was loaded with them. No discovering a long abandoned well for him, if you please.

Angelina loved it in Michigan he knew but didn't grow up there. She grew up in Hong Kong for the most part as a child and Maxwell spent a lot of time there with her. When he was not there he was in Monaco or on the Me Lady. Hong Kong was stop number three. First here, then the Me Lady, then Hong Kong, then he would go back to Devonshire if he was still searching. To be honest, he wanted to get onto the Me Lady badly. If there was one thing Maxwell loved that was it. He was settling for Monaco and also taking a much needed respite after his little run-in with the law in Florida.

Maxwell started keeping the Me Lady in Cannes several years after William and Joel showed up and found life in Monaco to their liking, much to Maxwell's chagrin. William knew Maxwell liked it here in this paradise. He also knew that Maxwell couldn't stand to be near the two of them. He took endless pleasure in depriving his rich uncle of the estate here. He could have forced them out any time he wanted, the spineless old asshole, but he never did. For some ungodly reason he tolerated them all. Maybe this was his way of taking his revenge out on them. It would be just like him. Not around to pay the piper but dying knowing they were all going to hell right behind him. Not

William. If he had to walk away from it, he would. He knew how to play poker and he was pretty sure at this point that Maxwell wasn't bluffing. The real trick is to know when to do the walking.

Monaco was not really an estate in the sense of a large tract of land with gardens and statues, stables and the like. It was just the entire three upper floors of one of the more prestigious buildings there, a parking spot or two and an absolutely perfect view of one of the places Heaven visited on a regular basis. It had a massive swimming pool on top of the building and you could sit and look out over the Mediterranean from the deck and see up and down the entire coast. The view from most of the rooms was just as spectacular.

Although the casinos were a considerable distance down from where it sat, it was easy enough to get back and forth to spend the money they stole from the house. All in all, living here was just like paradise for William, but now he would be so filthy rich he could pretty much indulge in every deprived fantasy he had ever entertained and never run out of money. He wouldn't even have to steal to do it, although that part he would actually miss. He might have to find some truly nasty way to use the money to sate his love of watching others suffer. He was sure that would be a pleasure he could afford when this was all over. With the kind of cash he would have he was pretty sure he could do just about anything his mind could conceive, legal or not.

His assistant, who laughingly called himself Mr. Jones, opened the door for him when they pulled up in front of the property. William got out, pulling his ponderous mass out with both arms and a few grunts that he could not avoid given the level of exertion it took to do it. Walking up the stairs, he looked at the doorman, a small man with a thick French accent, who he knew loathed him. He never tipped him though, and made sure to constantly annoy and disgust him, so in his warped sense of fairness, they were even.

"How good it is to see you again, Monsieur Madison! You are looking very fit today!" he offered disingenuously. He followed it up with an equally outrageous flourish to drive his point home.

"Thank you, Monsieur Dubois. You are looking very happy today!" William said, walking right past him without a glance in his direction.

"It is always a pleasure Monsieur!" the doorman threw at his back with a scowl and grabbed his nose before the odor he knew would follow William made it to his nostrils.

They made their way to the elevator and got in. The attendant winced as the machinery groaned in protest and apologetically asked Mr. Jones to wait for the next one. Mr. Jones took several steps backwards and out of the elevator, a hint of relief on his face. The elevator attendant knew the relief on his face was there because he got away from the ripe, noxious stench coming from William. What Mr. Jones didn't know was the elevator attendant could hold his breath the entire trip and had done so many times. William knew it too. William always tried to get him to speak and take a breath. All in all, a lovely game of cat and mouse.

As the doors shut, Mr. Jones saw the expression on the attendant's face rapidly changing. He hadn't gotten a big enough breath and was going to be forced to breath. He almost laughed, picturing the man getting out and running for some sort of deodorizer so the other tenants would not have to be subjected to that smell. All the while there would most likely be a stop in a bathroom to throw up.

Mr. Jones had taken to filling his nostrils with Camphor each morning to hide the smell somewhat. It was taking a terrible toll on the tender skin but was completely worth it. The technique worked well for decomposing bodies too! A fact he had learned long ago. A handy fact to know in his line of work, although he was usually long gone before the body got to that state of decay. What William wasn't aware of was how many dead bodies Mr. uh, Jackson, no, Jones had smelled.

After a time the elevator bell rang announcing its return. As soon as the door opened, the attendant sprang from the elevator and retrieved a can of deodorizer which he sprayed liberally around in the elevator. Mr. Jones, uh, Jackson, got in and rode it up to the penthouse. Between the Camphor and the spray he couldn't smell a thing. Unfortunately, the deodorizer wasn't strong enough to rid the tiny space of the noxious body odor of its previous passenger. Mr. Jones smiled as the attendant pulled a hankie out of his pocket and held it over his nose and mouth as they rode up. He started gagging. Feigning concern for his fellow passenger, Mr. Jones asked if he was OK. He nodded unconvincingly.

When Mr. Jones arrived at the penthouse and went into the main hall, he was treated to one of the more disturbing sights in his lifetime, and he had witnessed some pretty disturbing sights in his day. William was swimming in the pool nude, floating, his grotesquely large body rippling out over the water like a built in flesh raft. Mr. Jones was saddened by the fact that use of the pool was now out of the question, not that he would have used it, but he lamented the fact that he now couldn't just the same.

Mr. Jones was unable to watch. He had already put up with a lot on this assignment, this he did not have to endure. He just hoped the smell would at least be reduced to a level he could tolerate. Mr. Jones made his way into the main room and took a chair there and waited making sure his back was to the pool. He was silently praying he would at least dress before calling him for some meaningless errand. He was going to take a good long vacation when this was all over. It was going to be someplace where they had lots of soap and fresh air.

William wanted nothing more than to just lay there and float for an entire day. He had been afraid to shower in jail and he knew he was extremely ripe. He could see it in everyone's reactions to his presence. He didn't really want to be a dirty man but his size made it hard to get clean. If he didn't bath every day and sometimes more than once, he got pretty ripe, pretty fast because of the constant sweating his flesh suffered from in its many deep folds. Here, he usually just jumped in the pool for a few minutes which is what he was doing now. Ah, it was good to be back.

Maxwell's room was kept off limits in the past but now he was going in there and no one was going to stop him. If they tried, he would have Mr. Jones fix it for him. William guessed correctly he was a good fixer. It was the way he looked at people as if they didn't exist on the same plane as him or more correctly, as if their existence was not of any significance. William realized that Mr. Jones looked at him quite differently than other people. If they didn't matter, he, William, was prey. It was extremely unsettling.

There were five servants here full time, a cook, a house mistress, two maids and a butler. The butler was standing near the pool waiting with a robe for him when he got out, a deeply disturbed look on his face, as usual. William smiled thinking he must have lost the coin toss, but then, none of the maids would have come near him anyway, not even the butler was that cruel.

He had no illusions he was hated here. They all knew he stole and it angered them that Maxwell forced them to put up with it all these years. William figured he better not do it now, though. At least not until it was all his.

He fought to pull his highly buoyant shape underwater for one last rinse and made his way to the edge of the pool where he was unceremoniously handed the massive robe. The butler never once looked down at him, he held it out at arms length with his head turned as far in the other direction as he could get it to go. William thought he looked like an owl it was turned so far around on his neck.

"Have some dinner made up for me, please," he ordered.

"What would you prefer?" the butler responded tonelessly.

"A whole roast chicken and fried potatoes and a bottle of white wine sounds good," he said.

"Very well," the butler said, quickly moving towards the door in an effort to keep from getting any more orders.

"Before you leave, take my clothes out for cleaning. Empty the pockets first, though," William said, before the poor man could escape. He wanted to watch him pick them up knowing how badly they smelled. The man didn't answer back but reluctantly went over and gingerly gathered up the clothes holding them as far away as he could, grimacing each time he stuck his hand into the pockets.

William finished drying and wrapped the robe around his bulk. He felt much better now. Even his normally greasy, brown hair was semi-clean. He half expected to see an oil slick on the pool and the water a nasty shade of brown.

He sat in a chair near the pool for a long time, finally able to relax after his ordeal and finalize his plan of attack. After his little ordeal in Fort Lauderdale ripping the place apart was out of the question. It begged a simple fact, though. It would be something obvious, if one knew what they were looking for. He knew what he was looking for, and where. This was Maxwell's domain and his room was his and his alone. No one ever went in there except the servants to keep it sparkling clean in case Maxwell came.

William got up and walked from room to room taking stock in anything out of the ordinary. So far he saw nothing that jumped out as changed since he was last here. He was here when he got the call to New York so it wasn't that long ago since he had been there and his memory, although he certainly never paid attention at that level of detail, didn't' show anything he could immediately say was different. He still wanted to make sure it wasn't out in the open anywhere. The penthouse was huge with 5 master bedrooms, each with its own bath.

There was a study, a formal sitting room, a massive kitchen with a breakfast nook overlooking the Mediterranean, a formal dining area and a main room with an open ceiling that had a glass rotunda style roof that let in patterned light through its stained glass windows. Two sets of winding stairs circled to main room on either side leading up to the second floor where the bedrooms were. There was one additional stairway that went to the third floor. The entire third floor belonged entirely to Maxwell. There were still two thick red theater ropes across the stairs where they began on the second level to prevent visitors, or nosey types like William, from going up to that level uninvited.

The place was beautifully appointed and constructed almost entirely out of a pure white marble. Expansive windows offered the most incredible views from almost anywhere in the place and the furniture was exceedingly opulent, with a more than just a hint of roman influence. William always expected to see Caesar himself come out of one of the rooms when he was here, which was almost always.

William was very hungry. He was planning on going up to the previously off limits spaces reserved for Maxwell and his dead wife but decided to wait. He would go right after he devoured the chicken dinner, so for now he went over and turned on the stereo, Vivaldi filled the room and he sat down to relax and catch his breath. His assistant came into the room and went to a chair in the corner and sat there, not looking at him, just sitting there and pretending he wasn't even in the room, like he always did.

Mr. Jones worked for the agency for ten years now and couldn't remember a less palatable task. Maxwell had them do many unsavory things through the years but this, thankfully his last, was the pits. He had been assigned to do things most people would have tossed their cookies just imagining, but tailing and catering to this foul creature was beyond even what he could stomach.

He loved his work and it was a shame it was over, though. He made a lot of cash and was given a lot of lateral room to accomplish what was needed. The only real rule was you had to make sure the marks would never speak. If they did, you were finished. They never did, though. They all understood the ramifications that could have. That fact was always made very clear. Leverage of loved ones tended to make business deals go a lot smoother for Maxwell. He didn't care. Maxwell had a way of getting his way, thanks to his "Special Team" but then, that was what he paid them to do.

After a job was over he simply found money deposited into several accounts whose owners existed solely on paper. He had a number of these accounts and all the credentials for each one. Any one of the accounts could support him for the rest of his life. The thing was he knew he would never quit. He liked his job. He would quit when he got that one assignment to take a long vacation, meaning your time was over. His mentor received that call. He was now living in a tropical paradise spending his remaining days soaking up sun and playing hide the salami with the local pretties he kept around the place. It was definitely a nice way to end a long life of service.

The most important trait one had to have to do this work was you had to be a psychopath. They existed outside of the real world and out of sight of the main population. Soon they would be in business for themselves. This was the end of their relationship with Maxwell but they made a pact to keep together and continue their "work" for whoever could afford them.

Working for Maxwell, their founder, had been a very good run and they would finish the job but with the death of Maxwell, they were free to move on. There was more than enough work out there for people with their talents and connections and there were plenty of Maxwell's out there willing to pay for their unique services. Besides, rumor had it that Mr. Smith had a little something special up his sleeve he was waiting to share when this was over.

Mr. Jones smiled as he watched his charge nod off listening to the soft music. Soon he would be moving on, William's need for a personal assistant would soon be at an end. He pictured the man lying there and the look of surprise that would be on his face when he finally got the inheritance due him and smiled a deep satisfying smile. Oh, he truly loved his work and he had a very sweet surprise planned for this one.

While William slept and the help was all purposefully staying as far away as possible he slipped silently and unnoticed

up to Maxwell's rooms. Just a quick check to make sure
everything was ready for his charge. He would surely make this
place the first place he searched. It was up to him to make sure
he found what he had coming to him.

William woke to the smell of the food, he didn't need to
be called, he sensed it was there and his stomach was growling in
anticipation of the meal to come. He went into the dining room
and found a large covered silver tray and several other smaller
ones at the end of the table waiting for him. There was a bottle of
water and a bottle of white wine ready as well. They may not like
him but they still had to treat him properly although he could
imagine the chef doing all sorts of nasty things to the food as he
prepared it. Yes, he could envision many ways to prepare food
that would make the man feel vindicated and make William sick
with the knowledge. But that never stopped him from eating it. A
little spit or a slimy, green bugger or two wasn't going to make
him stop eating.

The chair normally sitting at the end of the table was
sitting in the corner and a bench capable of holding him was in
its place. He plopped onto the bench unceremoniously and
voraciously began to make his way through the doomed chicken.
The butler looked on, disgust plainly evident on his face, he
filled the wine glass over and over as William ripped off pieces
of the chicken with his bare hands and shoved it along with tiny
new potatoes into his gaping maw, the juices running down his
chin and onto the robe he wore staining it. Pieces of the chicken

and chicken juice flew around the room as he devoured the bird like a starved animal.

The culinary assault continued until there was nothing left on the table to be eaten. Satisfied at least for the moment, he stood up and wiped off his face and body with the sleeves of the robe not caring how dirty he got it. Carefully, so as not to slip in the mess he left behind for someone else to clean up, he made his way out of the five foot radius around him which was covered with grease splatters, crumbs, and chunks of food from the recent carnage. They were used to this behavior and William knew how upset they would be. The thought brought a broad smile to his face and he let loose a massive belch that nearly brought part of the recently devoured chicken back up for another go around.

Without a thank you, or a word, he left the dining area continuing to belch and make other equally disgusting sounds from both ends. He walked towards the stairs and began the laborious ascent. He had to stop several times to catch his breath from the exertion. When he came to the second landing and the stairs leading to the third level he reached to remove the red theater style barrier meant to stop people from going up to the third floor.

"You are not allowed up there, Monsieur!" he heard the butler yell up at him, as expected.

He turned to correct the man and saw his assistant standing there at the man's side, lightly holding his elbow, whispering in his ear. He watched with interest and waited to see what the outcome would be. The butler was frowning and eventually he winced and pulled his arm free from the man's grasp. He walked away, muttering under his breath.

His assistant gestured for him to continue and William decided to leave it at that, rather than push the butler, his recent stint in jail still fresh in his memory. Mr. Jones was good for something other than arranging for transportation or ordering food for him after all, just as he knew he would be if this type of situation ever came up.

He continued the arduous climb and finally, stood at the forbidden door to Maxwell's private domain. After catching his breath, he grabbed the handle and opened the door. He looked back down and saw his assistant sitting back down in his chair again, an almost excited look on his normally bland face as he watched on with an uncharacteristic level of interest and look of contentment. He must have threatened the butler, and he obviously enjoyed it. William shivered at the sight. He had to admit he feared this man, and the blatant joy he got out of the interaction and certain other aspects of his work was disquieting in a way.

Beyond the door he was greeted by the sight of a spacious foyer which opened into the main bedroom at the far end. The rooms were done in red and gold and the walls and columns made of white marble. A massive covered bed fit for a king lay in the center of the grand bedroom on a marble platform. Red curtains hung around the four posters and sheer white silk netting hung all around partially distorting the bed which was piled high with pillows. Every piece of furniture was covered in red velvet. William surmised Martha didn't have a lot of say in the décor. Something this ostentatious had Maxwell and his visions of grandeur written all over it.

There were several doors off of the foyer. One he found was a library lined with walls of books on mahogany shelves. Every inch of the room was mahogany, and it had a massive desk to match. The other room was a very feminine sitting room which must have been where Martha spent a lot of her time during the infrequent visits before she passed. Off the bedroom was a dressing room which led to a walk in closet large enough to house a family and a bathroom made of a rich black and white marble complete with gold fixtures on the toilet, bidet, and bath tub, which was large enough to swim in. The walk in shower was huge, doubling as a sauna.

One of the first thoughts William had as he surveyed these rooms was how selfish it was of Maxwell not to have let him enjoy these royal surroundings all those years. Not that the guest rooms were not richly appointed, but this was over the top luxury and he should have been languishing in here long ago. Thinking back, he wondered if anyone would have really stopped him if he was insistent. He could have lived off of some of the treasures in the library for a century. A few of the paintings alone he knew were original works of the masters and would be worth millions. He could have replaced them with fakes like he did in some of the other rooms and made a fortune selling them on the black market.

The place was so large he had no idea where to start so he went back into the library to think after he locked the doors to the master suite to prevent anyone from disturbing him. Sitting at the desk he tried to picture Maxwell sitting there and planning his grand schemes. The desk had a lidded wooden case on top which he tried to open. It was locked. Just on the off chance he tried his key. No luck there and all of the other drawers were also locked. Later he would need to pry it open if he was still looking. Hopefully, that act would not end with him in some deep, dank cell afterwards.

He got up and looked around the room. There was a large globe, of course, and shelve after shelf of curios and books. There were several tiny chests and other possible locations to use his key but none of them were a match. Maxwell would have to have a globe in his study, he thought. There was a suit of armor in the corner too. He looked it over for any signs of a hidden catch. The books on the shelves were so numerous he could never go through them all without leaving them in a big pile on the floor. He wasn't going to do that for fear of another stay in the local jail, one he would be left to rot in, for sure. Nothing in the room caught his attention so he moved on to Martha's sitting room. It made no sense it would be there, if his hunch was right, but he would look anyway.

This room was the total opposite of the study and the other rooms. It was well lit and spacious with only a few carefully placed pieces of furniture making up a sitting area. There was a round table with four chairs for afternoon tea, or, a social game of bridge with a few well chosen friends. There was a large fireplace near the table and a few small statues surrounding a clock on the mantle. On one wall was a small, dainty desk with a writing pad and picture of Maxwell in his younger years standing by a large tree leaning on his cricket bat. A small box on the table had a little keyhole in it and excitedly, William tried the key in the lock. No such luck. The desk was equally unproductive.

Over by the table was a tea service and there was a bowl containing several foil wrapped chocolates. The chocolate was probably dry, but what the hell. He could try at least one piece. He could use a little sugary pick me up! Besides, he knew eating them would piss the servants off.

He unwrapped one of the pieces and popped it into his mouth. Not bad considering how old it probably was, he thought. He grabbed them all up and returned to his search. He removed the wrappers on the chocolates one by one, moving around the room as he sucked on them, tossing the wrappers on the floor.

That would piss a few of them off too, he thought happily. It wouldn't be enough to throw him in jail for, though.

As he continued to look around the room he stuck the last remaining treat into his mouth. There was obviously nothing in here either and the long day was catching up with him, not to mention the large meal he devoured before he came up here. He went towards the bedroom with the intent of putting the mammoth bed to very good use. A good night's sleep was in order. He could get up and search in the morning.

William didn't sleep as well as he wanted to. After about eight hours he woke feeling nauseous and was having trouble opening his eyes. His arms and shoulders ached and his legs were beginning to ache. The worst was the feeling that he had no control over his facial muscles. His eyelids were drooping and would not fully open.

He fell back to sleep and woke again after a few more hours, the nausea still there but less intense. He tried to get out of bed and fear gripped him as his arms and legs refused the commands he was giving them. He had managed to roll onto his back and was now unable to move and for a man his size, this was not the best position to sleep in, in fact it could be down right dangerous, especially when he was having trouble breathing already. But despite his efforts, his arms and legs were still fighting his orders to move.

If only he hadn't locked the door. No one would come in here to help him. He knew that, and in retrospect, he didn't blame them. He always took full advantage of them and treated them poorly. If he stayed in here a day or more they might come in but right now they would just sit there and sigh in relief over the fact that they didn't have to look at him or deal with him. They would not lift a finger until he finally poked his head out asking for food. He also suspected the same would be true of his trusty assistant, Mr. Jones.

He felt like vomiting and fought against it trying to roll over onto his side. The bed was very soft and he was deep in its folds. He managed to roll partially onto his side but could not get far enough to remain there and he was getting weaker by the minute. The edge of the overly wide bed seemed a mile away. If he could get to the floor and crawl to the door he might be able to yell for someone to come and help him. It didn't help that it was so late now and dark. Another problem was he wasn't able to make any noise. He didn't have the breath for it in his current predicament.

Grabbing the sheets he willed his arm to do his bidding and managed to roll a little further onto his side. He couldn't imagine what was wrong with him. He was close to vomiting but seemed not to be able to do it. If he was sick from the dinner, he needed to vomit. But he was afraid he would choke laying the way he was if he did. He had to get to the floor. Maybe then, he could yell for help.

He remembered the two vases on the stands at either side of the stairs on the top landing and thought if he could get there he could knock them over. That would get someone's attention. He had to get there though before he could do anything. Every bit of his being was revolting and he felt a strange detachment coupled with an overwhelming need to vomit.

The exertion was making it hard to breath. He lay quietly for a few minutes and again drifted into sleep. A short time later he found he let go of the sheet while he was dozing and his massive body was again on its back and this time, he couldn't get his arms to follow a single command.

His breathing labored dangerously as he lay there suffocating from his own weight and the effect of whatever was wrong. Panic was setting in but he was literally becoming paralyzed and could do nothing as he began to gasp for what little air he could get. He could not get his lungs to cooperate and knew in that moment what it must feel like to drown. What horror it must be just before you take that breath of water into your lungs. After that, you were supposed to relax and calmly, as your oxygen starved brain floated towards the waiting darkness, you would just drift off to sleep forever.

Right now he was not at that point of suffocation. He was at the all out panic point of suffocation. The sensation of wanting to breathe and not being able to took him to an even deeper level of panic but he was helpless now to do anything about it. Fear gripped him as he realized he was dying and helpless to stop it.

Finally, he did vomit, and as he choked on the partially digested dinner he had so greedily put in his stomach he mercifully passed out. His body made a few feeble attempts to keep air coming in but it was too late. He expired on Maxwell's bed in a pool of vomit consisting of poorly chewed chicken and potatoes in a savory white wine sauce laced with delicate hints chocolate.

Botulism is a very serious sickness if not treated. The bacteria secretes Botulinum toxin as it grows which has recently become a popular cosmetic, a treatment we all know as Botox. In small doses it is a wonder, but if digested in a large dose along with active spores, it is a paralytic which affects the central nervous system, especially those muscles associated with breathing. It can oft times go undiagnosed but symptoms usually start with nausea and facial muscles suffering from flaccid paralysis followed by a downward paralysis in the arms and legs and eventually, if untreated, the muscles associated with breathing. It usually takes a day or so for the symptoms to start and they are usually slow but a large dose of the toxin can bring symptoms on much more rapidly. William had ingested a rather large amount of the toxin. William had ingested a dose large enough to kill a man of his size rather rapidly, or a small elephant.

Mr. Jones woke refreshed, wondering how his charge was making out in his search. He went to the kitchen and found no sign of him there. He went outside and nothing. He looked everywhere except the third floor. He wouldn't go in there until one of the other staff members gave him a reason to.

It took nearly all day for someone to decide they needed to see what good old William was up to. The poor maid found him lying on the bed apparently having choked to death on his own vomit. She ran screaming from the room and down the stairs to look for the others.

One of Mr. Jones' other highly developed skills was not being noticed. No one saw him up in the room. They had all gone down to the lobby to wait for the police to arrive.

Mr. Jones quietly went up and using a rubber glove, picked up several empty candy wrappers. Carefully, he used the glove pulled inside out as a bag to hold the wrappers. He was well versed in handling toxins. Touching the wrappers was not a good idea. He hoped the people that handled him were careful. It would be a shame for the chef to have to explain the botulism but that was his problem, not his.

Standing out on the balcony he saw the squad car pull up and he quietly let himself out when none of them were paying attention and took the stairs down, feeling the sudden urge to avoid the elevator and front lobby. There was a service entrance out back. He had checked last night, and with the police coming in the front no one was looking in that direction as he quietly slipped out.

Mr. Jones wondered what his next assignment would be. He was very pleased with the outcome of this one. It had good entertainment value at the end. The sight of William's massive body drenched in his own vomit was actually a little exhilarating. Mr. Smith would be pleased with him. For now, he was going to visit his old mentor. He liked chasing his bevy of young servants, too and there was more than enough soap and fresh air.

The servants never even thought to mention he was even there to the police. They simply all told them what a nasty disgusting man William was and how he ate enough food the night before to feed a third world country. It served him right for being such a pig. God had finally given him what he deserved for all those years of cruelty and thievery. The world was a better place with him not in it. They just couldn't decide who was going to have to clean up the mess.

The inspector left the place in a hurry, even though he had seen a lot in his day this was enough to turn his stomach and there were underlings for this type of nasty work. The coroner wrote the cause of death on the spot. He called it an accidental death caused buy choking which was brought on by gluttony. He had no intention, unless he was forced to do it, of conducting any type of autopsy on that foul lump of flesh. The servants told him all he needed to know and the vomit and body position were enough to confirm what had taken place, in his professional opinion.

Case Closed.

Chapter Seventeen

Martin was beginning to have a change of heart. At first, all he wanted was to get away from his bitchy slut of a wife. Now he wanted her right where he could keep an eye on her. One step in front of him, first to encounter whatever trap was set, ready to absorb whatever lay in store for him. He had more than a growing suspicion Maxwell meant for them all to die and this last piece of news from Thomas was the icing on the cake. The only one that seemed to be immune was that worthless son of a bitch, Sean. The irony was that he wasn't going to give up and scurry away. He was going to find some way to win. What did it matter? Maxwell had already stripped him of everything else.

As their jet landed at LaGuardia Airport, Martin sat with a growing sense of apprehension. He was afraid to ask his so called assistant to even arrange for transportation for them, and he was starting to want the enigmatic man gone... period. When he got to Thomas' office he would see to it the man was sent packing.

Jessica was still asleep and he half wanted to just leave her here to fend for herself. So far she hadn't been any help at all but now he was afraid to make a single move without her by his side. To shield him, that is. He was going to hole up in a hotel and wait for news on Sean. Sean didn't know it yet, but he was about to have some company. As a matter of fact, he was about to have a Siamese twin for company. Maybe they could work some kind of deal. At this point, all he really wanted was to live through this.

Maxwell must be just laughing his ass off by now. Martin pictured him sitting in a nice comfy chair next to Satan while they watched on a big screen TV, each with a tall glass of iced tea, as one by one, the potential heirs had their little "accidents". A demon served as the commentator giving a wonderful blow by blow description of the events as they unfolded. It was the third quarter, the score was 5 to 1 and the home team was set to receive another one.

Oh yes, how clever he must think he is. You can't blame him really, after what they did to him while he was alive. Leave it to Maxwell to follow through after he was dead and buried on what he must have dreamed about all those lonely nights. It was the perfect crime, really. Even Marin had to give him credit. You can't hold a dead man accountable. Yes, even Martin had to give him credit. It was brilliant. But he wasn't going to lose this fight. He was still alive, and he knew how to stay that way.

Jessica was either too blind or too stupid to realize what was going on. So far she was just counting all of the deaths as unfortunate accidents that increased her chances of success. Either she really believed that, or she was not facing the truth. It occurred to Martin she could actually fully comprehend what was going on and hiding that truth from him. So be it. If she wanted to play dumb that was all the more reason to use her as a shield. He could always beat what he wanted out of her, if he chose to later on.

"Wake up! We're here," Martin said, jabbing her roughly in the ribs where he knew a bruise already existed. A really nice purple one he put there himself earlier, when she had made some unacceptable comment, or other.

Jessica woke with a start and cried out for a split second before hiding the pain from his expectant face. She looked around, her eyes still glazed and unfocused with sleep. She sat up and rubbed her eyes for a minute and yawned as if the pain didn't bother her at all.

"I'm up," she said still trying to shake off the numbness and pain.

"We are going to see that fat lawyer before we get a room so get cleaned up," he spat at her. "I want some answers."

"I have a car waiting, sir," Mr. Jones said in that flat tone he always used.

"We won't need a car or your services for now, thank you. The two of you can remain here if you like or go wherever you want to go. If we need you, I will send for you," Martin said trying to gauge his reaction. Mr. Jones indeed! Whatever, and the other one was no Mr. Brown, either.

"As you wish, we will be here waiting. Shall I get the jet ready?" Mr. Jones said, turning and gesturing to Mr. Brown.

"Yes. We may need it on short notice," Martin said heading for the door, Jessica in tow.

When they got out on the tarmac, Martin headed straight into the terminal and straight for a cab. Jessica was yelling at his back for him to slow down but he maintained his brisk pace seeming to flee through the airport. Apparently he didn't really care if she kept up or not, she thought. What a pompous ass he was. He probably didn't think she had a clue about what was going on.

Once in the cab Martin gave instructions for the cabbie to take them to the offices of Talbert, Gibbins and Talbert. As the cab made its way out of the airport and onto the streets of New York, Martin kept looking back over his shoulder to see if Mr. Jones or his unsavory associate were following. Martin more than half expected them to be there, but if they were, he never caught a glimpse of them. He was certain they had something to do with this mess.

Eventually, they found themselves at the empire state building. How quaint, they kept their offices there, Martin thought. They probably had several entire floors, if he had his guess, and most of it paid for by Maxwell. He paid the cabbie leaving him a whole thirty cent tip and got out of the cab, Jessica right behind him. The cabbie just flipped him off and squealed away calling him more than one well deserved name.

The offices were on the 18th floor with nothing listed on the 19th floor. "Gee, just two floors," Martin thought, delighting in his intuition. They got into the elevator and rode it in silence until it finally stopped. As it settled, Martin grabbed Jessica's arm, hard.

"Let me do the talking, you hear?" he said. She gritted her teeth and Martin delighted in the pain he saw on his once lovely wife's face. It was a look he had seen a million times.

"Fuck off," she spat back ripping her arm out of his grasp as the door flew open to reveal a massive receptionists desk.

Martin pushed past her and went to the seemly woman behind the desk, a false smile on his gaunt face.

"Good afternoon. We are here to see Thomas Talbot. I believe he is expecting us?" he said to the woman in his most magnanimous voice.

"And you are?" she asked, a look of total indifference on her own face.

"I am Mr. Alderson and this is my wife, Mrs. Alderson," he responded in that same calm voice, the smile growing even larger under his thin, pointed nose.

He looked at her the way one looks at an ant just before they step on it snuffing out its insignificant life. He was thinking of things he could do with her she might not like. Things he himself would thoroughly enjoy. Too bad she wasn't a little bit younger.

"One moment please, Mr. Alderson," she said averting her gaze and shivering slightly as she fought the feelings that gaze brought out of her.

She picked up the phone and spoke in a trained, hushed voice that Martin could not hear clearly, even though he was no more than three feet from her. After a few words she hung up the phone and looked up at him.

"He will receive you in the main conference room just behind me, sir," she said pointing to a massive set of double doors behind her desk, glad to be rid of him.

Martin just nodded and moved in the indicated direction without another word, dragging Jessica behind him.

They made their way into the room and stood there just inside the door. A massive round table with approximately 20 chairs around it was the centerpiece of the room. Martin didn't want to sit down, he knew this trick. He knew any seat he chose would be the wrong seat, allowing Thomas to sit as far from him as he desired. Martin was no dummy, the room was designed to intimidate and control. He would wait until Mr. Talbot seated himself before he sat down, beating him at his own game. He was determined to be in control of this little gathering.

As they stood there, Jessica turned and looked at him. "Grab me like that again and I'll kill you myself and save Maxwell the trouble," she said expecting no response whatsoever. It was her way of letting him know she knew exactly what was going on and he could drop the "I'm all that and don't forget who's in charge" bullshit.

After a few minutes, Mr. Talbot opened the door and came strolling in. The anticipation was obvious on his face. Apparently, he must have thought they found something. At least it would seem that way. Martin had no way of telling what his level of involvement was.

"Ah, I got your message. So what it is you have discovered?" he asked.

"Only that this little game is getting a little out of control," Martin spat at him stopping him in his tracks.

"Yes. It seems there has been a rash of mishaps," Mr. Talbot said quietly. "I wish I could explain it."

"Oh, I can. Maxwell is trying to kill us all and those thugs you set us up with are in on it," Martin threw back at him.

"What proof do you have? I have no idea what you are talking about. As I stated earlier, my job was simply to administer the regrettable reading of the will, which I am somewhat ashamed of having been forced to do, and to award the proceeds when it was over. Neither I, nor this firm, had anything to do with this little treasure hunt or the choice of assistants. Maxwell arranged for it all himself."

It was obvious to Martin that this was all he was going to get, true or not.

"Well I want out. I want this whole thing called off or I will go to the authorities and have this will of Maxwell's annulled," Martin said, trying to gauge what affect the words had on him.

"You can do whatever you like, sir. I have thoroughly reviewed all of the mishaps and read all the police reports, there is no evidence that will stand up in court that they were in any way planned. For all intents and purposes, they are simply a series of untimely, and more importantly, unconnected events. If you have some proof otherwise, I will be happy to look into it, otherwise there is nothing I can do. Nothing that has taken place affects the validity of the will," he said dismissively.

"Fine, have it your way, but you and I both know there is more than meets the eye going on here. Where is Sean at? I demand to know," Martin said defiantly.

"Now, there I can help you. I just received word he will arrive in Hong Kong by tomorrow morning. The captain called in his intentions a few hours ago to the port authority. I was having this watched so I would know when and where they eventually landed. Pretty slick maneuver, if you ask me. I think he did a good job of avoiding all of you. No rule against it, really. I was actually working on a dispatch to inform you of his whereabouts when you came in," he lied, smiling.

"I bet you were," Martin said, turning to leave. "Come on Jessica, let's go. I am going to Hong Kong, with or without you."

"I'll make my own arrangements from here on out, thank you. I have just about run out of patience with you. Mr. Talbot, can you have someone call me a cab and call my assistant to ready my jet for Hong Kong? Mr. Alderson forgot one important fact. We came here in my jet. His is back in Monaco where he left it. Nice seeing you again," she turned and left Martin staring at her back.

"I will take care of that right away, Mrs. Alderson!" Thomas said, trying hard to hide the smug smile on his face. Oh, he did love a good snuffing from time to time, and this was one of the best he had ever seen. Martin was out in the cold.

Chapter Eighteen

Sean stood next to Captain Spencer as he eased the Me Lady into Hong Kong harbor. The atmosphere was one of calm and experience as the ship slipped effortlessly past the other boats and ships in the busy harbor. Sean just stood there silently admiring the man's skill and obvious love for what he did.

"OK. Tell me again why I cannot dock?" the captain asked him. The tension and strain of maneuvering the massive ship in this crowded harbor, and the abrupt change in plans coming through his normally calm demeanor just a little.

"From here you are in complete control of who comes and goes or even gets near the ship. Lift the gang plank and lower it only when someone is coming or going and the only other way on the boat is to climb the hull," Sean said to him.

"Do you really think we are in that much danger?" the captain asked him.

"I'm not sure. Like I said, I don't think the Me Lady is, but I don't want to see anyone get hurt here. Is there any reason to take unnecessary chances?"

"I'll do as you wish, Sean. It just makes the task of replenishing that much more difficult for the crew," Captain Spencer said in resignation.

"Sharon and I are putting an end to this here and now, sir. I promise you that," Sean said in a determined voice.

"I never had any children of my own. I was always chasing the big blue lady and she only takes. She never gives. I think of you two as the closest thing I ever had to a family, especially Sharon," he said, a little bit of emotion escaping his normally formal demeanor.

Neither one of the two men noticed Sharon coming in. She overheard what was said.

"Well we feel the same about you. Reload my boat for me and we will get word to you," she said sliding up to him and throwing her arms around his weathered neck and kissing him soundly on the lips.

"Ah my little spring flower, my little cherry blossom. You are dear to me, like a daughter you are special," he said returning the hug with one of his own.

Sharon kissed him one more time on the cheek and pulled away, her face down to hide the tears. Sean reached out and grabbed the captain himself and hugged him. He really liked this guy, liked him a lot.

"Uh, we need to have a chat about whose boat it is later on!" he said to Sharon to break the tension.

Sharon looked around at Sean smiling then turned and looked out the window. It finally dawned on her they were anchored out and not in a slip.

"Why are we anchored out?" she asked confused. "This was not the plan."

"It was Sean's idea, miss. He thinks we are safer out here where it is more difficult to gain access to the ship." the captain remarked turning back to his helm.

"Good point!" Sharon said admiring Sean's rekindled ability to think on his feet.

"Give me about thirty minutes and I'll have Me Lil Lady in the water," The captain told them.

Sharon was digging in a bag she obviously dug out of her closet. A massive, black leather thing left over from some bygone fashion era when it was considered fashionable to carry your entire household around with you in your purse. She finally pulled out three radios and brandished them both at the men triumphantly.

"Ta Daaa!" she said smiling. Sean just looked at her with a quizzical look on his face.

"Sean! Don't you know what these are?" she said, chiding his ignorance and getting a little boost from having come up with her own good idea.

"Um, radios?" he said still not sure what the big deal was.

"Captain?" she said turning to him.

"They are security radios. There are two sets both on their own private frequency. We use them in some ports where additional security is necessary or to communicate with the crew when they are working on the deck. I was going to break them out here for the guys to carry while they patrol the decks," he said, the realization coming to him. "Good thinking, Cherry Blossom!" he said.

"Ah. I get it. What's the range on them and how do you know they are secure? What's to stop someone from listening in?" Sean asked.

"Well, the range on a good day and with a clear line of sight is about ten miles. Here maybe five. Depends on a lot of factors but still pretty handy to have if you need to call ahead or you get separated. As for who will be listening, why would they? These are registered to me! I don't even think Maxwell knew about them or any record of them exists outside the ship's records and the registration with the FAA. You would have had to dig pretty deep to trace these. You would also need some pretty sophisticated listening equipment to pick this stuff up. The frequencies are far from the normal ranges used with this stuff. Hell, Secret Service uses ones like them." The captain said smiling. He enjoyed watching the realization come over Sean's face while both he and Sharon stood grinning at him like a pair of Cheshire cats.

"Here are the ear pieces and belt holsters too!" Sharon said pulling them out of her magical, bottomless bag.

"Well, if I had my guess, these guys are no dummies and might even think that far ahead. But it sure does give us a potential advantage, doesn't it?" Sean said taking one of the radios. "Are there any more that match these three?" he asked.

"Yes. I'll get them and lock those away. The crew will use the other set. You two take these and put them on. You can talk right away. I'll chime in a little later after it is quiet enough to grab the other three and lock them up. Could be a spy on here too, you know. I trust my crew, but people will do a lot of things for money," he said feeling a bit like Sherlock Holmes and reveling in every minute of it.

"Good point!" Sharon said.

Captain Spencer helped them put them on, "spy style", as he put it, running the wires for the earpieces under their clothes and showing them how to work them.

"Now, you can talk to each other and be in constant contact even when you are pretty far apart. I bet now they even have some kind of mini Bluetooth device to get rid of the little cord running to the ear bud." He said in a knowing tone. Oh, he was having fun.

"I'll talk to Mr. Kim. If anyone knows, he does. I bet he could get us some better ones too, ones that for sure could not be compromised, except by him, that is. Wish us luck, Captain Scott Spencer. If all goes well we will be back in a day or so." Sharon said saluting before reaching up and putting her hands on his broad shoulders and giving him one last peck on the cheek.

"Oh. I like things just the way they have been for the last few weeks. Just figure out how to keep the Me Lady and come back safe to me. If you need me, you call me, and I will be there. I know if I asked them to help you, a lot of the crew would be more than eager to do it, too. We all love you, Cherry Blossom. Sean, take care of her for me," he said tearing up slightly.

"I promise," Sean said solemnly. "We won't need the radios to talk to each other, just to you. I promise she won't ever be more than two steps from my side."

He turned and went out to watch them lower the launch. Sharon remained behind a minute longer, hugging the captain and speaking to him quietly. Sean saw she was crying and decided to leave her be. She was very fond of him. Sean vowed in that moment, he was going to finish what they started and he was going to make a lot of people happy afterwards, people that had spent a lifetime suffering because they worked for the most evil man ever alive. Everyone Maxwell ever shit on, or used, or abused was going to be taken care of if he had any say in it.

Sharon and Sean had already talked about it. Every servant Maxwell or his nasty relatives had ever mistreated was going to get a cut. He knew Sharon would approve when he suggested it. Hell, a few billion and they were all very rich and could live out their days in comfort as a reward for their years of agony.

They might hang on to the estates after all. Just so all of these people always had a home, and yes, he would rebuild the Michigan place too. Katy might enjoy living there, or Ben senior. That way Sean could visit and fish whenever he wanted. They would stay in the lake house every now and then when they needed a break. That would be a nice little present for Katy for all her years of friendship and loyalty. Katy! He needed to let her know he was OK! He imagined she was worried sick by now.

As soon as the Me Lil Lady pulled up to the dock Sean and Sharon got off and made their way to the nearest pay phone. Sharon spent a good ten minutes on the phone with Mr. Kim while Sean scanned their surroundings as casually as possible. He saw no sign of a Mr. Smith or Mr. Brown or anyone who fit the profile, but that didn't keep him from feeling uneasy.

"A ride will be here in about fifteen minutes, Sean," Sharon said when she hung up the phone. "We have a safe house to stay in, a private car, and a fleet of security, all compliments of Mr. Kim. All for the right price, for him, of course," she told him, letting a little snort of disgust out.

"Good. Just don't tell me what it cost," he said, still looking around for anything out of the ordinary. "I'm sure it would make me cry."

"You will have billions soon so stop being so stingy," Sharon said trying to keep the mood light.

"Oh, yea, I forgot about that!"

"I hope you have some cash now though. This is going to cost you about three hundred thousand," She said sarcastically. "Mr. Kim doesn't come cheap. He is a friend, but that is only because I pay him well."

"I told you not to tell me, and anyway, you know I don't have that kind of cash," Sean said. "How am I going to pay that?"

"Oh. I'll lend you the money, I guess. Daddy took very good care of his little girl. But it is going to cost you plenty!" she said laughing at him.

"You really are the devil. OK. What is my penance?" he said playing along to kill the time.

"You will let me keep the baby," she said looking at him sheepishly.

Sean didn't know what to say. He just stared at her. How could she have gotten pregnant? They discussed this! He was a bit angry with her for the deception.

"It just sort of happened, Sean. I know what you must think but I didn't do it to deceive you. I know that's what you must think. I didn't think about pills when we left and went to sea. I didn't have time to think about it and then we changed course. I wasn't expecting to have sex either. How could I have known? I thought I'd be OK with the timing but... well, you were there!" she said looking at him with pleading eyes, a hint of anger bleeding through.

"Sharon. You should have told me to be careful!" he said softening. "The timing couldn't be worse. This is just terrible," he said.

"Well gee thanks, daddy. It is yours, after all. I thought you might be excited. Maybe take me in your arms and tell me how much you love me or something romantic and sentimental like that. Not chew me out for letting you ravage my body so thoroughly you left a little bundle of joy in it," she said, the anger welling higher within her at his callous reaction.

"Sharon. I love you. I am worried you could get hurt, is all. I was going to tell you I wanted a child when this was all over. I want babies with you, but this changes everything. Hell, we aren't even married!" he said shaking his head. "You are going to stay at the safe house until this is all over. I'll go it alone from here."

"Like hell I am and like hell you are! I have as much skin in this game as you do now, Mr. Ryder. You seem to forget what is at stake here for me as well. I need to follow this through now, too. I have to know the truth. Besides, I am just missing my period right now. I think I am pregnant but I am not even sure. I just didn't want to keep it from you. If I am, just late, then there is nothing to worry about. I'll be fine."

"Stop it!" Sean laughed. "You win! But only if you do something for me."

Sharon realized she was half way into a very fulfilling tirade. She began to laugh, too.

Sharon leaned back against the wall in relief, putting her hands to her face, her fragile emotions all over the place. Sean reached out and put his hand to the side of her beautiful face, slipping his fingers under her hair, cradling her head and neck. She was wearing her hair down, which she rarely did, and her beauty, as always, overwhelmed him.

"Sharon. You just promise me one thing. You will not do anything stupid and you will not take any risks with yourself, or our child, if you are indeed carrying him, her," he said softly trying to absorb this new development.

She put her hand over his and cried into it nodding.

"Sean. I'm scared. I wish we could just quit, but I don't think we will ever be free if we do. If this never ends I don't get my money, and you don't either, and those men could follow us forever. That's all I really care about. Hell with the money. I want to be free of all of this," she said breaking down into sobs. "I have a lot of money. We don't need this, but, what if we can't get away from them? I hate Maxwell. I hate him!" she yelled in a high pitched screech that reminded Sean of nails on a chalk board. He had never seen her so angry.

"I know," he said taking her in his arms and trying to comfort her. "One more thing you need to agree to do for me."

"What," Sharon said, still crying.

Sean fumbled around in his pocket for a minute as he started talking.

"Well, I found something in Maxwell's desk right after I woke up from your kidnapping and drugging me," he said teasing.

"You aren't going to hold that over my head forever, are you?"

"Maybe, a man needs some kind of an edge around an imp like you," Sean laughed.

"Well, what was it already?" Sharon asked, exasperated.

"Only this," Sean said, holding out a ring.

"I sort of stole it a few days ago. If I am right, it was Martha's ring. Angelina's was in there, too, but I didn't think it would be right to offer that one to you. I was sort of looking for the right time," he said.

"Sean, what are you saying?" Sharon asked her eyes wide and wet.

He dropped to his knee right there. It seemed appropriate, after her news, he thought.

"I want you to be my wife, Sharon. I want to marry you and spend the rest of my life with you," he said solemnly. "This isn't quite what I had in mind, but it's as good a time as any."

He held the ring up to her waiting for her to react.

Sharon started crying again. She held out her hand and nodded emphatically. "Yes," she said, a little too loudly. It was all she could muster in her current condition.

Sean slipped the ring on her finger and stood up taking her in his arms.

"No matter what happens, know that I love you, nothing can take that away from us," he said.

Just then a familiar style of black sedan appeared. Sean braced himself and stood up putting himself in front of Sharon protectively. As the car approached, he could make out a single figure in the back seat. Jessica. Well, obviously the word was out.

The car stopped a few yards from them and the back door opened. Jessica slowly and unsteadily got out looking like she had been through a war, to say the least.

"Sean. Please. I want to talk to you. Alone," she pleaded as soon as she reached them. She looked at Sharon in a way that said she wanted her to leave.

"Talk away, but Sharon, my fiancée, stays right here," Sean said to her coldly.

"Oh! Congratulations. You'll make a nice couple," she said in a strangely casual and disconnected voice, surprising them both.

"Lets the three of us take a little walk then, shall we? Far away from the car, if you don't mind," Sean said, taking both of their arms and leading them down the pier. He noticed Jessica wince at his touch.

When they got far enough away from her version of Mr. Smith to make it safe to talk, Sean stopped and turned his back to the car to hide what he said.

"Jessica. You are in danger," he began.

"That's an understatement," Jessica snorted.

"No, listen to me. Maxwell is doing all of this somehow and those 'assistants' are his tools. We could all end up dead."

Jessica began to cry then.

"Sean what is going on? I am scared to death. I don't know what to do," she said, hiding her face in her hands.

"A car is coming to pick us up. If I were you, I would get into it with us and send your assistant on some far away errand. Tell him to go to some hotel to arrange you a room or something. Get rid of him. We have contacts and a safe place to go. We can offer you protection," Sean looked at her and waited for her to respond.

Jessica's face was bruised and swollen. Martin didn't think much of her plans to leave him in New York. He wasn't accustomed to her standing up to him and took payment for his aggravation by way of a pound or two of flesh as he always did. She was wearing huge sunglasses to try and hide it. Her so called "assistant", and Martin's for that matter, just stood and watched him beat the crap out of her on the plane. It wasn't until she screamed at her assistant to get rid of him that he finally stepped in and promptly, with great gusto, literally tossed Martin from the plane to stop it. She almost screamed when she saw the strange look of excitement on her assistant's normally cryptic face. He had been truly enjoying all of it and made no attempt to hide that fact.

Jessica was tired, hungry, and scared half to death. She had no one to turn to and she needed help. Sean had never done anything to hurt her even though she was always rotten when dealing with him and here he was offering to help her. Oh, what a fool she had been. She just wanted to live and get free of this nightmare. She nodded her acquiescence as the sobs wracked her body.

Sharon was watching the car while Sean spoke with Jessica. She could just imagine the look of hatred and cunning on the man's face. Just to prove it a car rounded the building and the lights shown directly on his scowling face. The jig was up. They knew now for sure that everyone knew what was going on and that made them all very dangerous men. Sharon didn't kid herself. They knew a long time ago. This was their game and they were enjoying it immensely.

The car was a beat up old taxi. The light on top knocked precariously to one side flashed on and off as the wiring was obviously near breaking. A small, nondescript man was driving it. He pulled up and spoke in Chinese to Sharon. Sharon leaned close and spoke back to him. Good to have someone who knew Mandarin with you in Hong Kong, Sean thought.

"Get in." Sharon said rounding the car and pulling the door open on the passenger's seat next to the man.

Jessica didn't hesitate one second. She got into the backseat of the car and looked imploringly to Sean. He sighed and went over to the sedan, and knocked on the driver's window.

"We will be going out to dinner. Mrs. Alderson asked me to tell you to arrange rooms for yourself and her at a good hotel. She will call you when she requires your services later," he said with the most casual voice he could muster.

"I will be glad to drive you all, sir," the man said.

"We already called the cab and, well, he knows his way around and hopefully a good place to eat where we won't be served dog! It won't be necessary, but thank you, all the same," he said turning and walking away before the man could answer back.

He strode swiftly to the cab as if he knew the meter was already running and got in. As soon as he was in, the cab circled to go back the direction it came from and Sean watched the driver as he kept one eye on the rear view mirror. He could see in it himself and he wasn't a bit surprised to see the car follow them.

"Not to worry. I spoke to my cousin. He is the gate guard tonight. Well, to be honest, he is not really my cousin at all. I just like to say that. I know I have a sick sense of humor," the man smiled. His English was perfect. "That man is going to have a very long delay trying to leave the port. If he behaves, he may be spared the body cavity search!"

Sean laughed. "Mr. Kim, I presume?" he asked.

"If you say so, you can call me anything you want. That is, as long as you are paying me enough!" the man smiled looking at him in the mirror, making Sean laugh even harder.

"Well I must say it is an honor and a privilege to meet such a good friend of Sharon's."

"We go way back," he said smiling. "She number one customer!" Sharon reached over and hit him.

"Stop talking like that. It's demeaning," she said indignantly.

"Oh, I'm just playing. Seriously now, he will be detained for about thirty minutes. He will need to show his passport and every other document he can think of, and I wasn't kidding about the cavity search if I know my cousin! I got you all cleared earlier. We won't stop when we hit the gate up here for more than a few seconds. I was only expecting two of you though, but no matter," he said, changing from a joking little man to a very serious and obviously well educated man.

"Then what do we do?" Sean asked.

"Well. Then we take a long trip around town and maybe change vehicles a few times if I think we need to. This is my cousin's cab. I have a lot of cousins at my disposal as you will find out, and they all know how to keep their mouths shut and eyes open. If you see other cars following us they are my tails, unless I say otherwise. I assure you, we will not be followed by this or any other goon he works with. But just to be safe, they are going to sweep our backside." He paused a minute looking in the mirror again to check the car behind them.

"We need a place to stay," Sean said.

"You will be staying with my, you guessed it, cousin, in his house. It is a very comfortable house and sits well up on a hill. He employs a lot of gardeners and such, if, you get my meaning, who do not allow strangers within the compound, or even near it," he was smiling at Sean in the rear view mirror, obviously pleased with his own cleverness.

"How can we thank you, Mr. Kim?" Sean asked him in all earnest.

"Pay my considerable fees and we will call it even!" he said laughing.

"If all goes well there might be a considerable bonus to boot. That is, if you accept that type of thing. I would not want to offend my new number one friend, or bring dishonor on him," Sean said teasing the man.

"Oh, I have no time for honor, sir! I went to Harvard! Where do you think I met Sharon? I tried to get her to, well, date me. She played hard to get. You are a very lucky man, Mr. Ryder," they all laughed at that, everyone that is except Jessica who was still crying.

Sean looked over at her. "It's going to be OK, Jessica." Sean told her. He actually felt pity for her. The only malice between them was on her side as was true of the entire family.

"Sean. I don't know how to thank you," she replied in a small, tired voice.

"We will discuss that later. For now, just relax and enjoy the scenery," he said dismissing her.

"Sharon. I was wrong about you, too. I am sorry. I am not a good person," she said unable to stop herself from trying to at least show some gratitude.

"All in a days work. Just make me one promise," Sharon said not turning to look at her.

"Anything," Jessica responded immediately.

"Do what we say and let's all live to see the sunrise. The rest we can work out later," she said leaving no room for misinterpretation.

Jessica knew she had to do what was being asked of her. It was, after all, her only chance. Martin would kill her for sure next time he saw her. She was sure of it. She never stood up to him like she did in New York and he knew how to treat a lady who did. He knew all the right spots to hit and kick her. Jessica had first hand knowledge with his considerable talents in that area and a barren womb as a result, not to mention a few broken bones.

Jessica knew another fact, too. She knew this was her one chance at salvation. She was the envy of everyone she previously knew. All the glamour and money they pretended to have. The reality was they really had nothing at all. Her entire existence was a lie.

She shivered as she rode in the back of that car. The memories flooded into her mind, coursing through it like icy fire, one on top of the other in an endless procession of lies, deceit, and much, much worse. She knew what a monster Martin was, always had.

She recalled what he did to 'turn out' their daughter. He might as well have been her pimp. He raped Melissa endlessly when she was young and even made Jessica hide in the closet and watch for his own sick amusement. The first time she refused, but he "persuaded" her by beating her to within an inch of her life. She stopped arguing with him after that.

Martin was not a big man but he knew he was stronger than her and he beat her like there was no tomorrow. Enough of that and anyone would get numb. What could she do? She had no money, no name, and no hope. In return for her silence and obedience she was allowed to live like a queen when she wasn't being abused.

If only she had been strong enough to put a stop to it. Why Maxwell! Why, if you knew, didn't you do something! She hated him and she hated them all. At least Maxwell was right about one thing. These two were the only ones who had been in that room that still had souls. She could never repay them now, not ever.

She reached up and put her hand tentatively on Sharon's shoulder. The tensing from that touch told her everything she needed to know. She reviled herself, why should this kind woman be any different?

"I will do anything you ask me to. I just want to be human again," she said in a small vulnerable voice she didn't even recognize as her own.

Sharon didn't respond with words. She responded in a way she knew was much more appropriate. She nodded her head softly and reached across and placed her hand on Jessica's in a gesture of friendship and forgiveness. She wasn't ready to do much more than that right now though, but it at least left the door open for later.

Jessica sat back in the seat and relaxed somewhat. Mr. Kim had observed this entire exchange and being no fool, knew he had a lot to learn. He also knew a woman who was badly hurt when he saw one.

"Mrs. Alderson? Do you need a doctor? I can arrange for one for you all nice and quiet if you prefer, or I can take you to the hospital, if you think it is better that way," he said in a quiet and tightly controlled voice.

He didn't like men who hit women. He might be a lot of things but he was not that. He did, after all, have certain kinds of honor.

"Don't call me that. I am no longer Mrs. Alderson. I just changed my name to Long, my maiden name, and yes, I think I am going to pass out soon. Please get someone for me but I am just not sure how I will pay you. No hospital though. Martin will find me and if he does…" she let it hang there.

"No charge ma'am. If you want to pay me, give me permission to educate the man who did that to you. I haven't had a lot of fun lately and I know a few restaurants that can use some fresh meat. The tourists need to eat too, you know!" he said in the most chilling voice she remembered hearing, ever.

"Robert! That is disgusting!" Sharon said, hitting him in the arm again.

"Oh, I don't think that will be necessary, Mr. Kim. I think if things continue the way they've been going he will soon get his education anyway and I won't lift a finger to stop it from happening. But if for some reason he does make it through this alive, you can do anything you want to him. I give you my permission, and my blessing," Jessica said drifting off peacefully. For the first time in as long as she could remember, she was looking forward to tomorrow and what it might bring.

"Robert?" Sean said disbelievingly.

"Yea, pop was a Marine officer stationed in Okinawa long enough to deflower and dishonor my mother. Robert is about all he left for me besides a free trip to Harvard, which is better than a father anyway," he said trying to be humorous but unable to hide the disgust he obviously felt for the man who left his mother the minute he was transferred. He was not without feelings, just a little world wary.

"Call me Po. This is the name I choose for myself," Robert said seriously. "The women love it. They all love to say hey it's Po Kim. Ha! Get it?"

Sean burst out laughing. He liked this guy, liked him a lot.

Chapter Nineteen

Martin knew he had at least one broken rib. The goon who tossed him out of the plane was going to pay. The goon he had for a so called assistant was going to find himself a very busy man doing his bidding. It was time he put this whole thing into high gear. If he was the only one left alive, he could take all the time he needed to riddle this out. Accidents seemed to be popping up all over the place! Someone might get hurt! That applied to Sean, and that little bitch Maxwell seemed to be so fond of!

Jessica might have won this round, but it must have slipped her mind that these kinds of fights had more than one round to them. Yes Sirrreeee folks! Round two, coming up! The knock out round! The money round! Yes sir, folks, stay right here, don't leave your seats! You don't want to miss this one! Please stay seated while the delectable bathing beauties parade around the ring and the champion catches his breath. He is going to come out fighting, I promise you that, and he is going to win!

Jessica forgot where they were when she left him lying there with this goon standing above him waiting to see if he would move. Lift a finger to help him? Not a chance. But they were in New York! His goon had a flight arranged in about ten minutes even if he didn't like doing it, he had no choice.

Maxwell's jets were not the only ones around, you know. This is the one reason to keep that goon here with him. He didn't care how the man looked at him. He knew what lovely tortures ran through the asshole's mind when he looked at him. All he cared about was winning! And if it pleases you all, he was going to win and kill every son of a bitch that screwed him over, starting with that whore he put up with all these years for the sake of appearances. Soon he would no longer need her to help him cover up his little habits. He would have an eighteen billion dollar shield.

Sean would get his too. He was going to be in the ring with Martin for the next title fight. He was going to find out why you didn't mess with Martin Alderson, too!

He was certain he was at most two hours behind her. He of course had insisted on the fastest jet his goon could find. As it touched down in Hong Kong he sat looking out the window envisioning all of the wonderful things in store for his soon to be deceased wife and that weak, pitiful drunk who obviously was the key to this whole thing. He was going to find him and stick to him like glue. He was going to make him miserable. He was going to have him killed. But that would have to wait until Sean found for him what he was looking for, of course.

"Mr. Smith. Please make sure we have a car as soon as we touch down and find out where Sean Ryder and my wife are," he said not bothering to look over.

He knew the man was there, staring at him, waiting for him to make a mistake. Well, he didn't make mistakes. They were all in for a big surprise. This was what he was bred to do. Win! He was an Alderson, after all.

"I will do what I can to find them but they seem to have disappeared again. A car is waiting already. I took the liberty of arranging it before we left," the goon responded.

"Never mind about that, my good man. We both know where they are going anyway, don't we?" Martin said to let him know he was onto him.

As the plane came to a stop next to a black sedan Martin got to his feet carefully, hiding the pain. He wasn't about to give this asshole the satisfaction. He moved painfully to the exit and down the ladder and let himself into the car. Mr. Smith got into the drivers seat and the other man, obviously another member of the goon squad, got into the front passengers seat.

"You are not invited, sir," Martin said to him.

"He is our interpreter," Mr. Smith said, not turning. "I don't speak the language here so I took the liberty of arranging for him to meet us. I hope you don't mind. It should speed things up for you," he said looking at his charge in the rear view mirror.

"Whatever," Martin responded, "Take me to the estate."

"Very well," Mr. Smith responded with a slight glance at his partner.

It took about one hour to clear customs and get to the estate. Martin never once came here before. He didn't know the lay of the land and felt at a slight disadvantage.

The estate was a traditional oriental style house which sat on a small rise surrounded by beautifully manicured gardens. Surrounding it all was a massive stone wall at least ten feet high and covered in some sort of flowering foliage, quite beautiful actually, martin thought. There were several buildings all connected by a raised wooden walkway that wound through the vast landscape of trees and flowers and pools, complete with ancient Coy. There were sand gardens and other sights all exquisitely maintained, a feast for the senses, Martin thought. Maybe he would hang onto this place. Especially if it upset that whore Maxwell assigned to Sean. He might need to educate her, too! She was a beauty, that one. Yes sir, she had caught his eye many times.

The main house was a massive stone and timber structure with exaggerated overhung eaves. Any emperor would be happy to live in it. A large stone stairway led up to the doors. As he came up the stairs with goons one and two in tow, the doors opened and a slight woman stood there chattering away. Martin had no idea what she was saying but he knew she was not very happy to see them.

"Tell her who I am and tell her I will be staying in the master's quarters. Tell her to find suitable rooms for the two of you and tell her to fix me some food. Tell her that for now, I am the lord of this house and she will do as I tell her," he ordered Goon Two.

Goon Two nodded and began to speak to the woman. As far as Martin could tell, she must have been expecting visitors sooner or later because she looked at him and moved to one side when Goon Two finished speaking. The obvious look of hate on her face made Martin wish he could fire her right now. Soon she was going to find herself out on her ear when he was truly the master of this place. She would be replaced with a nice young virgin, or three, willing to do what Martin liked to do with nice young virgins.

He stood inside the door as she closed it and followed her silently through the menagerie of ancient and obviously priceless artifacts that filled every nook and cranny of the place. Yes, he could get used to this. He liked it here, and right in the heart of one of the most corrupt cities on earth, if one knew where to look, that is. Here he could live like a true king. Visions of casino's and hotels ran through his sick mind. All owned by the new king of the Alderson family, Martin Mathew Alderson. No, Emperor Alderson sounded so much better. He smiled internally to himself in a wistful, hidden dream of grandiose proportions.

The Head Mistress opened a large wooden door which was at least two inches thick and led him into the main bedroom. The richness of the place struck him like a fine wine. It was obvious Maxwell had taste, or more likely, hired someone who did. This was over the top. The bed was large enough to hold half the city and covered in rich colors of red and purple sporting hand stitched scenes of dragons and warriors battling for their liege.

A tapestry as large as the entire wall was hung behind the bed. A scene of some long forgotten battle which Martin was sure the authorities would love to know the whereabouts of. It had to be worth millions or even priceless and most likely existed only in the minds of scholars and collectors of antiquities, supposedly lost long ago, but in reality, bought in the underground world of the filthy rich.

The entire room was soft, polished wood and fine silk. A chaise here, a screen there, hiding some detail around every bend that drew the eyes and fired the imagination. What a wonderful place this was. Why hadn't he ever come here before?

Martin bowed to the woman and signaled for them all to leave him. He continued surveying the spacious rooms finding a bathroom and study appointed in equally splendid fashion and there were other smaller rooms where once he could imagine servants sitting and waiting for the emperor to call to them for whatever purpose he had. Martin would again fill those tiny rooms with his many virgins and he would teach them what it was like to serve a true master, yes indeedy! He liked it here a lot.

He was definitely going to need to arrange for a little company very, very soon. His loins were practically burning with the idea of what lay in store for him here and from what he gathered, this city could provide it all. Ah, home sweet home. Fuck the rest of the places, he might keep them but then again there was the Me Lady, his floating castle, to take him any other place he desired.

Martin took a running start and threw himself on his new bed laughing like a little boy. He was barely able to contain himself. Laying there he let his mind wander. Oh this was going to be fun. He knew it was here, whatever it was, it was here. Of that little fact he had no doubts. Why else would that poor excuse for a man, Sean, and his oriental whore, have come here in the first place?

The knock on the door woke him. He had been drifting just this side of sleep, his mind deep in the diseased places only he knew about, well, a few others knew but most of them were dead or soon to be. He yelled at the door for whoever it was to come in and the door began to open slowly.

A young man in pure white attire came in with a large wheeled cart filled with delightful smells and colors. They certainly knew how to treat a guest here. He expected to be thrown a bowl of soup for not having been specific in his ordering but this was wonderful! At least the kitchen staff's jobs were secure!

He shooed the young man out and grabbed a chair sitting near the door. Tea, dim sum, noodles and meats, vegetables, and smells so enticing one could die eating them all sat waiting to be devoured! It was all here. He filled the tea glass and poured the rice wine then dug in. After trying a little bit of everything on the table he washed it down with the wine and went back over each dish again until he was fully satisfied. Stuffed, he made his way back to the bed.

After relaxing a little Martin began to forget how angry he was. This place was just too peaceful and visually stunning to allow one to harbor ill feelings for long. This nasty business could all wait until tomorrow when he woke. If he was lucky, there was a nice young maiden willing to help him bathe in the morning. He would need to ask his new goon to find out. Then he would tend to what needed tending to.

Martin slept like he had never slept before. When he woke, it was well past ten in the morning. He made his way into the bathroom and showered. No need to rile the natives just yet by asking for company, he thought. There would be plenty of time for that later on. His little playmates would just have to wait until he finished what he had to do.

He finished washing and put the same clothes back on. He should have asked Goon One to get him something else to wear. That could be remedied later. For now, he was going to search this place from top to bottom.

When he left his rooms and made his way down the stairs he wasn't at all surprised to find goons one and two sitting there, their heads close together whispering. Martin immediately felt a chill run down his spine. Careful, old boy, these two were nothing but trouble and he knew he had to watch his back. He walked over to them and smiled as they pulled apart and looked at him expressionless.

"I need a tailor, please. I need some clothes made. Mr. whatever your name is, can you tell the chef to fix me something? I will be in the gardens waiting," he said walking past them and out the door he had come in last night.

He needed time and privacy to think. The sun was out and the gardens were beautiful but none of that mattered now. What mattered was finding Sean. He was the key. Sooner or later he would show up. Martin was certain of it. For now, though, he would search for himself. If he found anything at all he would need to be careful.

He wasn't sure how it had happened to the others but he was sure of the fact that too many coincidental mishaps seemed to be hitting the Alderson family tree since their little get together to listen to the old fart spew his vile hatred in New York. Of course, there was that little slut Sean was hiding out with, too. Who knew what she had to do with the whole thing or why she was assigned to Sean. Martin knew she had a long history with Maxwell and actually with Sean too, but he wasn't sure if she was anything more than what she appeared to be, his personal assistant. Beyond that, he knew little about her. He would need to find out more about her, though. He might need to find out first hand! She made him think very nasty thoughts when he saw her!

After he ate he was summoned to be fitted for a few new suits. The tailor was amazing. Martin knew this city was famous for its suits, but this was his first experience with having one hand made for him. In a matter of a few hours he was decked out in the best suit he ever put on his skinny little frame. He looked like a million dollars, hell a few billion actually, even if he did have to say it himself.

He tried to talk to several of the servants but it seemed that if they did speak any English they weren't going to speak it to him so he was again forced to depend on Goon Two. He set up shop in the study in his apartments and had them called in one by one for questioning. So far they seemed unable to provide him with the key, or keyhole as it were, he was searching for.

He asked them everything from who came here and how often to what was Maxwell like. There were only a few people left here who apparently had even met him before. There was an old house mistress who died some time back and the new one who met him at the door was her replacement. The other woman apparently lived here from the time she was old enough to go to work to the time she died. The ones who knew her said she was a great lady and much loved by Maxwell. This got him to thinking. He decided when all of the other possibilities were exhausted he would need to look into her too. Maybe Maxwell had some secrets here no one even knew about.

He dismissed the idea that any of the newer servants here could be of any use to him. He needed to concentrate on the long time employees so he got Number Two Goon to put a list of their employment history here together for him. He needed to concentrate on the ones who actually knew Maxwell and his daughter. He hadn't thought about that! His daughter apparently was raised here and by the dead house mistress to boot! Her room was spot number one for his search if it was still kept in any kind of semblance to what it was when she lived here. Regardless, he would be spending a significant amount of time pouring over the room even if it was changed. That was item number one on his list.

Once G2 got the list together and Martin reviewed it, he realized he hadn't considered the kitchen staff. How careless of him! It turned out the head chef was by far the oldest member of the staff here and was certainly worth interviewing. G2 had him summoned and Martin watched as he entered the room, head down, all humble and afraid. Oh, this was going to be fun, Martin thought! He loved weak humans he could bully!

"Do you speak English?" he asked the man when he sat down. The man just looked at G2 quizzically. Obviously not, Martin thought.

"Ask him to tell me about Angelina," Martin instructed Goon Two.

342

Mr. Brown translated and listened as the man began to speak. He began slowly and then opened up as the memories came to him. G2 started to translate as he spoke to him.

"He says she was a little angel, the true master of this house. He says, she loved to play in the gardens and she loved to sneak in and steal the sweets he made sure to keep for her to steal. It was a game they played. He says, she was a bright and kind child and always wanted to know things, always asking a million questions. She used to play with Meiling's daughter, a girl named Sharon, he says. He says, they were like sisters and always getting into trouble with Meiling, the old house mistress," the man sat and reminisced and G2 waited patiently for him to speak again.

So that was the tie. Maxwell had hired that little slut that was with Sean. Martin was certain now he was on the right track! Whatever he was looking for had to be here. It was all coming together into one nice little package. Oh, Maxwell. Your little game is about to be blown out of the water and not by that little prick you are so fond of either! Martin knew he was close to beating him now. Why else would Sean have come here, he reminded himself yet again?

"Ask him what Maxwell's relationship with his daughter was like and what they did together," Martin instructed.

Again G2 turned to him and asked him the question. He sat for a minute and then began to speak again.

343

"He says they were very close. After her mother died, Maxwell stayed here for many years. He says Maxwell was a good father and always kind to them all. He says Maxwell loved and treated both girls like his daughters. He says Maxwell took them many places and did many things with them. He does not think they had a special place, though. He says Maxwell liked to do many things with the two little ones."

The old chef stopped and sat there smiling, he was short a few teeth Marin noticed, and the ones he did have needed a lot of work and were not very well cared for. Obviously, Maxwell did not have a dental plan! He almost laughed at his own quick wit but held back. He was oh so close now.

"Ask him which room was the daughters," he told Mr. G Man number two.

The interpreter turned back to the man and began speaking to him again. "He wants to know which one," he said shortly after the quick response he got from the chef.

"Well Angelina, of course!" Martin said sharply, exasperated.

Mr. Brown, aka, G Man Two, turned back to the old man and began the tiring interpretation for Martin again.

"He says he will not let you see it. It is still the same as she left it. He also says it should not be disturbed out of respect for the dead. No one goes in there, ever. He says you will upset the house guardians if you go in there and they will send demons to torture you," he repeated after the man stopped talking.

Martin snorted and motioned for him to show him. He stood and pushed the man out, a little rougher than he meant to but the day long barrage of questioning was wearing thin on his nerves. The man shuffled out into the hall and pointed to a door at the end of the hallway up the stairs speaking to the interpreter.

"He says it is the second from the end but no one goes in there. It is locked," G2 told Martin.

"Call the house mistress and tell her to open it, now," he said excited. "I am the one giving the orders here now, not Maxwell. If they refuse, break the door down."

"As you wish," the man said to him turning and heading down the hall to the stairs.

Martin shooed the others away and paced nervously up and down the hall as he waited. Eventually, two figures appeared on the stairs, the old woman babbling away to G2 as they approached.

"What is she saying?" Martin demanded.

"She says the house spirits will surely punish you if you defile the little master's rooms. She says you are a bad man and should leave before you do bad things and bring bad luck to the house."

Martin saw the amusement in the man's face and he also saw G1 coming up the stairs.

"I won't need the two of you while I am in there," he said dismissively. "Just have her open the door and I'll take it from there."

The woman continued to speak in a rapid upset tone and she got more and more agitated as she approached. She was wagging her finger at Martin and he didn't need an interpreter to tell him what she was saying. She wanted him to go away and never return, and she didn't want to open the door for him, or anyone else for that matter.

"Tell her to get on with it or I will force her from the premises," he said coldly, "tell her."

"With all due respect sir," G1 began, "you don't have the authority to do that, and neither do I."

"Well thank you, Mr. Brown," he said sneering at him. "Tell her anyway."

Mr. Brown looked over at Mr. Smith and Mr. Smith nodded. He turned and spoke to the woman again, maybe a little longer than was necessary, in Martin's opinion. When he finished speaking, she broke out into laughter and she reached down on the ring and worked an old skeleton key off of it and threw it on the floor chattering away the entire time and shaking her head back and forth, turning, she started towards the stairs still laughing and talking away, shaking her head the entire time.

"What did you say to her?" Martin demanded.

"Only what you asked me too, sir," G2 two lied.

"What was she babbling and laughing about then?" he spat at the man.

"She said you are crazy and she thinks the spirits here will punish you for all eternity. She said you were not in charge of even your own mind so you cannot touch any of them. She said she will be keeping an eye on you and she will throw a celebration when the spirits punish you. It kind of just went on and on after that," he said calmly.

"Oh how sweet of her to care!" Martin said sarcastically.

Martin greedily picked up the key and turned towards the door. He stuck the key in the lock and turned it. For a room that hadn't been opened in so long, it sure did work smoothly, he thought. A good sign someone had been in here recently. It was a good sign that something wonderful was hidden in it. He just hoped it was to put what he was sure he would find in there. Of course it could have been to put another 'accident', or trap, or whatever else you wanted to call what was happening to the now nearly extinct Alderson family in there, instead but part of him knew Sean was coming too and he seemed to be blessed. If Sean was blessed than it stood to reason Martin would be safe too.

"Be cool Martin. Don't blow it now," He thought to himself.

As he went to turn the knob he motioned again for his two little helpers to go away. They both nodded and turned to leave as he entered the dark room.

"What did you really say to her?" Mr. Smith whispered when they were well out of range.

"Well, most of it was exactly what I said," he said pausing to let Mr. Smith's anticipation grow.

"Give," Mr. Smith said eager to hear the rest.

"I just added that if she would allow him to go in I would make sure the spirits were awakened and punished him and in return, she and the rest of the staff would forget they ever saw us," he told his associate.

"Well let's hope she does. She is a nice lady and we have had to be way too much in the open here. I don't like it much. Too many loose ends," he said in a low whisper.

"Relax. I told her while he was talking to her earlier that he raped Angelina when she was a child. The woman wants him dead and neither she nor the others care how it happens as long as we promise he will pay. They will all have a case of the dumb ass when the time comes, I promise you. I added a little hint that this approach would be best for everyone, if you know what I mean," he said smiling at his longtime associate.

"Well, that will have to do. I kind of like the old woman. She has a lot of character and spunk. I'd hate for anything bad to happen to her or the rest of the staff. I never did like collateral damage. It always ends up getting very ugly and spreads out like wildfire," he said cryptically.

Chapter Twenty

Jessica was finally asleep. She had a bruised spleen and two broken ribs. She had a slight concussion, but apparently she would recover. Martin obviously knew how far he could go. She had a very large number of old battle wounds on her according to the doctor who was so angry Sean was afraid he might do something stupid.

Unfortunately, they all got a glimpse at the punching bag Martin had worked out on so many times and a glimpse of her torso and the most current bruises there. These overlaid on the ones that couldn't have been more than a day or two old. Her entire midsection and more was covered in a myriad of bruises of varying colors. How she was able to move was beyond them.

Sean wanted nothing more than to go out and find Martin and put his lights out once and for all. Sharon openly wept and cradled Jessica's head in her lap as the doctor looked her over and she would not leave her. Sean and Po were ordered from the room and waited outside while they finished up.

When the doctor came out he said he wanted her in the hospital but Jessica refused. He was angry and wanted to call the authorities even though Po told him he had to keep this quiet. Po promised it would be taken care of and the doctor, who was very familiar with Po, and had fixed many things for him and his "cousins" over the years, reluctantly agreed to keep quiet. He was no idiot. He had mended a few bullet wounds and worse in his dealings with Robert Kim. He was paid handsomely and he knew the value of remaining ignorant. It was easier that way. Nice and quiet, no questions asked. He knew what Po meant when he promised it would not happen again.

He left promising to come back in the morning and check in on her. He insisted that if they thought she was in any danger they would take her to the hospital and immediately call him before he would leave. They both solemnly promised him they would watch over her and call him if there was a change and this satisfied him. Po followed the doctor down the stairs and out the door. Sean carefully opened the door and silently went back into the room. He came around the bed and put his hand lightly on Sharon's shoulder.

"Sean, how could anyone do something like this?" she said fighting the sobs so as not to wake Jessica. "Oh, poor Melissa, I don't even want to know what he did to her. He deserves to die."

"Yes, he does. But that is not for us to decide. I promise he will be brought to justice as soon as I can figure out how to do it. This didn't happen here. I am not sure what the authorities will do. We need to talk to Po and figure out what to do."

"We have to protect her, Sean. I don't care about the rest of this mess. We need to help her."

"We will. I promise. This has gone far enough," he said trying desperately to control his anger.

"Kill the bastard for me," Jessica said in a weak voice startling them both.

"Jessica. We thought you were asleep," Sharon said still holding her head in her lap.

"I was until I heard the part about he deserves to die. I think that every day but it never seems to happen," she said smiling weakly, attempting to sit up.

"Jessica. You are hurt really bad. Please just lie there," Sharon said trying to hold her down.

"I have been a lot worse than this," she said shrugging her shoulders as she sat up in obvious pain. "Let's have a little chat then I promise I will go to sleep and do whatever you want me to."

"OK. But just lie there and we will sit here with you," Sharon said still trying to hold her down.

"OK. Yea, it hurts pretty badly now that I am stiffened up. That nice doctor could have at least given me something for the pain. He poked me in all the wrong places," she said trying to be funny.

She lay back and Sharon helped fix the pillows for her. Sharon was still fighting back the tears after seeing the woman's midsection. Sean left with Robert and didn't even see the worst part. Sharon didn't think she could ever forget what she saw, and she was sure to have nightmares.

"This changes nothing do you two hear me? You need to finish this or else he'll win. I don't want anything to do with it anymore. I just want to stay alive at this point but you two deserve to beat that nasty old man, both those nasty old men for that matter!" she said trying not to laugh. It hurt too much to laugh.

"We stopped caring a long time ago," Sharon told her. "I think it is time we shared a few things with you."

Sharon looked over at Sean and he nodded his approval. Sharon was a little reluctant to go into a lot of detail. She didn't exactly trust Po any further than she could throw him and was sure he would be listening in. She also didn't have a lot of reasons to trust Jessica other than the fact that she seemed to have had a change of heart towards her and Sean, an awakening hopefully.

She kept to the simple facts that didn't give away the money or their suspicions on what Sharon's connection to this was. They did this not out of a lack of trust for Jessica, but because of a deep and unshakable feeling it was necessary for their own safety. Sean caught on just fine and helped with details he felt were safe and cut her off when he was not sure where she was going with the tale. Basically, they shared all they knew about the deaths and the connections they suspected to the assistants.

Sharon even started to share details about their trip half way around the world and she shared the fact that they were now engaged. Jessica smiled and grabbed Sharon's hand then she reached for Sean's too patting it as she listened. A content and happy look he could not ever remember seeing there, a motherly look. His heart went out to her at that moment and he understood her situation better than he wanted to. He knew he had to help her, too.

She seemed genuinely happy for them so Sharon went into great detail on the account of their rough start and short, yet torrid love affair. She even started to go into great detail on the first night they were together and the part about how close they came to making love after fishing until Sean abruptly stopped her in mid sentence. She must have forgotten he was there because she headed straight into girl talk. Sean sat there blushing while Jessica laughed at him. He realized though, that Sharon didn't have anyone to share it with and she was, after all, a woman, and a very passionate one at that. It was natural to think she wanted to share the details with another woman, but did she have to do it with him there?

"Well. I think that about does it!" he said trying to hide his discomfort.

"Sounds like you got a good one, Sharon. Hold onto him," Jessica said longingly.

"I will. I love him. I love him more than anything in the world and best of all, I know he feels the same way," she said looking at Sean and loving him all the more as he sat there just being her own personal knight in shining armor, here to save the damsel in distress.

"I don't know that feeling. I don't know anything anymore. What am I supposed to do?" Jessica said starting to sob.

"We will take care of you, money or no money. I can take care of us all with what I have," Sharon said.

"Oh, I don't want the money any more, well maybe enough to buy a hit man for my husband. He needs to pay for what he did to me and to my daughter. After that, I'll gladly go and rot in hell where I belong for letting it all happen, especially to my daughter. How can I ever make up for that?"

She began crying in earnest now. The remorse and the overwhelming circumstances of the last few weeks were taking their full toll on her emotions. Jessica stopped fighting and let it all flow out of her unimpeded.

"I should have fought him. I just let myself be drawn into his sick world because he beat me and threatened me. I just finally gave in and became a weak, hopeless creature not to mention a real bitch. I am so sorry for how I treated you all these years, Sean. You didn't deserve it. I am so sorry," she sobbed.

Sean just sat there, tears welling up in his eyes. He looked over at Sharon and saw the same sorrow there he was feeling himself. Sean was so angry now he could barely speak.

"Maxwell, you are a real son of a bitch! Why didn't you ever do anything? Were you really always that sick and that cruel and was I just that blind?" Sean asked himself.

Jessica was openly and inconsolably crying now. She buried her face in the pillow. "I let him rape her. I tried to stop him once, and he almost killed me, but after that I. I just... That is when it started to get really bad. He did things. I."

She was so lost in her anguish now she was incoherent. Sean and Sharon just sat there trying to fight the vision of her demons and losing the battle with their own tears. Jessica kept it up for several minutes. She kept blaming herself and she started to sink deeper into her own depression. Sean began to fear for her health.

"Stop it," Sean said angrily. "We all make mistakes and we don't have to pay for them forever. If anyone knows that, it's me. Sharon taught me that, and now I am going to teach it to you. Let's call ourselves the three musketeers for now. Is everyone OK with that?" he said looking at the two of them in turn.

Sharon just nodded her head vigorously and Jessica just sobbed and squeezed his hand. He took it for a yes.

Jessica felt a little bit better already. If only Sean was right. If only there was salvation for her. She would do anything for that. She would die for that.

Mr. Robert Po Kim opened the door and stood just on the other side.

"I think it is time you gave me a clue on what the hell is going on here, Sharon. What the hell am I getting myself into?" he asked.

"Well I see you are still as thorough as ever, Po. You heard most of it so I guess we might as well fill you in on the rest," Sharon said in a stern voice. "If you want that you need to tell me we are alone and not being monitored by one of your cousins."

"Um, I'll be right back," Po said, leaving the room.

Sharon looked at Sean who was staring at her quizzically.

"What? I never said I trusted him completely, just that he was very good at being bad," she said in defense of herself.

Sean just shook his head and smiled. "We need all the allies we can get. I bet Po comes in real handy before this is all over."

A few minutes later Po returned with a mischievous look on his face. "Ok we can speak freely now," he said.

"I bet. Well we may need the tapes I bet you are making for later, my dear friend," she said smirking at him.

"I turned it all off and asked my cousin to make sure we had privacy! What?" he said in mock defense.

"Never mind that, I guess it doesn't matter now," Sean said, "we need all the help we can get and if you play nice, Po, we will make you a very nice offer."

"How nice?" he asked greedily.

"How does ten million dollars worth of nice sound to you?" Sean said. "If that works for you guys, that is."

"That works for me, maybe a little more if you are really helpful. The rest we split," Sharon returned, "All for one and one for all."

"That should be enough to buy a hit man for Martin." Jessica laughed. "I will leave the rest to the two of you in my will."

"Oh. Miss Long, it was, right? That little chore I do for free. That I do for all of mankind," Po said in a quiet, reflective, infinitely serious tone.

"You have my blessing. But so far the others have died in some pretty nasty situations and maybe, unless you tell me you are very creative, we should wait just a while to see what happens," she said.

"You could remember me in your will though, too!" Po said smiling.

"OK. It's time to put all of the cards on the table. Sharon?" Sean looked to her, leaving the final decision in her hands.

Sharon was very nervous. She was afraid, in fact. She trusted Po about only as far as she was able to control him and now they were bringing him in, full speed ahead. What choice did they have really? They needed help and he was the only one they had. Money he understood, this was enough, she thought, to regain control of him and his army of cousins. If all went well, his thugs would turn out to be better than Maxwell's. It was, after all, his home turf. She just hoped that was enough.

"Look at the bright side. If we are right, two of us are not the targets anyway," Sean said looking at Jessica. "She is though."

"The funny thing about targets, Mr. Ryder is that you can't hit what you can't see," Po said deviously. "Miss Long is now under my personal protection. She is invisible."

Po looked down at her not in pity but in a strangely protective way. He was no saint, but he was not a monster either. He was a monster killer though, when he had to be, and he was soon to be hot on the trail of one named Martin.

"Thank you. Mr. Kim. You are a true gentleman and if I were younger and not so beat up I think I would like you. You honor me as I have never been honored before. I am forever in debt to you, even now." Jessica said.

No one thought of the old Jessica, the one that tried to get Sean to compromise himself. This Jessica was the one that had been trapped for many long years in a life none of them could even comprehend. This Jessica was the one both Sharon and Sean decided they liked.

Mr. Kim bowed deeply to the lady. "You are welcome in my house as long as you wish to stay," he said sincerely.

"OK. Stop it or I'll start to cry again," Sharon said. It was already too late.

Sean saved them from any more embarrassment and began the tale start to finish with no details left out. Sharon added details when she thought he missed something and between them both, they learned that each one had ideas percolating they had not yet revealed to one another. When they finished, they sat there and looked at the stunned audience.

"Well dip me in Tempura batter and deep fry me," Po said finally.

Po had a way of defusing situations they all appreciated at that moment. Everyone laughed, Jessica too, although the pain the act brought on was plainly visible, it didn't stop the hysterical laughter she no longer held back. It was like a tonic to her and seemed to ease her pain.

"Wow. And all I did was act as Martin's punching bag! You have been a couple of busy bees. Now I understand why Maxwell had you two around," Jessica said approvingly.

"Harvard educated ma'am," Sean said disarmingly. They all laughed.

"So, the Me Lady, that's the name of the yacht? You think it is safe there? You trust the captain?" Po asked them, his mind already scheming.

"Absolutely, it is safe. Well, safe is a relative term these days. We turned it upside down and found nothing there," Sean said.

"So here is what we do. If you are both right, and from what I have heard I think you are, we put Jessica here on board, with a few of my cousins, and we send it back out, tonight, if you can take the move, that is, Jessica. I'll get the doctor to go on board, too. He will do it for me, he owes me," he added.

"What's wrong with this place?" Sharon asked him.

"If these guys are as good as you say, I am not sure I can keep her safe. They had the license plate from the taxi and if they are any good at all, sooner or later, they will connect the dots. They are pissed off at her already and sooner or later, they are going to get another chance. If it was me, I'd be ready and no antics you tried would keep me from following you. We aren't dealing with cut rate thugs here. We are dealing with the best there is," he said earnestly.

"What if it is already compromised?" Sharon asked him.

"Leave that to me. Miss Long will have a personal escort which I will provide. I live for this shit! In about two minutes, you are going to use that radio and tell the captain to expect a visitor. Tell him nothing about the destination if there even is one. Tell him to prepare to leave port. Tell him not to let anyone on board unless they say something only you would know to him. I'll get her there safe, that I promise. One of my cousins even has a nice fast boat that will be tagging along!"

"It will be watched now. We can be certain of that," Sean said mulling over the idea. "Jessica, do you trust us? I think you need a vacation. If you don't trust us, just say so."

"You are all I have to trust, Sean. I said I would do whatever you wanted, I meant it. I trust you," she replied. Not only did she trust him, her new found respect for them both was more than she could bear. He was still sitting on the bed and she reached up through the pain and put her arms around his neck. "Forgive me."

"I already have," he said weakly, patting her back, trying not to hit one of the many bruises he saw earlier.

"What do we do?" Sharon asked.

"You sit right here and wait until I get back. You are not invited on this little trip. We need to keep your location a secret for now. You will both be getting into a car and going for a little ride to a new destination. I need time to rally a few more of my cousins together though, to get this done. We will meet up later and go to the estate from there," Po said. He shouted something in Chinese and a woman came into the room almost instantly.

"Po!" Sharon said accusingly.

"Sorry!" He returned shyly. "She is my number one cousin and she will be with Jessica day and night. That is why she was out there. I already told her she was not to let her out of earshot. Can I help it if she overheard us a little?" he said in a disarming tone laced with sarcasm.

Sharon was up on her feet and had her arms crossed. "I think I am going to regret this."

"For ten million dollars, you just need to sit back and enjoy the ride, beautiful," Po responded as confident as ever.

"Just understand that comes with the completion of the task. No tickey, no washey!" Sharon said mocking his earlier display.

"Sharon! Don't do that! It's degrading!" Po said in mock dismay. "You said so yourself!"

Sean liked his style and just started to laugh. Oh, Sharon had absolutely met her match here. He was actually having fun, in a scary kind of way. He stopped laughing, almost, when Sharon glared at him.

Chapter Twenty-One

The room was nearly pitch-black when Martin stepped in. The thick shades were drawn and only a few dim beams of light, which made their way in through the occasional crack at the edges of the windows, illuminated it. Martin searched for a switch and eventually found it and flipped it up. A small lamp on a dainty white table near the door burst to life shedding enough light to make out the general layout of the room.

"Why hadn't they added a damn ceiling light?" Martin complained out load to himself.

It was obvious the room had been uninhabited for many years. The original fixtures, lights, and furniture still where they must have been when the former occupant lived here now sat silently covered in silk cloths and a fine layer of dust. The silence was palpable, and Martin actually felt a slight chill run down his spine at the memory of the old woman and her house spirit mumbo jumbo.

Martin wasn't a superstitious man but he wasn't a fate tempter either. He would search the room thoroughly but he wasn't about to offend any spirits in this foreign land. The spirit he was really afraid of offending was the old lady who might call the authorities on him and get him thrown in the darkest hole they could find for a very, very, long time.

He circled the room carefully looking for more lights to turn on. At the same time he began to open the shades and let what was left of the sunlight stream into the silent memorial of the dead girl he saw before him. His movements were slow and methodical. He was afraid of something much more sinister than a spirit. He was afraid of the fact that anytime one of his now deceased relatives got too close to something related to Maxwell or his daughter, they got dead, real dead, and real permanent. He had no intention of joining them.

As the shades were pulled back and the few lights in the room were turned on, the overall theme of the room began to be revealed. It was post little girl to teenage girl. This room was home to someone who spent their entire young life right here, and there were items of obvious emotional importance from each and every stage of her life up until she left this place. Even as a college student she must have returned here for summers and took down one item of importance and replaced it with the newest rage in her life, slowly setting aside her childhood to become the woman she was, but desperately trying to hang on the those other, more innocent memories. The thought of it began to have its usual affect on him. He was becoming aroused.

Along one wall were a number of teddy bears and other dolls. All dressed up and carefully set in their specific place of honor. Alongside of the dolls were games and other things a little girl might find important. Martin had a good idea what little girls liked. He spent a lifetime studying them. That was how he controlled them and fed his perversion.

This little girl could have easily been enslaved, he thought, in his sick mind. A candy treat here and a dolly there from that nice man, Uncle Martin. Once there was a little trust established they would begin to play a few secret games. Yes indeedy. Martin knew how to do it. Children actually loved secrets and games are wonderful ways to introduce secrets to them. Works every time! Once they know a secret and they keep it just once, the blackmail part they didn't expect comes.

"Oh, don't make Uncle Martin tell your secret to mommy and daddy. You will get into a lot of trouble. You don't want to be punished, do you? Now let's keep our secrets to ourselves and no one will be angry or mad and you won't get punished," he would whisper over and over, each time adding a new little secret they would need to keep until they no longer had an escape.

Oh, he was a seriously sick man. He knew it and made no effort to hide that fact, or change. There was no god other than himself, so one should do what made one happy and to hell with the ones who aren't brave enough, or smart enough, to look out for number one. No one but him knew the truth of how many times he had done it, or to whom.

Not even that bitch he called a wife knew about them all, even though he had found the secret to keeping her quiet, too.

She just needed to be knocked around and then made an unwilling accomplice and she was powerless to stand in his way. Just like them. But what he did to her fed the other demon within him. That one needed blood to survive and she was an excellent, if unwilling, supplier. His secrets were safe with her as long as he had control of her.

He reminded himself he needed to fix that little control problem he was experiencing right away where she was concerned. Yes, that was priority number two. Right after he got his hands on Maxwell's fortune, he would get her back. Death was too kind for her. He wanted to use her up and break her back down again, and again, and again like he had so many other times when she tried to escape. Oh, that was definitely Martin's idea of a good time.

He snapped himself out of his reverie and the near orgasmic episode it was bringing on as he thought about the pleasures that awaited him as one of the richest men in the world, and tried to focus on the task at hand. The menagerie he was in was profoundly affecting his ability to think. He was, after all, one of, no, the most prolific pedophile in existence. If mankind knew of his existence, it would shatter heir weak minds.

The room was done in mostly pinks, reds, and whites. The bed was a four poster job covered in an intricate floral pattern of roses and twisting stems with matching dressers, armoire and a mirrored boutique complete with lights. Martin found himself sitting at the boutique trying to picture the little girl and what connection he could muster to lead him to the waiting prize he sought.

He opened each of the drawers finding an endless array of girl's essentials. Make-up, combs, and brushes lay in abundance along with lipsticks and cosmetics all carefully arranged and undisturbed all these long years. He found things there, just as on the shelves, that one would associate with girls of different ages. Flavored lipsticks and balms gave way to more brash and bold colors a young woman would prefer as she blossomed towards womanhood.

The one thing he didn't find was a box he could put his key into to unlock the future for Martin Alderson. He stood and moved to the identically designed armoire and rummaged through it for anything unusual. He was beginning to get agitated and the mental state he was in from being so close to the possessions of a young woman wasn't helping matters, at all. The armoire was filled with sweaters and other articles of clothing, and his state of agitation was reaching monumental proportions. He could not help himself as he fingered and fondled all of her possessions, imagining what she would look like wearing them.

Hang in there! He thought to himself. Later tonight he would be making a trip to some seedy hotel and arranging for an equally seedy rendezvous with the youngest blossom he could find someone who understood him to arrange for him. His mind whirled and twisted down the paths true human beings found absolutely monstrous and deplorable, but not him! Oh no. Martin found those paths exhilarating! Profoundly exquisite and downright satisfying, in every sick, perverted way a man who devoted himself to the forbidden and unforgivable pleasures would. But right now, he just needed to work extra hard, and to remind himself of the need to prevail and remain focused.

His mind had forgotten all about the other "issues" his adversaries had suffered and he struggled just to maintain his focus on the task at hand. His hands were shaking and he reminded himself he had a weak heart and the excitement could trigger an episode if he were not careful. He didn't have his nitro pills with him, so that would not end well. This served to sober him a little and he moved on to the dresser.

The middle top drawer had the usual jumble of things one might find. He rummaged through watches with broken bands she kept intending to fix without ever actually doing it. There were broaches and other little girl keepsakes. Nothing here, he mused.

On the side drawer he found socks and below that undershirts. His urges were again beginning to get the best of him, and he battled with his desire to touch and relieve the intense erection he had been trying to get control of ever since he came into the room. He knew he was losing the battle, and just in case he might need to do something to relieve himself so he could focus, he went over and locked the door as quietly as he could. For all he knew, someone was standing just outside and that, of course, only fed his sickness. His entire being thrived on secrecy and sickness.

He returned to the dresser and admired the beautiful wood work and artistry of it. Running his shaking hand over its delicate features and fine detail, he moved it slowly towards the opposite set of drawers imagining the delightful things he might encounter there. Slowly, oh so slowly, he opened the top drawer. Eureka! Oh this was what he was hoping to find!

Martin stood there staring into the treasure chest he had discovered. Every nerve was on fire as he shook violently. Oh, how many where there? All those wonderful dainty pairs of panties! He reached into the drawer and oh so gently touched the dead girl's unmentionables with a feeling of unbridled ecstasy. Oh, and what is this! There was a small box that appeared to be a jewelry box, or something like one, hidden beneath the layers of panties.

"Oh, Martin, You lucky son of a bitch!" he thought to himself. Could he really be that lucky? Could he have stumbled onto both of his desires all at once?

"Oh, Maxwell, how careless of you to put these two treasures together for me," he whispered to the dead man, barley able to control himself.

"If this is what I hope it is this is going to be a very productive few minutes!" he uttered, grinning at his outrageous luck, if it was, indeed, the box he needed. If not, that was OK too, because he needed a short break to fix his little problem, and this drawer held just what he needed to do it.

He moved the pairs of panties off to the side stopping to pick one up and inhale its fragrance deeply into his lungs to feed his diseased mind. He then stuffed it in his jacket pocket for later use. He carefully pulled the box out, reminding himself it could be a trap. The first sign of disappointment crossed his flushed, ruddy face when he realized the box was not locked. "Damn!" he hissed. Well it was worth looking into anyway to see what little treasure awaited him inside. Not all treasures were of the monetary type, he reminded himself.

He set the box carefully on the top of the dresser and slowly lifted the lid. Maybe he didn't need the key at all. Maybe it was just a symbol. He hoped that was not the case though. If it was it meant that he could have overlooked the treasure he searched for a thousand times. It would be just like Maxwell to do that too.

The anticipation was driving him insane but was feeding his sick pleasure to even greater heights of unchecked perversion. Ah! Yes! Not what he had hoped to find but this treasure was just as valuable to him.

"Oh Maxwell!" he said in a tiny high voice which was nearly a squeal of enjoyment. "I bet daddy didn't know about this little item!"

He pulled the picture out of the box and ran his shaking hand over the ancient photo of the dead and gone Prom Queen and her Prom King. But this was not the treasure he wanted. He was so excited his zipper was nearly ready to pop and he feared the inevitable explosion he was about to have before he could even get it out, but what the hell? At this point, he didn't really care, let it happen. He loved it when it happened.

Beneath the picture lay the true treasure. If he found nothing else, he was sure to get years of happiness from this little trinket. There, beneath the picture lay a pair of panties, complete with stains. There was only one reason to keep something like this. Oh, and of course he knew why she kept these little babies! These were what she wore to the prom, and more importantly, what she wore when she lost her virginity! They had to be! There was really no other explanation!

"Oh, would you look at this! What a lovely little deep, dark, tasty stain!" he said, barley able to breath.

He greedily reached for the panties and shoved them in his face inhaling deeply as before. As his mind whirled in ecstasy, he licked and sucked and inhaled the odors in the hope of rekindling at least a bit of her essence. In an uncontrollable haze of sick and perverted visions he exploded into his nice new suit.

His body was violently shaking and waves of dizziness washed over him as he slowly stepped backwards towards the end of the bed to lie down. He never stopped sniffing and sucking and licking and rubbing as he let himself fall onto the bed, spent from the orgasm he had experienced.

Martin was unable to move and thanking his foresight for locking the door, he lay there immersed in his vile exploration of the treasure he was holding to his face. As the stain in his nice new suit pants grew, Martin drifted off slightly into the dreams only a twisted pervert like himself could fully appreciate.

It was at least fifteen minutes or so before he regained his self control. He just lay there enveloped in his perversion, a warm sense of satisfaction filling him as he continued to fondle and inhale the disgusting treat he had laid claim to. Martin had never in his life felt so much satisfaction. He knew deep down it was the thought of what his actions would do to that old buzzard if he knew about it. He planned many pleasures with this little treasure but soon he would need to get back to business, plus, there was cleaning up his little accident to deal with.

He slowly sat up on the edge of the bed and the dizziness hit him hard. He needed a little more time before he attempted to stand, he decided, and lay back down to continue to enjoy the olfactory and oral exploration of his treasure. He feared his heart might cause him trouble if he got up just now. His lips and face were a little numb from the contact, he presumed, and he felt like a giant head, a balloon head, floating in paradise as he tried to literally suck the juices from the treasure that his saliva was making as it mixed with the virginal stains in the panties.

As time passed he got somewhat worried, he was still dizzy and his mind was wandering aimlessly. He kept his focus on his prize but it was becoming a little difficult to hold his arm up to his face. His body seemed to either weigh a million pounds, or maybe his head was floating free of it, he wasn't sure which was the right description but it was exquisite, in its own way. He knew he was going to pass out, but he was too tired to care. The only real concern he had was that one of them would come in and find him with his treasure almost completely stuffed into his mouth as he tried to drain it of flavor. They would surely take it from him.

He drifted to sleep with his eyes still open and the panties hanging out of his mouth. What he did not know was that at that moment, Sean and Sharon were downstairs listening to the ravings of the house mistress as she complained about the strange and evil man in Angelina's room. She wanted them to make him leave. He was evil, she could tell.

Chapter Twenty-Two

With Jessica safely away at sea, Po made his way to the restaurant he sent Sharon and Sean to. He joined them in the private rooms above the place. Sean and Sharon were pacing back and forth when he walked in. With a sigh of relief they sat down with Po to decide what to do next.

It was getting dark and their sense of urgency was beginning to overwhelm them. They knew damn well that Martin was here and out at the estate by now. Martin wasn't stupid and would be tearing the place apart, not even bothering with the Me Lady at this point. He would assume they had already combed it thoroughly. They were actually counting on that in hopes Jessica would be safe there and far enough out to sea in a few hours to prevent his getting to her.

After a long discussion, they decided that all three of them would head out there. Po and Sean both tried to convince Sharon she had no business going but she would have none of it. There was no way she was going to change her mind, they both knew it but still felt obligated to try.

Po made a number of calls and set up some tails and a few escorts to meet them there to keep Maxwell's thugs that they were sure would be nearby at bay while they tried to solve the puzzle. If they found nothing, they were out of ideas. If they had misread the clues, they would need to start from scratch, and neither Sean nor Sharon thought they could deal with that prospect. They spoke of it only once and then put it out of their minds.

Po didn't bother trying to use the old taxi trick again. They piled into his Lexus and drove rather rapidly towards the estate.

"I can't stand the idea of Martin being there," Sharon said softly. "It's like the place is being defiled just by his presence, hell, just by the thought of it."

Sean was sitting in the front seat next to Po and Sharon in the back. He didn't speak but she saw his head nod slowly up and down, imperceptibly. He understood her feelings. This was her home. Several minutes later the car pulled into the drive and passed through the open gate.

"Let me do all the talking," Sharon said, mostly for Po's sake.

"As you command my lady fair. This is your show. I'm just a member of the band," he answered back in his usual light way.

Po had pulled up as close as he could to the front of the house but there were several other cars there. Surprisingly, there was no familiar black sedan. The cars that were there obviously belonged to Po's cousins or some other local, unless the Mr. Smiths and company changed their ride preferences. They got out and climbed up the stairs towards the door. Sean took

Sharon's hand and she squeezed back tight to stop it from trembling as much as she could.

"Sharon. Are you OK?" he asked her concerned.

She just nodded her head and pulled him up the stairs determined to put an end to this whole mess.

Po made it up to the top first and knocked on the massive door. They waited for what seemed an eternity for the door to open. An older woman dressed in traditional garb answered the door. Sharon bowed to her and began to speak. They exchanged words for quite some time and Sean poked Po and silently made expressions to indicate he wanted to know what they were saying.

Po moved over and whispered in his ear. "She just greeted the woman and gave her some traditional compliments and is generally working to earn her trust. The old woman asked her who she was and Sharon is telling her she grew up here and was the old head mistresses daughter," he said.

Sean waited a few more minutes and elbowed Po, whom he thought was doing a terrible job of keeping him in the loop. When Sharon stopped the old woman took up speaking in a rapid agitated voice and Sean couldn't wait any longer to know what was being said. He poked Po in the ribs hard.

"Stop it! The woman told her she was the new head woman and that there is an uninvited guest up stairs. She is very upset."

"I gathered that much," Sean said, sarcastically.

"Well then why are you asking me to translate?" Po said deviously.

"For a minute there I was really starting to like you, but I'm not so sure now," Sean said exasperated.

The old woman was beckoning them to come inside and they all complied. She was walking rapidly and talking away the entire time.

"Now what is she saying?" Sean asked. Damn! He wished he spoke some Chinese. He was going to have to get Sharon to teach him.

"She is telling Sharon how the man asked them all kinds of questions and then locked himself in the little master's room. She said no one ever went in there and she was not happy but the other one who was here earlier, told her she had to let him go in."

"Sharon," Sean cut in. "Ask her about the ones here earlier."

Sharon nodded to him and cut into the woman's continuous jabbering. Sean waited for a minute and looked back over at Po. Man, Po was really enjoying this. He was just standing there looking at him with a big grin on his face, just waiting for him to ask for a translation. Sean scowled at him and got nothing but a bigger smile. He was wondering why he thought he liked this guy earlier. He was a real smart ass, when he wanted to be.

"I'm messing with you, Sean. It is wise to keep perspective in these matters and humor brings perspective, well, something like that. Old Chinese proverb, you know!" Po said.

"Po!" Sean said a little louder than he wanted to. The old woman stopped and looked at him.

Sharon turned and stared them both down, then turned back to the woman.

"OK. She described your benefactor's associates pretty well and said they just got in their car and left a few minutes ago. Oh, and Sharon said we were both just being silly and she should ignore us." The smile on his face was just begging to be slapped off, but Sean instead just smiled back.

Again, the old woman started talking. Finally, Po translated without all the fun and games.

"She says he has been up there for about two hours and she tried the door, but he locked it from inside. She heard noises, like things being opened earlier but nothing for about an hour or so. She wants us to go in there and get him out of there."

Sharon nodded and turned to Sean. "Do we go up there or do we wait for him to come out?" she asked.

"I think we wait but then there is one thing nagging me a little."

"What is it?" Sharon asked him.

"Where did his errand boy get off too, and did she say there were two of them?" he said looking back and forth from Po to Sharon.

Before Sharon or Po had a chance to answer an elderly man in a brilliantly white smock came down the hall, apparently to see what was going on. Sharon squealed and ran to him throwing her arms around him and hugging him. A look of recognition came over his face and he laughed and pulled her to him. They began talking rapidly to each other as they stood there holding hands.

"I suppose you will want me to tell you what they are saying, too," Po said in mock resignation. "Oh very well," he stepped back just in time to miss the elbow to his ribs.

"They are talking about the little girl she was and how he missed her. She is telling him how much she has wanted to come home and see him. He is now complaining about Martin to her and telling her, yea, you guessed it, what a bad man he was and the ones with him, too." Po said adlibbing quite a bit.

Po walked over to the door and opened it. He reached out one arm and then turning back, he said something to the head woman. A few seconds later a couple of young, and rather well developed, Asian men came into the house and stood by the door.

"They are with me, cousins, you know," Po said to Sean in explanation.

"Strange, but I don't see the family resemblance, Po," Sean said mischievously. "They are all buff and fit and your just a scrawny little guy who needs a hair cut!"

"They eat a lot of fish. I am a rice man, myself. Besides, I am the brains not the brawn of this operation," Po shrugged, enjoying the fact he had a sparring partner.

"Po, I look forward to you and me going fishing, and swapping lies. I bet you are good at both," Sean said slapping him on the back.

"You can't imagine the size of the fish, no the shark, no whale, I caught just last week!" Po said warming to the idea.

Sharon motioned excitedly for Sean to some over. He made his way over trying to remember all of the proper etiquette he knew when meeting an older Chinese man. Bow deeply, no eye contact. Wasn't that right? Or, was it, you keep eye contact? He decided to take the safe route and just bow deeply and look down. As he neared the man he bowed all the way to his waist and then stood up and offered his hand. Hopefully, he got it right.

He must have done it, at least to some degree of acceptability, because the old man took his proffered hand and shook it vigorously, talking to him at the same time. Either he got it right or the man was just being nice. Sean looked over at Sharon who was watching the exchange with obvious pleasure and maybe a hint of pride.

"He says you are a very nice man and you honor him, and even though you do not remember him, he remembers you," she translated.

"I don't think I ever met him. I was only here two times, and that was years ago," Sean told her.

Sharon said something to the old man and he laughed.

"I told him you must not have gotten to eat his food because you do not remember him," she said.

"Well, come to think of it, if he would like to show off his talents I would be more than happy, and eternally grateful, to try anything he cooks. We haven't eaten all day!" Sean said smiling.

Sharon relayed the message and the head chef smiled and threw his hands up in celebration. He took Sean's hand in his and shook it again, just as enthusiastically as before. Turning back the way he came, he said something over his shoulder and disappeared.

"OK, musketeers, what do we do now?" Sharon asked turning to the two men.

"Oh, am I one now? That means I get a full cut, right?" Po said smiling at them.

"Your greed is showing, my friend," Sharon said sarcastically.

"One can only ask. No harm in that. So, the fact that you didn't say no, do I take that as a yes?" Po said raising one eye brow inquisitively.

"Po," Sharon said annoyed but amused.

"She still didn't say no. I wish she would just come out and give me an answer," Po whispered to Sean just loud enough for her to hear.

"Po!" Sharon yelled.

"You better cut it out," Sean said laughing.

"Cut what out? I something growing on me I don't know about?"

Maybe I should cut something off of you. Now there is an idea I can take hold of and run with. If you get my meaning, Sharon said in a low evil tone.

"We are going to your room first, just like we planned. We start in your room and your mothers." Sean said. "If we are right, and I still believe we are, we can leave Martin up there for a while to dig in vane and avoid a confrontation at the same time."

"Agreed," Sharon said.

"I love a good plan," Po chimed in. "What do I do, oh great and powerful wizard?" he just couldn't help but try to keep the little contest he and Sean had going alive. Who would choke who first? He knew he was a shoe in, to be choked first, that is.

"You patrol. You provide the security and watch our backs and let us know if any of the assistants show up," Sharon said, leaving no room for argument.

"Later Po, I'd keep the next words you were considering to yourself for now. Don't anger the natives," Sean laughed as he shook his head in warning.

Sharon looked disapprovingly at them both. She knew an inside joke when she heard one and was definitely not in the mood. Maybe it was a bad idea putting these two together. Po was beginning to be a bad influence on her otherwise perfect mate.

"If you insist, but I don't think that this so called plan of yours is wise. Which one of you knows anything about traps?" Po asked pointedly.

Po looked at them both in turn and then crossed his arms and tapped his foot, like a school teacher waiting for the answer that he knew was not forthcoming. Sharon shrugged in resignation. He had a point there, she had to admit and that is why he was here. He was absolutely the most qualified of the three and they should keep him close.

"Good point," Sean said before Sharon had a chance to respond.

"One other slight detail you are screwing up," Po said.

"Oh? What, pray tell might that be?" Sharon asked.

"Do you really want to leave that guy up there to come barging in on you later? I think he needs a few of my cousins with him to keep him company, not to mention keep him someplace safe," Po responded.

Chapter Twenty-Three

Tetrodox is a highly toxic substance. Voodoo experts can vouch for that, as can Japanese chefs. There are a number of sources where it can be found naturally, but the most common source of poisoning by it is from improperly prepared blowfish. A very select group of master chefs are trained and licensed in Japan to handle it, and it is usually served in the form of soup and sashimi. In Japan, it is considered a delicacy, and highly prized with a price tag to match.

Its allure for the connoisseur of foods is the potential poisoning a person risks from eating it and the mild sensations it brings on to the lips. In the world of Voodoo, it is the fact that someone who has been given just the right dose is physically paralyzed, while their sight, hearing, and other sensory functions remain intact. That is until their abdominal muscles fail, or their heart fails. You might be familiar with the term Zombie.

A properly trained chef knows what to do and how to prepare it but mistakes do happen and deaths follow. The real thrill in eating it is said to be from the intoxicating effect it has. Numbness occasionally accompanied by light headedness that can be quite thrilling if one knows the danger of ingesting it and enjoys taking risks. Unfortunately, those same desirable effects can also be the first signs of a lethal dose.

Hong Kong is a very popular tourist stop and many of the tourists don't know the difference between China and Japan so even there, you can get the dish and many of the chefs train for long periods of time and train under masters. It is a time honored system and considered an art. Others do it for the extreme profit they can demand, and don't give a damn about the potential danger, or the law.

Of course, one can always refine the poison and create a fine powder with it. Just ask someone familiar with Voodoo if you don't trust me. It only takes about 25 milligrams or so to kill an average sized man. No more than a light dusting, really. A little more just to be sure and the right medium to apply it is all you need.

A good medium might be a pair of panties worn by a diseased whore. A pair complete with stains believed to be something more than the juices of a menstruating woman with god only knows what else included in the bargain. This might be the perfect medium for someone who liked that kind of thing and thought the stains belonged to a long dead Prom Queen from the night she lost her virginity. A person could get themselves into a lot of trouble if they played with those unmentionables. Even more trouble if they did other, more perverted things with them, like put them in their mouth ingesting the fine powder on them. Let's say they decided to suck on the juices from their own saliva mixed with said fine powder sprinkled on them by someone who knew the demented habits of someone that sick.

Martin was just such a person and as a result, found himself in a pretty unpleasant predicament. He woke up to find he was unable to move. His eyes were somehow wide open, and everything seemed to work except for the dizziness from not being able to get enough oxygen. But other than that, he was A-OK!

Time seemed to be passing at a very disoriented pace as he drifted in and out of consciousness. He lay on the end of Angelina's bed with the panties still stuffed into his mouth, and although he was sure his pants were almost dry, he was also sure whoever finally found him would be able to tell there was a hard, dry semen stain there.

Jesus! What was wrong with him? Why was he unable to move?

Martin knew exactly why. He had gotten so bent out of shape, and so aroused, he forgot the cardinal rule in Maxwell's little game of death or glory. He forgot to be cautious. Now, he just lay there praying someone would finally pick the lock, or better yet, break down the damn door, and find him there, still alive and still breathing. He was breathing, wasn't he? Was he breathing? He wasn't even sure he was. It didn't feel like it but then he was having a lot of trouble concentrating.

In his sick way, he had to give credit to his thugs. They obviously had done their homework. They seemed to know exactly what would make each of them vulnerable. The only exception was Melissa. She was simply in the wrong place at the wrong time. It was quite ironic how this trap was placed, like it was there just for him, and him, alone. It has to have something to do with the panties. Oh, they were a slick bunch of devils. That was for sure.

Time was lost to him. He had no idea now how long he lay there. Finally! He heard a noise at the door and he heard voices. His mind was so out of whack he tried to convince himself he was screaming for help. But where was the noise? Please, someone, anyone! HELP!

Several figures appeared over him. The house guardian angels, he thought, and laughed to himself. Why didn't he feel his body responding to the familiar movement of laughter?

The figures stood there talking and yes! Sean! HELP ME! I take it all back, really. Just PLEASE, HELP ME!

Chapter Twenty-Four

Outside the estate, a black, but otherwise non-descript sedan pulled up to the gate. It made no attempt to pull in. The passenger's window opened just enough to let the occupants sunglasses peer out. One of Po's cousins, who had been assigned to the gate walked up to the car cautiously, one hand behind his back hovering near the gun in his waistband. If he was going to take a bullet, the creep in the dark glasses was going to get one back.

He didn't have to go all the way up. The man spoke a few short words and the car sped off. He stood there for a minute, his heart in his throat. You never knew in these situations, and Po had a bad habit of keeping his cards close to his vest, and keeping them in the dark. He smiled at his own cleverness and turned to his partner who was standing there with his hand in his jacket and shrugged. They exchanged a few words and he went to convey the message he just received to Po.

All Po told them was to keep an eye out for anything strange and especially for a black sedan. He didn't tell them it was going to leave them a message, but it wasn't his place to question Po. He did what he was told, and that was that. In payment, he and his wife and children lived quite comfortably. So relay the message he would.

Sean and Sharon were quietly discussing this latest development. The old woman had insisted they go in there and see what he was up to and they had finally given in. She would not leave them be until they did. Besides, Po was probably right even if it meant Sharon had to eat a little crow.

Martin lay there dead as a door nail. It was plainly obvious to them what had happened. They both knew he was a sick fuck, now that Jessica had shared the horrors of her and Melissa's tortured existence. But jeez! He had a big stain on his pants, and a pair of panties stuffed in his mouth. His heart must have given out, and thank the good lord for that! No more Martin. Secretly they were both glad it had happened like this. Let him rot in hell with Maxwell as company.

None of them wanted to touch him because this could just as easily, and almost more assuredly, was the work of Maxwell's little army of assassins. It was impossible to tell if he put the panties there or someone else did but if they did, there was almost a 100% chance they contained some exotic poison, or something else they should not touch. This was the gist of their current conversation.

Martin lay there wondering why no one was moving to call 911 or whatever version of it they had here.

"I am still alive here, you stupid idiots! Get me some fucking help!" he screamed.

They just continued to talk as if he said nothing and it dawned on him he could hear them but he didn't hear himself. Damn, this was not good.

The house mistress came into the room and Sharon moved as quickly as she could to try and prevent her from seeing Martin lying there, but it was too late. The woman was pointing and yelling in a high pitched voice and Sean stood there just imagining the things she was saying.

Sharon was trying to usher her and out and trying desperately to calm her, but nothing she was saying worked. She was pointing at Martin and shrieking and her distress was nearly unbearable. As if on cue, one of Po's 'relatives' came bursting into the room and went directly to his employer and whispered in his ear. Po turned from his cousin and looked at the body lying on the bed. He said something, and the man nodded and left the room. Sean was sure he saw both of them shiver.

Po stood there for a moment trying to think, and then went over to the poor woman who was still fighting Sharon and yelling. In a commanding tone, he spoke to her. The effect was swift, immediate, and profound. She bowed to him and turned and fled the room. Sharon stopped in her tracks and just stood there for a moment and then fell to her knees.

"What the hell was that all about?" Sean demanded of Po as he ran to Sharon.

"A man in a black sedan came up and he gave my guard some very distinct and specific instructions to pass on. He said, and I quote, 'Burn the man. Burn the contents of the drawer. Handle it all carefully. Make sure that is the case. We might feel threatened if you don't follow these instructions. There could be collateral damage. Do this and it all ends here' then he drove off", Po recited ominously.

"What about Jessica? She is still alive and if they follow suit, she would be on their list," Sean said.

"I am thinking that after what they watched this piece of shit do to her, she got a free pass," Po said, pointing down at Martin's still body.

Martin caught all of those words. He caught the part about Jessica being alive and well. He caught the part about it ends here, too. But what Martin especially caught, was the part about burning the body!

Martin always expected to burn in hell, if such a place actually existed, which he doubted. That was why he was able to live with himself. Enjoy the now any way you wanted, because when you died, you were just dead.

This little development wasn't quite what he had in mind, though. He always believed hell and heaven were strictly ideas for suckers who didn't have the courage to go after what they desired and needed, an empty crutch to fall back on as an excuse for their weakness. Martin decided it was time to see if god was really as merciful as he was supposed to be. Right now, all he was doing was praying for death.

"It's time for me to earn my fee," Po said. "You two get out of here, take her with you and leave this to me."

Po said something else to the Head Mistress pointing at Sharon. The woman obediently went over and helped Sean take her collapsed body from the room. Sean was just hoping that whatever killed Martin didn't get on Sharon, too. He was trying with little success to hold back his fear.

Po walked calmly over to Martin's body and stood there a moment. He then bent down and looked closely at the body. While he waited for help to come, he reached into his pocket and pulled out a pair of gloves and a baggie. Sean covered Sharon's face and watched in horror as Po put the glove on and pulled the soaking wet panties from his gaping mouth and put them in the bag.

Po looked over and saw Sean watching.

"Professional curiosity," he said casually as he carefully removed the gloves and put them in the baggie along with the panties. Sealing the baggie, he placed it carefully in his pocket.

Sean picked Sharon up and carried her from the room to avoid her watching the grizzly scene any longer. He decided he did not like Po as much as he thought he did. No, fishing with this man was definitely out of the picture.

After they all left the room, Po got down close to Martin and whispered into his ear.

"I think I have seen this before. Your eyes are not glazed over like a dead man's. You're still alive, aren't you? Well, it will be our little secret. Just so you know I'm going to have you burned alive, if you live long enough, that is, which, I truly hope to be the case. Call it a task I promised your wife I would take care of for her. No hard feelings, I hope. When I get to hell, long after you, of course, you will have to let me know if you felt it. OK? Call it, professional curiosity."

He put his face right in front of Martin's and smiled a big nasty smile. You might have easily mistook him for someone who worked for Maxwell, had you seen him in that moment. Po had no reason to hide his hatred from this guy. He preferred he was well aware it existed instead.

Sean carried Sharon down the stairs and followed the old woman who was waiting at the bottom of the stairs frantically gesturing him to follow. He was not going to argue. She led him to a series of rooms in the back and pointed to a bed for him to lay her on. He carefully lowered her down and he pointed at her belly and tried to make the woman understand Sharon was with child. The woman's eyes went wide open and she pointed at him and then pointed at her belly. Sean nodded. The woman put both of her hands to her mouth and broke out in tears.

The old woman literally pushed him from the room as she was yelling something loud enough to be heard all over the house. Sean saw a young girl come running out of an adjacent room. The two stood there talking and the old woman shut the door in Sean's face. He got the hint and turned to head back to talk with Po.

Sean walked back up the stairs and down the hall where he left Po. Po had several others there with him now and they were wrapping the body, and the other objects they had been instructed to burn, in the bed cover. They were all wearing gloves. Sean walked over to Po and tapped him on the back. Po turned and looked at him.

"What are you going to do?" Sean asked him.

"Exactly what they told us to do. It ends here. Remember? I will take that as a peace offering any day. I speak the same language," Po said in a very uncharacteristically, business-like tone.

"What about the servants?" Sean asked.

"They won't say a word. People die here all the time, Sean. People also disappear without a trace here all the time. How many people do you think knew he was here?" Po said in the same tone. "Let me do my job now, please."

"The old woman was pretty upset before you spoke to her. What did you say?" Sean asked knowing Po was getting a little annoyed by all of the questions.

"I told her that the bad spirit was exorcized and I would take it away for her if her and the others would forget it was ever here. I told her the other bad spirits that were here with him might come back if they said anything, and that would not be good for them," he said in an offhand way.

"Well it sure did calm her, it seemed like it, anyway," Sean said, recalling how agitated she was.

"Oh, she wasn't upset. She was just telling me she knew it was a demon and she was glad we killed it. She thinks I did it. She said she would not let those spirits back in here and she said that they had already forgotten they were here. She said the bad spirits told her to forget about them too and they would never come back. It wasn't them she was upset with obviously. Get it out! She kept yelling at me. That's all. As I said, let it end like the bad men suggested. You don't owe this monster a thing, Sean. None of us do. Not even a proper burial. Now, can I get this gruesome task finished, please?" Po said turning away from him, letting him know the conversation was over.

"I owe you Po," he said turning and leaving.

"Damn straight Skippy! For Jessica, this is free, but you and Sharon owe me big time!" Po said with a hint of his usual wit seeping back in.

Sean wondered how he could do this thing. True, Po was a bit of an enigma and scared Sean quite a bit, but it was obvious he was not an evil man. He just knew how to deal with evil people, and evil situations, is all. He let it drop after that. Sharon didn't need to know the details either, he decided. This was between him and Po.

Sean wanted to go and check on Sharon but when he got there the old woman met him at the door and wouldn't let him in.

The younger woman that came in earlier pushed past her and came out into the hall. She said something to the house mistress and quietly closed the door.

"She is sleeping now. She is fine. My mother said you should let her alone for now," she said in broken, but passable English.

Sean nodded. No need to agitate the woman and upset Sharon any further. But he had to know if she was OK. Seeing Martin like that had to be the worst thing she had ever seen, it was the second worst thing Sean had ever seen, the vision of his dying wife coming back to hit him dead in the stomach.

"She thinks she is pregnant. Is the baby OK?" he pleaded.

"Oh, she pregnant for sure. My mother knows these things. She says baby is OK. No demons touched it," she said with a smile on her face.

Sean let out a sigh and bowed to her and left.

He saw Po standing at the front door giving some more instructions to his crew. He waited until he was done and the men left. Po turned and went over to him, a solemn look on his face.

"It's all finished as far as Martin is concerned, Sean," he said in a tone that almost reached regret, but just could not get there. Not for Martin, it couldn't. "I hate this part of my work, but I promised his wife to see him burn too, so hey, that one is on the house, I guess."

"Well, I can't thank you enough," Sean said sincerely.

"How is Sharon?" Po asked concerned.

"Sleeping," Sean said.

"So what do we do now?"

"Well, I want to talk to the old chef. Can you translate for me?" Sean asked him.

"I am at your service!" Po responded cheerily.

"Could you please do it right?" Sean said remembering their earlier experience.

"What? I was doing it right," Po said back indignantly, or as close to it as he could muster.

They didn't have too much difficulty in finding the kitchen. The smell of food led them straight there. Sean had forgotten how hungry he was but his stomach was making sure he remembered. He just wasn't sure he could eat after what he saw upstairs.

When they entered the kitchen they saw three cooks busily working away under the watchful eye of the master chef, who saw them come in, and motioned for them to sit at an ageless table over to one side of the massive kitchen. Obviously, this was where most of the servants sat. Sean actually felt somewhat honored he would serve them here and not try and push them out to the formal dining room where most guests would be served.

"Po, tell him I need to talk to him," Sean said as they moved towards the table.

Po relayed the message and listened to the response while the chef literally forced them both into the old wooden chairs.

"He said, you can ask anything you want, to but first you have to eat something. He made you a bunch of dishes to try, not knowing what you might like," Po said, sitting in the offered chair rubbing his hands together. Apparently, his appetite was completely unaffected.

"I am not sure I can eat after seeing Martin like that," Sean said sadly.

"Oh, you will eat. He won't take no for an answer and you would offend him if you said no. Eat Sean. Besides, this is really good stuff!" Po said grabbing a set of chop sticks and stabbing a dumpling from the dish sitting on the counter.

They were poured cups of hot tea. The drink was soothing and delicious. Sean's belly growled and he decided he would most certainly be able to honor the man. The chef started by bringing bowls of hot broth and noodles and then one by one, different delicacies made their way to the table. Sean was delighted, and sampled every single dish the talented chef produced.

Sean had forgotten his manners for a minute. So intent on the food he even forgot to ask his questions.

"Po, would you tell him I would be honored if he would join us, please? Tell him I would consider it a privilege if he would sit with me, and share this wonderful food with me," Sean said.

"You learn fast, Sean!" Po said, turning to the chef and relaying the message.

The old man responded with a bow and sat down next to Sean smiling and nodding his approval. Sean reached out and took one of the delicate tea cups and poured it for the chef, bowing as best he could while sitting down. The man returned the bow and accepted the cup, sipping and smiling. They all sat there silently enjoying the dishes as they were presented.

"Thank him for the wonderful meal, please." Sean said to Po.

Po again relayed the message and the chef smiled and patted Sean on the hand speaking to him in a soft, respectful manner.

"He says you are an honorable man, and he is glad Sharon found such a good man," Po relayed.

"Ask him if Sharon's old room is still the same. Ask him, if he can show me where her old things are, and her mother's things. Tell him I am searching for something there for her," Sean said to Po.

Po began to talk to the old man and he answered right away.

"He said her room is just as it always has been. They keep it for her, in case she ever comes here. He said she used to come here more often, but not any more, and he would like to know why," Po informed Sean.

"Tell him she has been very busy, but I will make sure she comes here to see him as often as she can. See if he will take us to her room," Sean said to Po.

Po told the old man what Sean said and he stood and nodded his head, he beckoned them to follow him. They all got up and Sean and Po followed him out into the front hall and up the stairs. He stopped at the door down the long hall just past the door that was Angelina's and tried the handle. They kept Angelina's locked, but it seemed this one, they did not. Sean guessed it was because they kept it clean and ready for her at all times. She was not dead after all, and might come at any moment.

He went into the room and turned on a light switch. Unlike Angelina's room, which was basically a shrine, this one was well lit, and considerably more modern. Sean smiled to himself. Oh Sharon, he thought as he looked around. Even here, everything seemed all business and no fun. But, he realized that was only partially true. There were chests and shelves of girlie items here, too. Many of her favorite toys and dolls sat on the bed, and Sean smiled seeing little glimpses of her personality everywhere he looked.

The Chef bowed and left the room shutting the door behind him.

Chapter Twenty-Five

Martin was disoriented but still alive. He felt nothing, but knew he was in the trunk of a car, because he heard it close when they unceremoniously tossed him into it, and now he could hear the engine being shut off.

"Don't you realize I am still alive, you bozo's!" he tried to scream. "Get me the fuck out of here!"

On cue, he heard the trunk open. There were at least two of them he could tell for sure, because of the voices. In his mind he was screaming and yelling and trying to get their attention, but nothing seemed to work.

"Just at least check to see if I am alive, for the love of god!" he was yelling.

He couldn't understand what they were saying. All they did was spit out that same damn gibberish, just like the old lady. Jesus, these guys were stupid.

"Check and see if I am alive at least!"

They must have lifted him out of the trunk and tossed him on the ground. He was sure of it. God! They were dragging him across the ground, for Pete sake.

"Check me please! Hellp!" he tried screaming again.

What was the most exasperating thing of all was he could see a little, he could hear very well, hell, he could even smell, but nothing else seemed to work!

"You have to help me, please! Don't burn me alive," he tried again.

Nothing...

He heard the sound of liquid being poured onto cloth. He smelled gasoline! Oh god, no! They were going to burn him alive just like the other one said. How could they! He heard the sound of a heavy metal door opening as it screeched in protest. He sensed himself being lifted up. He heard one of them let out a slight grunt and then he smelled ashes mixed in with the overwhelming smell of gasoline as he heard and imagined his body thumped to the ground. The metal door slammed shut and he heard nothing for several minutes.

"Please, help me!"

There was a hissing noise and then the smell of natural gas and then a whoosh! All Martin did after that was wonder at how bright the light was and how bad his own flesh smelled as it burned. The last thing he remembered before he finally died was his own screaming as he was consumed by the fire on a pile of garbage in some smelly incinerator, somewhere in Hong Kong.

Chapter Twenty-Six

"Man, what a menagerie!" Po said whistling. "She sure has a lot of junk in here."

Sean laughed. Po had a point. The place was pretty well packed to the gills with junk, once you looked closely. He felt a little like he was intruding actually, and it made him think of what he had just seen in Angelina's room, and Martin in there, going through her things. Anger at the thought reared up in him, and he realized he was glad the man was dead. He had no remorse for him whatsoever and his own callousness shocked him a bit, but not for very long.

Sean walked over to the desk and sat in the chair. It wasn't a large desk, but was very nicely made of a dark wood, with a matching chair. He sat there, thinking about her, and wondered if she was OK.

"Don't you think you should have asked me for permission to go into my room?"

Sean's heart skipped a few beats and he almost let out a little yelp.

"Sharon. You scared the hell out of me!" he said. Po was laughing at him, after seeing how high he jumped.

"Is that all I get? No, are you OK? No, how are you feeling?" she asked him with fake anger in her voice he could read right through, crossing her arms in that way she had, to get the proper affect she was searching for.

Sean went to her and took her in his arms.

"The old woman told me you were pregnant," Sean said to her.

"She told me, too. She told me it is a girl and that she made sure the demons hadn't hurt her. She is a superstitious, but wise, woman," Sharon said quietly.

"I bet she is right, though!" Sean said laughing.

"I'll take some of that bet if the odds are in my favor," Po said, trying to remind them he was even there.

"So where have you looked, so far?"

Not really anywhere yet. Just looking at all the j... I mean stuff," Po said trying to cover his slip.

"Well this so called 'junk', is mine. Thank you, very much. I'm just afraid there is still some trap somewhere." Sharon said shivering, but letting him know she heard him.

"Seriously, we haven't looked anywhere yet. We just got here," Sean said.

"Yea and I doubt anyone could find anything in this mess," Po said taking another poke at her, and waiting for Sharon to respond.

"If you want to stay, you need to learn when to keep quiet, Po," Sharon said glaring at him.

Po moved away quickly and started checking the doors, a satisfied smile on his face.

Sharon went over to her desk and opened the top drawer and began to carefully dig around. She snapped her fingers and reached for the bottom drawer, while Sean and Po watched to see what she was going for. She reached in and pulled out a box of latex gloves.

"Hopefully these are still good. I bought them once when my mother was really sick and never even opened the box. Right now I would feel better if we all had something on our hands to protect us." She said ripping open the top of the box, "still good!"

She put a pair on her hands and handed the box to Sean who was standing on the other side of the desk.

"You too, Po," she said.

Po turned and held up his hands. They had gloves on them already.

"I am, as usual, many steps ahead of you, but sorry, I only had enough for me. I don't think to bring enough for everyone, like you. You humble me with your infinite wisdom and true foresight, oh wisest of us all," he said wiggling his gloved fingers at her.

Sharon just shook her head and resumed her search.

Sean walked around the room. He looked at the big cedar chest at the end of the bed and decided it was a dumb place to look. He saw an old pirate style chest and thought it had possibilities. He walked over to the dresser and surveyed the conglomeration of items sitting on top of it. Sharon sure had a lot of perfume, he thought, picking one up and sniffing gingerly at the ornate bottle.

Sharon was still digging through the desk and Po beat Sean to the pirate's chest and was slowly lifting the lid with the leg of a chair. Smart idea, Sean thought. He decided to try the top drawer of the dresser. It was a typical dresser with large drawers down the middle, and smaller ones on the sides. The lower ones ran the entire length of the dresser for holding clothes and what not.

Sean pulled on the drawer and it came grudgingly open. There was nothing but a lot of junk in it and Sean looked through it amazed at some of the things Sharon had in there.

"My goodness, Sharon, didn't you ever throw anything away?" He said jokingly.

"Get out of there Sean. That is my stuff! I am not sure I want the two of you poking around in here," she said peevishly.

"Oh, all your secrets are safe with us!" Po said mischievously.

Sean decided he didn't need to look in here and he would leave it for Sharon. She was looking a little upset and he understood how she felt. It was a bit invasive. He pushed on the drawer and it stuck a bit and then released and slammed into the dresser shaking the entire thing and making an awful clanking noise knocking over several of the dainty perfume bottles. He looked up from the drawer and saw a key hanging from a little hook on the side of the mirror. It was swinging back and forth hitting the mirror, over and over.

Tink... Tink... Tink...

What caught his attention was the size and configuration. He reached into his pocket and pulled his own almost forgotten key out and held the two together. He just sttod there and stared in disbelief at what he saw.

They Matched!

"Sharon. Over here," he said in an excited voice, holding the two up in front of his face.

"What?" she asked looking up.

"What is this key for?" he asked offhandedly trying desperately to hide his excitement.

Sharon got up and walked over to him. She took the key on its little pink string from him and looked at it for a second, recognition eventually washed over her face.

"It is for my diary! God, I forgot about that! I kept a diary when I was a little girl and this is the key to it. Why?" she asked intrigued.

"Where is your diary?" Sean asked in a strange tone.

"I kept it in the night stand over there, on the left side of the bed. You don't think..."

"I do think. Look," he handed her his key.

Sharon held the key Sean had up to hers. Po came over and looked over Sean's shoulder. Sean grabbed the key and turned to head to the nightstand.

"Stop!" Po shouted at him, "Don't touch it. Have you forgotten about all the dead people? My guess is several got the way they are because they forgot, Martin, first and foremost. Do you want to join them?"

Sean stopped in his tracks. Po walked past him and got down on his knees and began to look the Night stand over. He then got up and went back to the treasure chest and pulled out a ball of yarn that he saw earlier and broke off about ten feet of it. He went back to the night stand and tied one end around the handle and backed away.

"Go over by the door, just in case," he said, excited.

Po pulled the string half expecting it to blow up or something equally unpleasant, but nothing happened except the drawer opened. He pulled it out until it fell crashing to the floor. A pile of scarves and hair brushes and other things lay in a heap and mixed in was a small red leather book with a clasp on it.

"Right there," Sharon said pointing to it.

Sean went over to the desk and grabbed a pencil off of it. He went over to the pile and carefully pushed the book free of the other objects. It was lying face down, so he flipped it and examined it with Po right next to him. Sharon was slowly inching closer. She had the look of someone who had been asked to pet a snake, or a tiger.

"You all move back. I will be the one to try it," Sean said.

"Be my guest!" Po said and got up to stand by Sharon.

Sean carefully stuck his key in the lock and waited. Nothing happened. He then turned it slowly. Still, nothing happened. He heard the click as the hasp let go and pulled his hand back quickly. It just popped up a little, unlocked. He took the pencil and tried to lift the cover with it. It came open. He stared at the CD just inside.

Staring back at them, in bold black marker were the words, 'The Last Will & Testament of Maxwell Bartholomew Alderson.'

"Well look at that," Po said. "I guess I can count on that nice big bonus!"

"Not just yet," Sean said to him. "What if…"

He didn't get to finish the sentence, but they all knew what he was thinking.

"OK. I'll handle it," Po said in a voice that made Sean feel a little cowardly.

"I don't think we need to worry too much, if you think you can trust what they said about it being over," Sharon said.

"Well, let's leave it for Thomas to deal with!" Sean said smiling a little devious smile. "Po, you got any of those little baggies of yours left?"

"Sure do!" he answered.

Po reached down with his gloved hand and placed the CD in a bag and sealed it. Afterwards he carefully removed the glove and rolled it up in the other one placing them both in another baggie for disposal later. Seemed he was quite experienced in handling items like that.

Sharon took one last look around her room and sighed.

"I am not sure I can ever feel the same about this place, Sean," she said sadly.

"Well if you wanted to have someone take it off your hands. You did mention something about a little extra bonus?" Po said smiling.

"You can have it under one condition," Sean said looking at Sharon who nodded.

"You keep this room set aside for us and we can visit any time we want to. You also have to keep on all of the current help indefinitely," he said.

"You drive a hard bargain. I was going to give this room to my cousin! As for the help, I wouldn't dream of replacing the chef!" Po said smiling.

"You can't sell it either, unless you offer it back to us first," Sharon said getting her conditions in too.

"Done and done!" Po said before they could change their minds. He was rubbing his greedy little paws back and forth smiling almost to the point of gleeful laughter. Sean thought he looked almost like a rat. His nose was twitching above his sparse mustache and his head bobbing up and down triumphantly.

"Po, you are a one of a kind," Sean said to him.

"I know," Po said laughing.

Sharon went over and hugged him. As she pulled away she reached up and slapped him lightly on the cheek. "That's for teasing me and teaching my fiancée bad habits."

Po just laughed.

Chapter Twenty-Seven

Po drove back to his cousin's house and recalled the Me Lady. Although Sharon wanted very much to stay and visit with her old friends at the estate, she wasn't comfortable there after what they just went through. Sean didn't care one way or the other, and Po's cousin turned out to be a very gracious host. In time, Sharon would forget and he could bring her back for a happy visit.

When the Me Lady was back in port, Po took Sean and Sharon to the docks. They were still a little apprehensive about the recent events, but Po's cousins said there was no sign of Maxwell's agents to be seen. They had effectively disappeared off the face of the earth. No one was surprised.

Jessica must have been feeling better. She was on the Me Lil Lady when they got there, to greet them. She looked a hell of a lot better already. Once they were on board, the three of them found themselves sitting alone in the main cabin. At first, no one spoke. They had decided it would be better not to tell Jessica everything, unless she pressed them.

"Are you both OK?" Jessica finally asked, breaking the silence.

"We're fine. You look a little better yourself," Sean responded.

"It hurts, but I think I'll live. I just wish I knew what that meant for me right now," Jessica said sadly shaking her head.

"You're a free woman Jessica, and if it's all the same to you let's just leave it at that," Sharon said shivering a little.

Jessica sat there a moment fighting with her inner demons. "Is he?" she asked.

Both Sean and Sharon just nodded and left it there.

After a few minutes they reached the yacht. Silently, they went up the gangplank to the waiting figure at the top. As soon as they got there, Captain Spencer grabbed them both up and hugged them.

"I am so glad you are both safe. I was worried sick," he said, his voice breaking a little.

"We need to get to New York," Sean said.

"I'll get us underway right away. I already provisioned the ship and refueled. Is it safe to go out to sea with Miss Long in her condition?" he said all business.

"I'll be fine. For some reason I feel better than I have in years," Jessica said dismissing the notion.

There was no big meal that night. They all went to their quarters and slept. In the morning Sean found Sharon in the bathroom throwing up.

"Sharon! Are you OK?" he asked concerned. "Maybe this isn't such a good idea. You need a doctor!"

"Sean, leave me be," she yelled, burying her head in her arms on the toilet seat.

Sean paced outside the bathroom until she finally came out. He went to her and took her arm trying to lead her to the bed.

"Would you please stop that?" Sharon said half laughing at his overly enthusiastic attentiveness.

"You need to be in bed!" Sean said sounding like a mother hen tending her chicks.

"You are right about that. Get in bed with me," Sharon said mischievously.

"Oh I don't think so. You could get hurt. We could hurt the baby!" he accused.

"Sean. If you don't do what I said right now we are going to have a big fight," Sharon said taking her clothes off. "I want you to remember me this way before I get all fat."

Sean reluctantly obeyed and they lay together and made love slowly, gently. Afterwards, they lay there for a long time just holding each other. Sharon stroked Sean's hair as he laid there, his face nestled in her belly.

"See, I won't break, you know. You can make love to me any time you want to, at least for the time being, so take advantage while you can," Sharon teased him.

"Well, if you insist, my love. I promise I will be very gentle," Sean said dreamily.

"Not every time, I hope," Sharon said pulling his hair just hard enough for him to feel it.

Sean got up and pulled her to her feet. "Let's get cleaned up, and go see what's going on," he said.

They showered together and made their way to the main cabin where they found Jessica sitting and talking to the Captain. They seemed to be sitting quite close, Sharon noted. She was thinking Jessica and Po might be a good match, and they certainly looked at each other a little strange. But the way the Captain was looking at Jessica, she decided to forget about Po and work on these two instead. They were much closer in age anyway! There was the added benefit of the Captain's character compared to Po's to consider, as well. Jessica needed a good, gentle, loving man to show her what her life could be like, not someone like Po.

"Well, finally!" the Captain said getting up.

"Sit down, sir," Sean said. "Is there anything to eat? I'm starving. Sharon?" he said looking at her questioningly.

Sharon shook her head vigorously and winced, almost turning green at the thought. "Not yet. It's still a little too early for me."

The captain motioned to one of the servants and he left the room.

"So how long will it take to get to New York?" Sean asked.

"I will get you there in about three weeks. We will go through the Panama Canal. Once we get to the Gulf Stream we can pick up about three or four knots," he answered.

"We will go by the Baja peninsula that way, if I am not mistaken," Sean said sounding exited.

"We can, yes. Why?" the Captain asked.

"There is supposed to be some really good fishing there!" Sean said rubbing his hands together.

They all laughed.

"As long as I get to catch the first one, we can stop," Sharon said. "Otherwise I won't let you stop."

"You can't fish in your condition!" Sean said to her.

"Sean! If you don't get off the poor Sharon routine, and stop treating me like I am going to break, I'll scream," Sharon said hitting him in the ribs.

"What condition?" Captain Spencer asked.

"She is with child!" Sean said proudly.

"Cherry Blossom!" The Captain said getting up. "When did that happen?" There was a confused look on his face and they all just laughed.

Francesco saved them, just then, by coming in with a tray of goodies. He was followed by one of the crew with a pitcher of hot coffee. Unceremoniously, he plopped the tray down in front of them on the coffee table and took one of the treats himself, and began to eat it. Sean reached over and took one as did Jessica and the Captain. Sharon sat there enviously and decided her stomach was indeed ready for a little food and grabbed up a large cream puff and began tentatively licking the frosting from it.

"You're going to get really fat on me, I bet, just to spite me," Sean said teasing her.

"Really, really, fat!" She said smiling back as she slowly played with the morsel.

"What did I miss?" Francesco said confused.

"We were just discussing Sharon's condition, if you know what I mean," The Captain said cryptically, pointing at his belly.

"You are with child?" the chef said sounding offended.

Sharon put her head down and nodded.

"Well, this will not do!" the chef said. "You must marry her, at once!" he glared at Sean making him blush.

"As soon as we get back, I will. I asked her to marry me already, for gosh sake! I got on my knees, and everything!" he said defending himself.

"Well, don't make it sound like it was so hard to do, Mr. Ryder. Maybe, I should have made you beg," Sharon said peevishly.

"I have an idea!" the captain said.

"What?" Sharon asked.

"You know, that as the captain of this ship, I am able to perform marriage ceremonies. I always wanted to do that. That would be so romantic," he said wistfully.

Sharon and Sean looked at each other for a moment.

"It's perfect!" Sean said. "If you will have me that is, Sharon. You would make me the happiest man alive."

"You are like family to me. In fact, you are all the family I really have. I would be honored to be wed by you, sir," Sharon said, her eyes glazing up.

"I will be your bride's maid, if you want me," Jessica said shyly.

"Of course I do, and you will give me away!" She said to Francesco.

"Jack can be my best man," Sean said, warming to the idea.

"It's settled then. Let's get busy. We have a lot to do," the chef said getting to his feet.

"I have a request, please. I want to marry under the stars, on the front deck, by the pool, in the little garden," Sean said thoughtfully.

"Yes! It would be beautiful," Sharon agreed.

"Now Sharon, you come with me. We need to find something suitable for you to wear tonight," Jessica said. "Sean is not supposed to see you until then!"

Sharon and Jessica got up and left the room. Sean was left there alone as the Captain and the Chef left to get things ready. After sitting there in a haze for several minutes Sean got up and made his way to their stateroom to get ready. He had a long wait ahead of him, and nothing to do.

The Captain came in to see him at about two in the afternoon. He was cheerful and grabbed Sean's hand in a hearty handshake. He motioned for him to sit and Sean obediently got up and went over to where he waited by the fish tank. Sharon was locked in her old stateroom with Jessica. Jessica made one trip in to taunt him, and tell him if he so much as peeked, she would make him regret it. She also took the time to choose his clothes for him and lay them out and then, she promptly left him there alone, again. Sean was glad the Captain had come in. He was feeling a bit left out and alone.

"Sean, I wanted to tell you how happy I am. You have to make me a promise. You will never hurt her. If you do not promise me that, I won't marry the two of you," he said in a serious tone.

"I promise on my life I will honor her and protect her. I love her with all my heart," he said seriously.

"Good. That is what I wanted to hear. The ceremony will begin at nine. The stars should be in full bloom by then. It is going to be a clear, calm, beautiful night," the captain said. He got up and left the room.

Sean was dressed and ready by seven. One of the servants brought him some dinner earlier, which he picked at, but didn't really enjoy. His stomach was fluttering and he was a nervous wreck. He had Martha's wedding band in his pocket and he sat staring out at the sunset fiddling with it until finally, it was a half hour until the ceremony would begin. He could wait no longer.

He made his way to the forward deck. When he got there he was amazed at the transformation he saw before him. All accomplished in a few hours. There was an archway covered in flowers, freshly picked from the tiny greenhouse Maxwell has always insisted on having on the aft deck. The deck was lined with little Chinese lanterns and the crew was changed into their finest clothes and assembled there, still doing some last minute preparations, but for the most part, waiting for the ceremony to begin.

The first mate stood near the arch ready to stand in as the best man and one of the maids was standing in as a flower girl. Somehow they put together a buffet table with a beautiful spread and there was an ice sculpture as a centerpiece, why on earth the chef would keep an ice sculpture in the freezer was beyond Sean but it was just like him to be that prepared. The entire crew of twenty or so seemed to be present with maybe a few unfortunates monitoring the ship not here or doing other chores for the moment. Chairs for the guests were all set up and they all stood there waiting, staring back down the isle in anticipation of the bride's entry.

The captain was smiling at him as he approached the arch. He was dressed in his finest uniform, a bible in his hand. Sean fumbled in his pocket and got out the other piece of Martha's ring and gave it to Jack to hold. On the podium sat another ring. Sean wondered where it came from and deduced it must have belonged to Maxwell. He was planning on exchanging them when they could. He didn't want to wear these rings forever. It just didn't sit right with him. Sharon would have some say in the matter, but he bet she would feel the same.

Everyone took their seats talking and chattering away, obviously enjoying the break in routine. After a short while, Jessica came out and made her way down the isle in a beautiful beige colored dress. Everyone grew silent and strained to see the bride.

Francesco and Sharon finally appeared at the other end. The flower girl stepped in ahead of them as the bridal march began, strewing flower pedals for Sharon to walk on. Everything was perfect, and Sean waited for his bride to join him at his side as she gracefully made her way down the isle, all eyes upon her. Francesco was beaming at him as he stopped and placed Sharon's delicate hand in Sean's.

As Sean looked upon his bride he was overwhelmed by her sheer beauty. Her beige gown closely matched Jessica's. How they managed that he had no clue, but then, he never looked in Sharon's closet here on the boat. Sharon's gown had no shoulder and simply wrapped around her waist and chest showing just enough cleavage to be revealing yet respectable. It was floor length and as she walked her body moved in the semi-sheer material which highlighted every step outlining her perfect shape.

Somehow they had devised a veil which covered her pinned up hair and face falling about her shoulders to complete the look. Sean looked into her covered face longingly. She smiled shyly at the unspoken compliment.

There, underneath a perfect sky, filled with more stars than anyone could ever remember seeing, they held hands and made their vows. The Captain performed the ceremony flawlessly as he led them through the traditional vows. They exchanged the rings and kissed gently, as the captain stood smiling at them, several members of the crew wiping their eyes and Jessica outright crying. Finally, the captain announced them as Mr. and Mrs. Ryder and everyone applauded and threw rice as they ran down the isle way laughing.

There was dancing and celebrating and the music poured out over the open sea as the boat rocked gently on the calm waters. Sharon felt like she was living in a fairy tale world. The head chef had disappeared for several minutes returning with a beautiful two tiered wedding cake they had been busy making. Sharon and Sean made the obligatory first cut in the cake and gingerly fed it to each other kissing with frosting on their lips and large smiles on their faces.

Sharon danced with each and every one of the men and Sean danced with all of the women. Sharon could not help but notice the fact that the Captain seemed to be dominating

Jessica's time and she kept telling Sean about it. They were both becoming fond of Jessica and despite her dubious past, they wanted to help her in any way they could.

Finally they found themselves being thrust towards the 'honeymoon suite'. While the festivities were taking place, some of the crew snuck down and prepared it for them with beautiful silk sheets, trays of goodies, flowers, and a bottle of chilled champagne. Candles were placed around the cabin providing a warm glow and the door was shut behind them with a lot of cat calls and whistles from the other side.

Neither one of them said a word. Sean simply took Sharon in his arms and they stood there in a gentle embrace for a long time, Sharon resting her head on his shoulder in a vulnerable way that stole Sean's heart. Finally, Sharon pulled away and put her hand on his cheek, both of them still silent, no words were necessary. They helped each other undress and got into bed together, laying there together on the soft bed rocking gently on the open sea as man and wife. For a long time they simply held and caressed each other, neither one ever breaking the silence until finally, making love slowly and gently, they fell into a deep, satisfying sleep, wrapped in each others arms.

In the morning Sharon called the captain and informed him they would not be available all day. She also told him to have someone bring them food every six hours. They then spent the entire day just being man and wife.

On the following day they made their first appearance as man and wife and were greeted with a lot of cat calls, whistles, and knowing grins, again. They took the good humored bantering as well as could be expected. Sharon was teasing Sean and he couldn't help but blush a deep shade of red at some of the comments pointed his way.

Jessica was looking better than ever. They both noticed the occasional darkness that took her over and did their best to try and keep her from getting depressed. She had a lot of healing ahead of her and she kept insisting they didn't owe her anything. They were determined to see to it she had everything she needed and reminded her, again and again, they had agreed to split everything evenly. She would have none of it even though saying she had agreed under duress, and didn't deserve anything. In the end she made some strange remarks that the money would somehow hurt her. She genuinely didn't want it.

After a few days of badgering her to take her share she came up with an idea that no one could argue with. Instead of giving her part of the money she decided she wanted to earn it. She told them they had to employ her as the overseer of the Me Lady! Sharon smiled and gave her a knowing look as she shyly glanced in the Captain's direction. There was most definitely something going on there, she realized. They may not know it yet themselves, but Sharon hoped the woman could one day have a relationship with someone like the Captain. She needed it.

Although Sharon liked the idea, in the end they pushed Jessica into agreeing to be their partner. They intended to use the money to start a firm of their own, and Jessica was to oversee all of the properties, not just the Me Lady. They decided to keep them all for the time being, and she would see to it they were kept up and handle all of the employees while Sharon and Sean rebuilt a better Alderson Investments that would pride itself on building on new ideas rather than tearing down old ones. The concept was very different from what Maxwell's business had been and so would the name be.

They all agreed each employee who had worked all these years faithfully at the various estates would be given a very hefty bonus. The Captain also refused ownership of the Me Lady. He simply wanted to be her Captain, forever, now that they would be able to keep her. They reluctantly agreed, wanting to do much more for them all than was being allowed. But Sharon wasn't worried, the captain hadn't quite figured out yet what being intimately and emotionally involved with Jessica might mean later on. Sharon kept her plans secret, even from Sean, for now anyway.

They made their way slowly towards New York and ignored all of Thomas' requests for their arrival date and information on what they were bringing back. They didn't actually tell him they had found the will just to drive him nuts. He seemed to be getting more and more agitated at their total lack of response. They didn't have any reason to pity the man, and they all suspected he knew more than he admitted.

They fished several times and enjoyed the easy days the long ride provided. Sharon thrilled to the event each time they fished and afterwards would ravage her new husband. Sean teased her endlessly about her adrenaline laced lovemaking, complaining he was covered with bruises from her viscous attacks. He no longer worried about hurting the baby, Sharon made sure to tell him that just because she was pregnant didn't mean she was feeble. She was in excellent shape and had no issues in that area.

They thought about just staying right here and the hell with it all. It was very tempting, but Sean had a renewed desire to work, and Sharon had to admit, she missed it too. She would work right up until the child was born and then still work some. She would have Jessica to help her. The thought of letting her help raise the baby made Sean just a little apprehensive but Sharon insisted she be part of the family and she be given a second chance to get it right.

Jessica was like a doting grandmother to Sharon now. She watched over her like a hawk and Sean looked on as the two became close friends. Signs of her previous existence seemed to melt away as the days passed and she was looking forward to playing nursemaid to Sharon with an undeniable exuberance.

Finally, the trip had to come to an end and they made their entrance into the harbor of New York.

Chapter Twenty-Eight

Sean and Sharon sat in the same conference room Martin and Jessica had several weeks before, waiting. A CD in a baggie sat on the table in front of Sean. They came straight here after the Me Lady docked. Sean wanted to see just how agitated their slow boat from China trip had gotten Thomas. Hopefully, he was more than a little put out. Sean had made up his mind he didn't much care for a man who could be involved in what he had done, client or not.

When Sean called and told him what they had discovered he confirmed that it was a CD they had in fact, been searching for, and their description fit. He asked them to watch it but Sean had adamantly refused. He told him he would just have to wait until they got there. Thomas was not exactly happy with that, but there was nothing he could do.

Po contacted them every day to see where they were. He was a little put out too, by their slow trip back, but Sean and Sharon insisted he had to wait. The trip would be less stressful for Jessica and Sharon shut him up by chiding his lack of feelings towards the poor woman. Po reluctantly backed off but that was not going to stop him from nagging!

Po gave them a list of no less than ten accounts to make deposits in. Sean invited him for the trip expecting him to accept but he surprisingly declined. Apparently, Po already had a few plans of his own and said as soon as they came back to Hong Kong they had to look him up. They might be interested in investing in his plans. They made no commitments, though. Sharon cringed at the thought of what he might cook up.

Jessica was late to the meeting. The meeting was supposed to take place in about fifteen minutes. Sean and Sharon got here maybe a little earlier than they should have. They were eager to get this over with, and get on with their lives. The memory of Martin and the rest was fading fast, but the pure disgust with the entire thing was not. They wanted nothing more to do with anything Maxwell touched, except to make sure the promises they made were kept. They sat there, hand in hand, and waited.

The back door opened and Mr. Thomas Talbert came into the room with a small woman behind him. Sean almost laughed out loud. What was so funny to him was the memory of Sharon when she first got started. She was just so prim and so proper, and so obviously hungry to succeed his heart went out to her almost immediately. Sharon was staring at him and must have gotten the wrong impression because she elbowed him, hard!

Sean put his mouth close to Sharon's ear and whispered. "I was just thinking she reminded me of you. We will need a manager. Should we steal her?"

Sharon whispered back. "That better be all you were thinking. I am going to get really fat you know!"

Sean could not help it. He laughed out loud.

"Good afternoon. Mr. and Mrs. Ryder, isn't it?" Thomas asked.

"Good afternoon, Mr. Talbert," Sean answered back.

"I assume you have met the provisions of the will," he said to Sean.

"I don't know that, yet. We did find this CD. Have a look at the title, and you tell us. We haven't played it yet," Sean said.

"Well, shall we go ahead and have a look?" Thomas said gesturing to his assistant to get the CD and play it.

"Not so fast. Jessica Alderson is on her way here, too," Sharon said.

"What does she have to do with this if you found it?" Thomas asked confused.

"We invited her to this little party, and we would prefer to wait for her. She must have hit traffic. She'll be here, I'm sure," Sharon said.

"As you wish, it is, after all, your party," Thomas said.

"I heard Mr. Alderson, Martin Alderson, is missing," Thomas said casually.

"Yes. I hope he is OK, wherever he is," Sean replied sadly.

Just then the door leading from the front lobby opened and Jessica came in. To Thomas and his assistant, she probably looked fine, but Sean and Sharon saw how she moved. She was still in a lot of pain. Even the weeks at sea had not fully removed her years of abuse. She would need a lot of care and a lot of time to fully heal.

"Sorry. I got stuck in traffic," she said apologetically.

"No worries. We waited," Sharon answered getting up to hug her while Thomas watched surprised.

Jessica sat next to Sharon and Sean reached out and slid the CD across the table to Thomas' assistant.

"Let's see what this says."

She took the CD and went over to a cabinet and opened it. It was full of all types of audio-visual equipment. She stuck it into a slot in one of the components, fooled around for a minute or two and grabbed a remote. She went over and hit the lights and then made her way back to the seat next to Thomas. As she sat down she stuck the remote out and hit the "play" button.

The big screen TV flared to life and there was Maxwell in all his sick and demented glory. The irony was he didn't have a look of triumph on his face, like they expected. He looked old, tired, and defeated. They all waited as he sat and stared at them from the grave.

"Well. If someone is watching this they just won about eighteen billion dollars, or they think they did, anyway. The truth is I am not proud of what I did. I am not happy or vindicated or anything else that you might be thinking. I am just tired and ready to end this.

If my associates did what they were paid to do, Sean and Sharon are here. I was very clever, you have to admit. Sean? Did you solve the riddle first? I am guessing, yes. I am also guessing you went first to the place where I died while the monsters that I put up with all these years destroyed your favorite place. It served its purpose. I forced Sharon to kidnap you. Sharon that two hundred and fifty million is yours now. Thomas, see to that immediately.

Understand I had my reasons. I hope this little adventure served the real purpose I had in mind. Just a simple thing really;

A. Save Sean.

B. Get Sean and Sharon together and at least give Mother Nature a chance to see to what I wanted for you both. I know I deserve hell. I was destined to go there before any of this so I figured, why not go out in real style?

I know you both well enough to know that you figured out my little secret about Sharon. If you hadn't, you would have never found the CD. You were right, Sharon is my daughter. Sharon, my dear, sweet Sharon. To you, I leave everything. It is all yours except a few small details Thomas has to finish up with.

Sean. Don't hate me too much. If you love Sharon, don't hold my actions against her. I was not a stupid man or a blind man. I know you loved and honored my daughter. I know my Sharon loves you, too. It was always very obvious to me that you two had more feelings for each other than you let on. I am also proud that neither of you ever hurt my Angelina. Be at peace, both of you.

Sharon. Your mother got me through the worst time of my miserable live. She forced me to go on and we fell in love. She brought me back from the dead, just as I pray you forced Sean to remember he is alive. She made me promise I wouldn't tell you. She made me promise I would never tell until we were both dead. Maybe the method I chose to reveal this little truth was a bit extreme, but it served two purposes as I am sure you have figured out by now.

Sean, the Michigan estate is yours and I bequeath you one billion dollars, just in case I was wrong about you and Sharon. Angelina's spirit lives there and it should be honored. Everything else is Sharon's.

I thank you for this last chance to speak from hell. Maybe god will forgive me someday."

The screen went black.

"Well. This is a little bit different than I expected it to go," Thomas said. "What of Mrs. Alderson? She was not mentioned at all?" Mr. Talbert said.

"She is with us," Sharon said simply.

"Yes. We are related. Can't you see the family resemblance?" Jessica said in mock surprise.

"Well, we needed a third. We made her our partner," Sean said.

"I see. Well that is at least a bit of a happy ending," Thomas said.

"Well. Originally, we were going to make her our personal assistant but my wonderful husband here saw potential in your assistant there. What is your name miss?" Sharon asked sweetly.

"Miss Smith," she said.

Sean, Sharon, and Jessica all looked at each other wide eyed and applauded, laughing hysterically.

"Well. It was really nice to see you again Mr. Talbert, nice to meet you too, Miss Smith. We really need to get going. A lot of people are going to be very happy in a little while. We have a lot of debts to pay on behalf of the late, great, Maxwell Alderson."

"Am I one of them?" Thomas asked greedily.

"No," Jessica said.

The three of them got up and got ready to leave the room. Sharon stopped and turned back.

"Miss Smith. We will pay you double what you're making now, for starters, if you want to work for us. A fringe benefit will be never having to do anything dirty, underhanded, or immoral. The choice is yours," Sharon said to the young lady.

Miss Smith sat there a moment and looked at them with wide eyes. She needed about two seconds to decide.

"I'll just get my things," she said getting up and leaving Thomas sitting there with his mouth open.

"Jessica, could you wait on Ms. Smith and bring her back to the boat?" Sean asked Jessica innocently.

"Oh, it will be my greatest pleasure, Sean. You know, I always wanted someone named Smith as an assistant," she said walking out the door. "Hurry along, dear."

As the door closed Sean relished in the fact that Mr. Talbert was working so very hard, and yet, failing miserably, at hiding his anger.

The End